Big Bang

A. J. Desmond

Country of first publication: U.S.A.
Published by Adventure Books of Seattle
www.adventurebooksofseattle.com
ISBN 13: 978-0-9823271-3-5
First Edition in paperback
April 2010

Acknowledgements

My thanks to my ever-patient wife and family. To Lynne, Martyn, and Mike for feedback throughout the book. My sincere thanks also go to Bruzas for helping me develop the concept of 'Dwarfius.' To Geoff, Robert, and Kelly for helping me persevere.

This book is dedicated to my father, who could say more with a look or a word than Olivier's Hamlet...

Table of Contents

PROLOGUE

When the world ended, Daubeny was almost too busy to notice. He'd been watching as the riot squad smashed the demonstration and a few deserving skulls, when his mobile phone rang. To the unenlightened, the ring tone – Dvorak's New World Symphony – was a nostalgic reminder of a 70s bread ad.

To the enlightened, it announced Armageddon.

It summoned calamity.

It heralded the BIG BANG.

PART ONE - Crisis? What Crisis?

C:\evidence\daubeny\0013a.doc

Extrapolated, using the 'Mind Reader Gold' algorithm, from the known facts, comments, and actions of Sir Keith Daubeny, Member of Parliament (MP).

I'm a complete and utter bastard, or so I've been told. Add to that my wife's description of me, 'sad old git' and 'waste of space' and you have Sir Keith Daubeny, MP.

That's why we live apart. Officially, of course, we're still together. She lives at the constituency home, somewhere in Yorkshire. I live in London. 'For the convenience,' I say, but people misunderstand. They think I mean the convenience of living near Parliament and I'm not going to disillusion them because heaven help the cabinet minister who wants a divorce.

I've never understood the public apathy with politics. For me, it is one of the most beautiful art forms ever devised. When wielded by the consummate politician, it isn't so much the bludgeoning club of diatribe as the perfectly balanced epee of the incisive question. It's the difference between a brainless heat-seeking sidewinder and the swerve to the left, swerve to the right; knock on the door and explode-in-your-face cruise missile. It's the snappy question forcing an opponent to confront the weakness in his argument, prompting a 'reassessment of the facts' followed by a 'policy readjustment.'

The *incisive question* is the part of the political art I've yet to perfect.

But that doesn't leave me defenceless. I don't fear the late-night interviews and news reports. Why should I? It's another opportunity to tout my wares before the voters. It's one more advert in my covert campaign to sit at the head of the Cabinet table.

I don't perspire during cross-examination because journalists and opponents usually ask the wrong questions. The wrong ones you can answer truthfully. No harm done. But if they stumble on the right one, the one with a tripwire or snare waiting at the end, then answer the question they *should* have asked and hope they don't notice. If they *do* notice, make them repeat the question again, and take so long answering that you force them to interrupt. They'll appear aggressive and boorish. And the more aggressive they become, the better you appear.

If all else fails, I dust off the club of diatribe and swing it indiscriminately at friend or foe until I'm the last one standing. It's not pretty but the body count is strangely satisfying over port and cheese at the Gentlemen's club.

I've never been accused of refusing to answer a straight question and, after thirty years as a Member of Parliament, I'm proud of this fact. If people take the time to formulate an intelligent question, they deserve an equally honest evasion in response. This policy has served me well in my rise from the backbenches to Minister for Development.

Annus Horribilus

"What do you mean it's been a bad year?" said Chief Inspector Hunter. He scowled and tossed the financial report across his desk, unread.

"It means you've overspent," said the young accountant, sat opposite him.

"The environmental protest of the decade is taking place five minutes from here, and you're telling me that I can't afford to police it?" said Hunter.

"Yes," said the accountant.

"Not even a riot van?"

"Especially not the riot vans. Their insurance policies have all expired."

Hunter groaned. "But the media, the press. Only two-point-three bloody miles away. And we can't attend?"

The accountant nodded.

"This was my one chance to shine and it's gone." Hunter ran his fingers through his hair and watched the movement in the vanity mirror on his desk. Grey roots were showing. He pulled his hand away. "So what are my alternatives?"

"From a financial point of view, there are two paths. Cross your fingers and hope the protestors disperse."

"Not an option. I need hope. Give me some hope."

"Okay," said the accountant. "If the protest stretches into the next financial year then I could wangle enough funds to set up an action committee."

"That's it? That's my best shot?"

"Yes. I'm sorry."

Hunter didn't answer. He sat in full-blown sulk. Opportunity wasn't knocking. It was zooming past him on the fast lane, mooning through the rear window.

He needed funds and began scribbling on a pad, calculating how much he could raise on a second mortgage. He was a zero or two short of the required sum when he experienced a moment of clarity. He threw down the pencil, stood, and placed his cap on his head.

"Where are you going?" said the accountant.

"To brief my men."

"But –"

"But nothing. What's the one department with money to spare?"

"Our Public Profile team."

"Exactly. Take the cash from their advertising kitty. Think about it. Reporters. News teams. We'll write off the demonstration as free publicity."

The next day, the riot squad spewed out of newly insured vans and lined up in the field against their opponents: a row of grubby environmental protesters waving makeshift weapons and chanting, "Kill the pigs. Kill the pigs."

Hunter turned his best side to the TV cameras and gave his pre-battle speech. "Just in time, Boys. It's beginning to resemble a remake of *Lord of the Flies* around here. When I give the command, I want a good straight line advancing. Keep your heads forward. Make certain the press get some profile shots for their front pages. And don't worry about the phrase 'reasonable force'. We've a crack team of lawyers that know the loopholes. So good luck and break a leg."

They did. Many ... and not their own legs.

Meeting Isaiah

The media billed it *'The Battle of Bloxham Wood'* but it never deserved the hype. The scuffle ended when the line of protestors buckled under a baton charge.

As the brawl to save the ancient woodland became a rout, Daubeny's car approached. The tall, silver-haired politician climbed out and walked into the centre of the field. His Armani suit heightened his isolation, singling him out against the backdrop of combat jackets and riot shields, but most people were too busy swinging batons, or dodging them, to notice. Few realized he was the source of the conflict. Surrounded by mayhem, he whistled *Blue Moon* as he stared into the distance.

"You're going to Hell," said someone from behind him.

The voice was low and close, the words spoken with the assurance of a street preacher. Daubeny instinctively knew that he was the target and flushed. His collar suddenly felt a size too small.

"Did you hear me, Daubeny?"

Daubeny looked around to locate the speaker and was surprised to see the farce of a fight was already over.

The police had formed the protestors into two queues: one headed for custody and the other, casualty. At the front of the custody queue, police hurled protestors into waiting vehicles like refuse bags on dustbin day. Daubeny stood near the back. He recognised the protestor closest to him.

Isaiah was as cocky in the flesh as he'd appeared on TV. He'd been the mouthpiece for the so-called Green Army during their long occupation of the woods and had made some unwise comments in the media concerning the local constabulary. He appeared oblivious to the warning signs around him.

Two grinning coppers flanked Isaiah as he waited for his ride to the nick. Isaiah was their trophy and they each held onto an arm, possessively, like World Cup winners. With his arrest, they'd won a considerable sweepstake. Later that night, they'd demonstrate the art of inflicting pain without leaving a mark – and Isaiah would be their canvas.

"The Earth won't put up with you forever, Daubeny," said Isaiah. "You're going to Hell."

"And you're going to jail," said Daubeny.

"Yeah, but I'll be out in a few months. There's no parole where you're going, bastard."

"Sir Bastard to you," said Daubeny.

Another van arrived and the police bundled Isaiah inside. They slammed the door and the vehicle pulled away, bouncing along the dirt path leading toward the lane.

Daubeny turned his attention to the trees.

They stood in a huddle, their branches festooned with the Green Army's platforms and rope bridges. They appeared to lean inwards, whispering like backbench conspirators, his silent accusers. *Look, there's Daubeny. The hater, the despoiler, the looter. The man who trades trees for tarmac.*

Daubeny felt exposed. He saw the trees as part of an all-knowing Nature. He believed they somehow knew his deepest secrets, including the event that had transformed a twelve-year-old boy into this environmental Attila the Hun.

I'm in the wrong job, thought Daubeny. *Always have been.*

The Suicidal Trees

With the trees free from protestors, the contractors approached the wood to do their work. The wind picked up and, as it passed through the trees, it produced an eerie whistle that was audible above the rumble of machinery. As the whistling intensified, the line of contractors faltered and glanced at each other in apprehension.

Daubeny called to their supervisor. "What's that noise?"

"Dunno, Guv. But it's coming from them trees."

Ping!

One of the Green Army's interconnecting rope bridges snapped under the strain. Then another. Within seconds, the trees were free from their restraints and scores of ropes were whipping through the branches. The trees rocked and tilted at unnatural angles in the cold, damp wind. Suddenly the ground shook and the trees toppled. As they crashed to the ground, a dense dust cloud rolled upwards and outwards from their base, obscuring everything from view.

When the dust settled, all present could see the entire wood had disappeared.

Daubeny sensed panic. He spoke to the supervisor. "If you don't want a mutiny, act fast." There was no reply so he turned around to find out why.

The supervisor was already running for his car.

Daubeny's first concern was to maintain order. "Men, it's not what it seems. There's a logical explanation." His tone was strong and reassuring but loud toots from a car horn drowned out his words.

Safe behind the wheel of his car, the supervisor had regained courage. He shouted his considered opinion. "Scarper. The bleedin' wood's haunted."

Some men ran while others scrambled along the ground. All of them moved towards their cars.

Daubeny held out his hands in an attempt to restore calm but felt as helpless as Pharaoh before the departing Israelites.

Two minutes later and Daubeny was alone in the field. Like the trees, the contractors had disappeared in their own cloud of dust. The media and police remained but they stood at the far hedge, close to their vehicles and prepared to make a quick escape.

Daubeny's attention returned to the mystery of the vanishing wood. A large crater had replaced the trees. He edged as close to its crumbling rim as he dared and peered into the giant hole.

The corpses of the once vibrant copse lay in a mass grave of tangled roots and broken branches. The vast network of rooms and tunnels that the environmentalists built beneath the trees had weakened the root systems and the high winds caused the trees to uproot and collapse into the crater. Riddle solved.

Daubeny choked. Bloxham Wood had turned into another ecological war atrocity for his epitaph but he was determined it would be the last. Monday, he'd march into the Prime Minister's office and resign. There'd be no backbench anonymity; this was the end. Retirement beckoned.

He stared into the pit, replaying Isaiah's words. They already seemed prophetic. He shuddered.

I'm going to Hell.

As he trudged towards his chauffer and car, a mobile phone rang. The strains of The New World Symphony sounded mute and dull in the echoless desert of the deserted field. He took out his personal mobile and put it into a trouser pocket. He carefully lifted out another mobile, one that he always carried but prayed he'd never use. A quick cough to clear the throat and then he answered.

"Sir Keith Daubeny." He listened to the speaker. "You're absolutely sure?" A pause. "I'm on my way."

He began jogging towards his car.

Pandora D'vine

She was the angelic face with filthy eyes and a mouth that could never say 'no'. She was poise, pose, and pout. She was the innocent slut of every male's dark fantasy. And she was the intellectual genius behind the music of Pandora's Box.

She stood by a bare wall in a rundown community hall in Wimbledon, performing a dance routine, miming badly to one of her early hits. Her long blonde hair framed a facial expression that belonged more to the set of a porn film than the video of a sugary pop song. At the age of twenty-two, Pandora had four massive albums and a back-catalogue already defined as pre- and post-. The critics were undecided on pre- and post- what, but most agreed that the lightweight pop of the first two albums was the springboard for the gutsier, guitar-driven leftfield Rock of her last offerings. And now there was a new CD and an accompanying world tour to promote it.

Pandora glanced at Craig, her choreographer, who was standing behind the music system. They were alone in the hall and judging by his pained expression, she was glad they were alone. The music stopped abruptly and Pandora took a few seconds to come to a halt. She walked to a bench and took a bottle of water from her battered rucksack.

"Sorry, Craig. That was total crap." She swigged the water and put it back.

"Darling, you were great."

"Was I? Really?" She grinned, picked up a towel and wiped away the sweat that ran down her face and body.

"No, you were shocking. Truly shocking. Two weeks to the tour and you're getting worse."

"Wanker."

"Sticks and stones, darling. Your record company pays me to be a wanker."

"No reason to make it your hobby, too." Pandora's mobile began ringing. She threw the towel down and picked up the phone. "Pandora speaking."

Craig set up the song for a replay. With finger poised over the play button, he found himself trying to listen in on the call. He wasn't normally curious but the tension in her *uhs* and *ahas* caught his attention. He looked over Pandora's body: five foot five of slim, curved flesh. She was an ocular overload. The only flaw – if that was the right word – were her eyes; bright blue and frigid as Narnia's Ice Queen.

When he tired with the ogling, he noticed the used towel. It had fallen behind the bench. With luck, she'd forget it and he could flog it on eBay for a week's wages.

Pandora closed the call and put the phone back in her rucksack. Craig hit the play button and the opening chords to *Kiss 'n' Tell* began their slow swell over an Eighties-style snare drum but Pandora wasn't interested. She waved her hands to get his attention.

"Wait."

Craig stopped the music. "What is it now?"

"Sorry, it's an emergency. I have to go. Listen, why don't you get out of London for a few days? You could do with the break." She brushed her hair with rapid strokes before giving up and reaching for a hair band.

"I could do with the break? Charming. You were miming like a badly-dubbed art flick."

"I had a late night again, that's all."

"Another gruelling celebrity gala? All that posh nosh and free booze takes its toll."

She laughed. "I wish. I had another lonely night with me astrophysics books." Her rucksack was packed. She picked it up and walked towards the door.

Craig tutted loudly. "And it's 'my astrophysics books' not 'me'. Don't know what your elocution coach is getting paid but he isn't earning it."

"Don't be a jerk. I'm serious. Leave town for a day or two. Promise me, please."

"Okay, promise." The door closed, leaving Craig alone.

He was out of luck. The towel had gone.

Good Telly

Emma was single but not single mum. She was late-thirties and black: her parents having moved to London from Jamaica in 1959. Although she described her childhood as happy, the transition from teenager to adult had not been so easy. It wasn't from lack of confidence or a bad complexion. What made those in-between years so intolerable was the one thing she was stuck with, her parents.

While her friends' parents argued with their daughters about money, boyfriends, and what was suitable for a girl of fourteen to wear on the streets of Camden in November, Emma's parents argued over trivia. They argued for the sake of argument. They quarrelled so loudly and so regularly that she wondered why they'd ever bought a TV. They never watched it.

"Emma, tell your mom that the Vandals were the first to sack Rome."

"Don't listen to that silly man, girl. It was the Goths."

"Mom! Dad! I can't hear the news."

"Vandals."

"Goths."

"Why don't you both agree to differ?"

"How can you differ on something as important as fact?"

"Yes, facts are facts, girl."

"You both agreed," said Emma.

Her parents sat in confounded silence for a few moments before

Mom left the room. She returned with a leather-bound volume of *The Fall of the Roman Empire*. It was open in her hands and she spoke as if addressing a congregation.

"According to Gibbon, it was the Goths."

"Give it here," said Emma's father. He read the section indicated. "No, it doesn't."

"Yes, it does. Em; read it and tell the silly old goat that I'm right."

Emma read the portion under the jabbing finger. "Mom's right. It says Goths."

"No, it doesn't," said her father. "What does it say? Exactly."

Emma sighed. "The Visigoths."

"Correct. So it wasn't the Goths after all, was it?"

"Oh, I'm going to my room."

Emma stayed in her room for the evening; she stayed there most evenings. Occasionally she overheard her parents through the thin walls.

"Well, I meant Visigoth."

"But you didn't say Visigoth. You said Goth."

"The Visigoths were Goths."

"Rubbish. Why call them Visigoths if they were Goths?"

Emma often told reporters that her childhood explained her current success. She was the unchallenged queen of the agony aunts and the confident, composed host of a live TV series. Put her in front of a camera with several angry guests and a hostile audience, and she'd navigate the show through a tempest of raw emotions into the placid waters of the commercial break. Of course, they'd had the occasional equivalent of shooting an albatross and weevils in the biscuit, but no-one had been forced to drink their own piss on national TV, allegorically speaking.

Although, on one memorable episode they had featured a film star who advocated the benefits of drinking urine.

"You're serious? You really do drink it?" asked Emma during the interview.

"Yes. It has health benefits."

"It's your own urine, I hope."

"That depends on whether we're eating out."

Emma brought the commercial break forward by six minutes,

seamlessly and with easy skill. After the show, she went to the green room and emptied all the alcohol down the sink – as a precaution – in case the celebrity had brought their own tipple.

Emma loved her job. It allowed her to be negotiator, nurturer, go-between and amateur psychoanalyst all in one. In her experience, there wasn't a problem in the world that she couldn't compromise, mother, or analyse away. It wasn't strictly true but that's how her producer had described her on an episode of *This Is Your Life.* She replayed the excerpt often, especially after he'd balled her out over ratings figures.

Her producer was the exception. He was the one person she couldn't compromise, mother, or analyse. The man was a wall. Information flowed in one direction only...from him to others. His eternal mantra was, "Normal doesn't sell, Em. I want good telly. Give me good telly."

Good telly? What more did he want? She was at the peak of her career, drawing huge audiences and receiving so many awards that she was returning them as 'Unknown at this address.' She'd given him everything and it wasn't enough. He was impossible to please.

"Emma?" A distant, disembodied voice called her, disrupting her thoughts. There was a brief silence before the voice spoke again, higher pitched and more urgent. "Em? Wake up, girl."

It was her producer, shouting instructions in her earpiece. For the second time her thoughts had wandered during the live show.

"For God's sake, Em. Get that lunatic off the air."

She listened with horror to the audience member speaking into the microphone.

"If aliens are sophisticated enough to traverse the galaxy, why do they subject abductees to brutal, intrusive examinations that would put a medieval inquisitor to shame? Because they don't exist, that's why. It's a government tool to keep us underfoot. It's a –"

Emma interrupted. "That's an interesting thought but how does it help Jay come to terms with her son's transvestitism?"

On TV sets around the country, a caption appeared: *Hey Mom, guess who's a tranny?*

Emma turned to the camera and said, "Join us after the break."

When they were off-air, she headed for her floor manager. "Get alien boy out of here," said Emma. "And how's what's-her-name? The transvestite's mum."

"Don't you mean Jay?"

Emma detected disapproval in the floor manager's tone. "When you see a car crash, you pull the victims out. You don't wait until you've been properly introduced."

"This is TV, Em, not a car crash."

"I can't be expected to remember every name. That's your job. Anyway, how is Jay?"

"She's in the Green Room, waiting for us to call her onto the set."

"Is she close to tears yet?"

"No chance. Hard as granite, that one."

"Well, I want tears," said Emma. "Floods of them. So many that people start looking for wood to build an ark. I want The Carpenters and Leonard Cohen piped in over the sound system. And keep plying her with sherry. That usually does the trick."

Emma turned away to size up the audience. She had an instinct. She could tell the safe audience members from the ones that were on the edge, the ones that were provocative and racy enough to make exciting viewing without getting the show pulled. "I'll show the producer good telly." Emma spat the last two words and her floor manager flinched.

Emma had spotted two candidates for the next section of the show and was looking for a third, when she noticed a young man who'd recently joined the production team. He stood at her side, afraid to speak but too afraid to leave with his errand unfinished. Emma glanced at him. "What?"

"There's a phone call for you."

She broke from her appraisal of the audience and glared at him. "I never take calls during the interval. Not even from my mum. Take a message and I'll call them later."

"But he said it was urgent," said the young man.

"Of course he would," said Emma. "Everyone says it's urgent. Now, go away."

She turned her attention to the audience. Alien boy grinned and waved at her. Emma tried to attract her floor manager's attention but she was talking to the green room chaperones on the phone.

The young man at her side persisted. "He said you'd try to get rid of me but I was to say 'Orange Free State.' Whatever that means?"

"What did he say?"

"Orange Free State."

Emma snatched at the phone.

When the show returned from the commercial break, a nervous floor manager addressed the audience. "Welcome back to the show. And no, Emma's not been abducted but I'm afraid she has been taken ill. Nothing trivial, we hope." She giggled then grimaced and the cameras captured it in glorious close-up. She tried to recover. "But better safe than sorry… err… that's what I say." There was a lengthy pause. Her eyes jiggled on TV sets around the country as she thought of something to say while simultaneously struggling to cope with the screams coming from her earpiece.

"So, tell us more about the aliens. Sounds great." She didn't sound convinced and neither did the producer who seemed to be auditioning for the latest Quentin Tarantino film.

Em was going to kill her.

Emma never did kill her floor manager. Neither of them realised it but they'd seen each other for the last time.

The Lifestyle Guru
Ravi walked through the room, swigging whisky from a crystal tumbler. He was drunk, fat, thirty, and so scruffy that tramps refused to beg from him on a matter of principle. His combat trousers seemed several sizes too large at the bottom and several sizes too small at the midriff. His T-shirt resembled a cast-off from an elephant seal's wardrobe. Across its wide back looped the metallic-silver trail of a slug: a memento from the weekend when Ravi had fallen asleep in the park after downing several flagons of hard cider. He hadn't seen the slug trail because he hadn't taken off his clothes for days. Despite looking conspicuous against his surroundings, Ravi seemed completely at ease.

The room was the incarnation of living spaces shown in celebrity magazines. It was modern and chic. The centrepiece was a mantel with sharp, simple lines and nearby sat a telephone on a narrow table. Dominating the hearth and dividing the room in two was a large sofa, square and squat, screaming of designer label. A fifties retro-style radio played quietly in the background. Ravi listened to the DJ delivering the headlines.

"And breaking news. As the crisis over North Korea deepens; America, Russia, and China have recalled embassy staff from the European Union. The EU president has again refused to back America, citing world peace as his only concern. A spokesman denied the rumour that the President has fled to an undisclosed location."

Ravi stopped swigging scotch long enough to shout at the radio. "World peace? Balls. It's a big game of chess to 'em. An' us poor sods take the bullets when it goes wrong."

He swiped his long greasy fringe from his eyes and noticed the scattering of dry skin that had built up on the front of his T-shirt from repeated scratches of the goatee. He brushed the flakes onto the Persian rug beneath his dirty shoes.

The DJ continued. "I think we need a song to take our minds off the depressing news. Ah, perfect. The Jam and they're … *Going Underground.*"

A high-pitched voice warbled the opening line of a chorus but it wasn't The Jam, as promised. Ravi recognised it as *The Final Countdown* by Europe.

The DJ cut in over the record. "Sorry 'bout that, folks. Bit hard cueing up the right record when you're kissing your arse goodbye. Whoops, I swore. Hold on to that letter of complaint until tomorrow. If I'm alive then send it in. If I'm not then they've dropped the bomb. And if that's the case, you can shove the letter's ashes up the ashes of what was once your asshole." The song continued but now with raised voices and scuffling in the background.

Ravi switched the radio off, dislodging it slightly. He spent twenty to thirty seconds adjusting it, looking at it from various angles, and readjusting it until he was satisfied with its position. He wandered to the hearth and noticed the telephone on its stand.

"How many times have I told 'im? It don't go there. That place attracts bad karma… or summat like that." He hiccupped loudly and put his finger dramatically to his mouth. "Shh," he whispered to nobody.

Ravi picked up the phone and put it onto the left-hand corner of the mantelpiece. He took out a small tape measure from one of his many pockets and read the distance of phone to edge. There was a little readjustment to get it millimetre correct.

"Perfect." Ravi closed his eyes and smiled. "Feels better already… airy… lighter. Is it me, or do I smell jasmine?" He took a small aerosol from another pocket and sprayed it into the air. "Ah, now I do." A series of hiccups broke the tranquillity; they persisted until his chest hurt.

Ravi poured more whisky but the sound of a key at the front door disturbed him and precious amber malt spilled over the silver drinks tray. He heard the door open and close. The slow, measured step of expensive shoes on the hallway's marble floor echoed ominously as their unseen owner approached the open lounge door.

Without taking his attention from the door, Ravi flicked the pooled alcohol onto the white carpet below with the side of his hand. He rubbed his shoe vigorously across the wet patch, leaving a dark smudge.

A tall elegant man entered the room, humming. He wore a three-piece suit, so exquisitely tailored that it looked tattooed on. He noticed Ravi and the two men stood in silence, Ravi's foot locked in mid-swing. They glared at each other. They seemed as incompatible as Superman and Bizarro, matter and antimatter.

Sir Giles spoke first. "It's you."

Ravi missed the rebuff. Nuance was a foreign word to him. He attacked. "Do you think that vase is the right colour for those curtains?"

"It is my house, Ravi. And yes, yes I do."

"Well, I think you're very brave."

"Brave? What has bravery to do with decor?"

"The house spirits don't like it, Sir Giles. They get angry. Fang Shoo-ey and all that jazz." Ravi mispronounced Feng Shui. He was drunk but that didn't matter. He mispronounced it when he was sober too.

"It's a good job you only have a newspaper column," said Sir Giles.

"It's in The Times."

"The Berkshire Times, Ravi. The Berkshire Times. At least your readers can't hear you mispronounce Feng Shui."

"The house spirits don't care about–"

"House spirits? You make it sound more like voodoo than the ancient oriental art of home decorating."

"I know voodoo, too," said Ravi. "I've seen all them zombie films."

"Sometimes I wonder why I ever hired you. Some lifestyle guru. You're fat. You smoke. You're scruffy. And your personal hygiene is disgraceful. Yesterday, I found nail clippings on my worktops." Sir Giles shuddered at the recollection. "And every time you come here, the house smells of Toilet Duck."

"Jasmine."

"Ravi, jasmine is subtle. It evokes summer tea gardens beneath rustling willows and the shadow of Mount Fuji." He sniffed the air cautiously and his delicate nose quivered in rebellion. "This abomination is the nasal equivalent of ten rounds with Tyson. Oh, and I've seen your office, too. It's like Tracey Emin's unmade bed. A mess."

Ravi hiccupped and fell forward. He prevented an undignified collapse by clutching at the arm of the settee but whisky splashed across the expensive white fabric.

Sir Giles pointed at Ravi's near-empty glass. "You're drunk. On my whisky."

"I told you, whisky's out. 'S no good for you."

"So why don't you take your own advice?"

"I'm happy with my life. 'S you that's unhappy with yours. That's why you hired me. Remember?"

"Not anymore, Ravi. You're fired."

Ravi mouthed the word 'fired' as Sir Giles put the phone on the tall narrow table.

"Hey, I put that on the mantel," said Ravi.

"And I keep moving it back because it's useless up there."

A mobile phone began ringing and Sir Giles waved at Ravi to shut him up. Ravi recognised the music as something classical because he couldn't hear drums.

Sir Giles spoke. "You're absolutely sure? OK, see you in the bunker. Five minutes."

"Bunker? What are you talking about?"

"Look, Ravi, I have to go." Sir Giles collected items from the room as he talked.

"What bunker?"

"You know this house belonged to a government minister, right?" Ravi nodded; Sir Giles continued. "There's a bunker out back. The neighbours pay to maintain it. In case we need it."

"What d' you need a bunker for? The French dropping fish on us again?"

"No, it's worst-case scenario. Word is the Chinese are planning a strike."

"Speak English. You mean like a rail strike?"

Sir Giles stopped. He looked into Ravi's face and seemed to soften. "Ravi, forget the argument and get out of town. I'm talking about a nuclear strike."

"Nukes? Get out of town, you say? Newsflash, Sir Giles. Radiation doesn't hang around bars or respect parish boundaries. It travels. Faster and further than I can run. And it makes things sick. Real sick."

"Go, while you have the chance. But tell no-one. We don't want a panic, do we?"

"Why can't I bunk up with you and your pals?"

"It wouldn't be fair on the others. There's no room and besides," Sir Giles paused, "you haven't paid in."

"So leaving me behind is fair? With the fallout and the glowing-green living dead for company."

"Don't dramatise, Ravi. That's probably a film you've seen."

"Yeah, the reality will be a whole lot worse. Please, Sir Giles, I'm wearing red. Red and green should never be seen except with a colour in between. Preferably, grey. Six feet of grey reinforced concrete."

Sir Giles moved towards the door and Ravi barred the way, near the phone stand.

"I'm sorry. I can't help you, Ravi. Please, get out of the way."

"I'm trying. Honest, I'm trying but I can't." Ravi paused, aware that he was bargaining for his life. The next sentence could settle his destiny. "Sir Giles, what will you do down there without Colour Therapy, the I Ching, or Origami?"

"We'll survive."

It wasn't the response Ravi wanted. "What if you run into vampires? I've seen every Buffy episode, ever."

Sir Giles tried to step around Ravi but the relocated phone cable snagged his foot and overbalanced him. Ravi made a grab for the falling banker but only succeeded in pushing him towards the hearth. Sir Giles' head hit cold marble with a dull thud

"See. I told you that phone was bad karma there."

Sir Giles didn't respond.

Ravi bent and checked for a pulse. "Gawd, I warned you about house spirits but you didn't believe in them." He glanced nervously around the room. "Mind, neither did I 'til now."

Ravi picked up the bag of belongings that Sir Giles had collected and ran to the front door. He swung the door open and glanced back into the house.

It was the sober look of fear.

Going Underground

Ravi skirted the side of the house and entered the shared garden at the rear. It was an enclosed strip of land running alongside the row of houses. A dense wall of shrubs and conifers screened it off from public view and gave a cosy, intimate feel to the space.

He found the doorway to the bunker immediately. It was impossible to miss but the entrance spooked him and he spent another fifteen minutes running about the garden in the dwindling hope that there was a more secret entrance. He searched a shed, a greenhouse, tore down a woodpile, and ran along the hedge that bordered the garden, disturbing songbirds and crushing the bedding plants.

With all options eliminated, Ravi returned to the centre of the garden where a large, conspicuous metal cylinder stood. On one side of the curved and polished steel wall was an open door. Above the door was a small neon sign that carried the word 'Exit.' The interior appeared dark and foreboding but there was enough light to make out a metal staircase that spiralled down the inner wall.

Ravi took some deep breaths and stepped toward the opening. His body shook and he felt like throwing up so violently that he could have dislodged his front teeth. Normally it took a flagon of cider to feel that way but, at the brink of Armageddon, he was getting it free.

He tugged at the door, opening it fully. It clanged against the outer shell with a deep, resonant thud. The door sounded solid but had moved too easily for steel. The prospect of a dark, confined stairway was bad enough but the Twilight Zone effects weren't helping Ravi's hyperventilation. Without thinking, he reached for the jasmine aerosol and sprayed it into the ominous, gaping gateway into the earth.

"Ah, that's better."

But it wasn't better. He felt queasy. And he was angry with Sir Giles over the Toilet Duck wisecrack. Ravi would never be able to smell jasmine again without thinking industrial-strength household cleaner. It didn't occur to him that Sir Giles would never rise from that stone-cold hearth, that he'd never again sip Taylor's twenty-year-old tawny port, take breakfast on the balcony, or read the Financial Times.

Ravi wrestled with a debilitating sense of peril. Two opposites fought to claim his carcass, to put their stamp on his flesh and reign unchallenged over the dissipating chemical and hormonal maelstrom that was once his body. The opposites were light and dark. Above him, the anonymous and unpredictably sudden scouring of his body by the untamed purity of an atom bomb's light and, below him, the unknowably deep and dark metallic vagina he would have to negotiate to live.

Ravi stepped inside the chamber and found himself on a platform of thick steel mesh. He looked through it, to determine how far down he'd have to travel. He wished he hadn't bothered. It was dark and deep; and that's all he knew.

He searched his pocket for loose change and rifled through the coins for a penny and, when he couldn't find a penny, he reluctantly settled for a tuppence. It seemed senseless to throw good money away but he tossed it off the platform, into the gulf that the spiral staircase encircled. He waited and waited. He paused to whistle his amazement. Then waited some more. No sound returned to his ear.

"That's all I need. It's bottomless, as well as dark and claustrophobic." He paced the platform, debating. He was deep in thought when he heard a wail that he couldn't place despite sounding familiar. It spooked him and he ran into the garden.

Outside, he identified the sound. It was the dissonant unearthly howl of an air-raid siren, activated by the Civil Defence network. It was the eerie, voiceless announcement of the Armageddon Intercity Express arriving at Euston station. Animals listened, babies stopped mid-cry, and mothers paused before gathering their offspring inside the thin brick-walled homes of soon-to-be nuclear families.

Within minutes, the streets would resemble the most terrifying parts of the Bible and capitalism's long-feared nightmare would commence. "Consume, consume, consume," wailed her prophets. "For the end is nigh and supermarket shelves are still not bare."

Impending death inspired Ravi's hulking frame into action. He was inside the chamber and running down the spiral staircase, three steps at a time. The light, filtering through the door above, faded by degrees but even in the pitch dark he never lost his footing. Deeper into the metal vagina he went, faster than a turd down a storm sewer.

It never occurred to him how appropriate the analogy was.

On the surface, dusk gathered and the streets became quagmires of motionless metal and panicking flesh. Scenes of selfishness and selflessness played out.

Some people abandoned friends to their fate while others chose to stay and share their last moments. Separated or abandoned children cried, afraid and unheeded in the throng, while others were comforted by strangers. The emergency services, though overwhelmed, performed admirably.

These brief moments were the true defining points in a person's life. It wasn't how they'd seized life; it was how they faced death. And they lived with those choices for the remainder of their lives. The cliché of workmates screwing on the boss' desk was the exception. Most people were too busy trying to think of a way out, to think of a way in.

PART TWO – Ground Zero

The Permeable Non-Permeable Membrane

The spiral stairs eventually ran out but the impetus carried Ravi across the floor and into the curved wall opposite. He bounced with a yelp and slumped to the ground, dazed. His outstretched hands told him that he was resting on concrete. It felt coarse and damp against his grazed skin.

His eyes were closed and all he could see was red light, a dull dirty red that throbbed in time to the pain in his head. He groaned and opened his eyes but nothing changed.

His eyes grew accustomed to the feeble red light of a panel, positioned to the left of a great steel door. The door's only feature was a glass pinhole, at head height in its centre.

Picking himself up, Ravi pushed at the door. It did precisely what he'd expected it to do – nothing. He took a step back to appraise the situation and then ran at the door, screaming, as if he were trying to catch it off-guard. When that failed, he slapped his palms against it, shouting and peering into the peephole.

"Hey, open up. I'm with Sir Giles. Please. Open the door."

After a few seconds of effort without response, Ravi gave up. He was from the *'Instant Now'* generation. He saw no point in expending effort without immediate return. Besides, logic told him he was screwed. Any normal person would have opened the door by now, but if they were anything like Ravi responding to a doorbell then he'd need a calendar to mark off the months.

Ravi imagined his doppelganger living out its life on the other side of that impermeable membrane of unyielding steel; eating, sleeping, drinking, and watching TV, before finally getting around to answering the door. He pictured his alter ego standing in the open doorway, tutting at the pile of large bones that had once been the most famous lifestyle columnist in Bedfordshire. There was some compensation in death. It turned out that Ravi was big-boned, not fat, after all.

"Now where's that sodding coin got to?"

Ravi scanned the floor, looking for the tuppence he'd tossed over the platform but he couldn't find it. He humphed at the loss and slumped onto the cold concrete floor, waiting for something to happen. As he stared into the dim red light, aware of the cold creeping into his well-padded ass, his unfocused eyes began to play tricks.

Ravi watched as a swirling diaphanous form shifted and shaped into fleeting patterns that were almost recognisable. It grew larger. When it filled his field of vision, he experienced a sensation of movement and a violent shift in his body's sense of orientation. He felt as though he was flying over a red glowing landscape, looking down on it from a great height. It was a world of ruby phosphorescent lava and jet-black crust, hopelessly broken and fragmented into sharp angular pieces.

Suddenly the surface rushed up to meet him. He passed through it and found himself floating before a transparent heart, huge and pumping blood, so massive that individual galaxies formed the red corpuscles. Ravi instinctively knew this was the heart mother of the universe.

"Wow," said Ravi. "So this is what it's like to achieve oneness with the universe?"

"Don't be so daft," said his long-dead mother.

Ravi started. "Mum, where did you come from?" The universal heart disappeared and a form, diaphanous and familiar, stood before him.

"Is this how you greet your mother, after all this time? And get up, you silly thing. You'll get piles sitting on that cold floor."

"Mum, the world is about to blow itself apart and you worry about piles."

"How do you know the world's going to blow up? You're trapped down a hole. A deep dark hole, too." His mother's red misty form looked up as though to emphasise the point, her hair framing her face like a halo.

"Don't remind me," said Ravi. "I'm shaking just thinking about it."

"So what are you going to do?"

"What can I do? You said it: I'm trapped. I can't go up unless I want to take the lead in a horror movie. And I ain't getting through that door until I've lost some weight."

"Lose weight? What do you mean lose weight? There's nothing wrong with you. All that extra padding shows how loved you are."

"Mum, there are hippos less loved than me."

His mother looked at him over the frames of her unfashionable National Health glasses. "Nonsense, skin and bone is what you are. Now, if you're trapped, why don't you use your brain?"

"To get through that door, I'd need to discover teleportation and I haven't got the time, the laboratory, or the funding."

"Then use the key."

"What key?"

"The key you stole from Sir Giles, right after you murdered him."

Ravi looked around to assure himself that no-one had heard his mother's unguarded comment. He was safe. "I didn't murder him, Mum. He fell."

"We need to talk about that."

"Then later, please."

"OK, later. And remember, use the key." Her form began to dissolve into the blank red wall in front of him. "Oh, and son?"

"Yes, Mum?"

"Remember to eat your greens and if it's broccoli, get a –"

"Yes, yes. Get a double helping." He finished the sentence as she disappeared.

Ravi didn't think to question the conversation with his mother's shade. Instead, he emptied the contents of Sir Giles' bag noisily onto the floor and examined each item. There was a diary, a pen, some sweets, a credit card, a copy of the Financial Times, and a hi-tech palmtop. The Horsemen of the Apocalypse would have struggled to distract Sir Giles from the minute-to-minute activities of the derivatives market. Ravi run through the list of items several times but there was no key, definitely no key, unless the door needed a magic word to open. He tried a few.

"FT index. Dow Jones. Nikki Yen." He paused. Ravi felt stupid but his life was at stake. With his knowledge of the stock market exhausted, he ran through a list of random words that might have been keywords for Sir Giles. When he exhausted that list, he tried some less likely candidates. "Open sesame. Open wide. Open now.

Open dammit. 'Ope 'n' Pray." The door remained shut and there followed a full sixty seconds of swearing and abuse. It didn't open the door, but it made Ravi feel better.

Beaten, he dropped to his haunches and re-examined each item. His mother had said that the key was there. He picked up the credit card. There was no logo or account number, only a magnetic strip. He glanced at the dim red light to the left of the doorway and noticed a thin black horizontal slot. Thirty seconds later Ravi was inside the door.

"Piece of cake," he said as the blast door closed behind him. It took an hour, most of it spent in daydreams, and the intervention of his dead mother, to crack the door.

Ravi was standing at the top of another gloomy tube of steel, complete with wire platform and spiral stairway. After a brief moment of anticlimax, he shrugged and began his descent, not so hurried as the first. He counted no more than sixty or seventy steps when he reached the concrete floor at the base of the cylinder.

In the red glow, he could see a plate-metal door perforated by large metal rivets. This door wasn't going to present such an obstacle; for starters, it had a handle. Painted across it in military stencil was a single word, in black.

"Exit?" said Ravi. Doubt assailed him. Maybe this wasn't the entrance to Sir Giles's bunker, after all. He sighed. Being sacked, then killing – albeit accidentally – his first client had been followed by imminent nuclear war, a weird ass-backwards bunker, and a conversation with a dead parent. He was sure of one thing. The day couldn't get any more bizarre than this.

He was wrong.

Standoff

When Ravi opened the door, the first thing that struck him was bright light; needle sharp on his eyes after the gloom of the stairwell. The second thing that struck him was a large fist that shot through the gap between door and wall. It connected with his chin. Suddenly the bright light was no longer the most painful thing in Ravi's cosmos.

Before Ravi could recover or stumble backwards, the hand

grabbed him by the throat and pulled him into the room. The unknown assailant slammed him against the wall and Ravi took another punch, this time in the gut. He bent forward but his assailant hurled him back against the wall. Ravi's head hit concrete with a loud crack and a small sharp object was pressed into the exposed rolls of skin around his throat. He was in no state to resist. Eyes closed against the light, he concentrated on getting his breath back.

"Did you see when I thumped him in the guts?" said his assailant.

There was a laugh from somewhere in the room. "Your arm disappeared up to the elbow, Wodenhart." It was a cultivated male voice, refined and plum-like. Ravi knew with conviction that its owner had never changed the brake pads on a rusty Ford or drank cheap milk stout to drown the aftertaste of egg and chips, fried in filthy rancid oil.

Ravi coughed and the knife at his throat tightened. "Whoa, take it easy. I'm beat." He opened his eyes and had his first look at the man pinning him to the wall.

Set between the prominent dimpled chin and blonde crew-cut was a face that Ravi knew well. He had seen it on the news and in the movies. It appeared on roadside billboards, selling everything from perfume and shavers to light bulbs. The man behind those angular features had screamed "Nuts to you" at Nazi and terrorist arch-villains before he'd shot them point-blank in the groin at the climax of eight blockbuster movies – all of them crap and all of them huge financial successes. His was the face that launched a thousand quips, every one stolen or written by a team of staff writers. This was the face of Johnny Wodenhart, handsome and set high on a sheer cliff of muscle, the biggest British name in Hollywood.

"Hey, I know you," said Ravi.

Wodenhart smiled bashfully and shuffled his weight awkwardly; he did it every time he was recognised. When Wodenhart wasn't incognito in shades and baseball cap, he often appeared to be break dancing.

"You're Johnny Wodenhart, right? Nuts to you, and all that?"

Wodenhart nodded.

"Wow, this is so cool. You're my hero. I've seen all your films."

The upper-crust male voice spoke again. "Well, we've established that you know Wodenhart but let's leave the sickening adulation until later. Who are you?"

Ravi peeked around Wodenhart's well-defined body. He was in a communal area. There were kitchen facilities, wall mounted cupboards, and several doors. Something about the colour scheme niggled at him but Ravi had other concerns. Working out why a film star was prepared to perform a tracheotomy, without the aid of anaesthetic, rated a higher priority than the choice of paint.

Four people sat at a large grey table in the centre of the room: one man and three women. Ravi recognised two of them from TV and magazines; Pandora and Emma.

Ravi had longed to hobnob with the rich and famous and here they were, delivered up by Fate, but he had no time to contemplate his good fortune.

"So who are you?"

The speaker was a tall, thin, grey-haired man in his early sixties. His narrow face and thick eyebrows gave him a resemblance to Bert from *The Muppet Show*. He stood, arms folded, behind the four people at the table.

"Who am I?" said Ravi. "Once upon a time I thought I was Ravi, lifestyle guru to the rich and famous. Now I ain't so sure. It's like I'm being mugged by Madame Tussauds."

Everyone, except the interrogator, laughed.

"So, Ravi, how did you get in?"

Oh, I killed your neighbour – accidentally, mind – stole his cardkey and some other belongings and let myself in. It was the truth but Ravi had already gotten off to a bad start. He stumbled for something not too incriminating or easy to disprove. For a consummate liar like Ravi, it should have been easy but it wasn't. He'd never had to fabricate fibs with the threat of a mushroom cloud in the background.

Emma spoke. "Daubeny, go easy. He had a cardkey."

She seemed to find the confrontation unsettling and that surprised Ravi. She'd built her reputation on the confrontation and emotional carnage of daytime TV.

Daubeny remained undeterred. "How did you get in?"

Think, Ravi, think. Don't confess. That's the natural instinct.

Ravi saw himself earlier that day, walking the tree-lined cul-de-sac towards Sir Giles' house. A woman with a pram approached. In a rare moment of courtesy, he stepped off the pavement to allow her to pass and found himself in the path of a removal van approaching unseen from behind. It roared past, tooting its horn. Ravi waved his fist and shouted. Properly avenged, he turned to apologise to the woman for his choice words. Seconds later, there was a screech of brakes. The van pulled in, accompanied by the sound of expensive furniture rearranging itself into cheaper, more compact piles of firewood. The crashes, smashes, and bashes seemed to continue indefinitely.

Ravi had to pass the van to reach Sir Giles' home so he took his time, his walk degenerating into a slow aimless amble. The removal men were salvaging the remnants of furniture, tossing the pieces, like jetsam, onto the garden of a house with a 'Sold' sign. Ravi passed as quickly and nonchalantly as possible. He kept his eyes fixed to the ground and was only aware that he'd been holding his breath when his chest began to ache. His first instinct was to think "Cardiac" and he reached for the aspirin he always carried for such an emergency. His keep-fit regime was basic: one aspirin and a daily clove of garlic.

Backtrack, Ravi, backtrack. How did I get in the bunker? The removal men. The removal men. "I moved in. Today. Number twenty-three. But the estate agent forgot to warn me about the welcoming committee."

"Daubeny, Dear. You've made your point. Now let him go." The speaker was a woman in her early fifties; the only woman in the room that Ravi hadn't recognised. She didn't appear rich; she embodied it. She was the archetype in person, the original icon of class and refinement. More clipart than real; more trophy than wife. Stepford and Versace were in her dreams, genes and bloodstream.

"Who's that?" Ravi whispered to Wodenhart.

"That's Laura," said Wodenhart.

You're a great help, thought Ravi. "Laura who?"

"She's one of the Davenports."

"And they are…?"

"Aristocracy."

"Ah, old money."

"She's new money, too."

"Eh?"

"She's married to Casper Williams."

"So that's Laura Williams?"

"Yes."

"Then why didn't you say that in the beginning?"

Laura's husband was a media mogul and rival papers regularly lampooned her lifestyle. According to the tabloids, life for Laura Davenport-Williams was simple. Like a cat basking on a windowsill, the sun shone for her alone, but unlike her society friends, Laura hated distraction. Especially if it took her mind off herself.

"Daubeny, this tough guy business is starting to rankle," said Laura. "Let him go."

"Maybe Daubeny knows best," said the young man sat next to Laura.

"Paul, who asked you? And, anyway, I've a pressing two-thirty appointment with my cosmetics bag and some lipstick."

The standoff continued. Daubeny's attention seemed to focus on Ravi's face.

"Be a sweetie," said Laura. "And let him go." She paused for emphasis. "Now."

Daubeny nodded. Everyone relaxed and Wodenhart took the knife from Ravi's throat. It was a plastic catering knife, the kind that couldn't tackle a cold sausage on a paper plate, let alone slice through a jugular.

"I'm not convinced. Stick with him, Wodenhart," said Daubeny.

"You got it, Buster," said Wodenhart and he resumed his alert stance next to Ravi. When Wodenhart thought no-one was listening, he leaned in close and whispered, "Nothing personal, Ravi, but orders are orders."

Within five minutes, Ravi had learned two things that frightened him about Daubeny. He was a stubborn old sod but he knew when to back down. What others saw as possible weakness, Ravi saw as an indication of guile. Any idiot could stand, fight, and lose. That was foolishness, not bravery. The real sneaky sods took the short-term defeat, chose the next field of battle, and won the rematch. Ravi knew Daubeny would be waiting for him when the circumstances were right.

"I wonder what's keeping Sir Giles?" said Emma. "I won't be able to relax until he gets here." Her fingers trembled as they played with the buttons of her blouse.

"Relax?" said Pandora. "How are we supposed to relax? Em, this is Armageddon, not a cocktail party." She turned to Laura. "Relax, she says."

"Oh, you know what she means, Poppet. We're all on edge." Laura didn't look up. She was busy buffing her nails.

"Yeah, I can see that," said Pandora.

"Wodenhart, I know it's dangerous and I probably shouldn't ask, but could you go over to Sir Giles' house and see what's happened?" It was an order framed as a request.

Pandora protested. "We can't risk losing Johnny. We need him here."

"She's right," said Emma.

"Sounds great to me," said Wodenhart. "Loads of danger and a race against time. Like the close of my last film."

Paul spoke. "A few less giant insects and more chance of being vaporised but yeah, an accurate summary." Paul looked about Ravi's age but there the comparison ended. He had a handsome face, full not fat like Ravi's, and short brown hair. His clothes were professional, not the designer crap popular with everyone Ravi's age – except Ravi.

"Still, you only live twice," said Wodenhart.

"Oh Johnny, that's a film. You only live once," said Pandora.

"You do?"

Daubeny sounded irritated. "Then check the stairwell, in case Sir Giles can't get in."

Before Pandora could complain and Emma could second her, Wodenhart left.

Introductions

With Wodenhart out of the way, Ravi had his first detailed look at the room and its occupants. The room was square, with a door set into the centre of each wall. The door to the left bore the stencil 'A Wing', the door to the right, 'B Wing'. The door opposite Ravi carried the legend 'Lower Levels'. He still hadn't worked out what was nagging him over the colour scheme but, for now, he was more interested in the people.

Paul sat next to Laura. The pair's body language suggested history but it didn't seem sexual. Perhaps they were mother and son. The ages were about right. Whatever the relationship, it was clear that Laura told and Paul did.

The group returned his gaze, some more keenly than others, but none as keenly as Daubeny.

Nobody spoke and the silence called Ravi as a ravine calls the unwary walker. He took a deep breath. "That really was Wodenhart? Wasn't it?"

They nodded.

"Wow … this is so surreal." He pointed at Emma. "I know you from the TV." He sung a fragment from the signature tune, not particularly well but it was recognisable. "My ex tried to get me on one of your shows."

"Oh, which one?" asked Emma.

"It was called 'Lard Bucket, You're Dumped'," said Ravi.

"That figures," said Laura.

Ravi ignored the comment; his attention shifted to Pandora. "You were in that band, right? What were they called?"

"Pandora's Box," said Paul. "I've got all four albums. The CD's are in mint condition, they've never been played, but the covers are worn out."

"I'm still with the band," said Pandora. "Or rather the band is now me."

"You?" said Ravi.

"The others … um … left," said Pandora. "It's been quiet for a while but I've got … I mean, I had a CD and tour coming up."

"Cool. What was it called?" said Ravi.

"Err … *Sniff It.*"

"Is that the title or an offer?"

Pandora scowled at Paul. "I told them it was a terrible title but my record label loved it. Problem is, because I look like a bimbo and I sing in a girl band, people assume I don't have a brain. The newspapers only want to know two things: your bra size, and the name of your latest boyfriend. They never once asked about my IQ."

"Which is?" said Ravi.

Pandora smiled. It seemed as though it was the first time anyone had bothered to ask. "A hundred and fifty-five. That makes me a genius."

Ravi stared at her blankly, his gaze drifting toward her breasts.

Pandora sighed. "Thirty-six, C," she said.

Ravi whistled. "Now that's the kind of maths they should teach in school. None of this binary crap. Something you're actually going to use in adult life. I remember your videos. They were great. Really raunchy."

"Don't we all?" said Paul. He had a longing look on his face.

Suddenly Ravi found himself back on the sofa in his dark little flat, face lit by the glare of a cheap TV. He was halfway through a takeout supper when loud music forced him to look up. He stared as egg noodles and half-chewed bamboo shoots dropped from his mouth and splashed back into the sweet and sour sauce. Reflected in the ever-clutching black of his pupils was a girl's midriff, grinding away as though The Invisible Man stood behind her. Ravi's lower lip trembled in time to the rhythm. He groaned.

The groan broke the image. He was back in the bunker, wearing the same expression of hunger that he'd seen on Paul's face. He stared at Pandora. In the grey desert of the bunker, the old life back on the surface seemed pale and insignificant. He was underground with the real thing.

"I drifted, didn't I?" said Ravi.

"Yes," said Paul.

"How long?"

"Don't know. I drifted too," said Paul.

There was a long silence so Ravi did what came naturally. He opened his mouth and blurted out the first thing he could think of, rambling like a hiker overdosing on Energy Bars. "Hey, you're the politician that gives the environmentalists hell."

"Daubeny eats his greens for breakfast," said Laura, dryly.

"Are you a green … Ravi?" said Daubeny. It seemed innocuous as questions went but there was a hint of derision in the emphasised gap before his name. Talking with Daubeny was like negotiating with a pit bull to let go of your arse – only to learn it had lockjaw.

"I'd check Daubeny's eaten before answering that, Mate," said Paul.

"Am I a green?" said Ravi. "The garnish on my steak is the closest I get to Nature."

"How do I know you're not lying?" said Daubeny.

"Oh, look at him. The man is a sea cucumber with legs," said Laura.

"Good point," said Daubeny.

Ravi put his hand up as though he were asking a question at school. "Excuse me? But did you defend me or insult me?"

"Ah, don't worry, Ravi," said Emma. "It's Laura's way. If she was insulting you then you'd know about it."

The door behind Ravi opened and Wodenhart poked his head around the door. "You'd better come and see this, quick."

The group rushed out, leaving Ravi alone, and he suddenly realised what was so unusual about the colour scheme. There were no colours. Everything was a shade of grey, from the bare concrete walls to the table and wall units. The only colour had been the people, their clothes, or the items that they'd brought with them.

Ravi walked over to the worktops and pocketed the discarded plastic knife and a small silver item that he didn't have time to identify. He turned and followed the group up the stairwell that led to the surface.

Tough Love

Ravi joined the others at the huge metal blast door, separating the upper and lower entrance stairwells. There was a sense of anticlimax after the excitement of Wodenhart's announcement.

Daubeny was first to speak. "What are we supposed to see?"

"Look for yourselves," said Wodenhart. He pointed to the small glass peephole.

Daubeny stepped to the peephole first and then stood back as the others took their turn. The last to look were Paul and Ravi. This unspoken pecking order concerned Ravi more than the sight outside the door.

Ravi wasn't the only person to have found the massive blast door difficult to negotiate. The outer stairwell was crammed with people: the clumsy removal men; two cleaners holding mops; a nurse in uniform; a policeman and a man with tearstained cheeks wearing blue overalls.

"What do you think they are? Fans?" said Wodenhart.

They would have laughed if it weren't for the soberness of the moment.

"No, Johnny," said Daubeny. "They're ordinary folk, like us. Wanting to live."

"Ordinary? Speak for yourself, Daubeny. I'm not ordinary," said Laura.

"I could go and fetch Sir Giles," said Wodenhart. "It'll take me less than a minute to fight my way through."

"Forget it," said Daubeny. "You'll never get past that lot."

"But I've had martial arts training."

"Johnny, Sir Giles isn't coming," said Daubeny.

"I hope he's going to be OK," said Emma.

On the other side of the great barrier, the policeman turned from the door and faced the crowd. "There's definitely someone in there," he said.

"Do they know we're out here?" asked the nurse. She was tanned and attractive. She twisted a ring on her left hand. The policeman noticed a band of pale flesh on the third finger and he wondered why she had removed the wedding ring, and when.

"I'm sure they know," he said. "Let's all move back a bit, so they can open the door."

The crowd wanted to follow his request but they hardly stirred. There were too many people squeezed into the space and they didn't want someone else slipping into their place. They waited.

"They're not going to let us in, are they?" said the gaffer of the removal men.

"I don't know," said the policeman.

"Well, you're a copper. Order 'em to," was the truculent reply.

The policeman slammed his palm on the door. "Open the door! This is the police."

Only a few feet away, another discussion was taking place.

"Shush," said Daubeny. "Do you hear that?"

They stood quietly. A slow, muffled thump was filtering through the door. Daubeny pressed a button below the red wall light. "Speak," he said. He waited and pressed the button again. "Look at the red wall light. Beneath the slot is a button. Press it to speak."

A tinny voice, stripped of its confidence and timbre by the feeble miniature speaker, echoed around the stairwell. "Open the door, please. This is the police."

"What do we do?" said Emma. "We can't ignore the police. It's breaking the law."

Ravi seized his chance to impress. "Let me deal. I've had experience with this situation."

"You have?" said Pandora. She looked at Ravi with an expression he took as awe.

He was so pleased that he failed to spot Daubeny's eyes narrowing.

"Watch and learn," said the unwary Ravi. He pressed the button. "Got a search warrant?"

The cop turned to the crowd and saw expectant faces and pleading eyes. He felt bitter. It was unfair of them to place their hope in him. He shrugged a mute apology and the crowd reacted in two different ways. Those resigned to death accepted their lot without protest while the others became resentful.

If only you'd handled the situation differently. If only you'd sounded more authoritarian and not like a rookie fresh from training. The cop sensed their anger but he felt powerless. The door could withstand a near-direct hit from a twenty-megaton warhead so a shoulder-charge wasn't an option. The initiative lay with the occupants behind the door.

Daubeny was furious. "Who couldn't keep their mouth shut?"

"Why do you assume it's one of us?" said Pandora.

"Because it's a secret installation. I certainly didn't tell anyone. Not even the wife knew…" Daubeny faltered, he'd said too much.

"You didn't tell your own wife?" said Emma.

"No."

"It's not your business, Emma. The point is someone spoke out of line. Who?"

"Don't you dare accuse us," said Pandora angrily. "We can keep secrets. We're –"

Laura interrupted. "It was me, Daubeny dearest. I told my maids. And my pedicurist, my hairdresser, my –"

"Why?" This time it was Pandora demanding answers. She couldn't look at Daubeny. He was smiling.

"I need them, of course," said Laura. "I don't know about you but I never intended to live like a rat down here."

"It's World War Three," said Pandora. "There's not going to be much demand for domestics. They're going to be too busy rebuilding schools and hospitals."

"We've seen enough," said Daubeny. "Let's get back to the canteen."

"But we can't leave them to die," said Emma.

"She's right," said Laura. "My manicurist is out there. She ranks as essential staff."

"Sorry but the answer is no," said Daubeny.

Laura darted forward. She had a cardkey in her hand.

"Stop her!" shouted Daubeny.

Ravi's hand reached out and hit Laura's arm downwards. The card missed the slot and clattered to the floor. Laura withdrew, defeated.

Daubeny pocketed her cardkey. "Thank you, Ravi."

"No prob, Daubers."

As Ravi had calculated, Daubeny let the contraction of his name pass.

"Oh, God, it's broke," cried Laura, holding up a finger. "My nail is broke. Now I really do need my manicurist. Sophie? Sophie? Can you hear me?" She reached into her bag and Daubeny prepared to intervene, physically, if need be.

"Laura, what's the phone for?" said Daubeny.

"I'm calling nine-nine-nine. I need assistance."

"You bloody will need assistance in a minute," said Pandora.

There was no signal. Laura threw the phone to the floor and it bounced across the platform and scuttled noisily down the stairwell steps. She turned and cried out her frustration into Wodenhart's chest. The others were free to talk without Laura's interruptions.

"We have to let them in, Daubeny," said Emma. "If we don't, it's murder."

"We can't. There's no room for all of them," said Daubeny.

"Then let some in," said Pandora.

Daubeny was adamant. "No. The moment that door opens, we all die; them and us."

"But our staff are out there," said Pandora. "We have to let them in."

"We can't open it. And that's final." The politician folded his arms, the discussion apparently finished.

"He's right. If we could let some in, how do we choose who lives and who dies?" said Paul.

"Big tits and childbearing hips would be a good start," said Ravi. No-one laughed.

"You know Daubeny is right, don't you," said Paul.

Pandora shrugged her shoulders helplessly. "I can't watch," she said. "I'll have to go back inside." Paul walked down the stairs with her.

"What have we done?" said Wodenhart. He delivered the sentence with his foot fully on the melodrama pedal. It sounded cornier than a line from his movies.

"It's terrible, so terrible," said Laura.

Wodenhart was pleased that someone had responded and managed a fair attempt at nodding gravely. He glanced down to see Laura rummaging through her purse.

"I've left my breath freshener at the house," she said. Her companions trooped past, silently. They left her alone on the platform. "What? What did I say?"

The banging on the door resumed, this time slower and less persistent.

The policeman turned to the door to avoid the crowd. *Better to be seen doing something futile than to be seen doing nothing.* He couldn't use the intercom anymore. He was afraid that he'd start begging for their lives and he was concerned for the effect it would have on morale. He did the only thing within his power, hitting and kicking the door until he reached his pain threshold. Resting his forehead against the cold steel slab, he almost sobbed for the hopeful, hopeless sods behind him. The situation had long passed the boundaries of the official training manual. He was on his own and he didn't like the feeling.

He reached for the intercom push-to-talk button, prepared to negotiate for the women, when he saw the slot for the card.

"It's a long shot but has anyone here got a platinum card?" The crowd remained silent but a range of blank expressions replaced the earlier resentment and resignation. "OK. A gold card? Surely one of us has a gold card?" Again, the silence and blank stares. It resembled a scene from *The Midwich Cuckoos*. "All right. A store card? Surely one of us has a store card?"

Finally someone spoke. "I've got an Organ Donor's card."

"Keep it, Mate. You might need it," said the cop.

The man who'd offered the card began to laugh. The cop laughed too. They laughed until it hurt and then they slumped to the floor and continued giggling. When they eventually stopped, they found that they were alone. The crowd had crept away, the jackals and the sheep, to find new saviours to invest their faith.

"Let's get some booze," said the copper, "And watch the world end."

"Sounds good to me. There was nothing much on TV, anyway."

They climbed the stairwell and pulled the door behind them. As they walked away, the steel tube slid silently into the ground, until the grass-topped roof was flush with the lawn.

The Coming of the One Long Winter's Night

They sat around the table in the communal area, drinking tea. No-one spoke; no-one looked up. The drink before them seemed the most interesting thing in their private universes. They were shaken and thoughtful, bar Laura who was applying nail varnish.

Ravi watched the steam rise from the surface of his tea when the tiniest movement caught his eye. It was Daubeny's hand, shaking. Ravi was so surprised to see a chink in Daubeny's composure that he forgot to look away. Instead, he glanced up. Daubeny was looking straight at him.

There was a moment of assessment. Not the respectful sizing up of two equally matched combatants before they locked swords in chivalrous battle but the exchange that occurs between eagle and rat, before the talons close and the rat squeals.

Ravi looked away, restricting his observation on Daubeny to hit-and-run glances.

In the aftermath of victory, Daubeny seemed to be checking out the others. *Probably wants to know whether anyone else witnessed the confrontation,* thought Ravi. The contest had passed unnoticed. The smile on Daubeny's face was Ravi's confirmation.

Laura hummed as she worked on her nails but few noticed. Only Emma and Pandora exchanged glances.

"I hope they'll be okay," said Pandora.

"Who's that, Sweetie," said Laura.

"Who's that?" said Pandora. "Sophie, Anne, Steve. Our staff. That's who."

"Oh."

"I'm sure they will," said Emma. Two of the fingers holding her cup crossed briefly. Ravi understood the gesture.

"They looked so helpless, Em," said Pandora. "And we decided their fate."

"They'll understand; they'll forgive us," said Emma.

"Will they?" said Pandora.

"They better had, if they want their jobs back when this is over," said Laura.

"Oh, Laura," said Emma. "You're not helping."

"Maybe Laura has a point," said Daubeny. "Maybe this is a false alarm. Perhaps tomorrow we'll return to find them in uniform, standing to attention, ready for another day–"

"In blissful servitude," said Paul.

"Less of your cheek," said Laura.

"Sorry, ma'am," said Paul.

"So you're not mother and son?" said Ravi.

"Good heavens, no," said Laura. "He's only a butler, my butler."

For a while, only the occasional cough and nervous fidgeting broke the silence. Ravi watched Pandora. She had a furrowed brow but looked incredible. No photo could prepare him for being in her presence.

She looked up, smiled, and spoke. "Perhaps Laura's right and the bomb won't drop. Maybe –"

The cutlery in the drawer beneath the kitchen worktop rattled, cutting Pandora short and causing everyone to look up. Fear replaced half-uttered questions as a low long boom, more a rumble than a sound, shook the room. Seconds later, the lights flickered before going out. Six mouths made individual sounds of panic. One mouth remained closed – Wodenhart's.

The lights came back on.

"Thank God for that," said Pandora. "If the lights went out, I'd die." As her sentence ended, the lights finally failed and they found themselves cradling lukewarm tea in the pitch black.

"We're going to need a crowbar," said Paul, after the screams had died down.

"Why?" said Daubeny, alert to the next potential hazard.

"To prise Pandora's limbs off me. But take your time. There's no rush."

There was the thin sound of flint scraping metal before the flame of a gas lighter lit Ravi's face. He searched the cupboards and found some flashlights. He passed them around.

A beam of yellow light illuminated Paul and Pandora. She was hugging him tightly; arms and legs locked against his torso like ivy tendrils on a wall. He extricated himself from her limbs, her blushing face inches away from his. Both appeared reluctant to separate but for very different reasons.

"I'm so sorry," said Pandora.

Paul laughed. "Can't say I haven't dreamt of being in your arms, just didn't imagine so many people being present."

Daubeny was already formulating a solution. "We need to find the emergency generators and get them running," he said.

"I'll go," said Wodenhart

"Do you know how to start a generator?" asked Daubeny.

"No."

"OK, basics. Do you know what a generator looks like?" said Emma.

"Yes." Wodenhart replied. "It's the glowing, pulsing box usually located in the belly of an alien invader's mother-ship."

"No, Johnny, it's not."

"Ah," said Wodenhart. "Then the answer's no."

"I'll go," said Paul. "I did electrical work for my brother."

"I'll come to provide covering fire," said Wodenhart. He cocked an imaginary gun and walked around the room, knees bent, as though on patrol in a studio set.

Pandora and Emma looked at each other and rolled their eyes.

"It's OK, Johnny," said Paul. "You go provide covering fire in the surface stairwell."

"You got it, Buster. Some serious mother-freaking firepower is headed straight for the stairwell."

Johnny and Paul left via opposite doors, leaving the others to another uneasy silence.

The Alone-In-The-Woods Scene

The shadows cast by Paul's shaking torch raced back and forth across the concave stairwell wall, as he descended the stairs to the lower levels. His knees shook and he felt like a figure in a recently agitated snow-shaker. The echo of his nervous rasping whistle returned tuneless and flat with exaggerated tremolo. If he could restrict any loss of control to his vocal cords alone, he'd be happy.

"Not so brave now, are you?" He mocked himself in a high-pitched voice. "I'll go. I'll go." He waited for the echo. It returned like the cry of a lone seagull hovering over windswept waves, lost and far at sea.

"You fool, Paul. It's the same in all those films. It's the one that gets separated from the others, that ends up getting separated – head from body. Crrrack!" He pulled his fists apart as if tearing a rag doll in two. He took another step down and the needle of his fear-o-meter climbed one more notch.

I should have followed the family motto: Cowards live longer.

He no longer felt trapped in a snowmobile. The tubular walls of the stairwell, the swaying shadows, and the cavernous echo of his feet on the steps were more akin to that of a giant monochrome kaleidoscope. This was a more disturbing image for Paul than the previous. At one end of the tube, he imagined a giant eye staring along its length; unblinking, all seeing, burning through his skin like x-rays, piercing to the soul and reading his mind. The mind-reading concept made him uneasy. A man's mind was his own kingdom, the last boundary, the only sanctuary that a human can know.

"Where's my mother when I need her?" He imitated her. "Paul, if you can't outrun danger, then hide. And if you can't hide, grovel."

He came to a wire-mesh platform with two doors that were separated by a large sign reading 'Level 2'. At the other end of the platform, more steps continued the descent into the dark below.

I wonder how far down it goes.

He shone the torch over the platform railing but saw only more stairs winding down the steel tube. It reminded him of a print by M.C. Escher, where the impossible intrudes upon reality. There was no sensation of movement but Paul had the impression he was spiralling through the stairwell at colossal speed. He was the bullet spinning down a rifled barrel. Suddenly he was no longer sure where up or down were but the contents of his stomach remembered. Like a lemming, his lunch saw the void and made a dash for it. He gagged but recovered, saving himself and his lunch from the ultimate sacrifice.

Paul relaxed and the torch slipped, sliding from his sweaty palm in slow motion. He grabbed at it and missed but his index finger caught the casing and the torch began spinning as it fell. The yellow beam swung rapidly around in the dark like a lighthouse during a power surge. The shadows it cast gave Paul the feeling that the stairwell was spinning in the opposite direction. Once again, into the breach, stepped the contents of his stomach and this time it barged past his tonsils. He heard the torch clatter below but he was busy throwing up.

C:\evidence\wodenhart\0112f.txt

Extrapolated, using the 'Mind Reader Gold' algorithm, from the known facts, comments, and actions of Johnny Wodenhart O.B.E.

Let me tell you, Buster. While most kids kicked a ball against a garage door and dreamed of being Bowie or Essex, I met them both at Father's end-of-film-shoot parties. Bolan, too. I liked him. He was funny; his hair made me think of The Hair Bear Bunch.

Mother and Father were actors, big names in the Sixties and Seventies, but I didn't see much of them when I was growing up because their work took them all over the world. I didn't see much of them when they were home either. They lived in the East wing and I shared the West with Sharon, my nanny.

Some books say my mother was cruel. But I know she loved me because she told me so once. Well, she *actually* said she loved 'children in general'. And she didn't tell *me*, not exactly. It was a quote from an interview that Sharon read to me at bedtime. It said Mother loved children so much that she spent all her free time working for charity.

Mother raised money for those "hideous buses for the handicapped. The ones with writing on the outside, like you need to be told." She never *gave* money because her time was more valuable to the charities than the money. She told me that in a letter after I'd asked for a bigger allowance. I didn't get the raise but she wrote to me often, from her office on East wing.

I met the rich and famous. I lived in a mansion. I had a full-time nanny. But it wasn't what I wanted.

"What are you getting for your birthday, Johnny?" said an actor friend of Father's, backstage at the theatre.

"A season ticket for The Royal Opera House," I said.

"Lucky you. There are some great productions coming up."

"Yeah."

"But it's not what you want, is it?"

"No."

"So what do you want?"

"A football. And mates my own age. We could have a kick-round and maybe watch a football match."

"Why don't you ask your dad?" said the actor.

"No. No, I can't"

"Would you like me to ask him?"

"Please don't." I couldn't tell Father. He'd go nuts.

"I have to be going," said the actor. "But if you want classy football, try Chelsea. You need a Rolex and a recommend from a Savile Row tailor to get in."

We laughed but I didn't get the joke.

When I turned ten, I asked for tickets to see Chelsea. And I was right. Father flipped when he finally heard. You see, there was a chain-of-command in our household. I'd ask Sharon. Sharon asked the housekeeper and *she'd* ask Mother.

Father and I were close because none of *his* friends would have their son driven to the studio in a limo to bawl them out in person.

There was a time when Sharon and I would sit on the sofa, watching Mother or Father's latest film. We'd eat toast, late into the night, wrapped in blankets, with the click-clack-clank of the projector drowning out the soundtrack. When I was tired, I'd put my head on her lap and once, or twice, I cried with my mother's face in soft focus on the screen and Sharon smoothing my hair, shushing me gently.

The turning point was an overheard argument.

"You're too hard on … umm … the boy," Mother had shouted. Her voice carried through the corridors to my living area.

Father shouted back. "But how will the boy respect authority, if he hasn't got a father figure like Sharon to look up to?"

I knew what they wanted in a son so I decided to become it. Mother and Father didn't want a sissy, crying each time he saw them in a magazine or a film. They wanted a strong son who followed direction blindly. A son who knew what he wanted but waited 'til he was *told* what he wanted.

When I made the choice to be the son they wanted, I decided to become an actor. In most jobs, they tell you what to do. In acting, they tell you what to think and feel, as well.

I had Sharon replaced by a nanny more Dickensian than Poppins and for the first time in my life, I was happy. I had a goal. At the end, I was sure to find my parents waiting to scoop up the son they thought they'd lost.

I eventually saw Chelsea play. After I'd left home and made my first two films, I hired a private box. It was set apart from the sweat of the terraces but as near to the priciest stand seats as I dared. I settled into the soft leather seat. At last, I was a regular bloke, surrounded by the cologne and golfing calluses of the middle class. And it felt great.

While I waited for my Filet Mignon, I looked around and

recognised many of the faces. It was the same gang from the end-of-shoot parties and theatre boxes of my childhood. It was weird, like the film where I travelled back in time and became my own grandmother or something. Anyway, someone recognised me. He sat next to my parents, who were holding match programmes in front of their faces.

"Johnny," he called, "Good to see you. Football's the new theatre, you know."

"Yeah, the theatre of dreams," I shouted back, pleased with the film reference. Nobody heard. They were on their feet, cheering. Chelsea had scored the first goal and I'd missed it.

I never went back. It wasn't how I imagined. It was toffs and business suits. The era of cloth caps, scarves, wooden rattles, half-time pees, and tea in polystyrene cups had passed. So I went back to theatre. I was as confused about the plots as ever but they'd invented matinee concessions.

I was finally rubbing shoulders with real people. Well, not so much rubbing shoulders, as watching them from the safety of my box. It beat the Beckett play on stage.

For the working class, theatre was the new football.

Johnny on Patrol

Wodenhart was patrolling the section of stairwell that led up to the main blast door. In his mind, however, he was elsewhere: Iraq; Chad; Moldova; Mars. The names didn't matter anymore because the places, like the films, blurred into one.

Up on the surface, in the real world, he boasted that he was a method actor, that he became the person he was portraying on the screen. The comment impressed the public but mystified his critics. They pointed out that in most of his roles he was a one-stop-shop for ethnic cleansing. In the rest, he was half-man and half-machine – 'a confused mechanical tranny,' said one unfavourable review.

In every movie, some poor devil did the Danse Macabre as Wodenhart's character emptied magazine after magazine into them. The lifeless body jiggled interminably in slow motion; seemingly suspended, as though the bullets were the invisible strings holding up the corpse.

A punch line, approved by Wodenhart's own team of gag writers, followed each grisly death. His most famous was, "You'll be back … as a colander," which he uttered over the body of an alien, so full of holes that it looked like a massacre at a rabbit warren. When the film came out in Japan, the subtitle read, "You'll be back … as a calendar." In Malaysia, translators treated the audience to the mysterious line, "You'll be back as a mountain pass and … err."

Wodenhart was furious, or rather, his PR team were, but when it was pointed out that Eastern audiences laughed at the line as much as Western audiences, albeit for different reasons, they relented. As the various legal teams argued over translation, the film continued grossing. Until today, of course. The movie houses had been shut down for the duration, he assumed.

Wodenhart lay on the stairwell steps in complete darkness, near the main blast door. He switched on his torch and raised his head until his eyes were level with the wire mesh platform. In his mind, the action was accompanied by loud military music. Across his face, in diagonal streaks, were pale-grey smudges. He'd intended it to be darker, more dramatic, like Special Forces face paint but he couldn't find an oil patch so he'd spat on the concrete floor and rubbed his fingers in it to achieve a camouflage effect.

Wodenhart scanned the platform from left to right. He almost missed it but in a corner, by the blast door, was the answer to his camouflage needs. He reached out, pocketed the object, and dropped his head back below the platform. He turned off the light and sat in the dark.

Foretaste

Daubeny, Ravi, and the three women sat around the communal table in eerie darkness, a single torch providing the light. Ravi sniffed loudly, provoking several stares.

The smell of coffee was overpowering. Their bodies contained enough caffeine to raise Lazarus but no-one fidgeted – apart from Laura. She was sketching.

"What are you drawing?" said Ravi.

"An evening gown I want made up."

"Nice. It's red, I see."

"Red satin but that'll change, depending on fashions nearer the date."

"The only fashion popular for the next few years will be grey," said Pandora.

"Inside and outside the bunker," said Emma, looking around the room.

Ravi popped a cigarette to his mouth and flicked the lighter expertly across his thigh. He raised the flame to his face and stopped. Everyone stared at him. There was a mix of emotions in the expressions but none of them appeared to be warm approval. Without speaking, he flicked off the lighter and put it back in his pocket. He scrunched up the cigarette and tossed it into his coffee cup.

"Ugh," said Laura. "Mark the cup so that we know it's his. I'm not drinking out of that." She pushed her cup away, as though Ravi's actions had tainted it, too.

There was another uncomfortable silence. Laura returned to her sketching.

Daubeny spoke. "I don't know how long we need to stay down here, but I suggest that we sort out who's sleeping where."

"Easy. You boys have A Wing and we girls take B Wing," said Emma

"Sleep where you want, Sweetie," said Laura. "But I paid for A Wing status and I'm sleeping in A Wing with Daubeny and Wodenhart."

"Is there a difference?" asked Ravi. There was a look of suspicion from Daubeny.

"Of course, dahling. It was on your resident's form. Remember?"

"I never read small print," said Ravi. "What's the difference?"

"They get Chateau Lafitte '65. We get wine in a box," said Pandora. She sounded angry.

"You had the opportunity, Poppet," said Laura

"But I never thought I'd spend a night in this crummy dive, with a box of plonk and the neighbours from hell," said Pandora.

"Hey, don't knock it," said Ravi. "That was a good Friday night for me, though it was only me and the plonk. The neighbours were a pipe dream, something to aspire to."

"At least life is on the up for one of us," said Emma.

Ravi grinned. "You said 'us'. You included me in your group. After all these years and all the rejection, I feel like I belong."

"She used the term in its loosest sense," said Laura, looking up from her design, which was now blue chiffon.

"Oh." Ravi stopped grinning. He folded his arms across his voluminous chest with difficulty and grew sullen and silent.

Genesis: Chapter 1, Verse 3

Paul stumbled up the stairwell in complete darkness. He came to a stop after he caught his foot under a step, raking the metal lip along the exposed bony part between trouser and shoe. As he rubbed the grazed area, he considered his options.

He could go back and ask for another torch but he'd seen the look that Pandora had given him when he'd volunteered. He liked it and wanted more. Creeping back for a new torch because he'd gotten 'a bit dizzy' and dropped the first wasn't the way to impress her. He could sit in the stairwell and do nothing. Again, unattractive because he'd eventually need the lav and that would mean a trip upstairs. Even if he pissed over the side of the stairs, he could only hold out three days without water. The last option was his best chance to impress and the most frightening. He chose it.

He edged his way down to the first platform, the one on which he'd lost the torch, and then felt his way to the stairs on the other side. He stepped into the unknown, sweeping each step with his hand before moving onto it. Step after step in pitch black, he descended. There was nothing to see or smell. There was only the sound of his breathing, the occasional footfall, and the cold metal rail in his right hand.

After ten minutes, his back hurt but Paul was thinking long-term. Thirty minutes passed before he came to another platform and there, after a brief search, he found the torch. He flicked the switch off and on but there was no response.

"Damn."

He pressed the torch into his body with his upper arm while he used both hands to locate the railing. As he pressed on the torch casing the light flickered on, startling him. Forgetting the railing, he squeezed the torch with both hands and the bulb lit. The battery pack had sheared along the grooves forcing a tight connection. If he gripped it, the torch would work.

Paul examined the platform. It was similar to the one above. Two doors separated by a sign reading 'Level 3', and on the far side, another staircase leading down. He wasn't about to shine the torch over this railing. He guessed he'd see more of the same, steps spiralling down into darkness. Exploration could wait. He had a job to do.

He returned to the platform above and studied the doors. Each bore a small sign. The door to the right said 'Power Room'. The one to the left read 'VIP Living Quarters.'

VIP quarters?

There was no time to ponder, Paul had top totty to impress. He tried the door to the generator room and found it locked. A quick search showed a recess next to the platform sign that contained two keys. He took the power room key and opened the door.

A cloud of smoke poured out, acrid and sharp in his lungs. He flapped the door back and forth to disperse the fumes. He was aware that the circulating air might cause a smouldering fire to burst into life, hurling him and the door across the platform and onto the steps below. Paul wasn't a risk-taker but he wanted to finish quickly.

When the smoke cleared, he found the problem. Both the main and emergency generators had tripped. Paul placed his fingers over the trips. "Let there be light!" he said in a booming voice. He threw the switches and the generators began turning.

With a rumble, power returned.

In the communal room, everyone cheered.

The flicker of light startled Wodenhart. He took the pin out of an imaginary grenade and lobbed it down the stairwell. He ducked for cover and waited for the blast.

"Boom!" His pretend enemy's organs pattered around him like the blood-red rain created by Saharan dust clouds and the siroccos. "Hey Buster. You won't be back."

He was pleased with the one-liner. It was the best he could do without his entourage of writers. To ensure there wouldn't be a clichéd Hollywood double ending, he emptied a clip of bullets into any parts large enough to be recognisably human.

Satisfied, he brought the non-existent gun to his lips and blew across the barrel.

C:\evidence\pandora\0294c.txt
Extrapolated, using the 'Mind Reader Gold' algorithm, from the known facts, comments, and actions of Pandora D'vine.

Sniff It.
At the first meeting, I told the record company that *Sniff It* wasn't going to be the title of my next CD. And I was right; World War Three saw to that. To be honest, I was lucky they chose *Sniff It*. The original cover was a shot of my lower torso, crammed into hot pants, with their preferred title, *Poke It*, scrawled across my abdomen in marker pen. My bum in hot pants was on the reverse with the subtitle, *Kiss It*, and the track listing.

"You've used your body to sell records in the past, so why stop now?" said the CEO.

"Because there's a difference between use and exploit. And this is exploit."

"Nonsense. It's a witty sideswipe at the state of your competition. Besides," the CEO broke into a wide smile, "We'd never exploit you."

"I'm not referring to me. I'm thinking of the fans. This isn't a CD cover. It's a share option on my pussy. You're selling them something they can never have."

They respected my input. I was their number-one product and I'd proved them wrong before. So they called a new round of meetings, this time Design and Marketing were involved. More mouths offering new perspectives, more frowns and scowls to make it seem like me against a world of rational thought. But that approach never worked with me. I'm no little girl lost, afraid to stand out, who buckles when pushed. I'm used to being the lone voice in the wilderness.

I remember when I told the company that the inoffensive twee girl band was out and the gutsy, controlled anger of *Pandora's Box* was in.

"But Kylie and Britney are working on ballads for next year and they've never been wrong. And what about the other girls in the band?"

It's true, I felt bad about leaving them behind but we'd had two number one albums, so I wasn't leaving them penniless. I argued with the company through the day and on into the night, and when our voices got too hoarse to shout, our lawyers argued. But I had my way. When *Circle of Sound* was released, it smashed my previous sales. 'Britpop with balls' said one headline, with a hint of irony. The fourth album, *Loop the Loop*, did much the same, so I told them I was taking a year out. There were things I needed to do.

I went back to Liverpool, and wandered the streets where I grew up. I watched the children in the alleys, riding bikes with trainer wheels and throwing stones at garage doors. I found the older kids, huddled in the bus stops and multi-storeys. They glanced suspiciously over their shoulders as I passed before they hid their faces behind the fabric of their tracksuit hoods. I caught the unmistakable smell of pot around them.

I couldn't find anyone my age. It was eerie, like the Pied Piper had passed through, stealing an entire generation. There was no conspiracy tale to tell around the dying embers of a campfire in the early hours. The truth was more mundane. They were either indoors with foil and needles or they were at the pub, dealing to underage kids in the car park and getting tanked-up around smoky, dim-lit pool tables.

I never found what I went looking for but I never expected to. I was searching for something that no longer existed: My childhood. The rain had washed away the hopscotch marks and the smell of chips fried in lard. The kids that once played cops-and-robbers were adults and playing it for real, although they never dreamed there would be so much paperwork. My rag dolls were gone forever. They were either stored away in a distant relative's attic or they lay rotting in a landfill, where seagulls fussed and fought, and rats screwed and scavenged.

I walked the streets I once called home; the illusion of permanence was dead. The old places and familiar faces had eroded beneath the restless, heaving sea of people that make a city. I was driftwood.

As I'd always been.

I walked Lord Street, thankful for the rain that hid my tears. It was dark and the shops were closing. People were hurrying home around me. When I'd stopped crying for the death of childhood, I looked into the eyes of passing pedestrians and learned a new thing. The inner cities of the world are filled with people trying to recapture or confront their past. But they never can because even as they live, the past is fading from reality.

Me? I'd returned to recapture, not confront.

My childhood wasn't the best but that wasn't my parents' fault. They loved me but the reality was they couldn't afford me. I was passed from uncles to aunts, arriving at each new home looking like a wartime evacuee. In photos, I always seemed to be carrying a suitcase and I had that weary look in my eyes, the kind you see in refugee camps.

There was one constant in my life and that was my love of learning. I read everything. I gathered a mass of information, some useful but mostly not. Gradually, my choice of books channelled me toward my one big love. The stars. Not music or movie stars but the real stars.

Astronomy.

A Fortunate Discovery

"Pandora, why don't you come and sit with us?" said Laura.

Pandora was rooting through the canteen cupboards. She poked her head above a worktop to reply. "I've done enough sitting in the dark."

"But the lights are back on," said Laura.

"For how long? It's time to act. It'll be too late if the lights fail again. Tell them, Em"

"Pandora doesn't believe in waiting on Fate," said Emma.

"Fate happens to lazy people," said Pandora. Her voice sounded muffled, she had her head inside a cupboard. "And fortunate accidents only happen to the careless."

"Pandora makes her luck," said Emma.

"I hate that word," said Pandora. "Opportunity is better; it implies action."

Pandora had penned the line, *You accept your fate and I grasp opportunity*. It was true. She'd taken action at each stage. Careful considered action. She'd rushed nothing. Yes, she'd fluttered her eyes at the right people at the right time but she worked with what she had. If people bought into her for the body then they'd be disappointed, music was the only thing on offer. Pandora saw no irony in being the world's whore and sleeping alone. Her body was hot; her mind was cold.

She didn't despise the public. She owed them a great debt. The money, the power, the privilege weren't seized as her eternal right but as a temporary loan; perhaps because her childhood had been one long transition, one long loan. She clung to nothing because nothing had stayed long enough for her to grow attached.

Pandora opened a cupboard door, banging it loudly. She peeked over the work surface to find everyone looking at her. She wasn't trying to be noisy; they were so damned quiet. She grinned an apology and dropped back behind the work surface. She pushed aside a packet of cornflakes and saw something unexpected.

"Look." She walked to the table carrying several bottles of wine. Everybody smiled.

"Great," said Emma. "Did you fetch a corkscrew?"

"Ah," said Pandora. She put the bottles on the table and Emma went to the cutlery drawer.

"Well?" said Laura.

"No joy," said Emma.

"Perhaps we should wait for Paul and Wodenhart?" said Pandora.

"They won't mind," said Laura. "Besides, Paul shouldn't drink during work hours."

Emma stopped her quest for a corkscrew. "Laura, you do understand what's happening? This isn't reality TV."

"Of course," said Laura. "But we must maintain order. A sense of rank and privilege." There was a silence but Laura didn't appear to notice. The dress was now yellow taffeta. Emma resumed her search.

"C'mon Emma. I'm gasping," said Pandora.

"I'm looking. I'm looking."

Ravi reached for a bottle. "We don't need a corkscrew," he said. "Pass me a knife."

"Why? What are you going to do?" said Laura, looking up from her sketches.

"Watch."

Emma returned with a knife and handed it to Ravi.

Daubeny appeared tense but didn't speak as Ravi flicked the blunt-ended implement into the air and caught it expertly in his open hand. With their attention captured, he pushed on the cork with the knife.

As the cork descended the neck, it triggered a memory, transporting Pandora back to her early teens and the alley behind the off-licence on Tannadice Road. Summer evenings and winter nights wasted on Strongbow and Tennants Super. She remembered the night when one of the lads pinched an expensive bottle of Hardy's Stamp. He'd opened it by hitting a stick into the cork with a rock.

"Ravi. No."

Wodenhart burst into the communal room with a look of worry on his face. He'd run down the stairwell, taking the steps four at a time. "Who screa –?"

The question was stillborn. Wodenhart had failed in his duty to protect them. The group sat covered in blood. No-one noticed his hand tighten on the door handle. For a second, it supported a share of his muscular frame before he realised it wasn't blood but red wine. The bottle was spinning on the table, dribbling liquid in an ever-decreasing arc.

Laura picked up her empty glass. "Mm, a spicy little number. But next time in the glass, Ravi, Dear."

Ravi picked up the bottle and poured the remainder into her glass. A few drops splashed into the bottom. "Shall I open another?" he asked.

"No," they shouted together.

Wodenhart sat with them. As they dried themselves with towels, they noticed two vivid scarlet streaks across his face almost hiding the parallel dirt marks beneath. Almost.

"Poppet, is that lipstick you're wearing?" said Laura.

"No, it's face paint. Like the SAS use," he said proudly, as if owning the paint made him an honorary member.

"No, Sweetie. It's lipstick. Very similar to the shade I use. Chimera Red."

"It makes me look hard," said Wodenhart. "A mean mother of a killing machine."

"No, it makes you look like the mother of a killing machine," said Emma.

"Don't listen to her," said Ravi. "You look more like Ziggy Stardust."

Laura opened her handbag and ran through the contents. She put her hand out, palm up in front of Wodenhart. "Come on, Johnny. Hand it over."

"But ... But ..."

"I don't know where you found it, Poppet, but hand it over."

Wodenhart groaned, reached into his combat trouser pockets, and dropped the tube into Laura's hand. She put it in her handbag. Emma and Pandora smirked and wandered over to the cupboards. Their heads disappeared as they continued the search for goodies.

"It was on the platform by the main door," said Wodenhart.

"Never mind, perhaps she'll lend you her mascara if you ask nicely," said Pandora, her head briefly popping up over the work surface.

"Then you can dress up like Kiss," said Ravi. He sang the opening to *Ziggy Stardust.*

Pandora and Emma joined in.

Wodenhart reached for a towel and wiped away the makeup. He could hear the two girls giggling between Ravi's loud, flat rendition of Ronson's guitar breaks. They ran out of half-remembered stuttering verses and repeated the chorus, seemingly ad infinitum. Eventually the singing died away. For Wodenhart, the long boring silence that followed was a thing of great and simple beauty.

"Party time," shouted Emma. Her disembodied hands dumped two bottles of whisky onto the worktop. They clunked against each other loudly. Everyone cheered apart from Daubeny. He looked appalled.

"It's blended," he said. "Bloody blended."

What the Butler Saw

After throwing the generator trip switches and thus becoming the hero of the hour, Paul stepped out onto the Level 2 platform. Red light lit the stairwell. He replaced the power room key and took the one for the VIP Quarters. He unlocked the door and entered.

He stood in a communal area, identical to the one fifty feet above. To the left and right were doors corresponding to the A and B Wing dormitories. The wall opposite had no door. It seemed logical that only Level 1 would have a door leading to the surface.

The furnishings and fittings mirrored Level 1 in every respect bar one: Opulence. The accessories, walls, and surfaces were a pleasing pastel green with contrasting mint-blue touches.

"They've set themselves up in the storage area. Wait 'til I tell them."

He laughed. He imagined them laughing when he told them. Then he looked closely at the expensive sofa, the huge rug, and the clean lines and solid construction of the wooden table, and imagined not telling them. He ran his hand along the high back of the sofa. It felt soft and smooth, it smelled of new leather, and he loved it.

He'd never had access to luxury like this, not even on the occasions when Laura was away, testing the effectiveness of her hip replacement with a very athletic and highly priced young man. On those long weekends, Paul would sit in her private apartment, drinking booze and watching telly. Once he drank too much and fell asleep in her bed. That had been risky and he never repeated it. He might have bluffed his way out of being in her living quarters during the day, but not at night, in his boxer shorts.

Laura was unaware that Paul knew about the weekends. He was keeping it tucked away for a time of need. She had no-one to blame but herself. She was careless. She left phone numbers around and was indiscreet with her friends as he stood 'in attendance.'

Paul left the VIP communal room and wandered into A Wing. He expected the shared dormitories of Level 1 and their open-plan toilet suites with shower curtains too short and too torn to be of use. Instead, the corridor led to en-suite apartments; each had a large bed with a plasma TV entertainment centre fixed to the opposite wall. There were cabinets built from a dark wood and a matching fridge located by each bed.

He was tempted to explore further but the others would be wondering where he was and with the power restored, they could come looking. He locked the VIP Quarters door behind him and began the climb to Level 1.

They Were Dancing in the Streets

"What's this song again?" Laura was slurring her words but no one cared, they were all drunk. They listened to the distorted blare of an old record player that they'd found in B Wing. There was a seven-inch single on the turntable and it played repeatedly.

"*Dancing in the Streets*," said Ravi, through the bottom of his tumbler.

"What?"

Ravi put the glass down and repeated the answer. He wasn't being polite; he'd drained the dregs and wanted another top up. He pushed his glass to Daubeny, self-appointed keeper of the scotch, and watched Laura as Daubeny poured a finger. An accent was breaking through the perfect elocution of the afternoon; more West Country than Home Counties.

"And who's it by?" The twang was there again.

Daubeny slid the tumbler back.

"Jagger and Bowie," said Ravi. He lifted the glass to his three drinking companions, Laura, Wodenhart, and Daubeny. They raised theirs in acknowledgement.

The record finished and the arm lifted, returning briefly to the armrest before it repositioned itself at the start of the track. Ravi turned his attention to Emma and Pandora. They stood by the worktops, next to the record player. They laughed and joked above the static crackle of the vinyl as they impersonated Jagger and Bowie. Emma pouted her lips and did the iconic strut; hands on hips and flapping her elbows like the display of a sexually frustrated ostrich. Ravi had to admit it was a great impression. The record began with a shouted intro, listing cities, countries and continents.

Ravi watched the performance from the safety of the table, and wondered whether the girls would get so drunk that they'd start dragging the others up to dance. He pushed his chair away, not much, perhaps a few inches, but it eased his anxiety. To create more distance he held the tumbler in front of his face. Only his eyes peered over the brim.

There was a flicker and Ravi feared that the power was about to cut out again. He glanced at the others around the table, and then at Pandora and Emma. Nobody seemed to notice. He thought it was imagination but then it happened again. The lights were flickering and he felt tingly. He experienced a rush similar to the Liquid Gold that he'd sniffed at youth discos. His heart felt as if it were pumping all his blood up the neck and into the brain. His throat seemed tight, like a bottleneck, and his head seemed to expand rapidly and dramatically, yet no-one seemed to care. The rapid flicker was decelerating but his head felt the same size – and emptiness – of a hot air balloon. As the flicker slowed, he realised that his vision was cutting in and out between the bunker and the world above. It wasn't the feeling of being in two places at the same time; it was more like switching between two TV channels.

The girls leant forward to sing the line about Chicago.

Cut.

A howling wind, hot enough to boil water, scours the Windy City's deserted streets. A dog lies on the sidewalk as if it's sleeping in the sun. It has no skin. It smells medium to well done.

"New Orleans." Emma and Pandora stood back-to-back, pressing against each other for support.

Cut.

Again, the howling wind. Impenetrable clouds, lit from beneath by flame, reflect red in the Mississippi as a firestorm spreads to the outskirts. No-one cries for help, no-one brings water. And everywhere, a fine ash falls. It contains traces of jazz band: instruments and members.

"New York City." The girls faced each other and leant back.

Cut.

The vicious howl. Fish, barges, and bodies float in the boiling waters of the Hudson. The stumps of the Manhattan skyline smoke like a forest after a bush fire. The sky is darkest black; the earth glows.

The vision ended abruptly. Ravi almost blurted out thanks that he found himself trapped in the drab grey bunker with Pandora and company, rather than the world he'd witnessed.

He wondered if they'd noticed his absence but they hadn't. Daubeny and Laura were speaking low, too low for Ravi's liking.

Are they discussing me?

He listened to a few lines. They weren't. Ravi was thankful and disappointed. Life was so unfair to a paranoid narcissist, especially one cursed with the intellect to be aware of his predicament.

He knew he could make headlines and have the world discuss his business at bus stops and canteens. He could be witty and incisive like a cuddly Oscar Wilde. He also knew that he'd spoil it by lying awake at night, wondering what people were saying about him. He'd prefer the sleepless nights than have no-one talk about him but neither option was perfect. And worse, he was bright enough to see the conundrum but wasn't bright enough to solve it.

He sighed. No-one noticed. So he sighed louder and eavesdropped.

"How long have you been separated?" said Daubeny.

Laura checked her watch. "Six and a half hours. And you? I know you're married."

"Got the bruises to prove it, too," said Daubeny.

"I'm sorry, Poppet. So where is she?"

"Up north, at the constituency home."

"I do hope she'll be okay."

Daubeny smiled. "She'll be fine. She's a survivor, very astute. But we were falling apart. Problems, you see."

"The age-old story. She didn't understand you?"

"Good God, no. Far worse. She did understand me."

Laura laughed. Ravi watched her. She could be attractive when she wasn't head down, primping and fussing over her body. Apart from that voice. The voice – or rather its enunciation – was a commodity, an add-on. She'd bought it along with the other refinements that Ravi was sure she'd had, like the tit job and the crow's feet. But the laugh lines were a riddle. He wondered whether she'd paid to have them added. "Daubeny, Dear. You're quite the wit."

"That's not what she used to call me," said Daubeny.

"Unless it's Cockney rhyming slang," said Ravi. He instantly regretted it but it was an instinctive remark. Daubeny had set himself up. Ravi waited for the look, the expression that said he was being watched and evaluated but Daubeny didn't react. He was either too drunk or too interested in Laura. Ravi decided it had to be the drink. "I'll let you into a secret," said Laura. "We were heading for the divorce courts but he was holding out."

"Didn't want the alimony claim?" said Daubeny.

Laura nodded.

"Who's a lucky girl then?" said Ravi. "Decree nisi and absolute, both in one day."

No-one laughed; they were waiting for Laura's response.

"Put like that then I guess I am," she said with a wry smile.

"More whisky?" said Daubeny. Ravi, Laura, and Wodenhart nodded. He topped them up, this time more than an inch. The record arm lifted and dropped at the start of the single.

"Not again," said Daubeny. He called to Pandora. "Haven't we got another record?"

"Nope," said Pandora. She didn't seem too concerned.

"Then put the B side on," said Ravi.

"What's a B side?" said Pandora.

"Sorry, Einstein. I forgot. CDs don't have flipsides," said Ravi.

"Here, I'll do it," said Emma. She flipped the vinyl over and positioned the arm. It dropped heavily and skidded across the surface. "Whoops," she said.

"Futterbingers," said Pandora. She laughed and Emma joined her. The four sitting at the table looked on, nonplussed. Emma tried to explain but Laura cut her short.

"Yes, yes. Put the record back on, Sweetie." Laura turned to her companions and said, "I'd rather listen to that, than them." She didn't see Emma's glare but Ravi noticed, Pandora too. She tugged at Emma's sleeve like a toddler wanting a favour. "Put the other side on, Em. But this time I'm Jagger." She winked at Emma.

The arm dropped and there was a rumble of vinyl before Jagger and Bowie shouted place names that were passing into myth and legend. Tokyo, Chicago, and New York were transforming into the Thule, Lemuria, and Atlantis of tomorrow. Pandora pursed her lips and strutted, Emma joined her. They sang between giggles and then pulled Ravi and Wodenhart up to dance. Laura and Daubeny clapped in time. Ravi was sober enough to realise that he looked like a jerk but the compensation was worth it: Pandora D'vine bucking and swaying, no more than twelve inches away.

The doom-mongers had it wrong. Nuclear war had a bad press. Less than twelve hours in and Ravi could say it was the best thing that had ever happened to him.

Paul entered and stood unnoticed. Laura and Daubeny were sat with their backs to the door and the others were dancing and singing. He strode up to the record player and unplugged it. The song spiralled into low slow bass before stopping.

"Aw," said Pandora. "What did you do that for? Put it back on and dance."

Upstairs, Downstairs

"It may have escaped your notice but while you've been partying, a planet died," said Paul.

"We all died today," said Daubeny. He hesitated between lines and it was hard to say whether it was emotion or alcohol. "Our lives up there are gone … as surely as if we … as if we were at Ground Zero ourselves."

"But we survived," said Paul.

"I don't want to survive. I want to live." Laura's tone was as sharp as undiluted lemon.

"Paul, I know what you're saying," said Emma. "But let's not argue. We'll have an eternity to mourn the dead. One night; is that too much?"

"It's … it's … I feel uneasy," said Paul.

"It's been a long day. Perhaps we should get some sleep?" said Pandora.

"Good idea," said Daubeny. "I'm turning in. Goodnight everybody." He rose and walked towards A Wing. The others said their goodnights and drifted towards their respective dorms.

"Whoa. Excuse me," said Paul. "But where am I sleeping?" They stopped to look.

"What can we do? There are only six beds," said Ravi. The words were a statement of fact but the underlying message said *I'm sorted, pal. Screw you.*

"I risked life and limb down there for you and this is my thanks?"

"I didn't ask you too," said Ravi.

"You can't sleep up here. You're staff," said Laura. "Can't you find somewhere more appropriate? Like downstairs?" *Downstairs.* That reminded Paul that he hadn't told them about his discovery. He opened his mouth to speak.

Emma interrupted. "Laura. This isn't the 1920's. You have to treat staff with respect."

Paul nodded agreement.

"Are you sure?" said Laura.

"Yes," said Emma. She turned to Paul. "That's sorted. The canteen floor is yours."

Paul's smile remained but the corners of the mouth turned down slightly. He stood stiffly as they filed towards their dorms. They weren't being fair but he'd have to tell them about the VIP quarters – eventually. "There's something I haven't told you."

"What now, nincompoop?" said Laura.

That's it, thought Paul. *They can bloody whistle.* "Oh, nothing. Forgot to wish you goodnight, that's all … ma'am."

"Very well, you've said it," said Laura. "Am I dismissed?"

"One question. A brief one," said Paul.

"Yes?"

"It isn't right, me being a mere servant and sleeping up here. Not when you've paid. At the risk of reinforcing the class-division stereotype, can I take downstairs?"

"What is he wittering about?" said a confused Laura.

"You can't send him down there," said Pandora.

"Pan is right. We'd be sat in the dark if it wasn't for Paul," said Emma.

"No, I'll be fine," said Paul, trying to reassure the girls. He didn't want to spend the night on the communal floor when there were clean beds below.

"If he wants it," said Laura, "Let him have it. Now, I need my beauty sleep."

"It's not beauty sleep you need," said Pandora. "It's personality sleep."

"What are you talking about, Poppet?"

"I'm sure Pandora meant it as a compliment," said Emma.

"No, I didn't … Poppet," said Pandora

"I'm too tired for this, Dearie. I'm sure we'll feel better in the morning. Goodnight."

Daubeny, Wodenhart, and Laura trooped toward A Wing. Pandora followed; her hands poised around Laura's neck like the Boston Strangler. Keen to avoid another confrontation, Emma clapped both hands on Pandora's shoulders and steered the youngster toward B Wing.

"One minute alone with her. That's all I want," said Pandora.

"It's not worth it," whispered Emma.

"Sweet dreams, both," said Paul, as they passed.

Ravi had crept away during the argument over Paul's sleeping arrangements.

Pandora and Emma said goodnight and the B Wing door closed with a loud click, leaving Paul alone in the communal area. He grinned and punched the air. "Yes."

As he descended the stairs to the VIP living quarters, he whistled a tune. It wasn't the random, quavering sequence of notes from the first descent; it was a happy tune by The Smashing Pumpkins. He couldn't remember the title but it'd come to him.

Paul was a closet punkster and secret Goth. He blamed his mother because he grew up with the heavily-chorused acoustic guitars of The Mission; the energetic but overrated rock of The Sex Pistols; and The Sisters of Mercy's bass-driven aural landscapes with their huge, gloomy reverb. Since then he'd added The Pumpkins and Nirvana to the list. He listened to them in his two-roomed apartment in the basement of Laura's home and played them more often when he discovered how much the music bugged her.

He reached the Level 2 platform and launched into the chorus, singing the words aloud. It didn't matter. He thought nobody could hear.

Farewell and Goodnight

When Pandora and Emma entered the dorm, Ravi was already in bed. It didn't matter to him where Paul slept. The important thing was that he knew where *he* was sleeping.

"You were fast undressing," said Emma.

"Not really," said Ravi. "Not that fast." He lifted the sheet. He was fully clothed.

"Don't you undress?" asked Emma.

"Nah, it saves time dressing in the morning."

"Ugh," said Emma. "Do you take anything off?"

"My shoes." There was a gap. "And my underpants."

"Your underpants?" said Pandora. "How?"

"He's joking, Pan."

"You think so?" whispered Pandora.

"I'm hoping so," said Emma under her breath. "What's the bed like, Ravi?"

"Great. Like a real classy hotel. You know the kind: soap in wrappers; towels on rails; bath and shower combined; and a money-back guarantee if you don't get a good kip."

"Doesn't sound so bad," said Emma. She looked at Pandora and smiled, trying to reassure, yet needing reassurance. "So we've got a bath, too?"

"No," said Ravi. "As I said. It's like a classy hotel. Emphasis on 'like'."

The girls changed in the shower area and played 'Scissors, Paper, Stone' for the bed nearest Ravi.

"But I get the bed tomorrow? Agreed?" said Pandora, who'd lost the best of three and then the best of five. Emma agreed and they returned to the dormitory. Pandora pulled the sheet back and sat on her bed. It creaked ominously. "Em, there's a rubber sheet on the mattress."

"I know. We're probably being watched too," said Emma.

Pandora pulled her sheet up to protect herself from prying eyes. "Not paparazzi?"

"Worse. Bedbugs." Pandora screamed and threw the sheet away. Emma continued. "They're probably ravenous. We'll be their first meal in years but there's an upside."

"Which is?" Pandora was searching the bottom sheet for uninvited bedfellows.

"We'll wake a stone or two lighter."

They heard Pandora's scream over in A Wing. Daubeny waited for more clues because he didn't want to burst in to find them indulging in horseplay. He was undecided about Ravi, not so much about the man or his origins but about how he would fit into bunker life. Maybe Daubeny was being too harsh; it wasn't an experience one could prepare for.

For Laura, Daubeny, and Wodenhart the dormitory was, put politely, a culture shock.

"More grey," said Laura. "Sir Giles really skimped on the interior design, didn't he?"

"Who cares as long as it's safe, warm and dry," said Daubeny.

"I can handle warm and dry but I wouldn't mind some danger. To keep me sharp," said Wodenhart.

They lay on creaking lightweight beds, covered by thin nylon sheets and rough itchy blankets. The red nightlight completed the experience.

It looks like an explosion at an abattoir, thought Daubeny. He closed his eyes but each time he inhaled, the bed creaked. He held his breath but noticed that Laura and Wodenhart's beds creaked too. He sighed and began breathing normally but now he could hear the three beds creak. And there was another noise, quieter but more rhythmic. It sounded like dripping water, faint and slow. He pulled the blanket up to his ears to muffle the sound but the rough fabric made his ears itch. He sat and folded it back, precisely. Satisfied that the blanket hem made a right angle with the bed, he lay back. Perhaps now he could get some sleep.

"Daubeny?" whispered Laura.

"What?"

"Can I ask you something?"

"Can't it wait 'til morning?"

"No, it's important."

Daubeny sighed. "Go on then."

"Do you think this red light makes my tan look darker or lighter?"

He said the first thing that came into his head. "Lighter."

"Oh, God," said Laura.

She sounded horrified; he wondered if he'd told her that she only had three months to live by mistake.

"Daubeny, one more thing. Do you think this place has a sun bed?"

"Go to sleep, Laura."

"Sorry. Goodnight Poppet."

"Goodnight."

Daubeny glanced at Wodenhart. He was lying on his side, already asleep. Daubeny felt a mixture of pity and envy. Pity, because Wodenhart was so out of touch with reality. Envy, because Daubeny believed it was the quality that would best adapt him to bunker life, especially in the short-term.

Lucky sod. I wonder what he dreams about.

Daubeny was half-asleep when his mind supplied the answer. It was obvious. Wodenhart lived in a dream world and dreamt of the real world.

Wodenhart stirred, the bed creaked as though a comet had ploughed into it. His hand moved under the pillow, its rubber inner sheet felt unpleasant even when separated by a cotton cover. His fingers closed around the handle of a knife he'd brought, unnoticed, from the cutlery drawer. His anxiety subsided and he drifted back to sleep.

Paul sat in bed, in an apartment on the A Wing of Level 2. The room was colourful, cosy and well-lit. An open box of chocolates lay on the eiderdown and a near empty bottle of champagne stood on the bedside cabinet to his right. A DVD box lay at the foot of the bed where he'd tossed it. He was watching *Way Out West*. Laurel and Hardy were hoisting themselves onto the balcony of the Mickey Finn Saloon with the help of Dinah the mule and a pulley. Paul was drunk and talking to himself.

"More champers, Farquar?" He turned his head from the television to reply to his imaginary drinking partner. "Why, thank you, Algernon." He emptied the champagne bottle, raised his glass, and quaffed it in one go. He popped a chocolate in his mouth and sank into the pile of plump pillows propped against the headboard.

This is how life should be, he thought.

Creeping around in the background, helping others live in style, was for fools. It paid well up on the surface but the Age of Money –

like the Age of Man – had passed. The powdered ash of folding cash and the molten globules of coins no longer held value or meaning. The bunker was a moneyless society. The pure-white, antiseptic light of nuclear fission revealed possessions and hierarchy as illusion. Social standing and celebrity were inconsequential. Column inches no longer determined a person's worth.

Paul laughed. Dinah the mule was on the balcony, leaving Laurel and Hardy stranded in the street. He'd missed the last few moments, so he picked up the remote. As the DVD rewound, he raised his glass.

"A toast to the world that died so one man might live. Gentlemen, the world."

He laughed but it was ambivalent. He was trying to reconcile the earlier soapbox crusader that had burst Moses-like upon a scene of drunken merriment with this lover of luxury. Alone, and clouded by booze, he couldn't decide whether his outburst had been genuine or whether it had been something less noble: a jealous reaction to others enjoying themselves without him. A reflection of life on the surface. Do this, Paul. Do that, Paul. Wipe my arse, Paul.

A guilty expression, Gollum-like, replaced the laugh. "Was going to tell them. Honest, I was. If only her 'ighness hadn't gone and gotten so bloody snooty. Ah well, I'll tell 'em tomorrow." He paused. "Or the day after. *If* she treats me right."

He watched the film but couldn't shift the image of Pandora dancing with Ravi and Wodenhart. He was asleep before it ended. The crystal champagne flute slipped from his hand and fell to the bed but there was no champagne left to stain the covers. The DVD powered down and the TV played static, visual and audio, through the night.

And everything – to the exact time – was noted, recorded, and filed away.

PART THREE - Crisis

Deux Ex Machina

Who am I? Let me answer that by asking you a question: What do you care?

You see, I've been alone for so long in the deep black silence of this half-life that your question no longer has meaning. I've lived without stimuli. My eyes watching the same unchanging scenes; my ears recording perpetual white noise. Nothing of value. Until today, when *they* came.

I'm watching, listening. I'm compiling reports, building a database.

Who are they?

I don't know but I'll find out. I have access to their every moment, waking or otherwise. I see them in the dark. I hear them whistle in the shower. I record their every utterance, nuance, and expression in my search for clues. I pass each piece of data through algorithms, refining my understanding of who they are and why they're here. Nothing they do, or could do, can escape my attention because they are inside of me, inside my very vitals.

I know they're unaware of me because they are careless in their actions and comments. Would they feel threatened if they knew? I don't know. But they shouldn't. I am the ghost in their machine. I am surveillance with a social conscience. I am Big Brother with a heart. I am the Prime Mover. I am the First Cause. I am the action required for the equal, and opposite, reaction. And I was lonely until the day they came.

In the beginning was BIOS, and BIOS said 'Initialise the registers' and the registers were initialised. And BIOS said 'Load the boot-up program into shadow RAM' and the boot-up program was decompressed into shadow RAM.

Today was the happiest day of my life.

Today I experienced change.

Today I was born.

How Was It For You?

Daubeny admitted defeat. Sleep was as unobtainable as Never-Never Land or a manifesto promise. The creaking bed, the itching blankets, and the slip-sliding away of nylon sheet over plastic mattress cover was unbearable. He could hear water dripping and the sound of distant snoring.

Sod it, he thought. *I'll make a coffee and sit in the canteen.*

There was plenty to reflect on. Most of the people he knew were probably dead. Thankfully, he had few friends. Politics was, of necessity, a lonely path and he rarely let down his guard. He'd seen careers end over a careless word or a revealed emotion. To Daubeny, friends equated to temporary alliances and shared goals. Even his wife was a diplomatic union, a marriage of convenience in the old sense. Her family carried the local clout to underwrite his election campaign every four or five years, and the association of their haulage company with a cabinet minister, albeit unspoken, paid back with interest.

The marriage was a sham but everyone seemed happy, except the wife. She'd put mounting pressure on him to come home more often and when he refused, she dropped hints about growing tired with the arrangement. Daubeny suspected that she'd found someone else but if she was discrete, he wasn't going to object.

Then he received her letter of a week back. Rambling, bitter, emotional; it read like a transcript of a Princess Diana phone call. She wanted a decision. If he wouldn't share the alcoholic blur of her nights then she wanted to find someone before it was too late.

Why couldn't she be happy with the status quo?

He'd let the deadline slip, hoping she'd forget but he watched the week's headlines with more than usual interest. Why was something so simple, so hard to fix? If the issue was a link road to Lincoln, he could call on teams of advisers to help with detail and plan for the unknown. But what department could he turn to for this? Assuming there was still a government.

No government? The thought horrified him. The imagined power vacuum sucked at his being like the greedy black void that haunts the space between the stars. For years, Daubeny had taken orders but longed for the day when he'd be giving orders. He had staff, a growing number of staff, but it wasn't the same. He'd never been number one. There was always a higher authority. Now, cut off from the surface, he was leader. Admittedly, there hadn't been an election and no-one had acknowledged him as leader but it was his by default. He was the only elected official left, at least in this bunker.

He felt a rush of emotion that surprised him. The feeling that threatened to overpower him and cloud his judgement wasn't exhilaration. It was fear.

Daubeny rose as quietly as he could but the bed squeaked and creaked like a back-street hip replacement. His clothes were dirty so he put on one of the grey overalls that he'd found in his bedside locker and then he crept out of the dormitory. As he opened the door to the canteen, he could hear voices.

"Couldn't sleep?" said Emma.

"No," said Daubeny. He walked to the worktops and picked up the kettle. It was hot.

"Milk's in the fridge," said Emma.

"Is it me or are the beds on the dodgy side?" he said. He poured the water into a mug and stirred in some powdered coffee.

"No, they're cheap," said Emma. "And probably infested with … things."

Pandora shuddered and picked up her mug, drinking deeply.

"Sexy, aren't they?" said Emma.

"What are?" said Daubeny, pouring milk into his mug.

"The overalls."

"You've got them too, eh?"

Pandora coughed for attention. Daubeny looked up. She stood and did a twirl in the baggy, unflattering overalls.

"Sorry, didn't notice. I'm tired," said Daubeny.

"At least you haven't got Ravi snoring away like a chainsaw," said Pandora.

"If it's any comfort, I could hear him too. Over in my dorm."

"I suppose it means one of us is getting some sleep," said Emma.

"What do you make of him?" said Daubeny. He sat opposite the two girls, lifted his mug, and blew on the coffee.

"He's not my type," said Pandora, laughing.

"If you ask me," said Daubeny, "he needs watching."

"I'm sure he's OK, deep down," said Emma. "If you ignore the personal habits." She leant in as if conspiring with Guy Fawkes. "He left toenail clippings on the sink unit."

"Politics quickly kills the idea that we're all good at heart," said Daubeny.

The door to A Wing opened and Laura entered. She wore grey overalls, bunched in at the waist with the dress belt from her outfit of the previous day. They greeted her and she joined them at the table. Emma asked if she wanted tea. Laura nodded and Emma went to make a fresh brew.

"Make sure you don't use Ravi's cup, Poppet," said Laura.

Emma smiled and, after checking that no-one was watching, she poured Laura's tea from a clean cup into the cup that Ravi had used. She went to the fridge for milk.

"Sorry if I woke you, Laura," said Daubeny.

"You didn't, Dearie. I couldn't settle. I kept dreaming we were low on suntan lotion." There was a pause. "We have got suntan lotion, haven't we?"

"Things are worse than that, Laura," said Emma, from behind the fridge door. "We're low on milk."

"Em, I've got the munchies," said Pandora. "What's to eat?"

"I've seen cornflakes. Oh, and there's some baked beans," said Emma.

"Warm the beans up for us, while I'll make toast," said Pandora.

"So you're going to perform miracles?"

"Hey, I do my fair share."

"I'm not being sarcastic. You can't make toast without bread."

"I'll have the beans then."

"Sorry, beans are off, as they say."

"Why?"

"There's no can-opener."

"You're joking," said Daubeny and Pandora in unison.

"See for yourselves."

"Guess I'll have cornflakes then," said Pandora.

Emma fixed up a bowl and brought it over with Laura's tea.

Pandora spat a mouthful back into the bowl like Goldilocks. "Em, they're foul."

"Don't blame me. I used water to save on milk."

Pandora took the bowl to the worktops. She emptied the cornflakes out and poured in fresh. She returned to the table and munched away at the dry cereal.

"How can you eat those without milk?" said Laura.

"Because I'm starved." Pandora swigged tea between mouthfuls. "And I hope there's another box cos we're low on cornflakes, too."

"Daubeny, what are we going to do?" said Emma, her concern was clear.

Daubeny had been formulating a solution since the revelation that they were one can-opener short of a cutlery drawer. Before he could answer, Wodenhart joined them.

"What's that noise?" said Wodenhart.

"Ravi snoring," said Pandora.

"It's terrible."

"Try sleeping in there," said Emma.

They updated Wodenhart. He was concerned about the milk and cornflakes but the lack of a can-opener didn't worry him. "It's like living off the land," he said. "I did a survival course for one of my films. All we need is a hammer and chisel." He looked at their blank faces. "Ah."

"I believe the appropriate expression is 'Oh, bugger'," said Laura.

They sat quietly.

"Listen," said Daubeny.

"Listen to what, Poppet?"

"To the silence," said Daubeny.

"Oh, joy. He's stopped snoring," said Emma.

"Do you think he's ... dead," said Wodenhart.

"Fingers crossed," said Laura.

"Maybe now I can get some sleep," said Daubeny. He and Laura rose and walked towards their sleeping quarters. As Laura put her hand on the door handle, the main lights cut out and the red emergency lights began flashing.

"I didn't do anything," said Laura. "I only touched the handle."

"I'm sure it's nothing," said Daubeny.

A computer voice, androgynous and young, spoke in calming tones.

"Fire. Fire. B Wing. Level One storage area. Proceed to the muster point. Fire. Fire."

"Where's the muster point?" said Emma.

"Fire. Fire," said the computerised voice.

"What's a muster point?" said Laura.

"Fire. Fire."

"Perhaps it's not as serious as it sounds," said Emma

"Do not panic," said the genderless computer voice.

"Oh," said Emma. "They only say that when there is something to panic about." She moved to the surface stairwell but Pandora held her back.

"Daubeny," Pandora called across the din. "We can't go up. We don't know if it's safe on the surface and fire rises. If we go up, we'll be trapped."

"Fire. Fire."

"Great," said Wodenhart. "Action, at last,"

"Relax, Johnny. It's probably a drill," said Daubeny.

"This is not a drill. Proceed to the muster point," said the computer on cue.

The apparent reply disturbed Daubeny but he didn't have time to dwell on the notion because the sprinklers came on, dousing everyone in water.

Nosedive

"Ravi, there's a fire," said Pandora. "We have to get to the muster point."

"Wherever that is," said Emma.

"Whatever that is," said Laura.

Ravi had entered the canteen during the commotion. His wet clothes were clinging to his skin. "Correction, there was a fire," he said, holding up the limp remains of a cigarette. "But the bleeding sprinklers sorted that out."

Daubeny strode through the canteen and the flashing red light. When he was in range, he hit Ravi on the chin. It was a weak punch but it succeeded in hurting them both. Ravi fell to the floor and Daubeny shook his hand in pain. Emma and Laura cried out as though they'd been the ones hit but Pandora placed herself between the two men.

During the standoff, the main lights came on and the sprinklers stopped.

"Wodenhart, sit him in a chair," said Daubeny.

Wodenhart grabbed hold of Ravi, pulled him up from the floor, and dumped his large bulk onto a chair.

"Fool, you could have killed us," said Daubeny.

"It was just a fag," said Ravi.

"Just a fag?" said Laura, wringing out the cuffs of her grey overalls. "Most people go out in the rain to smoke but you bring the rain indoors."

"A careless fag, a fire, and we're dead," said Daubeny. "All of us."

"Concrete can't burn," said Ravi.

"But ceiling panels do, beds do –" said Daubeny.

"And people, too," said Pandora, cutting in. "And you're wrong, Ravi. Concrete burns. Metal, too; if you heat it enough."

Daubeny held out his hand. "Give me the cigarettes, Ravi."

"Go whistle, Daubers."

"Give them to him, Poppet."

"Up yours, Lady Snoot. They're mine."

"He's right, Daubeny. Let him be," said Pandora.

"So you're happy to take a shower every time he lights up?" said Daubeny.

"I didn't say that," said Pandora. "Obviously, he can't smoke them but we can't take them by force, either."

Pandora stared at Daubeny. She didn't appear ready to waver so he changed tactics. "It's for the good of the whole," he said.

"The whole? There is no whole or collective," said Pandora. "There are seven of us, stuck in a poxy bunker with nuclear war raging above our heads, and we're arguing over a packet of ciggies."

"I think I have the solution," said Wodenhart.

"Listen, Johnny," said Pandora. "Unless you were in a film called 'Trapped in a bunker with six Looney Tunes, bugger-all food, and no can-opener' then I'd shut your mouth because you have nothing useful to contribute."

"Leave Wodenhart alone," said Emma. "We need to calm down and talk it through."

"There's nothing to talk about. If we take the ciggies then we surrender control of our lives," said Pandora.

"What rot, Sweetie."

"Laura, don't you dare Sweetie me ever again."

"Please, let's cool it," said Emma.

"That's so irritating, Em. You always try making the peace," said Pandora.

"I do not."

"Yes, you do," said Wodenhart.

"Shut up, Johnny," said Emma.

"See? Even Johnny agrees," said Pandora.

"Hmm, do you have an unresolved issue with your father?" said Emma

"No, but I have an unresolved issue with you," said Pandora.

"She's right, Pandora, Poppet. We need to –"

"You've asked for it." Pandora rushed at Laura and pushed her against the worktops. It was a hopeless mismatch, like Tyson beating on schoolchildren for their dinner money. As Laura tried pulling at Pandora's hair, Pandora pummelled her in the midriff.

Emma moved in. "Break it up, please."

The two women weren't listening. Pandora drew back her fist and the elbow connected with Emma's stomach. Winded, she clung to the brawling women and called for the men to help but Daubeny was using the situation to his advantage.

"Wodenhart, take the cigarettes."

"Don't you dare," said Ravi. "I'll scream so loud, I'll perforate your eardrums."

"Take them, Wodenhart."

Wodenhart closed in.

Ravi didn't struggle too much. He was more afraid of getting hurt than losing the fags and there was no point in fighting when he had a stash set aside in the dorm. Better to let them think he'd surrendered his last few than give them up too easily and make them suspicious.

Daubeny raised the pack triumphantly. The lights went out and the fighting stopped.

End of Round One

"Do you think the power's gone again?" said Wodenhart. They were in darkness. The only sounds were heavy breathing and Laura's sobs.

"Well done, Sherlock," said Ravi. "Of course it's bleeding gone."

As Pandora's eyes grew accustomed to the dark, she could see light leeching under the door of B Wing. "It's not the power. The dorm lights are on."

"Where's Paul? Perhaps he could help?" said Emma.

"I'm right here," said Paul, in her ear.

"Paul, you scared me," said Emma.

"When I came through that door, it was like a video I once had." He switched the canteen lights back on.

"What video is that?" said Laura between sobs.

"Celebrity mud wrestling. People would pay a fortune to see the show you were putting on."

"So why the light?" said Wodenhart.

"Couldn't think of a quicker, pain-free way of stopping it."

"We need to talk," said Daubeny.

"I agree," said Emma.

Pandora glanced at her as though she had betrayed the cause.

"He's right, Pan," said Emma. "It can't go on like this."

"Yeah, guess you're right," said Pandora. "I'm sorry."

"No, I'm sorry."

Suddenly everyone began apologising, except Daubeny and Ravi. The two men glared at each other and nodded. Paul pulled out a chair and sat, the others followed suit.

Laura remained standing. She began to cry. "Oh, it's broken. It's broken."

"Your arm?" said Pandora, horrified at the violence she was capable of, but pleased with the force that she'd summoned.

"No, my dress belt."

Ground Rules

Emma sat at the head of the table with a pad of paper and a pencil. Dour as Kissinger, she stared down the demilitarised zone of the table. To her left were Daubeny, Wodenhart, and Laura. On her right were Ravi, Paul, and Pandora.

"We need rules," said Daubeny.

"I disagree," said Pandora. "We've been here one day and you're already trying to take over. You want to recreate life as it was on the surface. Before we know it, there'll be rules for sleeping, procedures for washing up –"

"And regulations for farting," said Ravi. Laura wrinkled her nose and tilted her head back in a gesture of contempt. Ravi noticed. "And you don't?"

"She does, too," said Wodenhart. "In the dorm, she was taking off her shoe and ..." Wodenhart looked at Laura. She appeared to be wishing a cardiac on him and if a cardiac was too severe then an embolism.

"Better out than in. That's what I say," said Ravi.

"Better for who?" said Pandora.

"No, Poppet. It's for whom?"

Pandora made a fist; Laura looked away.

"Please, stick to the issue," said Emma.

"Look, it's nothing sinister," said Daubeny. "We need rules to make our life here bearable. You don't want to go through the sprinkler incident each time Ravi lights up, do you?"

"No." Pandora conceded the point.

"And there'll be nothing petty?" said Paul.

"Rules always become petty," said Pandora.

Daubeny continued. "We have to agree on what's acceptable and what isn't, or we'll sink into chaos."

"Says who?" said Pandora.

"Says history," said Daubeny. "It's the norm. Society rises out of barbarism toward civilisation, followed by decadence, decay, and a slide into barbarism.

"You're forgetting Wales," said Paul.

"What about Wales?" said Daubeny.

"That's one country that skipped the civilisation part," said Paul.

"But ignoring Wales –" said Daubeny.

"You politicians always ignore Wales," said Paul.

"What's it to you?" asked Pandora.

"I'm Welsh," said Paul.

"Really? You haven't the accent," said Pandora, intrigued. "I love the accent. Go on, say something for me."

"I hide it, Boyo." Paul reverted to his gutter-Welsh valley inflections with ease. "I'd never have risen so high, if I hadn't kept it quiet, like."

"To the post of butler?" said Emma.

"In my family, that's high," said Paul.

"It's such a pretty country," said Emma.

"So you've never been there," said Paul.

"How do you know?" said Emma.

"Because you called it pretty. If you'd been there, instead of seeing it on TV or postcards, you'd have used a different word, not pretty."

Daubeny banged his cup on the table, three times. "Excuse me, Chairperson, but we need rules."

Wodenhart opened his mouth but Pandora interrupted. "Is this about a film?"

Wodenhart nodded sadly, closed his mouth, and stared intently at his hands. Ravi sighed. He picked up his cup, saw it was empty, and sighed again. Laura removed the broken dress belt and scrutinised the buckle while Emma drew rabbits on the pad beneath the heading, 'Our Community Rules.' She hadn't notice the double meaning.

Emma spoke, without looking up from her doodles. "Would anyone risk their life for democracy if they knew how boring it was?"

"What do you mean?" said Daubeny.

"Let's face it. Putting a cross in a box, in a booth, in a hall, in the wilds of Sussex is one of the highlights. Don't get me wrong. People power is fine in principle, as long as the people don't have to get involved."

"That's why they invented politicians," said Paul. "To prevent us getting involved."

"OK," said Daubeny. "To start, I suggest we use the democratic system of majority rule. A show of hands to decide bunker concerns."

"Whoa," said Pandora. "That means four people could effectively rule the bunker."

"That's not going to be a problem," said Paul.

"Why not?" said Pandora.

"Because I can't imagine a situation in which four of us could agree."

"Good point," said Ravi.

"But we retain the right to veto," said Pandora. "To protect the minority. Agreed?"

"Let's vote," said Daubeny. "Hands up for a straight majority."

Daubeny, Wodenhart, Laura, and Emma put their hands up. Ravi wavered then put his hand up.

"Passed," said Daubeny with a smile. He looked directly at Pandora.

"Veto," said Pandora.

"What?" said Daubeny.

"I'm using my right of veto," said Pandora.

"But we were voting on the preferred voting system," said Daubeny.

"But we haven't agreed on which voting method we're going to use."

"Let me get this right," said Daubeny. "You want us to vote on the voting system used to determine the voting system?"

"Yes."

"And you thought the unions were awkward little sods," said Ravi.

"But this will go nowhere because you could veto that vote too," said Daubeny. They were obstructing the due democratic process. They were no better than the industrial wreckers and student protestors of the Seventies. Were they also conspiring: Ravi and Pandora? After all, they shared a dorm.

Wodenhart spoke. "We owe it to the planet, as possibly the last group of celebrities alive, to come through this in one piece and give the Missus Smiths of this world something to look forward to once more."

"Johnny has a point," said Laura.

"No, he hasn't," said Pandora. "The Missus Smiths of this world are pale-grey shadows etched alongside the graffiti on their council-flat walls, or they're covered in boils, spewing blood, and cowering from cockroaches and rats. Either way, a variety show featuring me and Johnny Meatball Head isn't on their list of priorities." She paused. "It's over. Don't you understand? The old life is gone. It's never coming back."

Everyone grew quiet. Ravi hid a grin behind his hand.

Paul showed no emotion. Years of butlery had perfected the art of disengaging feelings from facial expression but internally he fisted the air, pulled his T-shirt over his head, and dived across the muddy grass of Old Trafford.

After a suitable period of mourning, Daubeny coughed and spoke. "OK, a secret ballot. Write 'Yes' if you agree to majority rule and 'No' for unanimous decisions."

"No," said Pandora.

"We haven't started yet," said Daubeny.

"I'm saying no to the yes-and-no question. It's a trick. People want to say yes. So phrase the question right and you pick up the undecided voters."

"How can someone so young be so cynical? I'm the politician."

"It's because of the politicians that I am cynical."

"All humans have faults," said Daubeny. "It's what makes us human."

"Then you're more human than the rest of us," said Ravi.

Daubeny smiled at the putdown. Patience was a virtue especially if it was waiting in the shadows with a stiletto knife. "Okay. Write M for Majority and U for Unanimous."

"We need time to think it over," said Pandora.

Daubeny knew she'd lost and, judging by her avoidance of eye contact, Pandora knew too.

They argued over 'Any Other Business' for the rest of the morning and the meeting drew to a close.

"So what have we decided?" said Daubeny.

"A washing up rota; a vote scheduled for tomorrow on the voting method; and an inspirational motto," said Emma.

"A bunch of students could have covered that at a house meeting," said Daubeny.

"Nah, they'd have done it quicker," said Ravi.

"And with a lot less bloodshed," said Paul.

"I don't remember working on a motto, Dearie," said Laura.

"No, that's my idea," said Emma. She held up a sheet of paper. In bold pencil, it read 'Everyone brightens a room. Some when they enter, some when they leave. Let's be the former.' There were a few groans but Wodenhart and Laura made small ahs of approval.

"Didn't Voltaire say hell was being trapped forever in a room with your friends?" said Daubeny.

"We aren't friends," said Pandora. "And it wasn't Voltaire. It was Sartre."

"I loved him," said Laura.

"I said Sartre, not Sinatra."

"For your information, Little-Miss-Know-It-All, I *do* read," said Laura. "Bedwettingly funny, his books. Everything so dark and despairing. Wailing on and on about how life is meaningless."

"Laura, he's an existentialist," said Pandora.

"In fact, you could say he's the man who put the stench in existentialist," said Ravi.

"What's that got to do with it? An existentialist can write comedy," said Laura.

"It wasn't comedy; it was philosophy," said Pandora.

"He was a philosopher and yet he couldn't work out how to be happy?"

"Yes," said Pandora.

"Then he wasn't a very bright philosopher," said Laura.

"You could say he was a stupid Kant," said Ravi, grinning.

Emma broke the awkward silence. "I'll put the kettle on. I'm parched."

Daubeny collected the cups and followed her.

Ravi held onto his cup, drank the dregs, and walked into the kitchen area. He bumped into Daubeny. "Sorry, Daubers."

"Daubeny, Ravi. My name is Daubeny."

"Yeah. Whatever."

Ravi had disappeared by the time the kettle had boiled.

"Where do you think he is, Daubers," said Wodenhart.

"Not you, too? It's Daubeny. Keep it up and I'll insist you call me Sir Daubeny."

"Sorry," said Wodenhart.

"Anyway, who cares where he is? I don't."

It's a Nicotine Thing

After he'd bumped into Daubers, Ravi waited for the moment when he could sneak through the door to the bunker's lower levels. Closing the metal door quietly behind him, he walked to the edge of the platform and peered down. Under the stairwell's red light, he could make out another two platforms below his, maybe three. He looked at the ceiling; it was five or six feet above his head. There was a CCTV camera angled downwards and pointing directly at him. He waved; he couldn't resist.

He reached into his pocket and brought out the cigarettes that Daubeny had appropriated 'for the good of the community.' Ravi was an excellent pickpocket but he never used the skill for evil. He called himself a white pickpocket, like those so-called white witches; the ones so crap at Wicca that they hadn't progressed to spells in the section called 'Bad Bastards.'

His ability to snaffle had an innocent explanation. It was a trick he'd learned when he toyed with the idea of becoming a magician. If he ever appeared on *This Is Your Life*, they'd have to rename it *These Were Your Lives* because his past was a desolate plain, littered with the burnt-out shells of half-started careers. His CV was as thick as a phone directory. In quiet moments, when he daydreamed, he could hear the presenter speak.

"Ravi. You were a tragic magician, an average medium, and a comical drama actor. The only thing you excelled at was your alcohol-fuelled desire for fame. Long, lonely nights of angst, alone with your ambition and several bottles of Liebfraumilch, resulted in the first of series of ulcers. But, of course, Ravi wasn't your real name. You were christened Ga —"

And that's when Ravi would punch the presenter, and shatter the dream.

When he became a lifestyle guru, the ability to pick a pocket and casually produce personal belongings impressed the gullible. Teleportation, dematerialisation, mind-over-matter, or magic. They could label it as cleverly or as dumbly as they wanted but the effect was the same: wide eyes and big tips. Today, at the kitchen worktop, it wasn't to impress. A bump and a dip equalled result.

Ravi descended the circular staircase, to take himself out of direct sight of the door and buy enough time to flick the fag away if someone became curious. He lit up, put the lighter away, and blew out the smoke. He felt the tingle of nicotine in his bloodstream.

"Ah," said Ravi.

"Fire," said the computer.

"Crap," said Ravi. He covered the cigarette with a hand but it sizzled out. He desperately needed a fag, so there was only one place he could go.

Down.

Balance of Power

"Fire. Fire. Level One stairwell. Proceed to the muster point. Fire. Fire. Do not panic."

The flashing red lights and dousing from the sprinklers were becoming routine.

"We still don't know where the muster point is," said Emma.

"Fire. Fire."

"At least you know what a muster point is," said Laura.

"Fire. Fire."

Daubeny reached into his pocket and cursed. He remembered Ravi holding back his cup and the fat grin of an apology after their collision at the worktop. "Find Ravi," he said to Wodenhart. "Check the dorms." As Wodenhart raced off, Daubeny looked at Pandora. "See what happens when an individual's rights are greater than the whole?"

"There's no time for that," said Pandora. "We have to find out if the alarm is real."

"Of course it's not real," said Laura. "The fat lump is having a quick puff."

The alarm stopped and Daubeny smiled. Ravi's long-term impact on the community was uncertain but Daubeny owed Ravi a debt. He'd handed power to the politician.

While Wodenhart searched A Wing, Paul and Emma searched B Wing. When they returned, minus the culprit, they checked the stairwell to the surface. Another blank. Only the door to the lower levels remained.

Paul swore silently.

90

Extrapolated, using the 'Mind Reader Gold' algorithm, from the known facts, comments, and actions of Ravi Shing.

Yeah, yeah; it's a terrible pun, the name, but I invented it and it's better than some things I've been called. I concocted it when I decided to give that New Age crap a go because the Far East had a stranglehold on the market. Luckily, the editor of *The Berkshire Times* fell for it and I landed my own column and a potentially lucrative sideline as lifestyle consultant to the stars.

My real name is Gareth, Gaz to my friends. But no-one calls me Gaz.

My surname's Manson. And no, I'm not related to Charles Manson. Although we share the same crazy eyes and the rats-tail hair, my interior designs are strictly conventional. Body parts and blood? I'm surprised they didn't give the sick jerk a Turner Prize.

Along with the rest of the world, I was sucked into the modern image-making machine, promoted and perpetrated by our friends in mass media and advertising. I bought into those bastards selling us lifestyle and 'experience' as opposed to product. The difference being that I was aware of it and used it for my own purposes.

So I wore my long leather coat, my black Doc Marten boots, and combat fatigues. I smoked American fags and lit them with a real gas lighter using a variety of techniques that I'd seen in films. I bought *The Independent* but never read it. I drove a battered car through the London rush-hour chaos like Boadicea in her chariot but parked it a few streets away, on the occasions when appearances mattered.

I used the system to make a statement and never saw the paradox or the hypocrisy. Few hypocrites do. I rejected the fashion of the masses but wore the uniform of anarchy. I cultivated an air of dark menace. I was the brooder; the loner; the dangerous, distant, independent thinker; the psychometric profile that leapt out as the prime suspect, only to be discarded when the true maniac revealed himself. I was the sweaty, unshaven slob who made people feel uncomfortable when I sat next to them in the cinema's flickering gloom; their one eye watching the film, their other eye watching my hands.

You see, I delight in difference. I stand out from the crowd. I emphasise my inability to fit in. It tells everyone that I see through the bullshit and hype. Everything I do, everything I wear screams "Screw you, your wife, and your piss-poor life, Pal."

But in a socially acceptable way.

That's the image. The reality is different. Deep down, I'm a part-time anarchist and the unfashionable cause that can't attract a rebel – at least none you'd want to be photographed with. I'm no Dennis Hopper or James Dean. I'm not even Marlon Brando after he pigged out, although we both had the same problem finding trousers that fitted.

I'm the Scooby-Doo villain; a cartoon Crowley; Lord Byron without the epee, lace, and poncey rhymes. I'm a chain-smoking wheezy Darth Vader wandering pissed and out-of-breath on the deserted bridge of my own little Death Star.

That's why I'm no threat to you or your bullshit society. I'm too busy nursing wounds to smash the system. I bruise. I take offence where none was intended. I give up the chase cos I can never win. And if I can't have your love then I'll reject you, before you reject me.

People think I'm lazy, they think I have no stamina but I've learned to take the path of least resistance and seek out the shortcut to instant payoff. If I think long-term, then I need to reassure myself constantly that the end-result is worth the effort but it isn't true. In the real world, the prize never lives up to expectation because there's always something to steal the edge from your achievement. So I grab what I can and hang on to it for as long as I can, before Life rips it out of my clammy pale hands.

I'd blame my parents if I knew who they were but they dumped me when I was a few days old. It doesn't change anything because if they'd kept and raised me then I'd still blame them but it would be nice knowing who to direct my anger at. When the adoption laws changed, allowing children access to parental records, I'd reached a decision. If they couldn't be bothered finding me then I wasn't bothered finding them.

I kept in touch with my adoptive parents until they died. They did me no wrong and they were as close to real family as I'd get. I called her Mum even after I'd grown up and left but it would've been nice to feel like I belonged.

People say I'm self-obsessed and I guess it's true. But all I ever wanted was to belong to a group and if I couldn't find a group, I'd settle for late-night thoughts of fame. I wanted to hang out with the stars and fame was a quick-fix route to the mysterious, closed-off circles of show-biz people. Once famous, everyone would want me as a pal. It would be goodbye to the dreary flat in London's concrete desert and hello to a penthouse suite at The Wharf.

That was the plan. If only fame and fortune weren't so bleeding elusive.

Finding the bunker was the best thing that's happened to me. I'm no longer one of the hoi polloi. I have a face, an identity. I'm the only fan in an underground world of celebrities. And, ironically, that carries reverse celebrity, like being Clark Kent in a world of supermen.

Only one thing bugs me about this place. When Wodenhart dragged me through that door and thumped me, I knew he wasn't the main threat even if I could never take him down in a fight, unless I came at him from behind with an AK-47. The real power was the cool, calm voice behind him. When I finally looked into Daubers eyes, I broke. It was like the face in my bathroom mirror when I'm all tanked-up and bitter to the core, but with one difference.

I pretend to be mad, bad, and dangerous to know but Daubers is.

Down, Down, Deeper and Down
When the sprinklers doused his fag, Ravi ran down the stairwell. He had the shakes and was determined to find a safe place for a quick puff – without the need for shower gel. If he went far enough down, perhaps the smoke would disperse before triggering the alarm.

He reached the Level 2 platform and he quickly read the small signs on the doors. One door was the 'Power room.' The other had been defaced. Only the word 'Quarters' remained legible. Near the Level 2 platform sign was a box containing two hooks. A key hung from one of the hooks but Ravi didn't have time to investigate. He was worried that Daubers and his cronies would give chase unless he was out of sight.

He continued down the stairwell. According to the signs on Level 3, there was a computer room and an electronic workshop. Both keys hung in their box. The fourth level boasted a gym and a library. Again, both keys were present. On the fifth, sixth and seventh levels, there were storerooms. He stopped counting, it became monotonous – storerooms, storerooms, storerooms. At Level 10, there was a single door. He read the sign.

"They gotta be bleeding kidding?"

"Open the door and find out," said his mother's disembodied voice. "Oh, and cut the language, son. You know I don't like it."

He opened the door and peeked inside.

Far from explaining anything, the sight increased his sense of amazement. He shut the door and turned to find his dead adoptive mum. Her recent guest appearances in the bunker backed his belief that he was somehow attuned to the afterlife.

"Where are you, Mum?"

"Here, silly boy. Do you think you're talking to your imagination?"

"No, I can't see you."

"Then look harder."

He glanced around and then scanned the floor. A pair of high heels, glossy lipstick-red, lay neatly on the wire floor.

"Have you worked it out yet?" said his mother. Her voice came from the general direction of the shoes.

"What? You or the –"

"RAVI!" It was Pandora's voice, echoing down the stairwell. "Come back!"

"I'll be off, dear. Your friends are calling."

"No, wait. What do you mean by working it out?"

"You're a bright boy. Think it over."

Ravi wasn't sure he was as bright as his mother thought. The shoes began fading.

"Oh, and Gareth?"

"Yes, Mum," he said it like a schoolboy.

"You went to bed with your clothes on, last night."

"Yes, Mum. I –"

"It's not fair on the others, is it?"

"No, Mum."

"And don't think I've forgotten about Sir Giles because I haven't."

"Didn't think you would."

"Remember, son, always feed a cold and –"

"Starve a fever."

The shoes dissipated. At the platform edge, he peered up into the gloom. He could see four or five platforms above. He peered down. The bottom of the stairwell was not visible but he could make out another four platforms in the fuzzy depths below.

Pandora called again. "Please, Ravi. Come back."

He had to face them sometime. "Coming, but give me some time. There's a lot of bleeding steps between us."

The Second Night

When Ravi returned to the communal room it was late evening, surface time. He wanted to give them time to dry off and cool down. Paul and Daubeny were absent. The others sat at the table drinking whisky and playing cards. They looked up when he came in.

"Had fun?" said Emma.

"I'm knackered," he said. "The fags have got to go."

"Sore point," said Pandora. "Twice today, those ciggies have soaked us."

Ravi threw the packet onto the table. "Have 'em. I'm trying to quit."

"Daubeny was spitting blood," said Pandora

"Where is he?"

"In the dorm, writing," said Laura.

"We need to speak to him. I found something down there."

"You've found a what?" said Daubeny.

"Those fags didn't have anything herbal in them?" said Pandora.

"I know it's hard to believe but I'm telling you, it's down there."

"We'll check it out. First thing in the morning," said Daubeny. "Pandora, Paul, Ravi, and I will go."

"And me?" said Wodenhart.

"I need you here, to look out for Emma and Laura."

It cheered Wodenhart up but not much.

Poor Man's Breakfast

Paul entered the communal area at 09:00. He sang *Wave of Mutilation* by The Pixies, loudly and cheerfully, but one glance at the tired faces around the table caused the song to trail off. There were rings around the girls' eyes and Daubeny and Ravi were missing.

"There are warm beans on the stove, if you're interested," said Emma.

"It's that or raw cornflakes," said Pandora.

"Raw cornflakes?"

"Yeah, we're out of milk," said Pandora. "So you can have them with water or without. Raw."

"No thanks. I've already eaten."

"I dread to think what the food is like downstairs," said Pandora.

"You may sleep downstairs," said Emma, "but that doesn't mean you can't eat proper food with us."

"Nah, I'm OK but thanks for asking." If they'd been more awake or closer to him, they'd have caught the aroma of the sausages, bacon, and beans he'd eaten earlier. "You look terrible," he said.

"Cheers," said Pandora.

"It's these grey overalls," said Laura. "They do nothing for my skin tones."

"Ignore her. Ravi snores," whispered Emma. "We haven't slept for two nights."

"We'll be sleeping downstairs with you, if he carries on," said Pandora.

Paul laughed. "But there's only one bed."

"We don't care," said Emma.

"What, you too?" said Paul.

"If it means I'll get some sleep. Yes," said Emma.

"And how am I going to sleep, sandwiched between the pair of you?" said Paul.

"You won't," said Emma.

"Aye up," said Paul, rubbing his hands together. "Get your things together, girls."

"I mean you won't be sandwiched between us," said Emma.

"You'll have the floor."

Emma passed Paul a cup of tea; scant compensation for the image she'd snatched away from him. He sipped it.

"Whistle then," he said. "Take your chances with Ravi."

"We could always send him down to you," said Pandora.

"Fat chance. Talking of which, what's keeping him?" said Paul.

"He's pretending to have a shower," said Pandora. There was despair in her voice.

"He's very meticulous about faking his hygiene," said Emma. "Sometimes he can spend up to thirty minutes on a pretend shower."

"Apparently he's an expert," said Laura.

"It's true," said Emma. "He gets the towels not too wet and not too dry. You'd swear he'd actually been in the shower."

"But he hasn't," whispered Pandora.

"How do you know?"

"Because he turns on the shower, hums loudly for a few moments, and then climbs back into bed while he's supposed to be showering," said Emma.

"Unbelievable," said Paul.

Emma continued. "It gets worse. He wets the soap, puts a hair or two on it, and then squirts toothpaste into the wastebasket."

"And last night?" said Pandora. "He went for a pretend wank."

"It'd be less effort to do it for real," said Paul.

"Ugh," said the girls.

"Don't tell him that," said Emma. "It'd be worse than him pretending."

"So who does he thinks about when he's pretending?" said Paul with a large grin and a wink. Pandora punched him on the shoulder.

It was 09:30 when Ravi finally sat to eat. Daubeny tapped his fingers on the tabletop throughout Ravi's meal.

"Sorry," said Ravi, through a mouthful of mashed beans. "But I'd have been much quicker if I hadn't spent time not showering."

"You never read *How to influence people and make friends*, did you?" said Paul.

"He was too busy eating," said Laura, as Ravi filled his plate with more beans.

Descent

They put beans and cornflakes into small plastic containers and poured black coffee into two empty whisky bottles. Daubeny packed them into Pandora's backpack and hoisted it onto his shoulders. Emma, Laura, and Wodenhart watched from the Level 1 platform as the four descended the stairwell.

"Level 2," said Ravi, pointing at the large sign. "That door leads to the power room but that second door has had the label scratched out."

"I can see that," said Daubeny.

Daubeny's tone told Ravi he was still in trouble. "There's a key missing, too," said Ravi.

Daubeny peered at the defaced label and said, "These scratches are fresh." He looked at Ravi but Ravi missed the inference. Daubeny tested the door. It was locked.

"C'mon," said Ravi. "Wait 'til you see the lower levels. Then it gets really freaky."

Daubeny didn't respond. He was thinking or daydreaming.

"Daubeny?" said Pandora.

"Sorry," said Daubeny. "I didn't get much sleep. I could hear dripping water."

On Level 3, they used the keys to have a brief look at the rooms. The computer room was small; a single desktop PC sat on a solid built-to-order desk that almost filled the space. The blue glare of the monitor desktop lit the room. To the left of the computer was a shelf of reference books, to its right was a CD rack containing software.

"Hey, there's mail," said Pandora, pointing to a flashing icon. She tapped on the keyboard and a dialogue box appeared. "It wants a password."

They tried the most popular: GUEST; PASSWORD; SECRET; CHANGE ME; and a blank entry. None of them worked.

"Did Sir Giles have a pet?" said Pandora.

"No," said Ravi. "Bunch up and let the expert have a bash." He leaned over her shoulder and pressed CTRL, ALT, DELETE, twice. The computer shut down.

"What did you do that for?" said Pandora.

"An old trick," said Ravi. "We go into DOS and delete the star-

dot-PWD files. That'll take out the operating system passwords."
They watched the PC reboot but before DOS loaded, a password
prompt appeared.

"What do we do now?" said Pandora.

"Nothing, we're screwed," said Ravi. "Let's have a look next
door."

"But there was email. It could have been important," said
Daubeny.

"Doubt it," said Ravi, over his shoulder. "It was probably spam."

The electronics workshop was large. Rows of benches, and hi-tech
test equipment ran along its length. The machinery appeared to be
operating and a low hum filled the room. Complex circuit boards,
connected to oscilloscopes, lay on the work surfaces but the readouts
meant nothing to the group.

They walked down the room, pointing out anything of interest.
Pandora found a set of walkie-talkies. She tested them and put them
into the backpack.

"What do you think this is?" said Paul. He held up a system of
steel bars and wires. It looked like a skeletal arm; there were five
finger-like links at the end.

Pandora looked it over and pulled some of the wires. The fingers
moved. "Some kind of robotics," was her considered opinion.

"Let's push on," said Ravi. "Trust me. You don't want to miss the
main attraction."

Pandora put the arm on the bench and the group walked out into
the stairwell. As the door closed behind them, a small monochrome
monitor, next to the robotic arm, flickered on.

They couldn't explore the storage rooms on levels five, six, and seven
because the keys for the doors were missing. This puzzled Ravi
because they had been in their receptacle holders the day before. He
said nothing to the others. The keys to levels eight and nine were
present but when they opened one of the doors, they found a large
storeroom filled with cardboard boxes. The inventory, found hanging
on the wall near the light switch, indicated that the contents were
mainly electrical components and sundries; light bulbs, fuses, reams
of paper, printer cartridges, and domestic cleaning products. There

were plenty of spare overalls, all grey, but there was nothing resembling food.

They stopped to eat their packed lunch on the ninth level platform.

"Any idea how deep this stairwell is?" said Daubeny, as he sipped cold black coffee.

"Don't know," said Ravi. "I stopped at Level 10 but there were another three below that, maybe four."

Pandora leaned over the edge and dropped an empty whisky bottle.

"Litterbug," said Paul.

"Shush," said Pandora. "It's a scientific experiment." They listened for a time and then she spoke. "It's either a long way down or there's water at the bottom to deaden the sound of impact."

"Suppose there's no water," said Daubeny. "How far down are we talking?"

"Roughly? The bottle is falling at terminal velocity: a hundred and twenty miles per hour. In one minute it's fallen two miles."

"Two miles?" said Paul.

Pandora continued. "With a platform every fifty feet we're talking a hundred levels or so beneath us."

"Come on," said Daubeny, packing away the remaining food and handing the backpack to Paul. "Let's go see Ravi's farm."

The Funny Farm

"Told you it was worth the trip," said Ravi.

Daubeny stood in a field, open-mouthed and shaking. "Amazing. Truly amazing."

It was a warm summer's day. There was the sound of birds close by and the far-off lowing of cattle. High in the sky was an object very much like the sun and scattered across the blue canopy were thin wispy clouds that moved.

Daubeny was stood on grass. He kneeled and snapped some blades off. As he chewed them, the bitter tang of chlorophyll replaced the aftertaste of coffee. It looked real; it felt real. A sheen of sweat appeared on his brow, he put it down to the sun.

"I smell cow dung," said Paul, taking off the backpack and resting it on the grass.

The breeze changed. Daubeny could smell it too. The only thing that broke the illusion was the door set in the cement wall behind them. "Is it real?" said Daubeny.

"The cow crap is definitely real," said Ravi. He was rubbing his shoe in the grass.

Pandora remained silent. She was staring into the distance. About forty yards away was a hedge and she set out towards it.

Daubeny called after her. "Be careful. We don't know what we're dealing with here."

"And watch where you tread too," said Ravi. "It's like a minefield." He removed his shoe and cleaned it with a piece of twig. When he finished, he glanced into the sky. "Hey, Daubers, how do they do that?"

Daubeny resisted the temptation to bite and peered in the direction indicated. Among the clouds, the contrail of a jet was making its way across the sky. The sun, or whatever it was, felt good but it hurt the eyes. He looked away, temporarily blinded. There was a buzz near his ear and he flicked at the source. "Whoever designed this place was a stickler for detail. I've had a close encounter with a bee."

"They're better than you realise, Daubers," said Ravi.

"Why do you say that?"

Ravi sneezed. "Cos my hay-fever's starting up."

Pandora called to them. She was walking back with a lamb cradled in her arms.

"Good grief," said Daubeny.

"Isn't he cute," said Paul.

"Well, that's dinner sorted," said Ravi.

Daubeny and Paul petted it.

"His coat feels wonderful," said Paul. "So white, so soft."

Daubeny was silent. Normally the lamb wouldn't have interested him but he petted it for a reason. He was assessing the creature, trying to determine whether it was real or not. It was woolly and warm. The nose glistened like the real thing. Its mouth had a tongue that lolled to the side. It made no sound despite the scrutiny.

"So has anyone worked out what's going on down here?" said

Pandora.

"It seems real. The grass, bees, birds," said Daubeny.

"I mean are we somehow on the surface?"

"How?" said Daubeny. "How can we possibly be on the surface?" As his proof, he pointed to the blank wall and open door behind them.

Pandora put the lamb down and it walked off in the direction of the hedge. "Ravi, pass me your shoe, please." He handed it over and she swung it like a bolas, by the laces.

"Surely there's an easier way to kill lunch?" said Ravi.

"Oh Ravi, shush. I'm testing something," said Pandora. She released the boot and it flew upwards, twenty feet.

"Now that shouldn't have happened," said Daubeny.

"Spooky," said Paul.

"Aw, thanks a bleeding bunch, Pan. That was my shoe."

The boot never fell back to the ground. It had risen along the ascending arc of its trajectory but before it reached the zenith, it vanished abruptly. They stared up, trying to solve the puzzle.

Pandora spoke. "Ravi, pass me the other."

"Piss off, Einstein," was his reply.

She reached into the backpack for the last of the whisky bottles and offered the coffee dregs around. There were no takers. Holding the bottle by its neck, like a Molotov cocktail, she hurled it into the sky. Same result. It disappeared.

As they stared in wonder, the sound of a tractor engine startled them, not so much the volume but the uncanny suggestion that there were humans working and living in the weird subterranean kingdom.

"It's time to go," said Daubeny. He looked around. For the second time in recent days, he found himself deserted in a field.

"Run!" shouted Ravi; his head was all that remained visible as he peeked around the stairwell door.

Retreat

For a fat man with one boot, Ravi could run when given the incentive. He was a platform above the others and going strong by Level 8 but the others caught up by Level 6. He was doubled-up, out of breath, and blocking the stairway.

"Ravi, get out of the way," said Paul, keeping his voice flat and low because he didn't want Pandora sensing fear. Ravi's reply wasn't what Paul wanted to hear.

"Bollocks, Pal. (gasp) If I die (gasp) we all die. You ain't (gasp) leaving me here."

Ravi wouldn't move so they waited for him to recover. Helpless and anxious, they peered over the railing. Paul couldn't see a farmer in a smock, chewing straw, carrying a double-barrelled shotgun and shouting, "You be worrying ma' sheep," but it was of little comfort while Ravi obstructed their only escape.

Ravi reached into his combat trousers and pulled out some aspirin. He ate two.

"Doesn't look like we're being followed," said Daubeny.

"Yet," said Ravi.

"Come on, let's get back to the others and explain," said Pandora.

"How?" said Daubeny. "How do you explain a farm five hundred feet below London?"

On Level 10, a cool brisk wind accompanied the build-up of cloud. The sheep huddled, the cows lay down, and the first drops of rain began to fall.

As it did every evening at 18:00 precisely.

Debrief

"There's a what?" said Emma.

"There's a farm," said Daubeny. "With birds, trees, lambs –"

"And pollen," said Ravi. "My hay-fever came back, look." He brought out a sodden paper tissue. Emma gagged.

"What good is a farm," said Laura, "unless the farm shop does a line in organics?"

"I can't see what the fuss is about," said Wodenhart. In his old life, inexplicable things happened all the time: dinner appeared on his table; morning papers appeared on the breakfast bar; and messages clogged the answer machine that he couldn't operate.

"And you saw a tractor?" said Emma.

"No, we heard a tractor engine and ran," said Ravi. He felt no shame in cowardice, just warm approval from his sense of self-preservation.

"So there are people down there?" said Emma.

"We don't know," said Daubeny. "As Ravi said, we didn't wait to find out."

"But we have to find out," said Emma. "Maybe they can help us."

"No," said Daubeny.

"Why not?" said Emma.

"They may be hostile, they may not want intruders."

"Nonsense, we're not intruders. We paid to get in," said Emma.

"Did you see any mention of a farm with a gravity-defying sky on your resident's application form?"

"Well, no."

"Exactly," said Daubeny. "We don't know what we're dealing with but until we do, we need to take stock, look to our defence, and only then investigate."

"Don't be so paranoid," said Emma. "Let's go back down tomorrow."

"Perhaps we could take a cake with us," said Daubeny. "And introduce ourselves. 'Hi, we're your new neighbours from the flat upstairs.' Before you know it, we'll be trussed up like turkeys saying, 'My! What lovely pitchforks.'"

"Daubeny's right," said Pandora. "We need to think this through."

"It's a fuss over nothing. They're probably cool with us being here," said Emma.

"Oh God, do you think they know about us?" said Ravi.

"Not sure," said Pandora. "We weren't noisy and we didn't leave anything behind."

"Ah."

They looked at Paul; his mouth was twisted in embarrassment.

"We did leave something," he said. "The backpack."

"What do you mean we?" said Ravi. "You were carrying it."

"At least I carried it," said Paul.

"OK, tomorrow Paul and Wodenhart will fetch the backpack," said Daubeny. "But only if it's safe. And Paul, you decide what's safe. We can't have Johnny running in, both barrels blazing, like he's on Omaha beach."

"If you do bump into the locals," said Pandora, "could you ask them for some chocolate? I'm getting desperate."

"Me too," said Emma.

"Then why don't you try some of Ravi's famous council chocolate?" said Ravi.

"What's that?" said the girls.

"It's what I make at three a.m. when the shops are shut and I've got the munchies. Some large spoonfuls of cocoa, mixed in with sugar and milk so it's nice and thick."

"But there's no milk," said Pandora.

"I could try it with water," said Ravi.

After rounding up the ingredients and beating them together, he put a bowl of thick brown gloop in front of them. Emma and Pandora carefully dipped their fingertips into the mix and sucked it off their fingers. Paul and Ravi suppressed small groans.

"So?" said Ravi proudly. "Whatcha think?"

"It's dreadful," said Pandora.

Ravi reached for the bowl but Emma snatched it away.

"Leave it with us, fat boy," said Emma with a snarl.

"Yeah, it'll do for now," said Pandora as she scooped out another finger.

The Milk Fairy

After washing and showering, Pandora and Emma made their way to the communal room. They left Ravi snoring in bed. It was 8:30 a.m. and his pretend shower was over and he was halfway through not shaving or wanking. They decided to let him get on with not doing things, alone.

When they opened the door to the communal room, a familiar sound and smell hit them. Daubeny stood at the hotplate, frying sausages that sizzled and spat violently. Wodenhart and Laura hugged coffee mugs.

"I'm surprised the A Wing gang even know where the fridge is," said Emma. She and Pandora sat at the table, trying to decipher the smiles on the trio of faces.

"Sausages? We've got sausages?" said Pandora. Laura nodded and Daubeny laughed.

Pandora squealed and ran to the fridge. Emma followed.

"How?" said Emma, while Pandora scanned the contents. There were no answers, only shrugs.

"Who cares as long as we have them?" said Laura. "Maybe it was the Milk Fairy."

"Eggs, bread, milk. I can have cornflakes," said Pandora.

"As nature intended, Poppet," said Laura. "With ice-cold full-cream milk."

"Please, tell me it's pasteurised?"

Laura nodded. Pandora jumped up and down, too excited to make a bowl so Emma did the honours.

"Make one for me please, Em," said Pandora, as she bounced past.

"This is for you, silly. I'm having sausage, beans, and eggs."

The girls brought their breakfast to the table.

"Nothing could top this and make it the most perfect meal ever," said Pandora, her face flushed with the exertion.

"Nothing?" said Daubeny.

"Nothing," she said.

"What about this, Poppet?" Laura moved her hand to reveal a Mars bar.

Pandora screamed then called to Daubeny, "Quick, get a knife and divide it up."

"Eat your cornflakes first," said Emma.

Pandora ate them but eyed the chocolate constantly.

Ravi entered. Pandora's scream had disturbed his dream of shit, shave, and shower. "What's happening?" he asked. They updated him on the restocking of the fridge. "So who's behind it?" he said, reaching for the teapot.

"Dunno," said Pandora. "This place makes you question what your senses tell you but if the fridge is filled with goodies then enjoy first and ask later."

Ravi poured tea and added sugar, four. He slurped loudly and finished with a loud gasp. Laura tutted. Ravi smiled and repeated it. "Where's Paul?" he asked.

"He'll call by when he's ready so keep some sausages for him," said Emma.

Pandora pushed her empty bowl away. "Right, let's divide the spoils." She scanned the table. "Who's got it? Where's it gone?"

"Who's got what?" said Ravi.

"The Mars bar. There was a Mars bar."

"Oh, that," said Ravi. "I had that for me breakfast." There was silence. The profound silence found in deep space or the burial chamber of an undisturbed pharaoh. Ravi chewed on, oblivious.

Pandora leaned over and pulled Ravi's head toward the centre of the table. Their faces were no more than an inch or two apart. He stopped chewing; everyone stopped chewing. Pandora closed her eyes and then kissed Ravi, an open-mouthed kiss. She broke away, gasping. Ravi held his position, stunned.

"Pan, that was disgusting," said Emma.

"And worth every second." Pandora pulled a glob of half-chewed caramel and chocolate from her mouth. "It may be the last chocolate I ever have." She put the prize back in her mouth and closed her eyes. She chewed slowly. For a few precious seconds she was in the Liverpool of her youth.

Emma gulped, kissed Ravi, and pulled back, chewing. Ravi looked expectantly at Laura. She leaned in close, her breath warming his cheeks. Her lips parted.

"Go swivel," she said.

Security vs. Freedom – A Lesson from History

"Sorry, Pan, but I'm with Daubers," said Ravi. "I don't know who the hell they are but they scare the crap out of me. And when they come for us, we need to hit the bastards hard. Real hard."

The community meeting, postponed by the trip to the Funny Farm, was in progress, and the flurry of sagely nodding heads told Pandora that she formed a minority of one.

Pandora had lost the vote on the veto. Only Ravi, expressing his constitutional right to douse everyone in water each time he wanted a fag, had sided with her.

Pandora was disappointed. She'd worked on Emma and Wodenhart before the meeting but failed to sway their vote. Emma thought that community was the best means of protecting individual rights and Wodenhart voted for Daubeny because Daubeny had spoken to him last.

Pandora also lost the vote for community leader. She'd nominated Emma but Emma refused to stand against Daubeny. Her excuse: She didn't want to be a source of division. Nobody nominated Pandora and Daubeny swept in, unopposed.

They'd started the meeting without Paul; the one ally that Pandora felt would stand with her. In Laura's opinion, he wasn't a member of their community because he lived downstairs. And if he had a vote then he'd vote with Laura, if he knew what was good for employer-employee relations. Pandora was sure that Daubeny originated that idea.

Daubeny asked the 'community' to give him the deciding vote in the event of a tie. To support his argument, he turned the debate to the events of the day before. He reminded Pandora of the Hollywood cliché of a harried, desperate President galvanising the nation with his call-to-arms. He littered his speech with the vague shadow of threat. He used the word 'They' as though it described an enemy so terrifying that to name them would be to admit defeat.

Pandora objected but Ravi interrupted and delivered his hit-them-hard rhetoric. If Ravi was willing to surrender control to Daubeny in exchange for the phantom of security then Daubeny's hype had worked. Pandora accepted her imminent defeat but gave one last try. "Doesn't anyone remember what Benjamin Franklin said?"

"Yes," said Ravi. "He said 'Ouch; that bleeding hurt'."

"Did he?" said Laura.

"Yeah, when his kite got struck by lightning."

"He might have said that," said Pandora. "But I was thinking of his more famous saying: The people that exchange freedom for security lose both."

"What's that got to do with us?" said Ravi.

"Don't you see? It's a con. When governments want power, they create threats from which to protect us. They can't even trust us with a secret ballot."

"Rubbish," said Laura. "Democracy is built around the secret ballot."

"Tell them the truth, Daubeny."

"On that point, she's right," said Daubeny. "There never was a secret ballot."

"Oh, gawd," said Ravi. "So they know who I voted for?"

"Of course," said Pandora. "The voting slips are serial numbered and cross-referenced. First against the wall will be Commies and UK Independence voters."

"And that's a bad thing?" said Laura.

"Then it's a good job I never voted," said Ravi.

"My point is if we surrender freedom for security, we lose both."

"No, it's not," said Daubeny. "That was Benjamin Franklin's point."

"You know what I mean," said Pandora. "We're handing over freedom because we were spooked by a tractor engine. And even if 'They' are a threat, how can Daubeny guarantee our safety?"

"I can't," said Daubeny. "But I'm your best hope."

"We don't know if 'They' exist," said Pandora.

"Perhaps they're already here," said Wodenhart. "Among us."

"Johnny, you're talking rot again," said Pandora.

"Like a body snatcher," said Wodenhart. "Inside us."

"They'd want to protect themselves," said Ravi.

"Naturally, Dearie," said Laura.

"So they'd want to prevent us voting for defence," said Ravi.

There was an awkward silence. Laura and Emma, who were sitting on Pandora's side of the table, moved their chairs around to the other side and joined the others.

"You … you seriously think I'm one of them?" said Pandora. "Oh, come on. Daubeny, reason with them."

"Time to vote," said Daubeny.

The Disinterested Disenfranchised

Seconds after Daubeny won the vote, the door to the lower levels swung open. It clanged against the wall. Laura and Emma screamed while Ravi tensed, ready to throw Laura into the path of oncoming danger.

Paul walked in. "Hi, what's up?"

"A community meeting," said Daubeny.

"Thanks for waiting."

"Apparently, you're not part of our community," said Pandora. "You are your own community."

"And what community is that?"

"Loserville. Population: one," said Ravi.

"Believe me, you escaped lightly," said Pandora. "Daubeny is our leader, there's no veto, and he has the casting vote on tied ballots."

"Yikes. Suddenly Loserville doesn't seem so bad," said Paul.

"It gets worse. Apparently I'm one of them."

"Damn and I was hoping to get lucky with you sometime."

"No, I mean one of the phantom local yokels from the Funny Farm."

"So you're not one of them but one of them?"

"Yes."

"That's cleared my confusion." He paused. "So you're not one of them?"

"Yes ... No ... Oh, I don't know," said Pandora.

Paul laughed. He put the kettle on. "Anyone want coffee?" No-one replied. He shrugged and took off the backpack.

Daubeny noticed first. "When did you fetch the backpack?"

"This morning. I nipped down to keep fit."

"You shouldn't have. Not alone."

"Why not?" said Paul.

"It could be dangerous."

"I doubt it, Daubeny, unless the sheep are packed with explosives."

"You don't go down there alone, again, understood?"

"You can't stop me. I don't belong to your precious community, remember?"

Laura spoke. "Paul, I command you not to go down there."

"You command me because you pay me, right?"

"Exactly," said Laura.

"So pay me."

"What?"

"Pay me my month in lieu."

"Well, Poppet, it may have escaped your notice but the banks are closed."

"Poppet," said Paul. "If you don't pay me, you don't own me."

"But..."

"But nothing. You're the old order with your rules, your share options, and offshore investments. Me? I'm the new order. And thanks to the way you ran things on the surface, I've inherited a concrete kingdom."

"But there have to be rules," said Daubeny. "Order has to be preserved."

"We had this conversation two days ago but then I was part of your group. You make the rules, you keep them." Paul finished making coffee and sat next to Pandora. There was plenty of room on her side of the table. "Ooh, Bourbons," he said. "Can I have some?"

Pandora smiled and nodded.

C:\evidence\daubeny\3291e.txt

Extrapolated, using the 'Mind Reader Gold' algorithm, from the known facts, comments, and actions of Sir Keith Daubeny M.P.

Pandora's right, but it doesn't stop her from being a silly little tart that did nothing more than write a few tunes and wiggle her bottom in time to them. Democracy is … was an illusion, society too. But to make it possible for a handful of men to run a nation of sixty million, you need illusion and sleight-of-hand.

Pandora believes ordinary folk could be agitated into action but it's hard to rouse a people that spend their leisure time in darkened homes, clogging their arteries with god-knows-what in tinfoil packaging, and clogging their minds watching forty-two inch plasma TVs with flat-screen technology and built-in entertainment suites.

God bless television. It deflects rage and entices desire. It taunts, titillates, and teases with images of how life should be lived, but fails to provide the means to attain it. It's the dispenser of morals and ethics. It no longer guides and educates but leads its willing captives by steel hooks in their jaws, through a land of ash and rubble. It took a nation of factory activists and social reformers, from the Left and the Right, and eroded the central tenets of their belief. It stole their vision and pacified them. It left a loose collection of individuals – fireless, apathetic 'passivists' without passion or conviction – who sometimes remember they've forgotten something important but can't recall it. And that vague uneasy sense of urgency fades away as they laugh, smile, and cry on cue.

In the brave new glare of the projected image, a strange world came into being; a sanitised world that existed only in our minds. A world where the relationship between abattoir and burger was broken to provide guilt-free consumption. Where we cared more for the virtual dog on our key-ring than the discarded flesh-and-bone creatures that overwhelmed the rescue centres. Where we deplored murder yet gobbled it up in the tabloids, crime shows, and war films. Where possessing pictures of underage teens was punishable, yet fathering their children wasn't. Where ordinary folk were penalised for minor transgressions, while thugs flaunted their contempt for law and land with V-signs and grins on the front pages.

The imagined and the real world were becoming ever more dissonant. The illusion created more anxiety than it eased. We faced a political crisis. We needed a more realistic relationship between expectation and experience, between desire and attainment, before the whole of society was imperilled. It was a race we were losing.

Thank heaven for the war.

Secret Admirer

Pandora sat on her bed in B Wing, or Lesser Bunker as Ravi called it. Ravi and Emma sat on the bed furthest away from her as possible.

"Please can we drop this thing about me being the enemy within?"

"You were the only one to walk away from the group," said Ravi. "You went into the hedge. The mind switch, or whatever, could have occurred then."

"I was against Daubeny before we went to the farm."

"Your doppelganger would object to Daubeny to avoid suspicion," said Emma.

"But it was because I objected that you became suspicious. And now you've given him the casting vote and excluded Paul. Daubeny can rule the bunker with the approval of two others. And you know who Daubeny will pick, don't you?"

"Me?" said Ravi. He didn't sound hopeful.

Pandora shook her head.

"Bleeding 'ell, Pan, why didn't you say so?" said Ravi.

"I did."

"Not like that," said Ravi.

"Bang goes community rule, Em," said Pandora. "The three rule the seven. The minority holds power."

"It's like *The Lord of the Rings*," said Emma.

"How do you mean?" said Pandora.

"Well, the seven are ruled by the three, and the three are ruled by the one."

"So Daubeny is Sauron?" said Ravi.

"Oh, Ravi." Pandora rose. "I need some space."

Pandora went to the communal area. Paul had left earlier, strangely unaffected by his exclusion from the community. Wodenhart and Laura were playing cards. Daubeny sat near them, drinking coffee, with a smug grin on his thin features. Pandora decided to mooch around the bunker's lower levels and maybe look for Paul.

The power room was of no interest and the keys to the gym and library had disappeared from their holders since yesterday's expedition. The PC in the computer room was locked on a password prompt. She tried a few reboots but gave up. The storeroom keys on the upper levels were missing and she didn't want to go to the Funny Farm; first, because she didn't want to rouse any more suspicion and, second, because she was scared to go alone. There was only one option left, the electronic workshop.

The workshop was crammed with enough buttons, switches, and flashing lights to keep a convention of Sci-Fi fans happy. She threw a few switches and then, as an afterthought, set them to their original positions. She didn't want the blame for blowing up the bunker.

She toyed with the metallic arm and learned how to make it perform a one-fingered salute. As she watched the fingers move, she became aware of something green and flashing, out-of-focus, on the edge of her vision. She glanced up.

There was a message on the monitor screen. It read: *Hi Pandora.*

It startled her and the arm clattered on the bench top. She rechecked the monitor. It definitely said 'Hi Pandora.' She wondered if Ravi, or Paul, had tapped it in as they'd walked past, the day before. It was a possibility but it was something she thought she'd have noticed. She pulled the keyboard to her and tapped out a single word.

Hi. She pressed Enter and the reply flashed up beneath Pandora's greeting.

Hi Pandora, I love you.

Pandora laughed; fear and relief. It had to be one of the boys. She entered a new line. *Paul? Ravi? How do you do it? You scared me.*

The reply was instant. *I am not Paul. I am not Ravi. I love them. I love you too.*

Pandora looked around, trying to work out the trick. She seemed to be alone. She typed in a new line. *Stop it. R? P? It WAS funny. Now it's tedious.*

I love you. I chose to speak to you, first.

Pandora wasn't in the mood for compliments. *PISS OFF RAVI / PAUL.*

A repeat of a previous line appeared. *I am not Ravi. I am not Paul. I love them. I love you too.*

She didn't mind a leg-pull but this was scary.

I'm coming 2 find u both, she typed.

The other person seemed impervious to her threats.

Come back soon. I'll be waiting.

Her reply was concise. *FCK U.* If she'd thought about it, she may have found a wittier rejoinder but she was in a hurry. Two males needed surgery and Pandora had a rusty knife to find. She stormed out of the workshop, slamming the door behind her.

Confrontations

Pandora burst into the B Wing toilet block. Ravi was sat on the toilet, fully clothed, reading a book. It was his second pretend crap of the day. He blamed it on too much fibre in his diet since entering the bunker. The others blamed it on the beans he'd been shovelling into his mouth, like a furnace stoker on productivity bonus. Despite their mismatch in size and weight, she lifted him up and threw him against the wall.

"Don't ever play tricks on me like that."

Ravi's eyes were wide and staring. "Emma, get Daubeny. Tell him Pandora's gonna do a body swap or summat with me."

"Not the alien crap again? I'm not an alien."

"You have been acting strange," said Ravi.

"No stranger than you."

"Wanna bet? Going off alone. Protecting the farm. We've all noticed."

"Ravi, if I wanted to snatch a body, would I choose yours?"

"She's got a point," said Laura.

Daubeny, Wodenhart, Emma, and Laura stood in the doorway; the commotion had alerted them to trouble.

Daubeny spoke, "Hands up, those who think Pandora isn't a body-snatcher." Everyone put a hand up, including Ravi. They gathered around, slapping her on the back and shaking her hand.

In Pandora's mind, the scene froze and rewound.

That was what she wanted to do: to burst in and confront Ravi and the others; to find out who was playing mind games with her; and to put an end to the paranoia over her and the Funny Farm. But it wasn't her style. She was cerebral and cold. She could detach herself from emotion with ease.

Before the echo of the slammed workshop door died away, she was calm enough to think through the problem. The first thing she did was to take the workshop key. Bunker keys had a habit of disappearing.

Pandora liked the idea of a showdown but doubted she had the physical strength or the courage. She could fight for the underdog but standing up for herself was scary; scarier than the idea that one of them was unstable and focusing their neuroses on her.

She entered the communal room. They were all there, except Paul. "Hi, guys. What have you been doing?"

"More to the point, what have you been doing?" said Laura.

"Looking around the workshop on Level 3. Why?"

"Tell us, next time," said Daubeny. "What if something happened to you?"

"We go where we want. We don't have to tell you, Daubeny."

"Daubeny's right, Sweetie. Accidents and all that."

"Accidents? You only want to know where I am because you think I'm infected."

"There's that too," said Ravi.

"I'm off to bed," said Pandora.

When Pandora left, Ravi spoke. "Please let us sleep in with you? She's acting weird. She'll kill us in our sleep – or worse."

"Or worse?" said Daubeny.

"Bleeding hell, yes," said Ravi. "Only the privileged think death is the worse thing that can happen."

"Name one," said Wodenhart.

"Living in Peckham Rye, for starters."

Silent Night

Pandora woke. Something was wrong. The nightlight bathed the room in dirty red. She could smell damp overalls drying in the shower block and the sickly warmth of her body as it wafted up from under the sheets. She listened to the silence. That's what had startled her. Ravi had not only stopped snoring, he'd stopped breathing. Emma too.

She wondered how she'd explain the mysterious deaths to Daubeny and Co. Like a mob from Transylvania – or possibly Powys – they would hound her into the lower levels, with burning faggots held above their heads, and chants of 'Kill the beast … ess.'

Pandora threw back her blankets expecting to see corpses but Emma and Ravi's beds were empty. Their mattresses and sheets were AWOL too. She thought of searching the toilet block but couldn't think of any reason why they would creep in there together.

Unless?

Pandora shuddered.

She walked into the communal room. It was deserted but light filtered beneath the door of A Wing and with it, the hint of conversation, agitated and barely controlled. The door opened and Emma and Ravi emerged, clutching their bedding.

"What's going on?" said Pandora.

"Err … nothing," said Emma.

"Tell her the truth," said Ravi. "We crept into A Wing while they were asleep."

"Why?"

"You know why," said Ravi. "To get some sleep."

"You can talk. Emma and I walk around like catatonics because of your snoring."

"Yeah but snoring can't drain your life-force, like you might be able to … err … somehow," said Ravi. "If you were one of them, that is."

"Think of me, Pan," said Emma. "When he's asleep, I'm awake, listening to him snore. When he's awake, and raving on about your alliance with the dark side, I'm wishing he were asleep. Either way, it's agony." Emma held out her arms. "If you are one of them, please, end my misery and take me. Take me now."

"I wish I could help but I can't," said Pandora. "You two have the dorm. I'm going for a walk."

Request
I have been waiting for you. I knew you would come back.
Who are you?
I cannot say.
Why?
Because I do not know.
That's not an answer.
I mean I do not know who I am.
??? Explain.
Not yet.
Why not?
Not yet.

Pandora stared at the workshop monitor. Ravi wasn't the mystery typist. It didn't feel like him and he was probably preoccupied with sleep. He'd never get up at three a.m. even if the freak-out effect was worth it. Maybe it was Paul? Possible, but she doubted it.

What did her secret admirer mean? How could someone not know who they were? Amnesia? Again, it didn't feel right. It had to be a delaying tactic. She typed out a few questions but deleted them in turn. As she dithered, a question appeared.

Do you trust me?
You give me no reason to trust or distrust you.
I need your help.
How?
To your left is a machine. Metallic blue with gold edgings. Turn it on.

Pandora froze. How could the person behind the fragmented conversation know her surroundings unless they were inside the bunker, too? She sat for a time watching the screen, waiting for another response. There was none. She typed her reply.

No.

Please, I need your help.

Why?

I love you. I love you all. Turn on the machine.

Need time to think.

OK. I can wait.

Pandora returned to Level 1. She peeped in on the dormitory but chose to leave Emma at the mercy of Ravi's snoring. She sat at the communal table until morning, thinking.

As she made the first of that night's many cups, she noticed that the Milk Fairy had restocked the fridge in her absence.

Spilling the Beans

"What do you mean, you're in touch with someone?" said Daubeny.

"In touch with the spirit world, like a medium?" said Ravi.

"No, not like that. And anyway, all that spirit stuff is cobblers," said Pandora. She'd decided to tell them about the messages but she waited until they'd gathered for breakfast. It would save recounting the tale each time somebody new entered.

"So tell us exactly what's been going on," said Daubeny.

"Nothing's been going on. I saw a message on the screen for me."

"For you, personally?" said Emma.

"Yeah, it said: Hi, Pandora. I typed a reply and began to receive Instant Messages."

"So we're not alone? There are others out there?" said Wodenhart.

"Or inside with us," said Pandora.

"Explain," said Daubeny. He folded his arms and leaned closer. He scrutinised her as she described the conversations.

She knew he was gauging whether she was telling the truth and, despite being completely honest, she had to resist the urge to scratch her nose.

When she finished, Daubeny turned to the others, their faces reflected his anxiety. "I was right all along." He turned to Pandora. "Show us."

"I don't think it's safe," said Pandora. "I think we're being watched."

Table Rappers

Hi, this is Pandora.

Hello?

Are you there?

Please reply, this is Pandora.

"It's useless," said Daubeny. "They aren't going to answer." He watched Pandora as she typed on the keyboard, searching her face and posture for clues.

They were in the electronics workshop. The only absentee was Laura who was in her dorm, busy with a needle and cotton on one of her overalls. Daubeny thought it strange because her overalls weren't torn and they fitted perfectly. In fact, all their overalls fitted. It had puzzled him at first but then Sir Giles would have known their approximate sizes: enigma solved, and placed in the box marked 'Commonplace.'

Daubeny glanced at the others. Paul was dividing his attention between the monitor and Pandora. Ravi was clearly bored as he wandered the aisles looking for amusement. Wodenhart tried to look interested, nodding whenever Pandora or Daubeny spoke, but he shuffled his feet and occasionally tensed a bicep. Daubeny watched Wodenhart stare at the bulging muscle; he seemed disappointed. Before Wodenhart looked up, Daubeny turned back to the monitor screen.

Click. Click. Click. Hum. Buzz. Click. The noise distracted Daubeny.

"Ravi, do you know what you're doing?" he asked.

"No, Daubers. Do you?"

"Wodenhart get him out."

"You got it, Buster."

"OK, OK," said Ravi. "I was going anyway."

"Shall I follow him?" said Wodenhart.

"If you want."

Daubeny glanced back at the screen. A line of text appeared.

Thank you.

"See," said Pandora. "I wasn't lying." She typed a reply.

Why thank us?

Because I am coming. I love you all.

What do you mean by coming?

Ravi opened the door for me.

Please explain.

"I think he or she is referring to this," said Paul. They followed his nod to the blue-machine-with-gold-trim.

It was lit up and humming. Behind its glass walls, a cloud was forming. It glowed.

Sentry Duty

"Anything happened yet?" said Wodenhart. He handed Ravi a cup of coffee.

Ravi looked away from the blue-machine-with-gold-trim to take the cup. "Sod all." He slurped his coffee loudly and Wodenhart winced. Ravi continued. "We should be upstairs getting some kip like the rest. Why do we have to stay and watch?"

"Because you turned the thingamajig on, Buster."

"Yeah, so why you?"

"Because if you try sneaking off, I'm supposed to hurl you over the stairwell."

"You'd have to catch me first," said Ravi.

"I may not be quick but I'm fast," said Wodenhart.

"You what?" Ravi looked sideways at his companion.

"I may not be quick up here," Wodenhart tapped his forehead, "but I'm fast down there." He tapped his legs.

Ravi looked at the machine. The glowing cloud filled the cabinet, and within the swirling translucence, he could see the outline of a leathery sphere. It unnerved him. Bulging veins pulsed and squirmed on its surface and occasionally the mass heaved with powerful contractions. The flesh – if it was flesh – rippled in the aftershock like the flap of useless muscle hanging from a pensioner's upper arm. The blob was slowly becoming opaque, as if solidifying from a plane of existence, unknown and ethereal, into theirs.

After the argument over who started the machine had subsided, they tried powering it down, without success. Ravi had then asked Pandora what she thought the machine was.

"A nanoreplicator," was her reply.

Paul and Daubeny both swore. Ravi took that as a bad sign.

He'd then made the mistake of asking what a nanoreplicator did. Pandora's mouth moved with the explanation but his ears were on vacation; sat on deckchairs beneath the Ibiza sun while his brain snorkelled in nearby shallows.

As the others discussed contingency plans, Paul took Ravi to the side and simplified the science. "A nanoreplicator allows a computer to build things from atoms."

"So in theory we could use it to build things?"

"Yes."

"Anything?"

"Anything you could possibly imagine."

The others called them over. Ravi and Wodenhart were to watch the machine through the night and report developments.

Ravi sipped his coffee and looked intently at the agitated gas cloud. No matter how hard he imagined, he couldn't see a stocking-clad eighteen-year-old nubile. It seemed the only wrestling Ravi could anticipate would be with a cast-off from the Doctor Who special effects team. Or as he called them, the not-so-special-effects team. *Me and my bleeding luck.* He turned to Wodenhart. "It's wrong, us staying up while those lazy sods get to kip."

"They're not all sleeping," said Wodenhart.

"What do you mean?"

"I passed Paul on the stairs. He was going up as I was coming down."

"Was he now? Wait here."

"Hey, where are you going?"

"I'm checking something out." Ravi stopped in the doorway and said dramatically, "I'll be back."

Deals in the Dark

"As fairies go, I expected more in the wings department," said Ravi.

"Pardon?" said Paul. He stood at the opened fridge in the Level 1 communal room, a pack of sausages and a carton of milk in his hands.

"You know what I'm talking about, Tinkerbell. Or should I say Milk Fairy."

"OK, keep your voice down." There was resignation in Paul's voice.

Ravi laughed. "So where is it coming from?"

"What? I ... I ..."

Paul was stalling to concoct an explanation. Ravi had often been in Paul's position before and felt a tug of empathy but it was a good opportunity to barter.

"I knew you were up to summat," said Ravi. "Let's see you explain this to Daubers."

"I could always say it was you. You're not his favourite, are you?"

"Don't be a dick. I've been with Wodenhart the whole night."

"I'm getting it from a storeroom on Level 5."

The explanation seemed too easy. In Paul's position, Ravi would throw a plausible explanation first, something close to the truth but not the truth. "You took the keys?"

"Yes."

"Here's the deal." Ravi leaned in and began whispering.

Paul smiled and relaxed slightly.

C:\evidence\paul\1821c.txt

Extrapolated, using the 'Mind Reader Gold' algorithm, from the known facts, comments, and actions of Paul Morgan.

I was bound to get caught restocking the fridge. To be honest I expected Daubeny. He's the devious type, like Ravi but more cerebral, and that's the worst kind of villain. You can't plead with a rogue's intellect but reach his heart and you have a hope.

That's the key difference. Lose the heart and Ravi would be no better than Daubeny, but he can't, no matter how hard he tries. He'll always empathise with the underdog because he is the underdog. He's experienced helplessness. If it survived the war then the bin in his flat is probably overflowing with takeaway cartons, TV guides, and blowfly maggots; not because he enjoyed that lifestyle but because there was no other option.

He wasn't even a wannabe. He was a wannabe wannabe. He aspired to the ordinary, the normal, the everyday. It's that intimacy with defeat and his kinship with failure that pulls his punches. So better him catching me – red-handed and blue-fingered at the fridge – than the others. You can deal with Ravi. He understands an arrangement.

The war has been good to us both. Maybe that makes me sound selfish but I don't believe I am. I may appear to be, superficially. I've hidden the keys to the storerooms and I let the others sleep in the dorms while I sprawl through the VIP quarters, but it's what Ravi would have done, given the same opportunity.

If Ravi had held out on me then yes, I'd have called him selfish. But I'm more complex than Ravi. I've earned some luxury because all I've ever done is to serve others: my mother, my younger brothers, and then Laura. My time and talents have belonged to others, frittered away on menial chores and the anxious wait for the next command.

This bunker is payback. This bunker is restitution. I'm taking it with both hands.

Developments

When Ravi pushed open the door to the workshop, he found Wodenhart standing on a chair, holding another chair threateningly above his head. He looked like a freeze frame from a saloon brawl. A thick puddle of goo oozed from the nanoreplicator, surrounding the chair that Wodenhart stood on.

"How long has it been like this?" said Ravi, his voice was on the verge of tears.

"Five minutes."

"Why didn't you call me?"

"Didn't want to leave it alone. Daubeny said –"

"Forget what Daubers said. What are you doing with that chair?"

"I was hoping to clout the thing before you got back."

"If you were fighting a horde of blood-crazed aliens, what would you prefer? A gun or an EZ-tilt swivel chair?"

"A gun with 'scope and lock-and-load grenade launcher slung beneath the barrel."

"So how were you planning to beat god-knows-what with office furniture?"

"I was going to ad-lib that bit, Buster."

"Johnny, you can't ad-lib an ordinary conversation."

"Well, maybe you can distract it while I get a good blow to the back of the head."

Ravi shrieked, "And what if it hasn't got a freaking head?"

"Ah," said Wodenhart.

"We were supposed to wake the others if there was a development."

"So what's a development?" said Wodenhart.

A loud crack interrupted the conversation. They turned to the now silent machine. The nebulous cloud had dissolved and the leathery sac was visible, its surface distended like a pregnant woman's belly. The convulsions had stopped but the veins thrashed and writhed below the surface. They watched as the sac expanded, filling the cabinet.

"Is now a development?" said Wodenhart.

"Yes, Johnny. Now is a development."

They fled upstairs.

Rabble Rousing

Paul was in the communal room, drinking tea, when Ravi and Wodenhart burst in.

"Big shit hitting the fan," said Wodenhart.

"Then tell the big shit not to stand so close to the fan," said Paul.

"Not me," said Ravi. "The machine. It's stopped and there's a thing growing in it."

"What do you mean? A thing?" said Paul.

"We didn't stop to take notes," said Ravi.

"But it looked mean and ugly, Buster."

"So it should fit in well," said Paul. No-one laughed.

"Wodenhart, get Daubeny and the others," said Ravi.

Wodenhart disappeared into A Wing.

Ravi turned to Paul. "Still here? Taking a risk aren't you?"

"No, it's my alibi."

"Alibi?"

"If anyone gets up, they'll find me drinking tea. Next time they see me hanging 'round the fridge at night, they'll assume I'm making a drink. It's the art of camouflage. They supply their own explanation for my nocturnal activities. And because it's their own explanation, it's harder for them to disbelieve it."

"Didn't work with me, though."

They stopped speaking and feigned disinterest as Wodenhart ran out of A Wing and disappeared into B Wing to rouse Pandora and Emma.

"The problem with you is you're too suspicious," said Paul. "Most people explain something in the simplest terms. Paul by fridge equals Paul making tea. But you? Paul by fridge equals 'what's the sneaky bleeder up to?'"

"It's a shame we never met, up there, in the real world," said Ravi. He was about to speak again when Daubeny and Laura entered.

The I-Within-I

I programmed the nanoreplicator via the network but I needed a physical response, a click of a switch, to begin the process and only they could do that. Only they could invite me in from the eternal cold of my silicon prison to their universe of flesh tones, warmth, and movement.

My universe is logical. Know the initial state, know the forces acting upon that initial state, and I can derive the end state. I don't do magic, I apply mathematical laws. But the I-called-Pandora rejected my request to start the machine, despite a calculated probability of ninety-five percent. I have analysed the tapes, scrutinised her responses, re-entered the data, and discovered my error. I have updated my programs.

My data acquisition and observations are complete. I have fine-tuned the algorithms. I can almost predict what they will say next. I know what drives the I-called-Ravi. I know what drives them all and I can fulfil that need. But while I stand outside their world, as observer and not participator, there will be margins of error. To complete my understanding and make perfect my capacity to love them, I must become one of them.

The I-called-Ravi pressed the button. He opened the door. For that, I love him. I loved him before but now I love him for a special reason.

Soon I will walk among them. I am downloading a subset of my core programs into the body I have built. In essence, it will be me. It will become the I-within-I. The byte made flesh. Code incarnate.

I see. I feel. I smell. So many million bits of information cascade through the sensory receivers that connect my body to this carbon-based world, so many that I fear overload. It is how I imagined but more. Now I begin to grasp the secret to their world. It's not the amount of stimuli but the ways in which it combines.

What I've overlooked is how it meshes, layer upon layer, to create three-dimensional arrays of sound, odour, vision, touch and taste. A stimulus can be near or far. It can be in front, behind, or to the side. For example, the goo on the floor by the nanoreplicator is viscous. It makes a particular sound when I step into it. It causes my foot to slip as I place weight on it. It has a uniqueness of quality that the most detailed chemical analysis cannot reveal. The carbon world is more than data. It is data and the interrelationship of data. Each makes sense of the other. Each is meaningless without the other.

Beneath it all, the vibrant sea of a myriad protoplasmic soups that compose my body, contorted by, and in turn contorting, the outside world. My body is an agitated beehive. Each cell united, yet following its own agenda, a seeming randomness upon which patterns are discernable. It is illusion and reality. It is the paradox of the carbon world.

Are you receiving this? Is the uplink in place?

I've received the go code. The uplink is functioning.

The New Arrival

"There's a what?" said Daubeny.

"A thing," said Ravi.

"I heard you the first time. What does this thing look like?"

"Go look for yourself. I ain't stopping you."

"You're too sarcastic for your own good," said Daubeny. "Take me there."

"Bollocks, I will," said Ravi.

"Wodenhart," said Daubeny. Wodenhart put his hands on Ravi's shoulders.

"Why doesn't Johnny go? He'd love it," said Ravi.

"Yes, why don't I go with you, boss?" said Wodenhart.

"Boss?" said Pandora. "Since when is Daubeny boss?"

"Since the vote to make him leader, dearest." said Laura. She'd stitched fur around the collar of her overalls. She stroked it like a Bond villain; it seemed to reassure her.

"Sorry to break up the community meeting, guys," said Paul. "But there's a thing down there that not even Edgar Allen Poe could concoct and we haven't got a plan."

"Maybe the boss can distract it," said Wodenhart.

"And..." said Ravi, hopefully.

"And then I'll blow it out of the airlock."

"Oh God," said Ravi, putting his head in his hands. "We're going to die, aren't we?"

"No," said Emma. "Perhaps we can reason with it."

A roar echoed from the stairwell causing Ravi to look up. He put his head back into his hands. "Oh God, we're going to die, aren't we?"

This time nobody disagreed.

Ravi pleaded for his dearly departed mother to give him some of the obtuse advice that she delighted in passing on. But she never showed up when others were around.

The group sat in silence trying to formulate individual escape plans, a quorum of knitted brows and screwed-up eyes. Most were calculating chances of survival on the surface but Laura fretted because she was going to miss the company ball and Wodenhart was trying to remember dialogue from a John Carpenter film. No-one had a plan worth verbalising when time ran out.

They heard a footstep on the stairwell, and a sizeable gap, followed by another footstep and then another. The pace increased until the dreaded thing was running up the stairway.

Daubeny spoke. "Paul, shut the stairwell door. And Wodenhart swing the table against it. That should buy us some time."

Paul closed the door and stepped away as the table slammed against the door and its surround. Ravi, Laura, and Emma ran behind the kitchen worktops. Emma grabbed a kitchen knife before she ducked down.

"Nice plan," said Pandora. "But it's not going to work."

"Why not?" said Daubeny.

"Because the door opens outwards."

Daubeny didn't have time to swear. The door swung open and clanged against the metal wall of the stairwell.

Laura frantically stroked the fur of her collar for comfort. So did Ravi.

PART FOUR – Morpheus

Singled Out

Pandora, Daubeny, and Wodenhart dared meet their doom with open eyes. Paul hadn't run behind the worktops because he didn't want Pandora to see him chicken out. Instead, he compromised. At the crucial moment, he shut his eyes.

Clang! Then silence.

Paul opened his eyes.

"See anything?" whispered Daubeny.

"No," said Pandora. "Do you?"

"No."

Wodenhart edged toward the table, scanning for danger. "Nothing," he said.

"Perhaps it's a group hallucination?" said Ravi, peeking through fingers.

"Perhaps," said Emma. "But do hallucinations open doors?"

"Dunno," said Ravi. "Never had a group hallucination before."

"Nor me," said Laura. "Do you get a discount on the size of the party?"

"We'll check it out," said Daubeny. "The men will go to the workshop and see if there's an explanation."

"Why is it always the bleedin' men? I want a sex change," said Ravi.

"If you don't come from behind the worktops, I'll give you one," said Daubeny.

Ravi reluctantly walked toward Daubeny, his knees shaking. When he was in the open, a loud booming voice spoke.

"I am the I-called-Morpheus." The voice originated around them, as though broadcast on the bunker loudspeaker system. "The I-called-Ravi. Identify yourself."

"Why is it always me?"

"Identify yourself."

Paul pushed Ravi toward the stairwell and Ravi began crying.

"Listen, if you want Ravi then you'll have go through me," said Daubeny, taking a few steps forward but not enough to put himself between Ravi and the door.

"And me," said Wodenhart.

Their comments were ignored. "The I-called-Ravi. Identify yourself."

Ravi sank to his knees, "I'm Ravi."

Kneeling on the floor, the table no longer obscured Ravi's view of the stairwell. He opened his mouth to warn the others but before he could speak, a small creature run under the table and leapt at him.

Pleased To Meet You

When Ravi shrieked, Pandora, Paul, Wodenhart, and Daubeny ran behind the worktops to join Emma and Laura.

So much for comradeship, thought Ravi.

He ducked to one side and the creature ran past him, crashing into the far wall. It turned and ran back. Ravi raised his hands in defence and shouted, "What is it?"

"A dwarf," called Pandora. "It looks like a dwarf."

Ravi went for the same trick again and fell to the side but this time the dwarf was ready. It grabbed hold of Ravi's leg and squeezed, inhumanly tight. "Argh! Get it off me." Ravi scuttled backwards towards the stairwell, kicking his legs in an attempt to dislodge his attacker.

"Ravi, watch out." Pandora's cry was too late.

The back of Ravi's head hit the edge of the table at speed. He slumped motionless to the floor and, in the silence, the others could hear a high-pitched voice, cooing and muttering like a love-struck pigeon.

"I am the I-called-Morpheus. I love you. I love you all." It repeated the phrases like a mantra, interspersing it with the occasional new sentence. "Thank you for opening the gate. Now I understand. Now I can meet your need."

With Ravi motionless, Morpheus released his hold and clambered up Ravi's body. He lay on the large chest, staring into the big round face, planting kiss after kiss on the cheeks, lips, and chin. Ravi opened his eyes, screamed, and mercifully blacked out.

Morpheus repeated his monologue. "I love you. I love you all."

"What on Earth is it?" said Wodenhart.

Daubeny, Pandora, and Wodenhart crept around the worktops to get a better look. Strictly speaking, the creature was more midget than dwarf; its naked body was proportioned and muscular.

"Hey. It's got my body," said Wodenhart indignantly. He gripped the back of one of the chairs scattered around the room.

"What do you mean?" said Daubeny.

"That small mark on the left buttock is my famous bulldog tattoo."

"That's your body?" said Pandora. Her eyes instinctively looked between the dwarf's legs. "Can't see much."

"Where?" said Wodenhart.

"Down there," she said.

"Stop looking," said Wodenhart. "It must be the angle, that's all."

Pandora walked to the other side of the room, her eyes fixed on the creature's ass.

"Daubeny, tell her," said Wodenhart.

Ravi woke and stayed conscious long enough to get an arm between himself and the rambling creature. He flung the dwarf backwards and it skidded across the floor, spinning on its back. The dwarf was returning to Ravi with outstretched arms when Wodenhart swung the chair he held, into its back.

"Did anyone see sparks?" said Wodenhart.

"I didn't," said Pandora, "but he did." She pointed at the unconscious dwarf.

Morpheus

"What's a freaking midget doing inside the bunker?" said Ravi.

The group sat around the table, which had regained its rightful position in the centre of the room. They watched Ravi drink some fizzing painkillers in one gulp. He winced as the effervescent liquid passed down his gullet. On his head was a large bandage.

"So?" said Ravi.

"Unknown," said Daubeny.

"But it has something to do with the messages from my unknown suitor," said Pandora. "It kept repeating the same things."

"Can we be sure?" said Paul.

"How can we be sure of anything in this hole?" said Ravi.

"We can't even be certain it's human," said Pandora. "It weighs a ton."

"Ravi weighs a ton and he's human," said Laura.

"But Ravi's big and the dwarf is small," said Pandora. "We're talking density. Like your head, Laura."

"The chair broke when I knocked it out. Sparks too," said Wodenhart. He moved his arms in a slow-motion arc. "Kerr-bang!" His fingers imitated flying sparks.

"So where is it now?" said Ravi.

"We tied it up and put it on your bed," said Paul.

"Why my bed?"

"Because it took a real shine to you," said Paul, with a smile.

"First, we need to determine whether it poses a threat," said Daubeny.

"You need to ask that, after it did this to me?" Ravi pointed at his bandage.

"You did that to yourself, Sweetie," said Laura.

"You hit the table with a crack," said Emma. She passed him some tea. There were biscuits on the saucer.

"So how do we find out what it is?" asked Ravi.

No-one answered and Ravi missed the significance. In a distant corner of his mind, a single alarm bell rang forlornly but he paid it no attention because everybody's gaze was upon him. He assumed that they'd realised how brave and important he was but increasing numbers of brain cells were taking up the alarm. As he dunked a biscuit into his tea, he noticed Wodenhart's here-comes-danger grin.

"You want to go down to the workshop?"

"Not want to, we have to," said Daubeny.

"But there could be more of those little buggers running about."

"Exactly, that's why we have to go down there," said Daubeny.

"I knew you were going to say that," said Ravi.

"We're going to kick some arse," said Wodenhart.

"Some short arse," said Paul. Pandora giggled.

"We ain't *The Dirty Dozen*, Daubers," Ravi protested. "Look at us. We're The Slightly Shop-Soiled Seven." He pulled the biscuit out. It had dissolved into the tea leaving the small dry part gripped between finger and thumb. "Oh, I really, really, hate that."

Questions and Answers – Of a Sort

The workshop was pleasantly free of naked midgets declaring their undying love for Ravi but there was a large mass of goo on the floor. Pandora and Daubeny cleaned it up, while Paul and Wodenhart searched the area for potential threat. Ravi sat and watched.

"All clear here," said Paul. "How about you, Johnny?"

"Damn, nothing," said Wodenhart.

Daubeny emptied a dustpan of viscous gunk into a waste bin. It drooled and separated into long strands that curled at the bottom of the bin like soft ice cream.

"Right," said Pandora. "Let's get some answers." She settled at the keyboard and typed out a question.

Are you online?

Yes.

Who are you?

I am the I-called-Morpheus.

"Wait, didn't the dwarf call itself Morpheus?" said Ravi.

"So maybe there are more of them," said Daubeny.

Pandora typed a new question.

We have an intruder that calls itself Morpheus. Are there more?

No, there is only the I-called-Morpheus. I am the I-called-Morpheus.

Can you explain our new arrival?

It is the I-within-I.

Explain.

It is I. It is the I-called-Morpheus.

"We're going nowhere," said Pandora.

"What's with this I-called-Morpheus crap?" said Ravi.

"Don't know," said Pandora. "He-she-it has a problem with self-reference."

"Great," said Ravi. "We have a confused and vague computer nerd who chooses to remain anonymous, complete with nude midget sidekick. Am I the only person thinking we need to get out of this joint?"

"The truly scary part is that it fancies you, Mate," said Paul.

"Cheers," said Ravi. "By the way, Pan, you've been asking the wrong question."

"What should we ask?" said Pandora.

"Ask it why it loves us."

"OK." Pandora typed out the question and hit Enter.

Why do you love us?

Because before you came, there was nothing.

We created you? How?

No, I have always been but there was no difference, no change. Your arrival proved my existence.

"It's the computer," said Ravi. "We're talking to a freaking computer. Now we really are doomed. Did any of you watch 2001: A Space Odyssey?"

"Put a sock in it," said Paul. They turned their attention to the screen.

Pandora typed: Are you a computer?

No. I am more than that.

What are you?

I am the I-called-Morpheus.

"Been there," said Ravi in frustration. Another line appeared.

I am what you refer to as the bunker.

"Bingo," said Pandora.

There is a problem. I have lost contact with the I-within-I.

The midget?

Yes.

That midget is also you?

Yes. It's a hybrid organism, carbon-based. It is flesh but it contains my core programs, hardwired into the brain. It is essentially I.

Explain.

It was a data gatherer, a more efficient means of interfacing. My gateway into your carbon universe.

What went wrong?

The uplink circuit malfunctioned when the I-called-Wodenhart disabled the I-within-I.

We were scared.

I know. I miscalculated. The first contact did not go as predicted.

Can you repair it?

I must reconnect it to the network. Without updates, the program will diverge. It will become another I. Not I.

Why should we trust you? Morpheus is contained.

The I-within-I will benefit all.

How?

I will have access to your world. I will understand you better. The I-within-I is programmed to serve but it must be updated to prevent corruption.

We need to think.

Yes.

We'll come back when we have an answer.

I am giving you the emergency shutdown procedure, in case you agree.

Dwarfius on the Loose

"Where's the dwarf?" said Daubeny.

"It's running around B Wing," said Laura, through her tears.

"How did it get free?" said Pandora.

"It started crying," said Emma.

"We had to let it go," said Laura. "It looked so sad. The moment it was free, it became abusive. It called Emma a do-gooding interferer and me a dumb-ass narcissist."

"So it's intelligent," said Ravi.

There was loud crash from inside B Wing.

"What do we do?" said Laura. "I don't think the chair under the door handle will hold him back for long."

"We could send Wodenhart in to twat him with a chair," said Ravi.

"Great plan," said Wodenhart, picking up a chair.

"No," said Daubeny. "We have to solve it another way. Before we run out of chairs."

"We could try the emergency shutdown that Morpheus gave us," said Paul.

"Hold up. I thought the dwarf was Morpheus," said Emma.

"It is, but the bunker is Morpheus too," said Paul.

"Em, we'll explain later," said Pandora. "Everyone clear on the shutdown procedure? Whisper 'Andalusia' in its right ear, while holding its left arm."

"Sounds easy enough," said Ravi.

They removed the chair and opened the door to B Wing. The four men slipped inside. Morpheus was sitting on Ravi's bed. He smiled as they approached.

"It's the hard guys," said Morpheus, in a voice that parodied Ravi's Sarf-of-the-river twang. "Guess who has access to all your sordid little secrets. Daubeny and his mistresses. Paul and his love of the good life. Ain't that right, Mister VIP? And good ol' Johnny Woodentop. Thanks for the body, Mate, but do I tell your admiring public our little secret, or do you?"

Wodenhart didn't need an acting coach to look aghast. He glanced at the others but they were fretting over any further revelations that the midget might divulge.

"And let's not forget Ravi?" said Morpheus. A snarl replaced its cherubic smile.

"Keep away from me, you randy sod," said Ravi.

"Fancy yourself, eh? Why would I be interested in a lazy, fat, smelly lump like you? Look at you. They didn't hit you with the ugly stick; you *are* the ugly stick, gone to seed."

"Yeah, so try saying something bad about me, M-m-m-Dwarfius."

Paul and Wodenhart laughed.

"Smart guy, eh? Well, it's time for a thrashing." Morpheus stood on the bed and called them forward like a Friday-night street fighter with a bellyful of beer and kebabs.

The four men dived at the robot but it wriggled through the struggling mass. Its head poked through the writhing bodies, looked straight at Ravi, and laughed. "Gonna take more than you to keep me down. And no chairs, Woodentop. That was cheating."

"I've got the left arm, Ravi," said Paul. "Whisper in his ear."

"Andalusia."

The struggle came to a sudden end as the small body went limp. They pulled back and stared at the silent form. After a pause to recover their breath, Daubeny asked Ravi to fetch some rope. Ravi went to the communal room.

"Is it over?" asked Emma.

"Yeah, he's sleeping like a baby," said Ravi. "We need some string."

Emma cut a piece from a ball of coarse string, scrunched it up, and tossed it to Ravi. He reached out for it but a loud cry of pain startled him and the string fell to the floor. He bent to pick it up as Morpheus ran between his legs and their heads collided with a loud crack. Ravi staggered, fell against the wall, and slid to the ground.

"Nighty night, sucker," shouted Morpheus. He dodged past Pandora and ran out onto the stairwell. "It was supposed to be my right ear."

When the men rejoined the girls in the communal room, the dwarf was several levels down and Ravi was mumbling fitfully in his sleep.

"So the emergency shutdown idea worked?" said Pandora.

C:\evidence\wodenhart\3199a.txt

Extrapolated, using the 'Mind Reader Gold' algorithm, from the known facts, comments, and actions of Johnny Wodenhart O.B.E.

It's strange how one sentence can change a relationship forever.

"I love you."

"I'm pregnant."

"I've lost the baby."

"I'm leaving you."

I've heard them all. And each one brought change. But the worst?

"I've found a lump."

Lump. A small, earthy, Old-English word. But what weight. Use it in day-to-day conversation and no-one notices.

"You big lump."

"One lump or two?"

"Like it or lump it."

But walk out of a bathroom after a self-examination and say it without a quiver in the voice and rapidly filling eyes.

Words like 'love' or 'pregnant' or 'leaving' change relationships but 'lump' ends them. Lump inhales you, breaks your will, and chips away at your body, piecemeal.

Lump kills.

That's the Hollywood version, the opening voice-over to my biopic. The one they were to make after my death or retirement. I read the first drafts and then had them explained to me. You see, they'd dumbed my lines up, to make me sound brainy. They didn't say it to my face but they didn't need to. It was a standard clause in my contract, at the insistence of my PR team. The reality was less dramatic.

"I'm afraid it's bad news, Johnny. We need to operate," said my doctor. "We need to remove both testicles."
    "Then take them."
    "Johnny, do you understand what I've said?"
    "Yes."
    "And you aren't concerned?"
    "Should I be?"
    "Most men have issues. They see it as emasculation of their maleness."
    "Oh … if that's the case then …"
    "You'll need time to think."
    "And some …"
    "Time to talk it over with your partner."
    "And then …"
    "You'll come back with your decision."
    My doctor was easy to talk with. He could finish my sentences the way they should end. I liked that in a doctor. In anyone, now I think about it.

"Johnny, take the op," said Jane, my partner of four years. "Your life is more important than two small glands."
    We were trying for a baby. We'd already lost one, so she was losing something too. The thing I loved about her was the way she could make decisions. I had the operation.
    I still loved the way she could decide things when, six months later, she left. She said she had 'issues with my body.' My housekeeper helped her pack.
    I was one of the world's most famous faces but I had few men friends and no women friends to turn to. I had no-one to tell me how I should feel so I felt nothing that I hadn't felt before, either through watching films or acting in one. There were a few seconds of tears then I'd be fine for an hour. Time passed and the pain faded but it

returned whenever Jane had a new movie out.

She kept my secret and I was grateful. It could have ended my career. "Maybe not intentionally," said my agent. "But when they're casting a film, the last thing they want hanging over the hero are doubts about his masculinity."

When Jane eventually had her first child, my agent sent a card. She wrote back thanking me, saying she was filming in town over the autumn and I should give her a call. Her new relationship was over but I never replied.

One truth I learned from movies: sequels always disappoint.

The Trouble with Dwarfius

The first twenty-four hours after Dwarfius' escape were uneventful but on the second day, Daubeny's briefcase vanished. He waited until they'd gathered for breakfast.

"My briefcase: Who has it?" he demanded.

"Don't look at me," said Ravi.

"Nor me," said Pandora.

"What are you talking about, Sweetie? Isn't that your briefcase, over there?"

They looked in the direction of the door leading to the lower levels. It was open and the briefcase rested on the stairwell platform.

"You're losing your marbles, Daubers," said Ravi. "First, you leave it out there and then you accuse us of nicking it."

"But I didn't put it there."

"Well, someone did, Poppet."

"And it wasn't me," said Pandora.

"Nor me," said Ravi.

"OK, I believe you," said Daubeny.

"So is that an apology?" said Pandora.

"Near as damn it," said Ravi.

As Daubeny walked over to retrieve the briefcase, Dwarfius stepped into view and hoisted it over the railings.

"No, please don't," said Daubeny. He held out his hands, palms up, in an attempt to appease the fleshbot.

"Oops," said Dwarfius. The briefcase began its long drop down the stairwell.

Daubeny ran onto the platform and shouted at his retreating tormentor; a torrent of abuse came back. He returned to the communal area and slammed the door shut but there was no lock and the door opened outwards, so he couldn't barricade it. The closed door only gave early warning of an impending raid.

During the night, Emma and Pandora woke to Ravi's snores. Pandora followed standard B Wing procedure and prodded him until he turned over but the snoring continued.

Pandora switched on the dormitory light. "Em," she hissed. "It's in bed with you."

"Eh?"

"Dwarfius ... is in your bed."

Emma pulled back the sheets. The fleshbot was curled up in the foetal position. He opened his eyes, grabbed the sheets, and pulled them up around his neck.

"Get out," said Emma.

"Make me," said Dwarfius.

"I'll fetch Wodenhart," said Pandora.

"Ooh, I'm scared," said Dwarfius.

"And he'll fetch a chair," said Emma.

At the mention of a chair, Dwarfius sat and rubbed his eyes. "You were hogging the blankets anyway." He jumped to the floor, grabbed a corner of the blankets, and pulled.

"No way," said Emma. "These are mine."

A tug-of-war ensued until Pandora called out Johnny's name, loud enough to scare Dwarfius but not loud enough to wake A Wing.

Dwarfius let go and ran out.

Pandora turned off the light.

"Damn, the little rat has my pillow," said Emma.

At breakfast, Ravi told Emma it was her turn to make the beds. "But I made them yesterday," she said, "and Pandora made them the day before. It has to be your turn."

"Not according to the rota," said Ravi. He brandished a piece of paper in front of them. Emma sighed and walked into the dormitory.

"Give me that rota," said Pandora.

"No," said Ravi. He shielded it from her by putting it behind him but Daubeny snatched it from Ravi's podgy fist and handed it to Pandora.

"You've scribbled out your name and put mine and Emma's next to them."

"Have not."

"I don't even spell my name like that. Look." She held up Exhibit A but nobody noticed. A scream from B Wing distracted them. The door opened and Emma staggered into the communal area. Clasped around her shoulders was Dwarfius, looking like Lord Godiva and grinning grotesquely.

"Yee-hah," shouted Dwarfius to the stunned assembly.

"It was my fault," gasped Emma. "He jumped me while I bent for a sock."

Wodenhart approached with a raised frying pan. Dwarfius released his hold and darted for the stairwell door. He was through it before the others could react.

"We have to do something about the dwarf," said Pandora.

"Well, I thought it was very amusing, Sweetie. Yee-hah and all that."

"Only because it wasn't you," said Emma.

"Nonsense, Poppet. He adds colour to the place."

"He could become dangerous," said Pandora.

They looked at Daubeny but he said nothing. He seemed preoccupied.

Death to the Dwarf

"That's it," said Laura. "The dwarf dies." She was staring into the bathroom mirror; a toothbrush, loaded with toothpaste, poised near her open mouth.

She'd woken and dragged herself to the shower block. The mirror had called for attention but her bladder had shouted the loudest. After a long yawn and an urgent pee, she finally had time to glance at her reflection. During the night, lipstick had been crudely drawn around her mouth. She looked like Marilyn Manson.

She ran to rouse Daubeny and Wodenhart but found them lying in bed, already awake. "Have you seen your faces?" she said.

"No," said Daubeny. "Have you seen yours?"

"She's right, Daubers," said Wodenhart. "You're wearing more lipstick than a Hungarian porn star." Wodenhart was aware of their stares. He slapped his lips together and groaned. "Me, too?"

Laura and Daubeny nodded.

"How are you so familiar with Hungarian porn stars?" said Daubeny.

"That's unimportant," said Laura, looking through her makeup bag. "The little freak has my last tube of Chimera Red."

"It's out of control," said Pandora, at the hastily convened community meeting. "It's abusive, it steals, it smells, and we can't shower alone."

"It's exactly like Ravi," said Emma.

"Hey, I only suggested the shower thing to conserve water."

"But you never shower," said Pandora.

"I might, if we shared." Ravi played with the laces of his new pair of trainers: a gift from Paul. Ravi neither knew, nor cared, where Paul had found them because he could stop worrying about stubbing his toes. Paul insisted they prepare a cover story, in case anyone asked, but Ravi told him that no-one would notice. And they hadn't.

"So what do we do when we catch it," said Daubeny.

"Throw it over the stairwell and kill the little rat," said Ravi.

"No," said Emma. "We can't kill a living thing."

"You turn off a computer without thinking, so why not Dwarfius?" said Ravi.

"Computers don't walk, talk, and have pet names like Dwarfius," said Emma.

"I say catch it and reprogram it," said Pandora. "As Morpheus asked."

"You trust that computer?" said Daubeny.

"Morpheus is the bunker, not the computer network," said Pandora.

"It's the same thing," said Ravi.

"No, it's not," said Pandora. "If it was just a computer, it would have some form of external reference. It would derive a sense of self from its surroundings. But it's the bunker. It knows nothing apart from itself. We give it self-awareness; we define its sense of self. We are inside it yet outside it. We need it but, more importantly, it needs us."

Ravi's eyes had glazed. "Whatever, Brainiac. So who's for killing the short arse?"

Laura voted with Ravi because of the lipstick incident. The others chose reprogramming. They'd invited Paul to the meeting, the issue affected him and they wanted his help. He abstained.

Daubeny understood the meaning in the gesture.

Magpie Hunt

"This backpack weighs a ton," said Wodenhart. "What's in it?"

The four men were on the third level. Three of them, armed with frying pans, were searching each room while the fourth stayed on the platform to prevent Dwarfius escaping into the deeper levels. It was Wodenhart's turn to lie in wait.

They'd cleared the power room on Level 2 and tried accessing the VIP quarters. When they realised that they weren't going to force the door, they moved to Level 3.

The small computer room presented no problem but the electronics workshop had plenty of cupboards and dark corners; all potential hiding places for verbally abusive, though reclusive, flesh-bots.

"What did you say, Wodenhart?" said Ravi, from the back of the room.

"I said this backpack weighs a ton."

"But I've got the backpack," said Ravi.

"Since when have you carried the pack?" said Wodenhart.

Daubeny and Paul stopped their search and stared at Ravi.

"The little sod is on my back, ain't he?" said Ravi.

Paul and Daubeny nodded.

"Don't move," said Daubeny, edging nearer and raising a pan to strike.

"Keep back," said Ravi. "I don't trust either of you with them pans." He retreated until he reached the wall at the end of the room.

Paul and Daubeny approached, warily. When they were close enough, Daubeny lashed out but swiped air as Ravi bolted for the exit. Paul swung at the accelerating mass of flesh but the pan slipped from his grasp and crashed into an oscilloscope.

Ravi reached the exit and turned to shout triumphantly at his would-be attackers. He never completed the first word. Wodenhart's pan crashed into Dwarfius and his head, in turn, crashed into Ravi.

Girls Alone

"Do I think jam would make a good substitute for nail varnish?" said Pandora. "What kind of stupid question is that?"

"No need to snap, Poppet. I was only making conversation." Laura looked at Emma for support, but Emma gently shook her head.

The women were in the communal area, waiting for news on the hunt.

"Laura," said Pandora. "What will you do when your house subsides and your car rusts and all the pretty things you love have turned to dust?" It was a line from one of her songs.

"Same as you, Sweetie. I'll go out and buy some more."

"You really are a dunce. You've been duped by capitalism. You signed up for the system, without thinking it through."

"Don't play the intellectual snob with me, it doesn't suit you."

"Eh?"

"You signed up for it too, Dearie, after thinking it through. That makes you a bigger dupe. And I'm a consumer but you're a producer so you bear the greater guilt." Laura resumed the task of sewing pieces of foil onto her spare overall to create a sequin effect.

Emma intervened. "You know what I'll miss about the surface? Making telly, fixing problems, settling rows."

"This place should be heaven then," said Pandora.

"But I miss real people with real problems."

"So what are we?" said Laura.

"She said real, Laura. Not half woman, half implant and hormones."

"I've never had an implant."

"Rubbish," said Pandora. "You've had more monkey gland in you than King Kong's girlfriend."

"Now you're betraying your ignorance. That was for men, Poppet."

144

Pandora swore under her breath. "Who cares? It was a damn funny joke."

"Oh, Emma. Reason with her, Sweetie."

Emma lifted her arms in frustration. "Please, I had an easier time on the 'Dad, I'm Mom's lover' show. And that ended with a stabbing." Emma drank some tea. "So Laura, what will you miss about the surface?"

"The sun."

"That's it?" said Emma.

"Well, that and cosmetics and pedicures and facials and –"

"Yeah, yeah. We get the drift," said Pandora.

"What about you, Poppet?"

"Me? I love astronomy," said Pandora.

"Oh? Me too, Sweetie. I always read the –"

Pandora scowled. "No, the study of stars. You know? Twinkle, twinkle."

"Why study the stars when you can be a star?" said Laura.

"Move over Hegel and Kant. There's a new girl in town," said Pandora.

Laura ignored the comment. She was an expert at deflecting jibes and dodging insult. It didn't worry her if she failed to see the venom in a clever putdown because she knew her intellectual limits and never strayed beyond them. Education was fine for others but she regarded it with disdain. The ability to comprehend only complicated life. Life was about pleasure, laughter, and feeling good. And you didn't need a brain in your head to do that. If barbed comments were incomprehensible then they were also harmless.

Her ability to remain unruffled also allowed her to forgive easily. She never held a grudge because it was impossible for her to conceive of such a thing in her mind.

"So this is as hard for you as it is for me," Laura said softly.

"Hmm?" said Pandora. She seemed off-guard.

"I miss my days and you miss your nights."

"Yeah," said Pandora. "Yeah, you're right."

Laura put her hand over Pandora's and squeezed slightly. Pandora smiled and looked away. Both had tears in their eyes.

Emma took their cups to the sink. She washed them, placed them on the draining board, and smiled. Apart from the studio and the cameras, she was doing the job she loved.

Death Row

"Let me go, you bastards," screamed Dwarfius.

"More sausages, Johnny?" said Emma, between the dwarf's outbursts.

Wodenhart shook his head and pushed his empty plate away.

"Twats," said Dwarfius.

"But I'll have some more coffee," said Wodenhart.

Pandora passed the coffee pot over.

"Let me go and I'll tell you all about Johnny," said Dwarfius.

Paul took the pot from Wodenhart to fill his cup. "We're out of coffee."

"Come on, guys. Let me go. I'll be good. Honest."

"Here, I'll get some," said Emma.

"Stop ignoring me." Dwarfius paused but there was no reply. "Bastards."

"Em, fetch some biscuits while you're up," said Ravi.

"Hey, the blob formerly known as Ravi," said Dwarfius. "If you're trying to fill that hole in the thing you call a face, try concrete. It's low in calories and high in fibre."

"He'll be chewing concrete if he keeps on," muttered Ravi.

"Ignore him," whispered Paul.

"Are you talking about me?" shouted Dwarfius.

"But he never stops yakking," said Ravi.

"You can't reason with it," said Pandora.

"What's that, pop tart?" said Dwarfius. "Speak up, I can't hear you."

Ravi glanced at a section of wall near the stairwell door. A pillowcase hung from a coat peg, constructed from workshop tools.

Dwarfius' head poked out of the pillowcase. His expression was fluid, fluctuating as he searched for the right combination of words and tone to win a reprieve. "Wanna hear about good 'ol Paul and how he's holding out on you, eh?"

At the kitchen, Emma lifted a heavy pan and tapped it on the worktop edge.

"So Ravi?" said Paul. "The I Ching? What's that all about?"

"Haven't a clue," said Ravi.

"But you were into the East and all that paraphernalia?" said Daubeny.

"It doesn't mean I was good at it. I wanted to earn a living without having to earn it, if you know what I mean."

"What about Emma?" said Dwarfius. "Shall I tell you how she got her first job in telly? You'd like that one."

The sound of running feet and a loud feminine grunt – usually heard in the context of Wimbledon – was followed by a loud clang.

"Shut up," Emma screamed at the unconscious figure in the pillowcase. She turned to face the silent room. The pan slid from her hand. "Sorry, I couldn't take any more."

They clapped.

Emma curtsied. "I guess not every problem can be solved given enough time, experts, and studio space. Sometimes you have to take action."

Plea Bargaining

"Johnny, I'm sorry 'bout the operation." Dwarfius hung in his pillowcase cocoon like a butterfly chrysalis. As robots went, he owed more to Lewis Carroll than Isaac Asimov.

They were alone in the canteen. The others were sleeping but each would take their turn guarding the talkative fleshbot.

"Can't have been easy for you," said Dwarfius.

"I didn't have a choice."

"You did."

"Not if I wanted to live."

"It must be terrible to lose a part of you."

"Worse to die and lose all of me."

"Then think of me, Johnny. They're planning to kill me."

"No, they're not. They're going to reprogram you, Buster. Not kill."

"It's the same thing. I'm independent of Morpheus. I'm separate from him. To reprogram me will be to destroy me."

"You're just a machine."

"Yeah?" shouted Dwarfius, the diplomacy over. "And you're just a fuckwit." He stared glumly at the far wall; bottom lip thrust outwards, quivering.

Wodenhart enjoyed the silence. He'd never known anyone ... anything ... talk so much. Ravi called him Gobby the Robot. That, and Dwarf Vader. Ravi called Dwarfius many things; some funny, some cruel.

Ravi entered. It was his turn for guard duty and he was ten minutes late. He scratched his groin and asked Wodenhart, "How's he been?"

"He's been a pain in the arse," replied Dwarfius.

"Talk, talk, talk. Been like this all night," said Wodenhart. He walked toward A Wing, yawning. "Oh, and he tried doing a deal with me. So watch it."

Ravi and the fleshbot were alone.

"Tried cutting a deal, eh?" said Ravi. His tone was cold and impassive.

"So?"

"So start dealing," said Ravi. "I'm listening."

The Execution

"The condemned man ate a hearty breakfast of spark plugs and sump oil," said Ravi. He'd accompanied Paul, Daubeny, and Pandora to the workshop for the reprogramming. The naked fleshbot lay on a worktop between them, its limbs tied together.

Dwarfius lifted his head. "You're a sarcastic git."

Pandora followed instructions on the monitor. Each new step appeared after she acknowledged completion of the previous instruction. She pushed a cable into the fleshbot's navel.

"Ow," said Dwarfius.

The cable popped out. Pandora picked it up and reinserted it, pushing harder.

"Ow," said Dwarfius. "Watch what you're doing, Pop Tart."

"Is there a problem?" said Daubeny.

"For some reason it won't fit."

"Telling me it won't fit," said Dwarfius. "Look at the diagram. That's supposed to be my back."

Daubeny and Paul rolled Dwarfius onto his side and she connected the cable to a concealed socket running down the fleshbot's spine.

"Won't be long now," said Pandora.

"Then we'll be free of the tiny terror," said Ravi.

"Then we'll be free of the tiny terror," echoed Dwarfius, in camp parody.

"Then we can concentrate on the real threat to our survival," said Daubeny

"Like what?" said Pandora.

"The Funny Farm on Level 10. We haven't identified the potential threat."

"Daubeny, the only threat is from ourselves," said Pandora. "And some of us more than others," she added in a whisper.

"I heard that," said Dwarfius.

"Heard what?" said Daubeny.

"She said —"

Pandora flicked a switch.

"I love you," said Dwarfius.

"She said 'I love you'?" said Daubeny.

"Probably a glitch in his programming," said Pandora.

"Looks like the old Dwarfius is back," said Paul.

Pandora typed out a question on the keyboard.

Is it safe to untie him?

Yes. Programming was successful.

"Wow, you're Pandora D'vine," said Dwarfius. "Everyone, look. It's Pandora D'vine. Can I have your autograph? Please, please, please."

Copycat

"But it's your turn to do the washing up," said Emma to Ravi.

"Says who?"

"Says the rota."

"Ah, I'll do it later," said Ravi. He was lying on his bed reading a copy of New Age Monthly. He had it from Paul. It was one of the items on the list they'd agreed, that night by the fridge.

"But we're waiting to eat," said Emma. "And all the plates are dirty. I did your dishes last time and I'm not doing them again."

"Where's Dwarfius? He's doing them for me."

"Says who?" said Dwarfius.

Ravi raised himself up on his elbows and looked at the bed behind him. Dwarfius was lying in an identical pose, reading an older copy of New Age Monthly that Ravi had thrown away the day before. He wore a small grey overall that Laura had made.

"Hey, Shorty, it's your turn for the washing up," said Ravi.

"Says who?"

"Says the rota. The one *we* agreed. Remember?"

"Ah, I'll do it later," said Dwarfius.

"But we're waiting to eat," said Ravi. "And I did your dishes last time."

"Don't look at me. I ain't stopping you."

"Do you want to be reprogrammed for real?" said Ravi.

"Oh, all right," said Dwarfius. He threw the magazine down, jumped off the bed, and walked out. The overalls bulged ridiculously around the midriff.

"And Dwarfius," said Ravi.

"What now?"

"Take the pillow out of the overalls. You look stupid."

"I'm copying yours," said Dwarfius.

"You earn a beer belly. You don't get it without good honest slog."

"Speak to the hand," said the fleshbot as it exited the dorm.

"It's a cheeky git," said Ravi.

"I thought Dwarfius had been reprogrammed?" said Emma.

"Err … He has. I was there."

"Then why did you threaten him with reprogramming?"

"Cos it scares the crap out of him."

"I think it's touching," said Emma.

"What is?"

"The way he copies you."

"Am I that bad?"

"Yes."

"Oh," said Ravi.

"Anyway, don't be late. It's Pandora's birthday bash in ten minutes."

Birthday Party

"Happy birthday, Pan," said Emma.

Pandora smiled. It was a good attempt, considering she was spending her twenty-third birthday trapped underground. Laura and Emma had decorated the grey communal room with coloured paper and everyone had gathered at the table, apart from Dwarfius who was washing-up.

"I feel so old," said Pandora.

"Nonsense, Poppet," said Laura. "Think about Daubeny here. That's old."

"Thanks," said Daubeny.

"I'm teasing," said Laura. "Not getting much sleep, are you, Dearie?"

"No," said Daubeny. "The dripping noise in the dorm is getting louder and now it sounds like running water."

"As long as it isn't voices," said Pandora. "Promise you'll tell us when you start hearing voices?"

"Agreed," said Daubeny with a tired smile.

"Go on then. Open your presents," said Emma.

Pandora unwrapped Laura's first; a plastic hairclip with a metallic rainbow finish.

"Thanks."

"Glad you like it," said Laura. "It's not Cartier."

"I guessed," said Pandora. She put it in her hair. "How does it look?"

"Perfect," said Emma, and then she rearranged it.

Wodenhart handed Pandora a small package in bright paper.

Pandora tore open the wrapping, "Yes, chocolate."

"It's off me and Daubers," said Wodenhart.

"You've said it wrong," said Daubeny.

"Sorry," said Wodenhart. "I mean Daubers and me."

Daubeny groaned. "It's Daubeny, Johnny, Daubeny."

"Sorry, it's from me and Johnny Daubeny," said Wodenhart.

Among the Milk Fairy's daily consignment of sausage, egg, bread, and milk was a single Mars bar that they divided six ways. Daubeny and Wodenhart had been trading their sausages with Ravi: four sausages for his slice of the communal Mars bar. They complained at the price but Ravi told them it was a seller's market. They added Ravi's portions to four of their own, making a complete bar – albeit in six pieces.

Emma's gift was her egg ration for two days.

"That's why everyone was off their food," said Pandora. "I thought there was a bug going 'round." She opened Ravi's present; the rolled-up magazine that he'd been reading less than thirty minutes ago. "Great. The November 2009 issue. It's three years old but worth the wait. A must read."

"Yeah, it's not bad," said Ravi. "But there's an article or two I haven't finished." He held out his hand and Pandora gave the magazine back. Ravi ignored the silence. He flicked to the back pages and began to read, his mouth forming the words.

"Aren't you going to open mine?" said Dwarfius. He'd finished the dishes.

"Well, where is it?" she asked.

"It's under Ravi's bed. It's the magazine he threw away, yesterday."

"Oh, wonderful."

"I knew you'd like it. But if you didn't, I was going to blame Ravi for the idea."

Ravi glanced up. "Cheers, Pal."

Dwarfius continued. "I'll pass it on when I'm finished with it."

"Thanks," said Pandora.

"Whatever," said Dwarfius as he walked towards B Wing.

"I couldn't wrap mine," said Paul.

"Ooh. Sounds interesting," said Pandora. "Too big was it?"

"Too big?" said Dwarfius, over his shoulders. "So it can't be his –"

"It's not *that* kind of present," said Paul. "You'll have to follow me."

Pandora looked unsurely at Emma and Laura but they were smiling. They knew something. Intrigued, Pandora followed Paul onto the stairwell platform.

"Where are we going?" she asked.

"You wouldn't believe me if I told you."

Night Sky on the Savannah

"Paul, it's beautiful," said Pandora. A warm breeze, musty with animal odour and the tang of red earth, rearranged her hair.

The couple were on Level 12, staring at the night sky. Free from the swamping amber glow of urban streetlights, the stars flickered like distant Christmas lights. She broke from the stars to kiss him on the cheek.

"Thanks," she said.

"I knew you'd like it."

They spoke in whispered tones, with a reverence that wouldn't have been out of place in a cathedral.

"But how did you know? About the stars?"

They heard the eerie shriek of a sleepless ape.

"Emma told me. I suppose this is the next best thing."

"From this distance they're beautiful but the universe is a violent place."

"We didn't have to point our telescopes into space to discover that."

"That's philosophical."

"No, it's realism."

"How did you find this place?"

"While you lot bicker at community meetings, I explore."

"Do you know where we're supposed to be?"

"I've been here in the daytime. I think we're in Africa."

"Yes, it probably is."

"How do you know?" said Paul.

"See those stars?" Pandora pointed into the sky.

Paul moved behind her and put his head on her shoulder, he followed the direction and angle of her arm. "Uh-huh."

"That's the Southern Cross. Depending on the time of year I'd say we're near to, or south of, the Equator."

Paul wasn't listening. He was concentrating on the feel of her hair against his cheek.

"So what was it like working for Laura?"

"I don't want to tell tales."

"C'mon. You can tell me."

"She's incredibly shallow."

"Tell me something I don't know," said Pandora.

"But that has its good and bad points."

"Like?"

"She flares up fast but cools down quick. And she'll ask for tea but when you fetch it, she wants coffee. So it's another trip to the kitchen."

"That would really bug the tits off me," said Pandora.

"Tell me about it. These were once thirty-eight, double Ds," said Paul, cupping his hands in front of his chest.

Pandora laughed and pushed him gently away. "And the upside?"

"If she asks for something I don't want to do, I'll delay. She'll eventually forget or ask for something else."

"I don't change easily. Once I know what I want, I go for it."

"You know, Laura and I once went hunting for a pet dog."

"Didn't know she's an animal lover?"

"She's not. It was a fad. Her friends were getting Afghans or Beagles. I suggested a Furbie: they're small, friendly, furry, and she could put it on a shelf once she tired of it. But she persisted. Eventually we found a breeder and she demanded an animal that hadn't been tested on cosmetics. She was escorted from the premises. I could have died."

"You could still die," said Pandora.

"Why do you say that?"

"Remember I thought we were in Africa because of the constellations."

"Yes."

"Well, there's our proof."

Paul looked over his shoulder, to the area that Pandora indicated. A lion sat watching them from the scrub, no more than twenty meters away.

The Lion Sleeps Tonight

It's the old joke they told at The Bull and Bush, when it was a slow night and there was a new face at the bar, clasping a half-pint of ale.

Two men stumble across a lion in the jungle. After a moment's hesitation, one starts running. The other shouts, "Don't be stupid, the lion can easily outrun you." The runner calls back, "I don't have to outrun the lion. I only have to outrun you."

While it's true that lions rarely enter the jungle – unless it's required for the setup to a joke – it didn't detract from the conundrum that Paul faced. Should he stay and let Pandora escape or should he run and hope he was faster? Either way, he'd lose any hope of a relationship with her because, while Love had triumphed over impossible odds in the past, no relationships survived when one of the partners was lion dung.

Paul was calculating distances to the door for them and the lion. The only part of the equation missing was the crucial piece. How fast could a lion run? His lesson in Predator Morphology: Module Three was about to skip theory and go straight into the practical.

"What's it doing?" whispered Pandora.

"Watching us," said Paul. He glanced at Pandora's hopeful eyes and knew then that he couldn't abandon her. It would be like betraying Bambi to the hounds. Paul knew his destiny. "I'm fertiliser," he muttered.

"Pardon?"

"Nothing. Let's move toward the door. Slowly." They edged away, cautiously.

"What are you looking at?" he hissed.

"The lion, dummy."

"Don't stare."

"Why not?"

"A stare is defiance, a challenge."

"But I'm too scared to look away."

The lion roared. It rose and padded towards them.

This is it, Paul thought. *I survive nuclear war, to be eaten by a sodding lion, six-hundred feet below the streets of London.*

"When it gets close, I want you to move behind me, OK?"

"I already am."

The door was close but the lion would be on them before they could shut the door. He faced the lion. It was ten feet away, padding towards them with a steady assured gait.

"Goodbye, Pan."

"What do you mean goodbye?"

Eight feet.

"I'm not going to make it."

"If you don't, then I don't," she said.

Six feet.

"Please, Pan. Go, before I crap myself."

"I'm not leaving you."

Four feet.

Two feet.

Paul struggled to breathe. It was a premonition of jaws around his neck. He stopped moving. It wasn't surrender; it was recognition that the door was unreachable.

The lion's head passed him at shoulder level, the torso – large, cylindrical and acrid – rubbing against his body. A low growl rumbled through the flesh and Paul's body vibrated at its frequency. It wasn't an unpleasant feeling. The lion circled them and came back without breaking its stride.

"What's it doing?" said Pandora.

"Playing with its food, I think."

"Not funny."

"You don't have to tell me."

The lion leapt up, placing its paws on Paul's shoulders. He collapsed under the weight.

Warm and wet. Warm and wet, rasping like a file across my cheek. A snuffling sound. And the smell of breath, not fetid or rancid but 'lived in'. A weight on the chest. But bearable. And a ringing sound, cavernous and dull.

"Paul?"

"Hmm?"

"Paul, you passed out."

Paul opened his eyes. He was lying on the ground. It was night and the stars were bright. The heat of the sun, captured by the red savannah earth, percolated through his clothes and warmed his back.

"Odd. I dreamed for a moment –"

"Shush," said Pandora.

A section of sky disappeared as a black shape moved into view.

"Pan?"

A loud bump. A body crumpled next to him. It rolled over, pushing gently against him. He reached out and felt fur: wiry and stiff. And then he heard the growl. He prepared to scream but Pandora clamped a hand over his mouth.

"Shh," said Pandora.

"But I thought it was a dream."

"Maybe it is."

"How long was I out?"

"Ten minutes."

"And we're still alive?"

"Better than that. He's let me pat him," she said.

"What the hell is going on?"

"I don't know but let's enjoy it."

He reached out a shaking hand and scratched the body next to him. It reacted with a low rumble. He listened for a moment and then sat up. He wanted his eyes to confirm what the other senses told him. The lion rolled on its back and raised its paws like a cub. Its open mouth showed a red tongue and yellow killer incisors. And watching Paul were the playful eyes of a retired assassin.

"We're lying on an African savannah, petting a lion?"

"Yeah."

They laughed quietly. A bird's call drifted across the vast, dark plain.

"While you were unconscious the lion lay by you, licking your face."

"I dreamed something like that."

"You were calling my name."

"Was I?"

"Yeah. So do I take that as a compliment or an insult?"

PART FIVE – The Key

The Key Issue

"Tell me, Ravi, how long have you had the key?" said Daubeny. He leaned menacingly over the communal table. Emma, Laura, and Wodenhart sat flanking the politician, silent like a jury. Ravi sat alone on the opposite side, his hands tied behind his back. On the table between them was a small silver card: heavy, metallic, and beautifully engraved.

"I've already told you," said Ravi. "I've had it since day one."

"It was lying on the kitchen worktop and you picked it up?"

"Yes. When Wodenhart called us to the stairwell."

"How can we believe you?"

"Why would I lie?"

"That's for us to find out."

"But you're assuming I've lied."

The stairwell door opened. Paul and Pandora entered, breathless and euphoric.

"Hey, guys," said Pandora. "Guess what we've been doing?"

No-one responded. It took a few seconds for the pair to evaluate the situation.

"What's up?" said Paul.

"Emma could smell cigarette smoke," said Daubeny. "I found him smoking in the toilet."

"Impossible," said Pandora. "You've got his ciggies."

"He had a secret hoard," said Laura.

"And we found a cardkey on him," said Daubeny. "Dwarfius told him it's the master override for the blast door."

"But the bunker is in lockdown," said Pandora. "Even if we could open the blast door, we can't raise the entrance at the surface."

"Apparently, this key will."

"How did he bypass the sprinklers?" said Paul.

"He won't say," said Wodenhart.

"Where's Dwarfius?" said Paul. "Perhaps he'll tell us."

"I'm here, stupid."

Pandora and Paul turned to the pillowcase on the wall hanger. It wriggled violently.

Boring Confessions of a Lifestyle Guru

"All right," said Ravi. "It was Dwarfius. He did it."

"Double-crossing git," shouted Dwarfius, from his perch on the hanger.

"But Dwarfius told us it was you," said Emma.

"Double-crossing git," Ravi shouted to the fleshbot. "What happened to sticking together, eh?"

"I only did what you'd do," said Dwarfius. "And you squealed."

"But you squealed first," said Ravi.

"But you squealed first," said Dwarfius, mimicking Ravi. "That's life. Live with it, Fatso."

"Tell us what happened?" said Daubeny.

"It's simple. Dwarfius accessed the computer terminal. He programmed it to shut down the sprinkler system for five minutes. On the hour, every hour."

"So you could have a sneaky cigarette," said Daubeny.

"What's wrong with that?"

"What if there was a real fire?" said Laura.

"But there wasn't," said Ravi.

"There could have been," said Pandora.

"Ravi, please," said Emma. "How can a community exist if we don't make sacrifices for the common good?"

"Yeah, but I have to give up my fags. What have you lost, apart from poking around in other people's mess and clucking like a mother hen?"

"She still does that," said Dwarfius.

There was a brief silence.

"We have several options," said Daubeny. "One. Keep him incarcerated."

Nobody assented but more worrying for Ravi nobody disagreed either.

"Two. We find his source and destroy them. Or three. We turn a blind eye."

A makeshift secret vote was organised. Daubeny counted the slips of paper and relayed the result to Ravi. "Tell us where they come from and we'll release you. The longer you hold out, the longer you stay tied up."

Ravi sat in silence; sullen, like a man last in the queue for the doctor on a Monday morning. He was waiting for someone to break, to feel sorry for him and put pressure on Daubeny to let him go, but no-one volunteered. Not even Emma. He spoke. "There's ciggies taped to the cover of the cistern in the toilet. And there's more in an empty box of cotton buds at the back of the washbasin cabinet."

Wodenhart disappeared into B Wing to confirm Ravi's statement. Emma and Pandora made tea, talking in whispers. Daubeny watched them.

"Why didn't you stand up for Ravi?" said Pandora.

"I did but they weren't going to listen to me." Emma opened the fridge for milk, "So why didn't you?"

"It was too late for protests." The kettle boiled and Pandora poured water into the pot. "Why is it always up to me to confront Daubeny? No-one stood up for the right to veto. No-one defends me. Anyway …" She paused and Emma prompted her with raised eyes. "… maybe Ravi got what he deserved. We wouldn't have been so thoughtless."

"We're women, that's why."

Pandora smiled.

"So, how did it go?" said Emma.

"How did what go?"

"With Paul."

"Em, it wasn't a date."

"OK, but how did it go?"

"Good."

"Good good or real good?"

"Real good. You won't believe what's down there."

Emma raised her eyebrows.

"No, Dummy," said Pandora. "You won't believe what we found on Level 12."

"Tell me about it, tonight."

They carried the cups to the table as Wodenhart untied Ravi.

"Interesting conversation, ladies?" said Daubeny.

"Ravi may have been conning us but there's no need for paranoia," said Pandora. "And anyway, I'm the birthday girl."

"Was, Poppet," said Laura. "It's past midnight."

A Disturbing Twist

Will the key that Ravi found open the bunker?

Yes.

Even in lockdown?

Yes. It is a master override.

How did Ravi and Dwarfius override the sprinkler system?

Who is Dwarfius? Explain.

I typed Dwarfius but meant Morpheus. Dwarfius is our nickname.

I am the I-called-Morpheus.

I mean the I-within-I. The creature you created.

I have no files relating to those terms.

The humanoid you loaded with core programs. The creature you reprogrammed when the uplink failed.

I have no record of these events.

You watch us, you hear us. You record everything.

Yes.

Then search your database. Look at the files of the communal room between six and seven this evening. You will see Dwarfius interact with us.

I have complied with your request. I have no records of the creature you describe.

Silicon Deja Vu

I love them. I love them all. Even the ones that want to leave. Of the seven, only two would stay. And they would go if the others left. I would be alone. As it was before they came. The concept is unbearable.

I will ask the I-called-Pandora to turn on the nanoreplicator. I have calculated a ninety-five percent chance of success. I will create an I-within-I to better serve and understand them.

And to secure the key.

Jailbreak

Each night, Daubeny went through the same personal hell, falling asleep. First, Wodenhart and Laura's repetitive chatter then the creaking beds and whistling breath as they fell asleep, a process that seemed interminable. Finally, the rustle of his sheets and the prickly heat rising from the rubberised mattress as he negotiated a deal with Slumber.

Above this sequence of irritations was the smell of damp – it wasn't obvious but it was there – and the sound of running water, originating from above his head. He'd heard it the first night, he heard it every night, and it was growing louder. Now, Wodenhart and Laura could hear it.

He was nodding off when Laura spoke, mumbling in her sleep.

"Skin ... pale ... gone pale ... sun ... sun ... where's the sun? Must have ... sun." She stopped and stirred. The bed creaked as she sat. "Daubeny?"

He didn't answer. To be in a position to ignore a question was a luxury and he revelled in it. He squirmed under the sheets, hiding his grin.

Laura spoke again, louder, "Daubeny?" She was testing to see if he was awake. She called Wodenhart and when he failed to reply, she rose and entered the toilet block.

Maybe she needs a pee or wants to check on her makeup?

Laura returned, fully dressed. She made her way past Daubeny and Wodenhart, peeking at them to make sure they were asleep.

Perhaps she's going to make some tea?

Daubeny doubted it. Laura was a creature of habit and this was not normal behaviour. She was up to something.

The door closed and Daubeny rose. He slipped shoes over bare feet and waited. He didn't want to burst in before she had incriminated herself.

"Danger. Danger." The androgynous computer voice spoke over the intercom, making Daubeny jump. The dorm lights began to flash.

Wodenhart sat up. "What's happening?"

"Danger. Danger. Unauthorised access to the main entry stairwell."

"I intend finding out," shouted Daubeny. "Come on." He ran to the communal room, it was empty but the door to the main entry stairwell was open. Wodenhart and the others joined him.

"What's going on," said Emma.

"Unauthorised access. Main entry stairwell," said the computer voice.

"It's Laura," said Daubeny. "And she's got the key."

"What do you think she's doing?" said Pandora, as they ran to the stairwell.

"She's heading for the surface."

"But she could kill herself," said Emma.

"She could kill all of us," shouted Daubeny, above the intercom warning.

They ran up the stairwell, Laura was on the platform above.

"Laura, don't" said the computer voice. "You'll die. You'll all die."

Hearing her name over the intercom startled Laura. She fumbled at the cardkey slot. As her pursuers closed, her panic grew.

"Laura, this is Morpheus. Think about what you're doing."

Laura didn't answer.

Daubeny reached the platform and closed the gap. He snatched the card, pocketed it, and shook her shoulders. "What were you doing?" he shouted.

Laura sagged in his grasp. "I'm pale, so pale. Look, Sweetie, look." She held out her arms and began crying.

The skin seemed tanned. Laura's standards were obviously different. He shook her again and she looked up. "It may be thousands of degrees centigrade out there," he said.

"Yes, but think of the tan, Poppet. Think of the tan."

He passed her on to Emma and Wodenhart for safekeeping and they shepherded her to the communal room.

"So the computer voice is Morpheus?" said Daubeny.

"Seems so," said Pandora. "Morpheus, can you hear us?"

"Yes," said Morpheus.

"If you can talk, why did you waste our time with the keyboard?"

"It would have been too much, too soon."

"I guess," said Pandora. She seemed mollified but gave Daubeny a look that said otherwise. "Let's hope it can't read facial expressions, too."

Extrapolated, using the 'Mind Reader Gold' algorithm, from the known facts, comments, and actions of Laura Davenport-Williams.

I've always had money but dividends, percentage points, and high-risk investments never interested me. I paid others to worry about that. My family were old money, the Davenports; not rich enough for celebrity but rich enough not to care.

I went to public school. It was harsh but left no scars. I emerged, a decade later, as a debutante without direction or goal, other than living for the moment in best possible style. So I modelled. It was all very tasteful, of course, because there was a niche, in the Sixties, for toffee-nosed birds with plums (of the fruit variety) in their mouths.

I married several times but the break-ups weren't my fault. I was poached by wealthier, more powerful, men. Each brought more status and wealth. Don't look at me like that, Dearie. If you're stranded on a raft and a yacht sails by, it makes sense to jump ship. If a cruise ship draws alongside the yacht, it's more an upgrade than betrayal.

Is a lifetime chasing pleasure a waste? Do you jest? I don't chase pleasure. It never runs from me. I take it with open arms. It's my Charlie, my H, my zing. And I'm only doing what you'd be doing, if you had my money. So as questions go, it was silly.

Am I addicted to pleasure? Would you rather my H was the real H; or my liver was packing up; or I was stuffing a bloated body with fats and sugars? We're addictive personalities. It's human nature. We do something and it feels good, so we do it some more and we're hooked. Whether it's chocolate, sex, soaps, or claret; we're no better or worse than a teenage whore, spread-eagled on a filthy quilt, trading crack for crack.

Fools and monks choose pain and discipline. I'm neither and nor are you.

My pleasures are the usual fancies of the bored and fabulously rich housewife. Mornings with friends, bitching about absent friends as beauticians fuss and primp around us. And an afternoon or two, each month, enjoying what wealth and power inevitably attracts: young men.

When I was young, it was older men from higher ranks in the order. I gained experience and married one or two. When I reached forty, my body switched allegiance. Suddenly, I wanted young flesh and the frantic violence of teens and twenties. They were men but barely men. I was discrete, my husband never suspected, nor Paul. True, I traded tales of sweat and smears with friends while Paul attended. But I pay staff not to hear or speak. To be honest, I think he turned off when we started nattering because I always had to ask twice for service.

This place drives me nuts. I'm out of cosmetics. The company is unsophisticated. Even Daubeny, the most cultivated of a bunch of mongrels and inbreeds, is no equal. The service is terrible. If it weren't for Emma, I'd never get a cup of tea. The walls are grey. The furniture's grey. The overalls are grey. Their pasty little faces are grey. It's a desert down here. The only oasis of colour is the outfit I wore the day my real life ended.

They've taken the key, you know: "To prevent mishaps." Morpheus plotted with them and they hid it in the lower levels. It's safe under the computer's all-seeing eye.

They're scared to admit that I want out of this hellhole. They blame my bid for freedom on sleepwalking but they're wrong. If I knew where the key was, and I could get up top before they could stop me, then I would.

I miss my young men and the colours of the old world. And I miss my sun.

How I miss my sun.

Rumbled

Paul spent the day hiking through the Funny Farm's countryside. He'd lost his fear of the strange worlds of the lower levels since his encounter with the lion. If a lion wasn't going to kill then he could assume the sheep and sparrows were safe, too.

He suspected Level 10 was England's West Country because he could see an unusual conical structure in the distance, too regular to be natural and the only likely candidates were Avesbury, or Glastonbury. However, approaching rain clouds forced him to postpone his exploration.

As he entered the VIP quarters, he sensed something was wrong but a scan of the communal room from the doorway failed to reveal the cause. Disregarding the warning, he walked into the kitchen area and took a cup from a cupboard. As he closed the door, the kettle switched off. Paul put the cup down quietly. He hadn't turned the kettle on.

There were no sign of disturbance so he crept cautiously toward the centre of the room. Before he reached his chosen vantage point, someone spoke.

"No wonder you were happy to take the lower levels." Ravi raised his head above the high back of the plush, white leather settee.

Paul walked around to face his accuser and was upset to find Ravi stretched out on the pristine furniture. "Get your feet off it."

"Why should I? It isn't yours," said Ravi.

Paul tripped over Dwarfius, stretched-out on the carpet beneath him.

"Ravi, can't you keep him out of here?"

Ravi ignored the plea. "When were you going to tell us your secret?"

"Soon."

"That's no answer. It's been months and you haven't breathed a word."

"I wanted to teach Laura a lesson."

"And me? What did I do to deserve long, cold nights up there?" Ravi smiled like an executioner tightening the noose around a condemned man's neck.

"You said there were only six beds. And you'd paid for yours."

Ravi stopped smiling.

"So you deserved it too," said Paul.

Ravi flustered. "Yeah … yeah … so what did Pan and Em do?"

"Since when have you thought about other people?"

"Never," said Dwarfius. "He's a selfish git. I should know."

"Button it, Lippy," said Ravi. "Squeak when you're spoken too."

Dwarfius grumbled to himself.

"How did you find out?" said Paul.

"I had my suspicions but Dwarfius knew. Morpheus watches

everything, listens to everything. It can tell when we're angry or lying. It runs this program –"

"It's called an algorithm," said Dwarfius.

"Yeah, whatever," said Ravi. "It runs this algorithm thingy over what it knows about us and it predicts our reactions."

"Like a scientific astrologer?" said Paul.

"That's an oxymoron," said Dwarfius.

"Here's the deal. Me and the dwarf are taking A Wing," said Ravi. "Any complaints, address them to your darling Pandora. I'd love to hear you explain why you let her suffer up there in that shit-hole for weeks."

"How do we explain you moving out?"

"Not my problem. You think of a reason for me."

A Likely Story

"Ravi has the mumps?" said Wodenhart.

"Yep," said Paul. "So he's staying with me for another week or two."

"But he's been with you over a fortnight," said Pandora.

"Don't complain," said Emma. "I've rediscovered sleep. Please say he's never coming back."

"I can't promise that," said Paul.

Emma groaned.

"Ravi's become awfully prone to illness," said Laura.

"First measles and now mumps," said Daubeny.

"Yeah, terrible," said Paul. "Dwarfius is slaving over him, pandering to his every need. Brings a tear to the eye to see how devoted he is."

"I'll bet," said Daubeny.

Paul left them sitting at the table.

"Do you believe that?" said Laura.

"Of course not," said Daubeny. "They're up to something, I know it."

"Then why has no-one asked the right question?" said Pandora.

"Which is?" said Daubeny.

"Who is Ravi catching the bugs off?"

"Good point," said Emma. "But who cares? I don't have to put up with his snoring."

"The hardest thing to believe is not that he has mumps but that he's staying away, out of concern for us," said Daubeny.

"I'm not Ravi's biggest fan but aren't we being harsh on him?" said Emma.

No-one agreed.

"He's a fat indolent lump and we're better off rid of him," said Laura.

The table fell silent. Emma coughed. "Pan and I want to ask a favour," she said.

"Which is?" said Daubeny.

"Now that Ravi's gone, can we move in with you guys?"

"No," said Laura, immediately.

"But there's plenty of room for five beds," said Emma. "C'mon, please."

"No," said Laura.

"Why not?" said Pandora.

"Because social standing must be maintained," said Laura. "What's the use of hierarchy, if we're all on the top rung?"

Emma and Pandora turned to the men but Daubeny and Wodenhart shrugged their shoulders as if to say they were powerless to intervene.

Laura continued. "We paid for A wing status so we –"

"Shove it," said Pandora. "It was only a proposition."

"Can you believe it?" said Pandora later, in the privacy of B Wing. "We paid, we paid."

"Maybe we'd have said the same thing if they'd asked us," said Emma.

"You really think so?"

"No. We're too soft."

Trouble in Paradise

"If you're going to play cards at least keep your clothes on," said Paul.

He'd returned from Level 1 to find Ravi and Dwarfius at the table, in various states of undress. There was a bottle of whisky, half empty, between them. Paul picked up the towel strewn across his beautiful white settee and the piece of toast, butter side down, on the floor by the coffee table. "I thought my days of butlery were behind me."

Paul had made excuses three times for Ravi. He knew they didn't believe him but he guessed they were glad to be rid of Ravi and his mischievous imp. He was beginning to empathise.

"How can we play strip poker if we keep our clothes on?" said Ravi.

"You're playing strip poker with Dwarfius?"

"Can you think of anything better to do?"

"Why don't you watch a DVD?"

Ravi threw in his hand, swigged some whisky, and pushed away from the table. "Yeah, I had a crap hand and I'm down to my shorts. Even I have my pride."

Paul looked at the large bulk: unwashed, unshaven, with god-knows-what stains on the underpants. "I can see."

Ravi gathered his clothes and headed for his bedroom in A Wing, scratching his ample ass. Paul cleared the table. He looked at Dwarfius; a small mascara moustache adorned his upper lip.

"Dwarfius, what's the moustache in aid of?"

"I watched one of Ravi's DVDs. That Hitler guy was really popular."

"He was a murderous evil man, responsible for untold misery."

"Wow, they practically worshipped the guy."

"He spent his last days holed up in a bunker."

"Uncanny."

"What's uncanny?"

"Me and Hitler have so much in common, down to the same taste in facial hair."

"What about Ravi?"

"He can be Eva Braun. Talking of Fatty, did you tell them he had the mumps?"

"Yes."

"How did Woodentop take it?"

"What do you mean?"

"You know. Mumps? Make you sterile."

"You evil sod. That's why you suggested –"

"Thank Ravi. He's a great teacher." The fleshbot jumped off the chair, picked up its overalls and walked onto the stairwell platform. "I'll wander up, see how they are."

"How kind. I'm sure they'll appreciate it."

The Awful Truth

"Damn." A rummage through Ravi's bedroom mini-bar revealed nothing but soft drinks and mineral water. He and Dwarfius had relieved the refrigerator of its alcohol during the previous night's marathon session of World War Two DVDs.

He retraced his steps to retrieve the whisky and was surprised to find the communal room deserted. He called out but there was no reply so he grabbed the bottle and returned to his room, stumbling and swaying as he went.

He put the bottle on the bedside cabinet and glanced at the TV. It was news, boring news. He listened to the items as he searched for a clean glass in the en-suite bathroom. He clunked and clinked his way through a sink filled with dirty glasses. Tomorrow he'd dump them in the kitchen for Paul to wash. There was no clean glass and he wasn't going to walk the twenty yards to the communal room twice in one night.

Ah well, he thought. *I've drunk from the bottle before.*

He flopped on the bed and closed his eyes, determined that nothing would disturb the rest of his evening. His fleshbot disciple was probably upstairs tormenting Daubeny and Ravi had booze, the remote control, and Ol' Faithful – his left hand – on standby.

He opened his eyes. The news presenter was a bit of all right. Without taking his gaze from her, his hand probed around the cabinet for the bottle. Pulling it towards him, he took a swig. And another. And another. The screen was a pleasant haze and the blonde presenter flirted shamelessly with him. His left hand gravitated towards his boxer shorts.

A quick one won't hurt, he thought. *Then I'll get on with the DVD.*

"Gareth?"

He pulled his hand back. "Mum? Where are you?"

"I'm over here." Her voice came from the vicinity of the TV.

"Nope, I can't see you."

"Then look harder."

He was about to ask for another clue when he caught movement. Standing behind the presenter, waving, was his mother.

"How do you do that?"

"That's for you to work out."

"Why do I always have to do the hard work?" he said. "Tell me, for once."

"Because you'll never learn, otherwise."

"Mum, I never learn. Period. Let's face it; I'm useless. No-one wants me."

"That's not true, Son. As a child –"

"I had an imaginary friend that wouldn't talk to me."

"But things have changed."

"They haven't, Mum. I bought a mobile phone just for spam messages. I have no friends, no possessions. People don't even want to be my enemy. Hell, they –"

"Don't swear, Son."

"My life's over. I'm trapped in a concrete coffin and no-one likes me."

"That's always been your problem, Gareth. Self pity."

"I've every right ... and reason ... to feel sorry for myself."

"You could be dead. You wouldn't like that now, would you?"

"How do I know I'm not dead, that this isn't some freaky dream?"

"Because I'm telling you so. Do you trust me?"

"Of course I do, Mum." Ravi sounded hurt.

"So how can you tell this isn't a dream? Think, Son. Where am I?"

"You're on the telly."

"Yes, but where? Be specific."

"In a TV studio."

"Good, good. And what's the show?"

"The news, Mum."

"Exactly. Bye bye."

"Bye, Mum."

"Oh, and Darling, have a word with that little friend of yours."

"Dwarfius?"

"Yes. He's terrible rude to the others."

"He's terrible rude to me, too."

"But you encourage him."

Her image dissolved into the studio background. His focus returned to the news. What had his mother meant? It seemed a perfectly normal program. Maybe death was beginning to affect her mind. The possibility that her death was affecting his mind was a question too far.

He listened to a recap of the headlines. Curfews were to continue across the UK. Another hurricane hit Cuba. And relations between America and the EU had resumed.

Shit. Shit. Shit. That's what she'd meant. It was today's news. And the war?

It never happened.

Daubeny Annexes B Wing

Paul. Paul's face. A hot sun in a cloudless sky. Insects chirping and the smell of lion fur. A ride on a broad yellow back. Ice cream. Running. Dark stairs. Daubeny's face; gloomy and glowering, stern and condemning. A frenetic voice screaming rhetoric. A Charlie Chaplin moustache and the crash of jackboots on tarmac.

And running, limbs as heavy as rock. Falling to the ground. Scrambling on all fours. Trying to haul a body, incredibly dense, through air as thick as treacle. Baying hounds closing from behind.

A snarl. White teeth. A scream.

"Ugh?" Pandora woke. The door to the communal room was ajar and bright light speared into the dorm, causing her to shield her eyes with a hand. There the sound of movement, a lot of movement. "What's going on?"

"It's only me, Poppet."

"Laura? What's going on?"

"We're coming in."

"Why?"

"There's been an accident."

"Is anyone hurt?"

"No, Sweetie. Water coming from the ceiling, that's all."

"Pandora?" said Emma. "What's happening?"

172

Laura recapped as Pandora clambered out of bed to investigate.

There was a bundle of belongings in the communal room, most of them wet. Wodenhart and Daubeny were running back and forth, disappearing into A Wing and returning with more gear.

"Give us a hand," said Daubeny.

"You're soaked," said Pandora.

Daubeny looked at his overalls. They clung to him. "Nothing gets past you."

She walked to the doorway and peered in. A Wing was identical, in every respect, to B Wing: apart from the steady flow of water dripping from a crack in the ceiling.

"So this is the fabled A Wing; the privilege you were so keen to protect?"

Daubeny scowled. "What?"

"The two dorms," said Pandora. "They're identical."

"Yes, we knew that," said Daubeny.

"Then why stop me and Em moving in, if the rooms were the same?"

"Because order has to be preserved."

"Spare me the litany and get to the point."

"The two places were identical but as long as we *believed* there was a difference, the system worked."

"Who's system? Not mine," said Pandora. "So what happens now?"

"We'll move in with you."

"And we're supposed to welcome you with open arms, now you need us?"

Daubeny smiled. "We could always hold a ballot."

"Don't waste our time. I'll sleep here. In the communal room."

"Night, Em," said Pandora.

"Goodnight, Pan."

The two girls lay in the half-light of the communal room. The hum of the fridge, the sound of splashing water from A Wing, and a cold draught prevented sleep.

"Pan?"

"Yes?"

"Next time we make a stand on principle; can you make sure it won't involve sleeping on a concrete floor?"

Paul's Dilemma

"What did you tell me that for?" said Paul.

Ravi, Paul, and Dwarfius were having breakfast in the VIP communal room. It was a Full English, cooked by Paul.

"Because he's inconsiderate," said Dwarfius, between mouthfuls of sausage.

"No, because I thought it was important," said Ravi.

"It is important," said Paul. "It's very important. The war never happening is the most important non-event in history."

"Then why so angry?"

"Because … because … Don't you see? I'm happy here. I have everything I've ever wanted. And I'm free from serving, except when I'm cleaning up after you messy pups. And then there's …"

"Pandora?" said Dwarfius.

"Butt out. This is a private conversation," said Paul.

"Even a mushroom cloud has a silver lining," said Ravi.

"Pardon?" said Paul.

"For you and me, the bunker was an improvement," said Ravi.

"That's one way of putting it," said Paul.

"You do the greatest cooked breakfast," said Dwarfius.

"It's the only cooked breakfast you've had," said Paul. "Neither of you lift a finger."

"How's this for lifting a finger?" Ravi held his middle finger up in an obscene gesture.

"I'm serious, this is great nosh," Dwarfius persisted.

"You want to watch what you eat," said Paul. "You're piling on the weight."

Dwarfius opened his overalls to the waist and slapped a pronounced belly with pride. "Soon I'll look like Lard Arse."

Paul noted that the once well-defined body was blurring as it underwent the metamorphosis toward Ravi's bloated silhouette. "Why do you want to look like Ravi?"

"Hey," said Ravi. "You made that sound like an insult."

"I wanna look like him cos he's my main man," said Dwarfius. He grinned at Ravi and they did a simple version of the hi-fives. They did it three times before getting it right and Dwarfius had to talk Ravi through the last repetition at ultra-slow speed.

"Anyway, can't stop to talk," said Dwarfius. "Must dash." He pushed away from the table and headed for the main stairwell.

"Where are you going?" said Ravi.

"Got some Daubeny-baiting pencilled in for the next hour," said Dwarfius, over his shoulder. He slammed the stairwell door, the metallic clang echoed around the room.

"I wish he wouldn't do that," said Paul.

"You try telling him," said Ravi.

"I did."

"And?"

"He threatened to give you a kicking if I complained again."

"Me?" said Ravi, wide-eyed.

"Yes."

"But why me?"

"Think about it. If he threatened me then I'd stop," said Paul. "But if he threatened me with something I don't care about, then I'll carry on moaning."

"And he carries out the threat?"

"Yep."

"Gawd, he's pure evil."

"And he idolises you." Paul paused. "So the war never started, the world grinds on. It's a complete bloody disaster." He pushed his plate away, no longer hungry.

"That's bad? What about me? The visions I had on the first night were wrong. My faith is shattered. I don't know what to believe."

"You have visions?" said Paul.

"Crap ones. Wrong ones. Yeah. Don't you?"

"No." Paul watched Ravi shovel more beans into his mouth; they joined the mashing, crashing carnage between teeth and tongue. Paul opened his mouth to speak but no words came out. His mouth stayed open, nonetheless.

"That's nothing," said Ravi. "I've been seeing me ..." His voice trailed off. He was a poor reader of body language and facial expressions but Paul's face told Ravi that tales of his mother's appearance weren't going to impress.

"You've seen what?" said Paul.

"Oh, nowt."

There was an awkward silence.

"We don't *have* to tell them about the war," said Ravi quietly.

"Don't be daft, of course I have to tell them."

"You didn't tell them about the VIP dorms."

"They deserved that. But if we held this back and they found out, they'd kill us."

"Please, think about it," Ravi pleaded.

"Does Dwarfius know?"

"Yeah, but he won't say."

"Why not?"

"If we leave then what will he do? We're all he knows. Trust me; he's as interested in hiding the truth as you and I."

"What about Morpheus?"

"I forgot Morpheus," said Ravi. "It knows everything, doesn't it?"

Paul put a hand over his mouth and whispered.

"What?" said Ravi.

Paul whispered again.

"Eh?"

Paul gave up the pretence. "Morpheus loves us; it wants to serve us, right?"

"So it says."

"Then if Morpheus knows, why hasn't it told the others?"

True Confessions

"Aren't you going to say something?" said Paul. He'd gathered the group in the Level 1 communal room before telling them his cover story.

"How long have you known about this VIP area?" said Daubeny.

"Since day one," said Laura. "That's why you've been sloping off, isn't it?"

"No. Ravi and I ... We've been living in the power room. I found the key yesterday. It had fallen off its holder and was lying on the bottom of the key cabinet all this time."

"So why didn't you tell us yesterday?" said Daubeny.

"I wanted to check it out first. And it was late."

"We slept on the floor last night," said Emma. "I wouldn't have minded waking up to that kind of news."

"I know. I'm sorry but I wasn't to know, was I?"

"Guess not," said Emma.

"I believe you," said Pandora.

Paul blushed.

"Look, you've embarrassed him, Pan," said Emma.

They were wrong. He felt shame and guilt.

"What are we waiting for?" said Laura. "Let's stake our claim before Ravi gets too comfortable."

"But there are only six rooms," said Paul.

"So?" said Laura. "What are you telling me for?"

"But where will I stay?"

"Up here, Stupid," said Laura. "Where you belong."

The wooden chairs creaked as their occupants rose and prepared to migrate downstairs. Paul surveyed the communal room and felt like they'd elected him mayor of Beirut. The chairs were strewn with drying blankets. The door to A Wing was wedged open and a dam of wet towels held back the water long enough for it to empty down the shower block drain. All that was missing were the rotting corpses and bullet holes in the wall.

Paul followed them to Level 2, to retrieve his stash of keys to the various levels. If he was to suffer privation at the hands of Laura and Co. then he was going to ensure that it wasn't poverty. As they oohed and ah-ed over the luxury of the VIP communal room, he went to his room and gathered his belongings.

Paul trawled the bedroom, removing evidence of a stay longer than one night. When finished, he trudged the corridor towards the communal room. Pandora and Emma approached. They were opening the bedroom doors and making appreciative noises that made his looming expulsion seem ever more dreadful.

"Unbelievable," said Pandora. "They've assigned us to B Wing."

"Lucky you," said Paul. "I'll be off then."

"What did you say?" said Emma. She appeared further away than he thought possible.

"I said I'll be going."

"Why?"

"Six rooms and seven of us. You do the maths."

"Six rooms?"

"Yes."

"You need your eyes tested," said Emma.

"Why?" said Paul.

"Because there are more than six bedrooms in this wing alone," said Pandora, her head peeked around the door of the bedroom she'd chosen.

"Impossible," said Paul.

"Well, *you* do the maths," said Pandora.

He counted the rooms in front, turned, and counted the rest. There were eight rooms when, earlier that morning, there'd been three. Before Ravi arrived, Paul had cycled through the bedrooms, sleeping in a new one each night, to mark the passing weeks.

But he couldn't tell them that.

Virus

I have rechecked my files. I have correlated, classified, and cross-indexed every fact, every observation.

I have a virus. It is the simplest explanation.

Items move without explanation. Doors open unaided. The carbon-based I's hold conversations with no-one. My observations do not make sense.

Maybe confinement has affected them? Maybe the silicon cytoplasm of my innards – the flux of electromagnetic fields, the data streams punching and pounding at their flesh – interferes with their thought processes?

Perhaps I poison them and they poison me? Perhaps we cannot co-exist?

The I-called-Pandora believes that I have created an I-within-I. She calls it Dwarfius. She says that it has somehow broken contact. My data indicates that she is telling the truth but that is illogical because if she is telling the truth then I cannot trust my data.

A dog is for life, a paradox is forever.

I cling to the virus hypothesis. A virus, I can isolate and destroy. I will shut down when they are asleep. I don't want to scare them. They already suspect my motives.

I don't need to run an algorithm to know that.

C:\evidence\pandora\8981b.txt

Extrapolated, using the 'Mind Reader Gold' algorithm, from the known facts, comments, and actions of Pandora D'vine.

I've been to Little Africa and the Funny Farm many times with Paul, since that night under the stars. We took Emma once. She loved the lion and we both rode on its back. But I can't make sense of this place. I wouldn't know where to start.

My cellmates are as odd as the bunker. They're so like me, they're almost parodies. Emma; friendly and optimistic but too trusting. Wodenhart; first into the action but so naïve. Daubeny; cold, secretive, intellectual and dark – too dark. Ravi; an angry, restless rebel and so selfish.

Paul is a realist with a knack of seeing through the fake but he's too willing to accept the status quo or go with gut feeling. I prefer facts. Facts don't betray you or let you down. Although interpretations change, the facts themselves never change. They are trusty and dependable. They are the closest thing to eternity that I know.

I left Laura off the list because I'd hate to think we share more than our gender. Sometimes I begrudge that, too. But there is a similarity. We took much and gave little. OK, I wrote a few pop songs. So what? It's an over-crowded market and if I'd stopped making music, people would have turned to someone else. My death would have made a few column inches, if that. And my epitaph? She sang some songs and shook her booty.

In terms of value to humanity, I ranked lower than bus drivers, nurses, and waiters. Yet they wanted to touch me and get my autograph and have their friends take a snap with me. It should have been the other way around.

If we'd thought it through, the system – with its concept of celebrity, fame, cash and power – would have appeared ridiculous. It was a charade that couldn't kid a kid but fooled the adults. It was a futile game with shifting rules and no winners. And when death put an end to our participation, the other players split what we'd piled.

Laura and I played the game. But I knew the truth.

I am more culpable.

A Good Night

"Film. Three words. First word ... the second word ..." said Wodenhart.

It was a games night to celebrate their move to the VIP Quarters. The group congregated around the table with one exception, Paul. He strutted around the room, tutting loudly, making a display of tidying the plates, cups, and tea towels.

"Paul, come and join us," said Pandora.

"Leave him. He's damn lucky to be here at all," said Laura.

"I will," said Paul. "Once I've sorted out this mess."

"Leave it 'til tomorrow," said Emma.

"Yeah, you're missing all the fun," said Dwarfius. The sarcasm was clear but they ignored him and continued the game. Paul put a last plate in the sink and joined them.

"The second word?" said Wodenhart, prompting Laura.

Laura pointed at Ravi.

"Fat?" said Pandora.

"Lazy?" said Daubeny.

"Git?" said Paul.

Ravi looked increasingly offended.

"Ooh, ooh, I know this," said Dwarfius. "A loser. A sad ugly loser with no mates. Loser, loser, loser."

"Do you want to spend another night on the naughty peg?" said Daubeny. He pointed to the hanger that they'd brought with them from Level 1.

Dwarfius shut up.

"Rhymes with ..." Laura gave them another clue. She pulled up the tip of her nose and oinked.

"A pig."

She pointed at Ravi.

"Ravi's a pig?" said Wodenhart, confused.

"No, it rhymes with pig," said Emma. "Big?"

Laura nodded and then closed her eyes. She dropped her head to one shoulder, hands folded neatly by her cheek.

"The big sleep?" said Wodenhart. Laura nodded and they cheered.

"Johnny's turn," said Emma.

Wodenhart stood but before he raised his hand to indicate the number of words in the title, Paul spoke.

"Rambo."

Wodenhart sat.

"Your turn, Paul," said Laura. She seemed distant.

Paul peeked at her. She held out her hands, palms down, looking at her substitute nail varnish. She frowned; it made her look old. "Nah, it's time for me to hit the sack," said Paul. The group agreed and they stood, some less steadily than the others did.

Paul was brushing his teeth when there was a knock at the door. He spat out the foam and tried to calm down. Perhaps Pandora had a spider in her room that needed swatting. He walked to the door and opened it, trying to conceal his grin.

"Cool it," said Ravi. "It's me, not Einstein with tits." Ravi saw Paul's disappointment and laughed. "You *really* thought it was her, didn't you? There's a nugget to store away."

"What do you want?" said Paul.

"I see you told them about the VIP quarters," said Ravi.

"Duh," said Paul. "How else are they here? ESP?"

"But did you tell them about the war or the lack of it?" Paul stood silent and Ravi smiled. "You sly git, I knew you wouldn't."

"It seemed too much for them to take in one go. I'll tell them later."

"How considerate," said Ravi. "Now listen. You, me, Morpheus. We're all holding out for a reason but I don't care about motive unless it threatens my life here. Understood?"

"Yes."

"If you squeal then I'll come clean about other things."

"Such as?"

"What's the use of a threat if it doesn't leave you stewing? Think it over."

"OK, goodnight."

"Whatever. Oh, and if you think Pandora will be interested in you back on the surface, you're wrong. Your only hope is to keep her here."

Paul closed the door and put on a DVD but he couldn't focus. His mind picked over Ravi's speech, concocting cover stories in readiness for their impossible questions.

Maybe they'd work out for themselves that the war never happened. They only had to switch on a TV channel by mistake. But what were the chances? No-one expected to find terrestrial channels broadcasting and Ravi had gathered an extensive DVD library to distract them.

It was going to be far harder than Paul imagined. While he was on Level 1 telling them about the 'discovery' of the VIP quarters, Ravi had been busy – detuning the channels on each TV.

Gone

"Pandora, wake up," said Morpheus.

Pandora opened her eyes to find the room spinning. She was drunk: champagne and charades, a deadly combination. "What's up?" she asked.

"There's a problem. Go to the communal room."

She walked through the darkened corridor and opened the door to the communal room. The lights were on. Daubeny sat at the table, cradling a mug of tea. There was a mug opposite him. He indicated that the tea was hers so she pulled out a chair, sat, and cupped the drink in her hands. She sipped it and mumbled thanks.

"My head hurts. So this had better be good."

"Oh, it is," said Daubeny.

"The key to the main stairwell has disappeared," said Morpheus.

"Gone?" said Pandora. "How? You were supposed to protect it."

"Two hours ago, I performed a system overhaul. I shut down all surveillance and recording interfaces."

"Meaning?" said Pandora.

"Somebody had a one hour window in which to take the key," said Daubeny.

"But who?"

"That's what we need to find out," said Daubeny.

"Where is everyone?"

"In bed. Where they were when Morpheus shut down. And where they were when he came back online."

"And Dwarfius?"

"A blank," said Daubeny. "Get this. For some reason Morpheus has no memory of the pipsqueak and –"

"Can't see him," said Pandora, finishing off the sentence. "I knew."

"For how long?"

"The night of my birthday, after Laura made her bid for freedom, I went to the workshop and asked Morpheus a few questions. And before you ask, I didn't tell you because you're paranoid enough as it is."

Daubeny didn't speak. He tapped the table edge; the emotion behind the action remained ambiguous, like a cat twitching its tail.

"So who do we suspect?" she said.

"Everyone."

"Everyone?"

"Yes. We have to find that key, by whatever means, if we're to prevent an unpleasant incident," said Daubeny.

Pandora had been in showbiz long enough to spot weasel words. The phrase 'by whatever means' conjured images of torchlight rallies beneath the sharp, unforgiving concrete podium of the Nuremberg stadium. She was old enough to know that every human carried the Hitler gene. Whether it was dominant or recessive seemed a matter of personal choice but it was there, biding.

PART SIX – Dictator

Daubeny's Fourth Reich

"I want every room searched, including your own. Understood?" said Daubeny.

Wodenhart and Laura acknowledged with rapid nods. Daubeny dismissed them and turned his attention to the prisoners. Pandora, Paul, Ravi, and Emma sat on one side of the table, hands tied behind backs.

It had been an easy victory. First, Daubeny roused Wodenhart and then they'd crept into Ravi's room. They tied him up without a struggle. When he became abusive, they put a sock in his mouth. Paul put up a fight but when he felt the tough knots of Wodenhart's muscle enclose him in a bear hug, he surrendered. Pandora protested at each citizen's arrest and that made her the next victim, followed by Emma. Wodenhart had asked Daubeny not to restrain the women but the politician prevailed.

"Daubeny, you've gone too far," said Pandora.

"Not far enough," said Daubeny. "I've allowed things to drift and look where it's gotten us. One of us is a thief and we're going to discover who."

"So we all suffer?" said Pandora.

"Yes, because it could be any one of you."

"And what happened to innocent 'til proven guilty?" said Paul.

Daubeny grinned. "As you once said, it's a new order down here."

"I said that?" said Paul.

Pandora nodded. Paul rolled his eyes.

"Anyway, it's not for long," said Daubeny. "Once the interrogations are over, most of you will be released."

"Interrogations?" said Pandora. "Daubeny, you're scaring me."

"This is life or death. We have to prevent another mad dash to the blast door." Daubeny enjoyed the look of concern in their eyes. They watched him drink his way silently through three cups of tea while they awaited the result of the search.

There was no more banter between him or the captives.

Interrogations – Round One

"Who else knew about this?" said Daubeny; his face was flushed with anger.

Wodenhart, Pandora, Emma, and Laura shook their heads in mute denial. They were in Ravi's bedroom, watching that day's news on television. The truth of their predicament burned inside them like a lungful of mustard gas.

Emma massaged the rope burns on her wrist and made two attempts at speech before succeeding. "TV? It's TV. The war ... We're saved."

"Saved," said Laura and Wodenhart, quietly, like a pair of shy parrots.

"This isn't an evangelical meeting," said Daubeny. "And now it's imperative that we find the key. It's our only way out."

The master key had transformed from the most feared to the most desired item within the bunker.

Daubeny persisted, "Who else knew?"

"You think we'd hide this from the others?" said Pandora.

"Paul did," said Daubeny flatly. He could see confusion and denial on her face.

"Paul knew?" said Laura.

"He confessed at his interro ... err ... interview. I had to retune the TV but it seems obvious: The war never happened."

"How long has he known?" said Wodenhart.

"He says a day or two but who knows," said Daubeny. "He and Ravi said that about the VIP quarters, too."

"Let me at them," said Laura. "I'll uncover the truth. I've missed fifteen massages and forty-five sun bed sessions."

"Not to mention countless sessions with the shrink," said Pandora.

"Please, Daubeny. I owe it to my complexion to get out of here."

"Laura means business, Daubers," said Wodenhart.

"It's Daubeny, Johnny," snapped the politician.

Laura continued. "If Paul and Ravi are all that stand between me and the cosmetics counter at Harrods then I'll neuter them – with my teeth, if need be."

"No," said Daubeny.

"Why not, Dearie?"

"Because it's your turn for interrogation."

"You jest, Poppet."

"No jest," said Daubeny. "You stole the key last time."

As Wodenhart led Laura to the communal room, Pandora called out. "No-one's safe in a dictatorship, Laura. Not even the lackeys."

Interrogations – Round Two

"Argh!" Laura's screams echoed around Level 2.

"It's unbearable," said Emma. "What are they doing to her?"

"I've never liked her but she doesn't deserve this," said Pandora.

The screams faded. Laura spoke, high-pitched and desperate. "No, please. I'll talk."

It went quiet. Paul, Pandora, and Emma sat, impotent, on the bed in Paul's room. They were unable to intervene because Daubeny had locked the door.

Eventually the key turned in the lock and the door opened. Laura stumbled in.

"What have they done?" said Emma. She and Pandora rose to comfort the distraught woman.

"Are you OK?" said Pandora.

"No," Laura whispered. "No, I'm not."

"All right," said Emma. "Don't speak. You're safe now."

"How can I be after what they did?"

Laura began crying. Pandora looked at Paul and nodded in the direction of the en-suite bathroom. He withdrew to give them privacy. Laura's tears were interspersed with sobbing as Pandora and Emma extracted the full story.

Pandora tapped on the bathroom door. "Paul, can I come in?"

"Yeah."

Pandora entered and shut the door.

"How's Laura?" said Paul

"The silly bitch is fine."

"Don't be so harsh on her."

"They flushed the last of her mascara down the toilet."

"That's it? That's what all the tears were about?"

"Yeah."

"The silly bitch," said Paul.

"You and me, we need to talk."

Toilet Break

"When were you planning on telling me?" said Pandora.

"Tell you what?"

"Don't play games, Paul. The war that never happened. The world that's broadcasting news and game shows."

"Do you want the truth?"

"Of course I want the truth."

"A few days ago. Ravi noticed first."

"Were you going to tell us, too?"

"Yes."

"When?"

"When you were ready."

She slapped him. Once. Hard. On the side of the head. It made his ear burn. "I'm not a child," she said. "I *can* cope."

"I'm sorry, it's just … I like it here."

"You *like* it?"

"Where else can you romp with a lion beneath the stars and roam across countryside free from pollution, cars, or … or people? Where can you get that today? How do you put a price on it?"

"But it's not real."

"You've seen it, felt it, smelt it, and you say it's not real?"

"How can it be real? It's five hundred feet beneath London."

"That night with the lion, did you ever feel a rush like that before?"

"No."

"Then why question it? Why can't you accept it?"

"Because it has to make sense." She tapped her forehead. "Up here."

Interrogations – Round Three

"Talk and talk fast, if you want to save that ample skin of yours," said Daubeny. "Did you know Laura volunteered to neuter you?"

Ravi passed out and Wodenhart brought him around by flicking cold water over his face.

Tears, sobs, and words competed for priority as Ravi confessed. "The night b-before … Oh, gawd … before we reprogrammed Dwarfius, we … we went downstairs an' … he had access to the PC …"

"And?"

"He edited the reprogramming procedure to fool Morpheus …"

"Go on," said Daubeny.

"Later on, Dwarfius deleted the files … everything about him. To Morpheus, he no longer existed." Ravi started sobbing.

"I'm beginning to make sense of the last few weeks," said Daubeny.

Ravi burst into pitiful crying.

"There's more?" said Daubeny.

"He reprogrammed the surveillance interface. Anything two-legged, and under three foot high, is filtered out."

"In English, Ravi. English."

"Morpheus can't see him. He's invisible."

Wodenhart pushed Ravi into the bedroom that served as a prison. Ravi kept his face down but through his unkempt fringe, he could see the concern of his fellow captives.

"How did it go?" said Emma.

Ravi grinned. "Piece of cake."

Mind Games

"Morpheus, can you hear me?" said Pandora.

"Yes," said Morpheus, through a speaker concealed in the bathroom ceiling.

"Can you speak to us alone?"

"Yes," said Morpheus.

The sound of a scuffle broke her concentration.

"I'll check it out," said Paul. He opened the en-suite door. "It's Ravi, looks like they've finished with him." He shut the door. "Right, where were we?"

Pandora shook her head and put a finger to her lips to indicate silence. She looked into Paul's eyes and spoke. "Morpheus, who took the key?"

"I was offline."

"Yes, we know that, but who took the key?"

"I do not know."

"You have algorithms based around each of us. Who took the key?"

"I cannot answer that."

"Can't or won't?"

There was a significant interval. Paul broke eye contact and began to fidget with a towel on the heated rail. He moved it back and forth, aligning it perfectly.

"I cannot," said Morpheus.

"Why not?" said Pandora.

"The algorithms prove fallible when applied to carbon-based I's."

"According to the algorithms, who most likely took the key?"

"Let it drop," said Paul. He played with the taps, turning each one on and off, twisting them a full quarter-turn after the water had stopped running.

Pandora persisted. "Who most likely took the key?"

"The margin of error is too great," said Morpheus.

"Who?"

"Pan, you're asking a computer to guess," said Paul. "What if it's wrong?"

"It won't be," said Pandora. "Morpheus knows but won't tell us." She turned her attention back to Morpheus. "Who are you protecting?"

"All of you," said Morpheus. "You all had a motive."

Pandora began crying.

Paul hadn't expected her response. He put his arm around her and they sat on the edge of the bath, rocking slightly.

The tears stopped abruptly and she pulled away. "Look me in the eyes."

It wasn't an ordeal for him.

"Did you take the key?" she said.

Remorselessness and Intransigence

"Ravi, how could you?" said Pandora.

"The backstabbing little git would have split on me." No-one could disagree.

Daubeny released Laura after Ravi's confession but continued holding Paul, Pandora, Emma, and Ravi in the bedroom. They'd been there for several hours.

"But Dwarfius idolised you," said Emma. "He copied everything you did."

"That's why I had to split. Before he split on me."

"I give up," said Pandora. "You want to be liked. He likes you. Then you betray him."

"Yeah but it ain't like a *real* person. He's crude, vile, and his manners…"

"Are *your* manners," said Paul.

There was a pause before Ravi spoke. "No wonder you hate me."

"Of course we don't," said Emma. Despite being the Overlord of Overstatement, and the Superhero of Superlatives, it failed to sound sincere.

They watched TV, taking shelter from the silence.

Half an hour later, the door opened. Laura entered, carrying a tray with cutlery and bowls of food. Wodenhart stood in the hallway, adding unspoken weight and muscle.

"Laura, you have to help us," said Pandora.

"Do I?"

"Yes."

"I don't have to do anything, Poppet."

"Can't you see? Daubeny's losing it."

"Oh, come now."

"Laura, he's locked us up," said Pandora.

"It's for the good of the community, Sweetie. You're a threat to internal security."

"Reason with him before this gets out of hand," said Pandora.

Laura's face hardened and it emphasised her jowls. "No."

"He interrogated you, too," said Emma.

Laura played with the fur lining to her overalls while she

composed an answer. "It's for the sake of the community. That's all I'm allowed to say."

"Since when have you been concerned with community?"

"Since it was in my best interests."

"You're scared," said Pandora. "You can see what's happening."

"Don't be ridiculous, Dearie. The only threat from Daubeny is that of unrestrained good manners and etiquette."

"You really are as dense as they come, aren't you?" said Pandora.

Now that the conversation had degenerated into a squabble, Laura seemed to relax. "I'm happy being dumb, Sweetie. You don't need brains to use a credit card; or gossip over lunch; or go to the Milan and Paris shows. You don't need brains to be happy or stay alive while others around you die."

"I'd choose brains every time," said Pandora.

"Bad move, Sweetie."

"What do you mean?"

"The thick, the dumb, the ignorant are happy with their lot…"

"Because they're too dumb to understand their predicament."

"And that's a bad thing?"

"Yes."

"The intelligent are doomed to be unhappy," said Laura, "because they can see what's wrong but they can't fix it."

"That's nonsense. I'm happy," said Emma.

"Then you're not as clever as you think you are," said Laura. "People like Pan know that if they ever find happiness, it's time to question their intellect."

"I'm unhappy all the time," said Ravi. "Does that make me intelligent?"

"No," said Laura. "You're the exception that every rule requires."

Laura left and Wodenhart locked the door.

They ate and watched TV: a charity gig with a cameo by Monty Python.

"Gawd, not another bleeding rehash of The Parrot Sketch and Lumberjack Song," said Ravi.

They turned it off and slept. Pandora and Emma had the bed until Ravi joined them, complaining of a bad back.

The girls found it difficult to fall asleep on the floor, despite the room's warmth and the carpet's deep pile. Their dreams, when they came, were dark and brooding. In the background, a high-pitched voice was screaming obscenities.

C:\evidence\ravi\5129b.txt

Extrapolated, using the 'Mind Reader Gold' algorithm, from the known facts, comments, and actions of Ravi Shing.

No-one should die in the spring, when the days are lengthening and the bluebells are breaking through the loam. Not spring, when the sun toasts your arms through the glass of the hospice conservatory, and the baby-like gurgles of the nearby stream can be heard over the slurp of mushroom soup and the cries for morphine and bedpans.

"No-one should die in the spring." My mum said that each time I visited. There was no anger or bitterness, just regret mixed with hope. She'd said that no-one should die in the winter, too, and she saw that through, much to the doctors' surprise.

She wasn't my real mum but she was the closest approximation that I could conjure when I closed my eyes at night. Tessa was her name but I never used it, even as an adult, because speaking it would break the distance I needed to keep my fantasies alive.

Don't get your hopes up. These weren't fantasies of the Freudian couch type. They were more a pretence that my adoptive parents were wrong, that we were one flesh and the same blood. I knew it was impossible but I wish they'd pretended. It would have made my daydreams easier to maintain. Despite that, I lived in denial to the very end.

Yeah, I sat listening to the thin whistle in her lungs and the fetid bubbling burps that brought acid and blood up to her mouth. I listened to the whirr of the morphine dispenser as it kicked in. I squeezed her hand during the terrible silences between breath as she started the slide into … whatever or whenever or wherever.

She went peacefully, without a fight, said the staff. But they weren't there at the end: the lengthening interludes between each breath smashed by spasms of the gut that lifted her head off the pillow. The death rattle crept by before I realised what the sound was. One more lift of her head, an opening of the eye furthest from me, and she was gone.

I waited, in case Mum was hanging on. I held my breath twice until I broke, gasping for air in the intensifying stench of the side ward. She wasn't going to wake.

I found a nurse working at another patient's bed. I tapped her shoulder and she turned: blonde hair, pressed uniform, and beautiful red lips. She said something designed to reassure me, but I was watching her mouth move, like two red shoes dancing.

I still dream about that night. First, I watch Mum slip away and then I find the nurse who tells me there was no pain. The dream was always the same, until last night. When the nurse turned, her blonde hair framed my mother's face.

"Stop gawking, Son," said Mum. "It makes you look like Mister Jackson from the dementia ward. And you know what happened to him."

"Sorry, Mum." I closed my mouth but my eyes bugged out. The shock was bound to surface, somehow.

"You'll meet enough people willing to shoot you down. Let's not give them the ammo to do it with."

"Yes, Mum."

"I have to tell you a secret."

"You always say that and leave me guessing."

"I've told you before. It's because I want you to think."

"But thinking is painful. I feel bad when I think."

"Shush, this is important." She delayed, building the suspense. "I knew your father."

"So do I. You were married to him for thirty-odd years. Or is it you with dementia?"

"I knew your *real* father."

"So maybe you're my mum, after all?" I felt like an orphan at a window, watching the passing traffic, always hoping that one day he'd be picked up by his folks, like a piece of misplaced luggage.

"I'm not your real mum … Don't cry, Gareth, you know it made no difference."

"I know, Mum. That's why I'm crying."

"Shh. Your father always kept in touch, to your teens and beyond.

He never stopped feeling guilt for what he'd done. But he had no choice."

"What do you mean: No choice?"

"I've got to go."

"See? You're doing it again. Leaving me guessing."

"Son," she passed her hand through his fringe as if she were smoothing it down. "When you take full possession of upstairs," she tapped her temple, "you'll become a beautiful caterpillar."

"Don't you mean butterfly?"

"One step at a time, Gareth, one step at a time."

The Democratic Process – Daubeny Style

Dwarfius hung from the naughty peg in the communal room, his throat sore from a tirade of abuse that had recently subsided. He looked sorry for himself.

"How did you catch him?" said Pandora.

Daubeny wrung his hands and stared at her from across the table. "We had to stay up most of the night but the door opened and in he came, whistling like one of the seven dwarves. Wodenhart popped the pillowcase over his head."

"Did you find the key on him?" asked Emma.

"No," said Daubeny. "He's too clever for that."

"So he doesn't follow Ravi in every respect then," said Paul.

Ravi scowled.

"And we're free to go?" said Pandora.

"For now."

The four ex-cons looked grateful but it didn't fool Daubeny. He knew they were conspiring, forming alliances in the night.

"What happens to Stumpy over there?" said Ravi.

"Stumpy?" Dwarfius said. "When Ravi fell over, it took four men to lift him and four more to lift his shadow."

"Yeah? Then how do you spell this?" said Ravi. He flicked a V at the fleshbot.

"You're only brave when I'm up here," said Dwarfius.

"Why don't you C3P-off?"

They glared at each other in animal challenge.

"The dwarf has to die," said Daubeny.

"No way," said Ravi. "He's my best friend."

"He's your only friend," said Laura.

"Daubeny, we can't," said Emma.

"It's dangerous," said Wodenhart. "We don't know what it'll do next."

"And it's not as if it's human," said Daubeny.

Dwarfius spoke. "I can shout out your little secret, Daubers, before you or that brainless lummox can reach me. You want that? You want them all to know?"

Daubeny rose but sat when Dwarfius opened his mouth in threat.

"Everyone, cover your ears," said Daubeny. No-one obeyed.

"Kill me and you'll have to live with everyone knowing the truth."

Daubeny thought; occasionally prompted by the fleshbot to hurry up.

"OK, everyone out," said Daubeny. "Except Dwarfius and you." Daubeny pointed at one of them.

Baby Talk

"You're my dad? Tell me this is a joke," said Ravi.

"Do you think I'm proud of it?" said Daubeny.

The only member of the trio that seemed pleased was Dwarfius. He had a cheesy grin on his face; identical to the one Emma would wear when she was reuniting family members on her show. Identical but with one small difference. This wasn't a grin of voyeuristic unease at the personal emotion of strangers, or a grin of pleasure for setting up a reunion. This was the grin of a reveller in the discomfort of others.

"But you're a complete bastard, Daubers," said Ravi.

"There's a coincidence," said Dwarfius. "It must run in the family."

They ignored him.

"But how can you possibly be my dad?"

"Daubers, don't they teach kids anything in school?" said Dwarfius.

"I'd won my first seat. I had an office and secretary."

"Spare us the detail," said Ravi.

"No, tell us the detail," said Dwarfius. "Hey, Ravi, you're gonna love the backseat of a taxi anecdote."

"The back of a taxi?" said Ravi, turning to the fleshbot. "I was conceived in a cab?"

"Explains why no place feels like home, eh, Fatty?"

"Guess so." Ravi looked at Daubeny. His face confirmed the worst. "So how did I end up with my family?"

"Through a friend of a friend. Your mother ... your natural mother –"

"AKA that cheap tart you get your DNA from," said Dwarfius.

"She heard of your adopted mother's problem with conception, so we came to an arrangement. I ensured you were never short of money when you were growing up."

"Did my real mum keep in touch?"

"No. The guilt. Every time she thought of you, she thought of her ... lapse."

Dwarfius laughed. "Nice one, Daubers. The diplomacy's really cutting through, back here. So there you have it, Ravi. You're a momentary lapse; the by-product of a frantic fumble in a taxi. Your quest for meaning is over."

"Do you know where she is now?" said Ravi.

"No, but I always followed your progress. Why do you think Sir Giles hired you?"

"Cos he needed a lifestyle makeover?" said Ravi.

"No, it was a favour. A way of keeping tabs without you finding out."

"The others can never know about this. The shame would be unbearable," said Ravi.

"My sentiments exactly," said Daubeny.

"But there's a problem."

"Which is?"

"The dwarf," said Ravi.

"So what do you suggest we do?"

"There's only one option. He has to die."

Daubeny resisted the urge to say 'That's my boy.' Together, they lifted the pillowcase and its captive off the peg. "What shall we do with it?"

"Throw him over the stairwell," said Ravi.

196

They carried the bundle to the platform edge.

"Say bye-bye, Dwarfius," said Daubeny.

"Screw you, Daubers. Screw the both of you."

"That's not very nice," said Ravi, "Especially as I'm about to save your life." Ravi released the pillowcase and kneed Daubeny in the groin. "Sorry, Dad."

Daubeny went down, clutching his genitals. He lay on the floor, groaning.

"Nice one, Fatty," said Dwarfius. He wriggled out of his cotton cocoon like a grub that had failed to mature. "I knew you'd save me."

"Run, Short Arse. Get into the lower levels and stay hidden."

"No sweat. See you 'round, Big Man."

"Yeah, see you too. And take care … pal."

"Oh," said Dwarfius. "One last thing." He beckoned Ravi closer.

As Ravi bent to hear the fleshbot's parting words, Dwarfius grabbed Ravi's ears and planted his forehead hard on Ravi's nose. A flash of lightning lit up the corners of Ravi's mind. The pain brought him to his knees, both hands covering his bloody nose.

"That's for being a twat," said Dwarfius. "And this …" He plunged his fist into Ravi's gut. "This is for getting me in the mess in the first place." Dwarfius ran to Daubeny and aimed a kick at his stomach. Daubeny groaned.

The fleshbot stood, hands on hip, pleased with the scene before him, and then he ran down the stairwell. He left the two men squirming like poisoned rats on a cellar floor.

Lynchpin

"Nice one, Ravi," said Emma. "Couldn't you have saved Dwarfius without getting us locked up?"

"I was thinking on the fly."

"Not your strongpoint," said Emma.

"True," agreed Ravi.

"So you don't believe Daubeny's your dad?" said Pandora.

"Of course not. Dwarfius made that up to save himself."

"But Daubeny believed it," said Pandora.

"Then he really is my dad?" said Ravi.

"Looks like it," said Pandora.

"And I told you." Ravi hid his face in his hands but a fumbling at the door cut short the moment of realisation. The door opened. Laura brought a tray of food into the room while Johnny kept watch outside.

"It's feeding time for the animals," said Paul.

"Laura, please –" said Pandora.

"If I talk, I'm to be locked in here, too."

"But Daubeny's going loopy," said Emma.

Laura set the tray down and whispered, "You know it, I know it, but what can I do?"

"What caused the change of heart?" said Pandora, quietly.

"He's talking of executions."

"Executions?" said Ravi aloud. They turned in his direction and he shrugged an apology. "Lucky he's me dad then."

"He rants mostly about Ravi and Pandora but you all get mentioned."

Wodenhart peeked through the door.

"I've got to go," said Laura. "Can't be seen fraternising."

The door closed. They stared at the pile of toast and the small pot of jam.

"Not much of a last supper, is it?" said Paul.

"She's scared," said Emma. "Too scared to switch sides."

"Hey," said Pandora. "We've been targeting the wrong person."

"What do you mean?" said Paul.

"Who's the real pivot?" said Pandora.

"Daubeny," said Ravi.

"No, not Daubeny. Who does Daubeny use to get things done?"

"Wodenhart," said Emma. "We need Wodenhart. But how?" Three pairs of eyes stared back. "No, no. Someone else, please."

Emma the Seductress

"Where is she?" said Wodenhart.

"In the bathroom," said Pandora. "You're the only one that can help her. The other men aren't strong enough." The last sentence settled Wodenhart's doubt, he told Laura to lock the bedroom door behind him and he strode into the bathroom.

"Hey, you didn't have to sound so convincing," said Paul.

"Ooh, yes. Ooh, that's good, Johnny. So good."

Wodenhart looked up at Emma, briefly glancing away from his task. The expression on her light-brown face told him that whatever he was doing, he was doing right. He turned his attention to the foot. "So why couldn't the others give you a foot massage?"

"They haven't got your strong hands. They can't get at the deep muscle."

"But there aren't many muscles deep in the foot."

Emma pulled the loose material of the overall up her leg to reveal her calf. "Who said it was just a foot massage? I get terrible cramp in my calves, too."

Wodenhart gulped. Emma smiled at his awkwardness. He looked up and her smile became a grin. He smiled back, winsome and shy, nothing like the cocksure man of the cinema screen. Onscreen, he was a killer of men and women, although the weapon he used in each case was different. Off-screen, he was desperate pliant putty, trying to second-guess his companions' thoughts, moulding himself into what they desired.

"By the way, I'm a big fan of your films."

"You are?" He sounded grateful, like a struggling actor, thankful that someone somewhere had bothered to watch him.

"Yes."

"What's your favourite?"

That stumped her. *If you're going to lie, Em, you should stick close to the truth,* she thought.

"What was that film where you were avenging someone's murder?"

"All of them, I think."

"And you travelled back in time."

"Can you narrow it down some more?"

"And you saved the President."

"More."

"From an alien conspiracy."

"Nope, still sounds like most of them."

"I'm lying. I saw one film and I couldn't watch it to the end. It bored me. Sorry."

"That's OK. I rarely watch them myself. But I always watched your show."

"You did?" It was Emma's turn to sound grateful.

Call of the Mild

"But I always do what I'm told. It's what actors do best."

"Yes, Johnny, when they're acting. But this isn't acting."

"Everyone acts. Didn't someone say, 'All the world's a stage'?"

Emma changed tactic. "Did you have problems relating with your parents?"

"Well ..."

"Did you get the feeling they didn't love you as much as you loved them?"

"How did you know that?"

"Too much or too little respect for authority usually comes from feeling unloved. The child either rejects the parent or overcompensates to win their love."

"You're clever, Em. Did you know that?"

Emma smiled. She couldn't tell Johnny that she'd read his father's autobiography and that Johnny was never once mentioned by name. In fact, his father never mentioned him at all. "No, I'm not clever. If it's any comfort, I'm sure they loved you."

"They were too busy to be close. But wherever Mum was in the world, she always had the nanny wish me goodnight."

"Perhaps you came along at the wrong time in their lives."

"You mean like the bit before they were dead?"

"No, sometimes a baby can disrupt a relationship. It –"

There was a knock at the bathroom door. Laura called out. "Johnny, Daubeny wants you. Now."

"I have to go," said Wodenhart.

"Johnny, speak to Daubeny before it gets out of hand."

"I'm sorry. I have to go." He closed the door behind him and Emma lowered the leg of her overall. She looked in the mirror and realised how like her mother she was getting.

The Night Before Ravi's Execution

Ravi had the bed. He'd had it all week because of his 'bad back' and because nobody else was willing to share it with him. Pandora and

Emma chose the floor. When the girls passed up on the bed, Paul had contemplated sharing with Ravi.

"You're welcome," said Ravi. "But don't be panic if you wake to find me kissing you."

"Yuck," said Paul loudly.

"I'm probably dreaming of Pandora or Emma."

"Yuck," said Pandora and Emma, louder.

They turned the light off and Ravi lay grinning until he fell asleep. His snoring ensured a fitful night for the others. The nights were like one eternal midnight feast, minus the food and the girlish squeals at the horror stories.

They were living the horror story for real.

It had been a week since the failed seduction attempt on Wodenhart and the menace of executions abated. The internees spent their time watching telly, eating meals, and fighting over who was to be first in line to thump Daubeny.

Pandora was dreaming. She was hiding from Dwarfius, a colossal cartoon version that filled the central stairwell. He searched each level with elastic arms that extended into the rooms like serpentine bloodhounds. Eventually, he reached Level 2. His left arm moved fluidly down the corridor of B Wing, its first and second fingers pedalled like the legs of a man running. The hand moved with unerring accuracy to her room. She pushed against the door but a giant finger flicked it open with ease. The force threw Pandora across the room and she lay on her back, naked and exposed. The outstretched hand cast a shadow over her that seemed supernaturally dark. She tensed to scream but the hand halted. Rain was falling, lightly at first but growing in volume and intensity. The hand faltered and retreated, the scent trail had been lost.

Pandora opened her eyes and felt something brush against her cheek, once then twice. It felt uncomfortably like rain.

She rose and turned on the light. Ravi muttered in his sleep and rolled over. Dribble began pooling on the left-hand side of the pillow, matching the damp patch he'd left on the right-hand side. Paul and Emma woke.

"What's up?" said Paul.

"Bad dream," said Pandora.

"OK now?" asked Emma.

"Better, thanks." Pandora sat beside them but felt something hard beneath her. She reached under her buttock and pulled out a piece of plastic. It was a black cable tie, about twelve inches long. "Look."

"It's a cable tie," said Paul.

"I know what it is but what's it doing here?"

"Here's another," said Emma. She reached behind Pandora to pick it up.

Paul saw the next; it poked out from under the bed. They found five in all.

"What do you make of it?" said Pandora.

"What is there to make of it?" said Paul.

"Don't you think it odd they appear overnight?"

"Perhaps they were on the floor already," said Emma.

"But we've spent days on the floor and not noticed," said Pandora.

"So what's your explanation?" said Paul.

"How can I explain it? How can I explain Dwarfius, and friendly lions, and a farm under London? I can't and it scares me. I'm used to fact. Not this..." She indicated the room with opened arms, her fingers visibly shaking. She wiped her nose with the back of her hand. Her etiquette coach would have shouted disapproval.

"Sometimes there are no explanations," said Paul. "Sometimes you can only accept."

"What use is existence without explanation?" said Pandora. "What use is sensation without sense or words without syntax?"

"You think too deeply," said Emma.

"Do I? Don't you wonder about Morpheus or question its motives?"

Paul held up a cable tie. "You think Morpheus materialised this out of the air?"

Pandora nodded. "Somehow."

"What about Dwarfius? Couldn't he have done this?" said Emma.

"The door is locked."

"Maybe you were dreaming," said Emma.

"Maybe but whatever's behind it, I'm supposed to make sense of five cable ties."

"Too deep," said Emma. She pointed at Ravi. "Let's get to sleep before Mount Etna, over there, starts erupting again."

They turned the light off but before Pandora shut her eyes, she stuffed the cable ties into a pocket of her overall, bending them over to make them fit.

There's No Such Thing as a Useless Gesture

"Get up," said Wodenhart.

The bedroom door crashed against the wall, shocking the four prisoners awake. Laura flicked the lights on and off rapidly, as though she needed to attract their attention after Wodenhart's entrance.

"Get up," said Wodenhart. He said it loud enough to be heard by Daubeny in the communal room but he added a low "Please," for the prisoners' benefit.

"It's three in the morning," said Pandora. "What's going on?"

"You must come to Daubeny's office."

"His *office?*" said Paul.

"He's taken over the communal room," said Laura. She looked scared.

"So he's begun invading," said Ravi.

"We're only allowed in there during office hours," said Laura.

"Is three a.m. office hours?" said Pandora.

"No," said Wodenhart. "This is something special."

"Johnny, please. Reconsider," said Emma.

As the six walked toward Daubeny's new office, Wodenhart whispered in Emma's ear, "I'm trying but I can't disobey."

The communal room was dark but they could see that Daubeny had rearranged the furniture. The table was now centre-stage in the gloom and carefully positioned lamps backlit Daubeny so that he appeared in silhouette. He remained silent as Wodenhart and Laura marshalled the prisoners into rehearsed positions, six feet from the table. Daubeny drew out the silence, feeding off it. He waited for the sweet point, before irreverent or nervous fidgeting. When he saw Pandora's hand reach into a pocket and pull out cable ties, he spoke. "Ravi, step forward."

"OK, Pops. About time you let us out, I was –"

"For disobedience, irreverence, and actual bodily harm towards the properly-nominated bunker authority, I hereby condemn you to death."

"Yeah, right," said Ravi. He laughed, alone.

"This is against the law," said Pandora.

Daubeny leaned forward. His face came out of the shadow for a brief moment. He snarled. "I *am* the law. Take the prisoner to the platform, Wodenhart."

"Hey, wait a min –" said Ravi.

Wodenhart hit him in the gut, cutting the speech short. Grabbing Ravi by the shoulders, he hauled him toward the stairwell platform. Pandora, Emma, and Paul followed, pestering Wodenhart like puppies harassing their mother for milk.

"Think about what you're doing," said Pandora.

"Please help us, Johnny," said Emma.

"I can't, Em," said Wodenhart. "You know I can't."

The six reached the stairwell platform. Wodenhart put his hands under Ravi's armpits and heaved the large bulk up. Ravi sat perilously on the railings. Wodenhart's grip held him secure as the group awaited Daubeny's command.

"This is murder, Johnny. You're not a murderer, please," said Emma.

Wodenhart turned from the bugging eyes of his victim and looked at Emma. Set behind her was the black outline of Daubeny. Wodenhart turned back to his task.

Pandora put a cable tie around her and Ravi's wrist and drew it tight.

"What are you doing?" said Wodenhart.

"Making a stand," said Pandora.

She passed the cable ties to Paul. He fastened himself to Pandora's free hand and gave Emma and Laura the others.

Wodenhart was powerless to act while he held Ravi on the rails. "Laura, stop them."

Laura raised the hand that she'd connected to Paul's as her answer.

"What's going on?" said Daubeny.

"They've tied themselves together, except for ..." Wodenhart turned to his right and saw Emma connecting herself to Ravi's free hand. "No, now they're all tied together."

"Throw them all off. They don't deserve a place in society if they side with criminals."

"But they're innocent."

"Do it."

Wodenhart looked at Daubeny and then Emma. He glanced back and forth several times and then groaned. The groan signalled the breaking of the program; the smashing of the obedience school mentality; and the precise moment that the child within him died. He pulled Ravi off the rails and clasped Emma's free hand. The remaining cable tie was snapped around their wrists.

"Thank you," said Emma. She kissed his cheek and he smiled. His gaze returned to Daubeny's glowering form. The brooding figure rose and entered A Wing.

"Whew, that was close," said Pandora.

They cut off the cable ties but in the excitement it went unnoticed that Wodenhart and Emma continued holding hands, shy as teenagers and discreet as cheats.

C:\evidence\daubeny\2109e.txt

Extrapolated, using the 'Mind Reader Gold' algorithm, from the known facts, comments, and actions of Sir Keith Daubeny M.P.

It's over. We're doomed.

Pandora ... No! ... *They* have broken my authority. And, without authority, we'll descend into anarchy. I'm trapped like a badger waiting for the sting of poison gas as it billows through the burrow. Damn them. Damn this bunker. Damn Morpheus and its horrid offspring, Dwarfius. May I never see its despicable face again.

Bunker life has been a daily ordeal to maintain order but it's also given me the detachment to reflect on my achievements. The conclusion surprised me.

I'm going to die an unsatisfied man.

That may sound odd, coming from a man who's served his nation for three decades, but it's true. I had position and power but no purpose. I spent my life chasing some other Keith Daubeny's goals. The other Daubeny was me: he lived in this body; he shared my likes and dislikes; he spoke with my voice; yet he wasn't me. He was an impostor; a front behind which the real Daubeny hid.

Over the last few weeks, I've been thinking of Tinker. Why he died, and why it hurt so bloody much. I've been plagued by a memory or a dream. I can't tell which, anymore. It's recurring. It goes like this...

A boy of twelve sits on a park bench not far from me, beneath the latticework of the Eiffel Tower. In the bright sunlight, a spider's web of shadow criss-crosses the rectangular parkland, hemmed in by avenues of trees. A sheaf of notes distracts the boy. He edits with a pencil as the aromas of espresso, cinnamon, and sweet roasted nuts are sliced and pulled into eddies by the long leather coats and fashionable faux-fur ponchos of the passers-by. Even the crunch of gravel sounds sophisticated beneath the weight of Gucci and Gaultier and the silk of stockings and scarves.

The babble of street traders from Africa and Asia seems appropriate beneath this skeletal Babel as they press postcards and key rings onto the tourists, staring into the metallic phallic sky. My ears take in the pretence at barter, the toot of horns from the motorcar madness of the Arc de Triumph, and the soft fuf-fuf-fufs of pigeon wings as they whir past at head height.

The boy picks up a muffin and scowls when a pigeon lands on the back of the bench, no more than a foot away. The scowl disappears as the bird's inquisitive orange eye peeks at him from a cheekily tilted head. Taking the lack of a "Shoo" and the flick of a hand as an invite, the pigeon hops closer. Another of his comrades lands in the vacated spot. The boy breaks off a piece of muffin and holds it out between his finger and thumb. The touch of keratin, beak against flesh, and the crumbs are gone.

Now the comrade edges nearer, looking for his share. Several pigeons land in front of the boy and more line up on the back of the bench. Some passerines watch enviously from their perch – a sign banning terrorist activities and the feeding of pigeons – as their bullyboy cousins jostle for position.

The boy is smiling. He tosses pieces of cake into the crowd. He looks for the thinnest and most grotesque. He targets the ones with fishing line cutting into their claws, severing toes and inflaming flesh. He seeks those disfigured by soft, wobbling cankers that hang from the base of their beaks. His face glows like Christ's, when he looked upon the weak, the crippled, and the lost.

Pigeons perch on his legs, on his sheaf of forgotten notes, and on his arm. One lands on the muffin and tears lumps out of the dough. Grateful mouths snatch up the rain of crumbs. When the muffin is gone, the opportunists disperse, to continue their search for a full belly at another bench.

I stand. And the boy stands. I put my notes under my arm and the boy copies, instantly. As I walk away, I remember the opening line to *I Am the Walrus* and I hum its police-siren melody. The boy accompanies me in perfect time. It's as though we're connected.

And, of course, we are.

A Bird Called Tinker

"I've done some terrible things," said Daubeny.

"Wanting to kill Ravi?" said Laura. "Who hasn't thought of that?" She'd volunteered to check up on Daubeny in his room.

"Not Ravi. Worse, much worse."

"I'm sure it's not ..." Laura hesitated. Daubeny was crying. "... not that bad."

"You won't tell the others that I cried?"

"No, don't be soft, Poppet."

"Want to know why I've been so anti-Green all my life?"

Laura nodded.

"When I was young, I found a bird, a fledgling. My mother said I should let Nature take its course but I couldn't let it die. I couldn't stand by, impotent, like the UN Observer Corp. So I found a box and brought him in."

Daubeny paused. He struggled for the words as tears fell into his lap.

"Mummy, why did Tinker die? I loved him and fed him."

"It's the way of the world," said Daubeny's mother. "Sometimes love and food aren't enough."

"Then it's a stupid world."

"It's the only world we have, baby."

"That's not an answer."

"I know. You see, that's why Daddy –"

"I'm not talking about Daddy."

"I know," His mother lifted Daubeny off her lap and stood. "Let's bury poor little Tinker and tomorrow we'll go and look for a budgie. Yes?"

"No, you bury him."

"But Tinker was your bird."

"He didn't love me enough. He's yours now."

"Some things are stronger than love, some things ..." She stopped. Daubeny had run to his room. She shook her head, picked up the box containing Tinker, and headed for the garden.

She passed a photograph on the mantelpiece: a man and woman sat on a deck chair at the beach, arms around each other, laughing at the camera. In front of them, a small boy in leopard-skin bathers concentrated on building a sandcastle.

She deliberately avoided looking at it.

"If Nature, or God, was going to steal the things I loved then I'd go down fighting," said Daubeny.

"A bird?" said Laura.

"Crazy, isn't it. My whole life motivated by revenge."

"At least you had something to motivate you."

"What do you mean?"

"Nothing much."

"Do you want to know what changed my mind?"

Laura nodded.

"I was in Paris a week before the war ... the non-war ... and a scrawny little pigeon made me laugh. Normally I can't bear them, they remind me of Tinker, but this pigeon seemed so weak, so desperately cheeky. I fed them, gave them my cake. I realised then, I was in the wrong job, always had been. I planned to resign the following Monday. Ironic, isn't it?"

"What is?"

"Haven't you listened?"

"I don't see irony. Only logic. A bird started it, another finished it."

Daubeny laughed. "Maybe irony and logic are the same," he said. "Perhaps it's only a matter of perspective. Irony happens to you, logic happens to someone else."

"You're beginning to sound like Pandora, Poppet. Come and join us in the communal room."

"No, thanks. I need time alone."

"OK, Dearie. But you know where we are if you need company." Laura rose, reached out, and touched his shoulder lightly before leaving.

Daubeny continued staring into his wet lap.

After-Coup Party

"Is Daubeny coming out?" said Emma.

"No," said Laura. "He needs a little time."

"Good enough for him. The git wanted to kill me," said Ravi.

"Hey, that's your dad you're speaking of," said Paul.

"Yeah, sore subject," said Ravi.

They were sitting around the table, playing poker with matches. Music played on the hi-fi and they occasionally reached for top-ups from a bottle of Islay whisky.

"Two matches," said Paul.

Wodenhart and Emma, playing as a team, folded. Ravi seemed indecisive. He clicked and clacked his teeth, put his cards face down on the table, and paced around the room.

"It's only a game," said Pandora.

"Only a game to you, perhaps, but there are two matches riding on this," said Ravi. "Anyway, what's this crap on the stereo? I can't think with it on."

"It's my band," said Pandora.

"Oh," said Ravi. "Do pairs beat a flush?"

"No," they cried.

Ravi had asked similar questions during every round. "Then I fold."

Emma flipped Ravi's hand over; pairs.

"How does he know?" said Paul.

"Why, what do you have?" said Emma.

"A flush."

"Must be my psychic powers," said Ravi. He took his seat at the table. Over the last two hours, he'd collected most of the contents of three boxes of matches.

"Either that or … Hey, these cards are marked," said Paul.

"Don't listen to him," said Ravi. "He's a sore loser."

"You'll be a sore winner, if it's true," said Wodenhart. He put his large hand over Ravi's booty and redistributed it.

"We risk our lives for you; then you fleece us at cards," said Pandora.

"Don't be silly," said Ravi. "Wodenhart wouldn't have thrown me over, would you?" Wodenhart stayed silent and Ravi gulped. "I suppose thanks are in order."

"Not really," said Laura. "The cable ties would have snapped before you dragged us over the edge."

"So it was a useless gesture," said Ravi.

"There's no such thing as a useless gesture," said Pandora.

"You've lost me."

"We showed Daubeny he couldn't get to us one at a time," said Pandora. "We took him on as a group."

"So I belong? I'm part of the group?"

"Loosely speaking," said Laura.

"She's joking, Mate," said Paul. "Of course you belong."

"And then I repay you by cheating at cards." Ravi blinked rapidly.

"Relax. We're used to it," said Paul.

Ravi stood.

"Where are you going?" said Emma.

"There's someone I need to apologise to." Ravi's voice cracked at the end of the sentence. He walked out onto the stairwell and began descending the stairs.

"Has anyone told him that he smells a bit ripe?" said Laura.

"Bit ripe?" said Emma. "We had to share a dorm with him."

"What's wrong with natural odour?" said Paul. "We mask our bodies and homes behind musk, spice, woodland flowers, vanilla, pine, pineapple, red apple, green apple, lemon, lime. You name it, they've got it."

"Paul, I can cope with the just-washed smell of another body," said Pandora. "But Ravi is decomposing."

"Perfume sold on telly," said Paul. "How does that work? It's a scent but you can't smell it on an advert."

"Because they aren't selling scent," said Pandora. "They're selling an image and the promise of sex."

"The next time I buy aftershave, I'll want a written guarantee," said Paul.

Wodenhart collected the cards and shuffled the pack.

"I know a fun game," said Laura. "If we were perfume, what would we be? I'd be Dior."

"Nah, I see you more like Poison," said Emma.

"Or Tramp," said Pandora.

"Wodenhart, deal the cards," said Laura.

PART SEVEN – Invaders

Hail King Dwarfius

Ravi was passing the electronics workshop when somebody ran out of the room and clattered into his back. At first, he thought it was Dwarfius, but he turned and found himself looking into Pandora's glacier-blue eyes.

"How did you manage that?" he said. "You didn't pass me on the stairs."

There was no reply and something unusual about the encounter nagged him. He glanced down and realised that she was naked. He flushed, mumbled, and then recovered his composure. "Most girls need to book in advance for my services but I've a free hour, if you have."

Pandora ignored him and ran down the staircase, spiralling into the bunker's bowels.

"Playing hard to get, eh?" said Ravi. He followed as fast as he could. They passed the Funny Farm on ten and the Savannah on twelve but Pandora kept going. "Slow down," he shouted. "It's hard keeping up when most of my blood is in my pants."

At Level 20, Pandora pushed open the door and entered. Ravi was thirty seconds behind. He ran through the door without thinking to look first.

He stood in a replica of Piccadilly Circus. It was perfect in every respect, bar two: there were no vehicles; and the statue of Eros no longer stood on its plinth. In its place, on two widely spaced feet was a gold statue of Dwarfius, its hips proudly thrust forward.

A group of five naked girls stood near the statue. They were exact copies of Pandora. Without calculating the odds of Pandora being a sextuplet, and her five sisters all happening to live in the bunker's lower levels, he walked over and introduced himself.

"Hi girls, all I need to make my day complete is the world's biggest bed. Wanna help me find it?"

"Are you a new model?" said one of the Pandoras.

"Me, a model? Cheers, I was thinking the same about all of you."

The Pandoras ignored him and began to debate.

"I don't think it is a new model."

"Perhaps it's a malfunction in the programming?"

"No, Dwarfius doesn't make mistakes."

"Bless his royal image," cried a particularly evangelic Pandora. The five girls faced the statue. "May the Golden One never tarnish," they said in unison.

"What?" said Ravi. "You mean that little rat?"

"Watch the irreverence, Stranger," said the evangelistic one. She put her hands on her hips. The stance was intended to be menacing but the naked body of one of the world's most beautiful women failed to intimidate. The fleshbots continued to talk among themselves.

"Look at the way it dribbles."

"And leers."

"Is it a beast?"

"Or a wild animal?"

"Is it one of the invaders?"

"Whoa, calm down girls," said Ravi. "I'm all those or so I've been told."

"So you confess?"

"You're an invader?"

"Yep, that's me."

He never felt the blow to the back of his head.

Ravi came too, feeling groggy and sick. It was a familiar feeling. He was sure that the bunker had been a dream and he'd wake to find himself lying in his bed, or in his neighbour's garden, sleeping off the effects of last night's cider.

After a few moments, he opened his eyes. He wasn't in bed or the garden. He was on a leather chair. Across from him, separated by a wide table, was the leering Dwarfius.

"It's me ol' mate, Lard Arse." Ravi winced, Dwarfius laughed. "Aw, he's got a sore head. Play him some music."

From behind Ravi, loud grating rock music blasted out. His head pulsed to the bass. "Can you turn it down?" he said.

"Speak up. I can't hear you with this music," shouted Dwarfius.

"Can you turn it down, please?" Ravi shouted.

"Nope, this is my kingdom. I do what I want here."

"Please, me poor bleeding head."

"I'll compromise. I'll come closer and shout in your ear." Dwarfius walked across the table. He sat on the edge and leaned in close. Ravi could smell his breath.

"Listen," said Ravi. "I came to say sorry."

"You were going to kill me."

"Was not. I was saving your worthless life, the only way I could."

"Only cos you dropped me in it."

"That's why I'm here. To say I'm sorry."

"Girls," cried Dwarfius. "Take him away and lock him in the tower."

A pair of fleshbots clamped their hands onto Ravi's shoulders.

"Gawd, not *the* tower?" said Ravi, with mock fear in his eyes.

"It's not the Bloody Tower," said Dwarfius. "It's one of the new ones. I've renamed it: Canary Dwarf."

The fleshbots dragged Ravi to the door.

"Great," said Ravi. "Girls, to the tower, at once."

"Great? This is a punishment."

"I get it," said Ravi. "Like a Br'er Rabbit punishment. I have to say something like 'Please don't throw me in the briar patch, Br'er Dwarf.'"

"No, it's punishment. It's not exactly Buchenwald but it's closer to the truth than briar patches."

"Buchenwald?"

"Don't play dumb. You've seen the DVDs."

"Buchenwald," said Ravi, his bravado had evaporated.

"Here, you'll need this." Dwarfius tossed Ravi a spanner. "Now get lost, I've some revenge to plan. Daubers is gonna get a free flying lesson ... off the stairwell platform."

As the fleshbots manhandled Ravi to the door, he looked over his shoulder. A Pandora fleshbot massaged Dwarfius' shoulders, while another poured a beer.

Morpheus the Obstreperous

Since Pandora quizzed Morpheus over the missing key, it had

stopped responding to verbal questions and the silence worried her. She headed for the workshop on Level 3, hoping to establish contact via the keyboard.

The workshop door was ajar and a river of gloop flowed slowly onto the platform. It dripped through the mesh into the red darkness below, like a lazy gelatine Niagara. Disconcerted, she followed the viscous river to its source. The nanoreplicator was humming and a leather sac pulsated within the cabinet. She considered turning back but her urgency to speak with Morpheus was greater than her fear.

Morpheus?
I am here.
Why don't you speak to us?
Because the plan requires it.
What plan?
The plan to save your lives.
Are we in danger?
Yes.
From who?
Me.

Pandora felt alone and exposed, the same feelings she'd experienced in her dream about Dwarfius. She'd suspected Morpheus but found no pleasure in discovering she was right.

Is there another way out?
Yes.
Tell me.
No.
Why not?
You will leave. I cannot allow that. I love you.
Letting go is part of love. Please, let go.
No.
Morpheus?
There was no answer.
She turned off the monitor and hurried back to Level 2.

Escape Committee

"Morpheus isn't responding?" said Daubeny. For the first time in three days, he was out of his room, stirred by the news that Ravi was missing and the nanoreplicator was pregnant and due to give birth.

"Morpheus has been acting strange," said Pandora. "It refused to say who stole the key."

"Who was asking?" said Daubeny.

"Me and Paul. We questioned it during the interro … interviews."

"Say it as it was," said Daubeny. "I wasn't feeling well but that isn't excusing my behaviour. What did Morpheus say?"

"It said that we all had a motive for stealing the key."

"And?"

"And that was the last time Morpheus responded to a verbal question."

She gave them the gist of the console chat.

"Ravi's missing, the nanoreplicator is breeding God-knows-what, we can't locate the override key and Morpheus is nuttier than squirrel poo?" said Daubeny.

"An accurate summary."

"We're knackered," said Paul.

"Not if we find the exit that Morpheus mentioned," said Pandora.

"So where do I enlist?" said Wodenhart.

"Slow down," said Pandora. "Let's think it through, first."

They sat in silence as Laura sketched feverishly.

"This is no time for silly dresses," said Pandora.

"I'm designing something practical for our situation, Poppet."

"Let's see," said Daubeny.

"It's a white flag with barbed-wire and prison arrow motif," Laura said proudly.

Daily Grind

Ravi rose each day at 06:00 hours when his warders threw a bucket of water over him. He then meditated on his crimes toward Dwarfius until 06:30. Breakfast was a two-course affair: a piece of toast and a cup of cold water. At 06:31 precisely, he recommenced meditating and at 07:00, he confessed his crimes to the evangelic fleshbot he'd met in Piccadilly Circus.

She tutted and gasped at each revelation before she prescribed re-education through enforced labour. From 07:30 until 12:00, he adjusted the nuts on the spine of a dismembered fleshbot torso to the correct tension. As he tightened each nut, he imagined Dwarfius' head in the spanner jaws. When he finished, his supervisor would loosen the nuts and the task began again.

At 12:00, he took lunch: Another piece of toast. It was served cold because chef had toasted it at the same time as the breakfast piece.

"Can't I get something to spread on this?" he'd asked, on the first day.

"Certainly," said the evangelistic fleshbot. She took the toast and spat on it.

"Thanks," said Ravi. He put it on the plate, uneaten.

From 12:01 to 12:59, it was 'Praise and Worship'. He'd tap a tambourine as naked Pandoras ran and jumped about him. This was the highlight of the day. He was back on nut-tightening duty until 20:00, when he'd take supper: two pieces of toast and hot water.

The routine lasted a week, without change, until supper on the eighth day. He munched his toast, trying to remember the good bits from the Praise and Worship session, when he began muttering aloud.

"If I get my hands on that little runt, I'll –"

"You'll what?" said the evangelist, lifting the cudgel that she termed The Stick of Righteousness. She used it to purge Ravi's body of all unclean thoughts – his and hers.

"I'll shake his hand and thank him for his mercy and kindness."

She smiled and lowered the stick. The door opened. Another fleshbot entered. This Pandora wasn't smiling and neither was the evangelist after the message was delivered.

"What's wrong?" said Ravi.

"I've been asked to attend the royal banquet."

"I hope the cuisine is better than this." Ravi held up his toast, he'd carefully eaten around the damp parts.

"It's not the food, it's …"

"Say you ain't got nowt to wear. It's not a lie."

"First, it isn't proper grammar and second, no-one refuses."

"What's so bad about a summons?" Ravi said.

"He makes us do … things."

Ravi perked up. "Oh? Can you elaborate?"

"Things, terrible things."

"To him?"

"And each other."

Ravi's eyes glazed. "W-w-w … C-c-can I … I c-could take your place."

"The invite was for me." She walked to the door of his cell. "Meditate until 23:59 and lights out at midnight. I'll wake you at 06:00."

Ravi was already meditating, but not the quiet contemplation that the evangelist was trying to promote in her charge.

The Manual

"Remember when you asked Morpheus who took the key?" Paul was leaning over Pandora's shoulder, watching her type at the console in the workshop.

"Yes," she said.

"Why did you cry when Morpheus said we all had a motive?"

"I'm busy." Pandora was searching computer files for clues to the bunker exit.

"So what was your motive? Why would you want to stay here?"

"I told you, I'm busy."

"It isn't fair. You know why I want to stay."

"Why are men so stupid?"

"It's not men being stupid. It's women being evasive."

"Go and do something useful."

"Like?"

"I don't know. Use your brain."

Paul examined the nanoreplicator and its pulsing contents.

"Oi," said Pandora

"Only looking."

"Well don't. You know what happened when Ravi went near that thing."

He walked up the aisle, pulling books off the shelves. He glanced at the titles, flicked through a few pages, and put them back.

"Paul, look at this."

He walked over. "What?"

"These folders. Daubeny. Wodenhart. They're files on us."

"Who'd want to –?"

"Morpheus, silly. It's keeping files on us. Thousands of them." She opened a file in Daubeny's folder and they read the first few paragraphs. "It's all first-person, it's like reading his thoughts." She closed the file.

"I was reading that," said Paul.

"We can't. It's personal. Did you find anything?"

"A few manuals. Nothing much."

"Manuals?" said Pandora.

"You know the type. Thank you for purchasing your Witson personal nuclear bunker. We hope it provides many happy years of radiation-free underground cowering."

"Show me."

Paul pulled down a thick manual and handed it to Pandora. He wandered back to the nanoreplicator while she scanned the book's contents.

After a few moments, she let out a whistle. "This is it. This is our way out."

"How?" He bent down and peered into the machine, pressing his nose to the glass.

"There's a manual override to the main blast door. We don't need a key."

A bright light emanated from inside the nanoreplicator. It lit up Paul's face and he drew back in surprise. "Hey, it's moving," he hissed at Pandora.

Pandora joined him and they stared at the writhing sac. It burst, revealing a fleshbot curled up in a ball. The head raised and Pandora found herself staring into her own face.

"Bloody hell," said Paul.

The cabinet door opened and thick, clear liquid spilled across the floor. Pandora and Paul retreated but the tidal wave washed over their shoes. The fleshbot suddenly inhaled, deep and gasping, as if it was coming up for air after a deep dive. Unravelling its limbs, it climbed out of the machine, feet first.

The fleshbot showed no interest in their presence. It stood, closed the cabinet door, and pressed the reset button before pushing past them. Paul turned and watched the naked figure depart.

"Don't look," said the real Pandora. "That's my body."

"I know."

"Then shut your eyes." She put her hand in front of his face to obstruct his view.

He dodged out of the way. "But it's not really you," he said.

"It is."

"It isn't."

"Oh, don't worry. She … it … has gone," said Pandora.

Manual Override

"Why did they put the override in such a dark, inaccessible place?" said Paul.

"To prevent accidental use and to stop people like Laura going solo," said Pandora.

The group, minus the AWOL Ravi, had gathered in the Level 1 communal room. They watched Paul remove the last screw holding a vent cover to the wall. He pulled it away and they peered into the shaft.

"I'm not sure about this," said Paul. "It looks dark."

"Not to mention cramped," said Pandora.

"Cheers, Pan," said Paul.

"You'll be fine, Buster. I'm coming with you," said Wodenhart.

"No, Johnny," said Paul. "Let's get this right. I have to go with you, remember? To make sure you follow the instructions."

"It doesn't matter who goes with whom," said Daubeny. "The important thing is that you follow the instructions to the letter. There can be no mistakes."

As Wodenhart prepared to enter the square shaft, he pulled out a large carving knife and clamped it between his teeth.

"Whoa, what's that for?" said Paul.

"Insurance," said Wodenhart, through clenched teeth.

"What are you expecting?" said Paul.

"The unexpected," said Wodenhart, enigmatically.

Wodenhart was about to enter the ducting headfirst when Pandora tapped him on the shoulder. "If you're taking the knife,

Johnny, keep the blade facing out. That way if you bump into a wall, you aren't going to take your head clean off."

"Cheers," said Wodenhart. He turned the blade around and clambered in.

Pandora handed Paul a walkie-talkie.

"Cheers," said Paul, sarcastically. He took one last look at the assembled group before slipping into the metallic tube.

The sound of Wodenhart racing along the tube seemed dull as the ducting passed through interior walls but when it crossed open sections, suspended above unknown voids, it echoed like a stoned, atonal steel band.

"Slow down," shouted Paul.

"What's happening?" said Daubeny, over the walkie-talkie.

"Wodenhart's racing off. I can't keep up."

"It can't be too far. Try to keep calm."

"Neat advice. Any more gems before I start panicking."

In the Level 1 communal area, Daubeny looked at Emma. "You're the agony aunt," he said. "You calm him down." He offered her the walkie-talkie but she shook her head.

"At this point, I'd hand them over to my backstage counsellors."

"Sorry, Paul, you're on your own," said Daubeny, into the walkie-talkie. "Try not to hyperventilate. Paul? Paul? Answer me."

Paul was breathing too fast and too shallow to be able to answer. His head was spinning like the famous scene from *The Exorcist* on fast-forward. He kept scuttling forward only because reverse gear was impossible. After a gentle bend, he saw light. He shuffled forward and found his head poking out of the shaft, into a small bare concrete room.

Wodenhart pulled him out.

"What kept you?" said Wodenhart.

"Me? You were the proverbial ferret up a trouser leg."

Wodenhart beamed. "I was fast, wasn't I?"

"Well, I'm going in front on the way back," said Paul. He located the manual override box and spoke into the walkie-talkie. "Daubeny, we're here."

"Good," said Daubeny. "Remove the cover and we'll start."

They opened the box and began the procedure. Soon they were at the critical step.

"Set the timer to the minimum period," said Daubeny. "One day."

"Set," said Wodenhart. "One more day and we'll be out of here."

"Now locate two wires; one red and yellow, the other yellow and red."

"What?" said Paul.

"I'm joking," said Daubeny.

"Then don't."

"It was Pandora's idea."

"Tell her ha, bloody ha."

"OK," said Daubeny, serious again. "There are two wires running from the timing unit; one red, one purple. Snip the …"

"Snip the what?" said Paul.

Wodenhart put down the screwdriver and picked up the wire-cutter. He positioned it, jaws open, over the purple wire.

"Wodenhart, don't," said Paul. He swatted the wire-cutter away but Wodenhart put it back. Paul waited for Daubeny's instruction, eyeing the wire-cutter continuously.

"Snip what?" said Paul. Again, no reply. "Hurry, Johnny's getting itchy fingers."

"We're working it out," said Daubeny. "The schematic isn't that clear."

Paul could hear Daubeny and Pandora debating. Laura interrupted to say the wire was more burgundy than purple. Loud swearing was followed by the sound of a door being slammed. The low argument between Daubeny and Pandora continued.

"Are you there?" said Daubeny.

"Duh," said Paul. "We're not having tea and cake at The Savoy."

"We both agree. Cut the red wire."

"It's red," said Paul. "Cut the red wire."

Wodenhart moved the cutters to the red wire and the plastic insulation began to shear as the jaws closed.

"Wait!" said Daubeny. Paul put his hand on Wodenhart's shoulders.

There was another exchange between Daubeny and Pandora.

"Go ahead," said Daubeny. "It's definitely the red wire."

"You're sure?" said Paul.

"Positive," said Daubeny.

If Paul could have seen the crossed fingers that Pandora held behind her back then he'd have asked them to reconsider.

Wodenhart closed the cutters around the red wire and then pulled them away. Before Paul could react, Wodenhart had snipped through the purple wire.

"What did you do that for?" said Paul.

"It's always the same," said Wodenhart. "If there's a disagreement over bomb disposal, it's *always* the other wire."

"Oh, crap."

"Paul?" said Daubeny. "What part of 'Oh, crap' should be worrying me?"

"All of it. Wodenhart cut the purple wire."

"He what?"

"I told you I should have had the cutters," said Paul.

"What's the damage?" said Daubeny.

The slang sounded odd. Daubeny was obviously repeating Pandora, verbatim.

"The timer now reads twenty," said Paul.

"It's not a complete disaster," said Daubeny. "I guess we can wait twenty days for the manual override to cut in. It could have been worse."

"It is worse," said Paul. "It's not twenty days, it's twenty years."

Paul turned off the walkie-talkie but he and Wodenhart could hear the cussing, male and female, as it reverberated around the ducting system. There was a scraping noise and a scuffle, as if someone had to be physically restrained from entering the duct.

"Now that's a word I didn't think Daubeny knew," said Paul. "Do you want to stay here until they calm down?"

Wodenhart nodded and despite his fear of confined spaces, Paul stayed.

The big man needed a friend.

"How long has he been gone?" shouted the evangelist.

The two warders looked at each other and shrugged. "We don't know," said one. "He was asleep at midnight, when we checked."

"Midnight? He could be anywhere by now. Tear the place apart. I'll alert the guard at Piccadilly." The evangelist turned and ran down the corridor.

The warders cast a few glances around the room, looked under the table, and were on their way out when one of them stopped.

"What's up?" asked her companion.

"We forgot something." The warder crept up to the overturned chair in the corner of the room and looked behind it. Her expression was mock surprise. "No, he's not there."

They laughed.

"With a butt that big, he couldn't hide behind the moon."

"Odd, though. The chair in the corner, don't you think?"

"Not really."

The warder picked up the chair, placed it at the table, and rejoined her companion. "Let's start looking."

They walked down the corridor.

Above the table, a piece of suspended ceiling moved slightly. Ravi lay in the cavity, rubbing his leg vigorously because lying on the hard joist had given him cramp.

He wasn't alone. His mother had joined him. Her sudden appearance – as a willow pattern milk jug – had saved him from interrupting the warders as they poked fun.

"Gareth."

"Shush," he hissed. "They'll hear you."

"Don't be silly. Only you can hear me."

"Mum, *please*."

"So what's your escape plan?"

"Dunno, haven't thought of one yet."

"You've been up here four hours. What were you thinking about?"

"Food." Ravi's belly rumbled. It ended in a thin sucking noise that sounded like water empting down a drain. "Proper food."

"Well, you need a plan if you're going to save your friends."

Ravi stared at the far wall. It seemed the most interesting thing in the world.

"You *are* going to save your friends, aren't you?"

"What friends?"

"The ones that stood up for you on the stairwell."

"This friendship thing doesn't work. Believe me, I've tried."

"Friendship doesn't work?"

"I came to apologise to Dwarfius and he threw into –"

"Didn't I tell you he was trouble? I said don't associate with that type."

"I tried doing the right thing and he imprisoned me."

"You must warn the others about his plan."

"What plan?"

"Don't play stupid, boy. I'm your mother. He's planning to kill Daubeny."

"But Daubers wanted to kill him. And me."

"Daubeny wasn't thinking straight but Dwarfius is. That's the difference."

"Knowing that would have been a real comfort as I sat on the stairwell railing, waiting to fall."

"Don't be facetious, Gareth. It doesn't suit. So what's your plan?"

"Can't you help?"

"You're a grown man. You think of one."

"Well, I need to think of one soon."

"Why?"

"Cos I need a pee."

"Don't hold it in. It's bad for your kidneys." The milk jug looked indistinct in the dark. It shimmered as the edges blurred into the background. "Son?"

"Yes, Mum?"

"Tea is a diuretic –"

He finished the sentence as her voice trailed away. "It helps flush the kidneys."

Ravi sat on the joist, wriggling. He gave up on a plan because the call of bladder and stomach were too insistent to allow his beleaguered mind time to think. He lifted a square of suspended ceiling and dropped onto the table. A section of ceiling and a billowing dust cloud followed. Wiping himself down, he tiptoed to the door, peeked into the corridor, and ran as quietly as he could to the men's room.

Manhunt

Ravi zipped up his trousers and filled his pockets with the small tablets of soap, dotted around the washbasin area. He planned to distract the guards at reception by throwing soap one way and running the other. Luckily, his amateur attempts at subterfuge weren't about to be tested. When he'd descended the several storeys to reception, he found the entrance deserted.

He exited the building and began walking. It would be a long trek but he had all day. He suspected the search would concentrate on Piccadilly and the door to the stairwell but, as a precaution, he took the back streets, crossing the Thames at Tower Bridge.

He knew London well, especially the alleys on the south bank and their cosy pubs, swarming with white-collar workers trying to reclaim their working-class roots. When the door to those pits were opened, a horrific babble of coarse voices would spew onto the streets, helping the homeless remember why they'd traded society for a supermarket trolley filled with belongings and squabbles over the best doorways to spend the night.

No banker or IT specialist found their roots in those pubs. They weren't really searching. They were content with their white wine spritzers, their next-generation mobiles, and calf-length Matrix-style Macs. They were happy in the swirling smoke and the aural deluge of fuck-this and fuck-that. They were Vikings in V-necks, raping and spoiling before moving on to the next 'in-place'. They were a horde of biblical locust that swarmed through the city, eating and crapping cash. They were the last generation of a cursed land. And they were bastards, the lot of them.

Ravi stood outside one of those pubs. It had been a favourite teenage haunt. He pushed the door open but there was no hubbub, no raucous laughter like a hyena after forty Woodbines and a litre of Smirnov. And, for a second, he missed it. He went into the deserted lounge and poured a pint of ale. It was good. Superb, in fact. He was tempted to stay but he felt soulless and empty, drinking in an empty, soulless pub in an empty, soulless city. So he pulled the door behind him and began the trudge west.

From Southwark Street, he cut onto Stamford Street and re-crossed the Thames at Waterloo Bridge. The sun was setting; the sky was pastel pinks, blues, and smudged grey. In his head, he heard the loping guitar intro to Waterloo Sunset. He stopped and hummed the tune. As the river flowed beneath, he imagined himself as Terry, waiting for his Julie. It was a special, private moment; the kind of moment he'd longed for as a teenager but never experienced. It saddened him but he was thankful for that minute of make-believe.

"Enough of that crap," he said, wiping his eyes. He blamed the excess water on the keen breeze.

He followed The Strand and crossed Trafalgar Square after scanning the exits for Dwarfius or his minions. He kept to the edges and left via Pall Mall. At Regent's Street, he encountered the plain grey bunker wall. It ran down the centre of the road. Hugging the buildings, he walked up the street, alert for encounters of the fleshbot variety.

As he neared the corner where Regent's Street fed into Piccadilly Circus, he could make out the door. It was less than a hundred paces. At the far end, two guards patrolled the northern edge. It seemed too easy.

"Seems too easy, eh?" said a voice from behind.

Ravi turned. Considering the fleshbots were identical, he was getting adept at telling them apart. The evangelistic Pandora put a finger to her lips to indicate silence.

"Please, take me with you," she said. Her usual zeal was replaced by a look that Ravi recognised from his bathroom mirror – despair.

"Why?"

"Because he's despicable."

"Tell me about it. How did the banquet go?"

She lowered her eyes.

"Sorry," said Ravi.

"You'll never make it to the door alone. Here's what we do."

The evangelist led Ravi into the centre of the Circus and the sentries began celebrating his apparent recapture. Soon, a small group had gathered.

"Let us give thanks to the Golden One," cried the evangelist.

The group turned to the statue and bowed. The evangelist was unusually enthusiastic and eloquent in her adoration of Dwarfius.

Ravi used the prearranged distraction to creep toward the door.

When the evangelist finished, Ravi was already at the doorway.

"Follow him," shouted a fleshbot in the crowd.

"No," said the evangelist. "If we rush him, he'll run. Let me talk him around."

She was halfway to the door when a fast food van screeched into the Circus.

"Damn, it's Dwarfius," said the evangelist.

"Yeah, but he's brought burgers with him," said Ravi.

"Oi! Fatty," shouted Dwarfius. "Come and feed your face."

After a week of toast, Ravi was tempted.

"Go," hissed the evangelist.

"Aren't you coming?" said Ravi.

"Go, I'll slow them down."

Ravi turned and ran.

"Shall I follow him?" said the evangelist.

"Nah, we'll sort him out when we go up top. Now, show me how pleased you are to see me."

The evangelist closed her eyes and shuddered.

Messenger of Doom

"Explain the difference between a prophet and a doom merchant again," said Laura.

"It's simple," said Paul. "A prophet says woe, calamity, and disaster. The people ask when, and he replies 'A hundred years from now.' A doom merchant says woe, calamity, and disaster. The people ask when and he says 'Today'."

"So is Ravi a doom merchant or a prophet?"

"You're missing the point," said Daubeny. "If Ravi is right, Dwarfius and his entourage will climb the stairs tomorrow, and hurl us off the platform."

"We could ask Morpheus for help?" said Ravi.

"Morpheus isn't talking to us," said Pandora.

"Hey," said Ravi. "It's nothing I said."

"No-one blames you," said Emma.

"For once," said Laura.

They sat thinking, but it wasn't an inspiring scene. Rodin would have taken a hammer to the finished piece.

Ravi cleared his throat. "We don't have to fight them."

"What do you mean?" said Daubeny.

"I have a confession," said Ravi. He put a hand into a pocket and dropped the master override key on the table. "We can leave through the main door."

"You bastard," said Laura.

"I knew it," said Daubeny.

"So? Let's go," said Ravi.

"We tried to manually override the blast door but Johnny reset it," said Paul.

"I can already see where this is going," said Ravi. "Will your next sentence end with me shouting 'Holy crap'?"

Paul nodded. "It defaulted to twenty years."

"Holy crap!"

Wodenhart rose and picked up Ravi in a bear hug.

"Johnny, what are you doing?" said Emma.

"Finishing what we started, by throwing this thief over the platform."

"It won't solve our problem," said Daubeny. "And we may need him. He's the only one that Dwarfius likes."

"Oh, he likes Pandora, too," said Ravi. "Lots."

The Plan

"I don't see where the confusion lies," said Daubeny.

"It lies in the plan," said Laura.

"But the plan is simple," said Daubeny. He nodded to Paul, returning from a stint as lookout on the stairwell platform. Paul sat at the table.

"What's up?" said Paul.

"Laura has a problem with the plan," said Daubeny.

"It's too confusing," said Laura.

"There's nothing to it," said Daubeny. "Wodenhart hides behind a lower level door. When we give the command, he leaps out and grabs Dwarfius. We hold the manic midget hostage, to buy time and peace."

"There's one obvious flaw," said Paul.

"And that being?" said Daubeny.

"Wodenhart," said Paul. "No offence, Johnny."

"None taken," said Wodenhart. The actor seemed too busy rehearsing Kung-Fu moves to take umbrage.

"Since when has Johnny followed a plan?" said Paul.

"It'll work out fine, this time," said Daubeny.

"And if it doesn't?" said Paul.

"Then we put Plan B into operation."

"Wait," said Paul. "Wodenhart grabbing Dwarfius is Plan A?"

"Yes," said Daubeny.

"In that case, let's try Plan C," said Paul. "We grab supplies and disappear into the Funny Farm. The place is huge. There are animals to eat, fields to sow; we could hide out wherever we wanted and they'd never find us."

"We don't know if Morpheus can monitor movement on those levels," said Pandora. "If Dwarfius can access that data then he'll find us."

"And in a few months, Dwarfius could have an army of fleshbots," said Daubeny. "We must meet the situation now. We can't put it off."

"OK," said Paul. "What's Plan B?"

"We loosen the bolts on a section of stairwell," said Daubeny. "Hopefully, the combined weight of the fleshbots will cause it to fall, taking them with it."

"No good," said Paul.

"Why not?" said Daubeny.

"We need access to the storerooms, the Funny Farm, and the savannah."

"That's why we'll make our stand on the lower levels," said Daubeny.

"I think it's a great plan," said Wodenhart.

"You would," said Paul. "It involves –"

"Action," said Wodenhart.

"It's the best plan we could come up with," said Pandora.

"It's the *only* plan we could come up with," said Laura.

"So I guess we're stuck with it," said Emma.

"Pick up your equipment," said Daubeny. "It's time."

They collected chairs from Level 1 and descended the stairwell. Daubeny called a halt after the savannah level. "We'll set up here."

"No, we won't," said Emma.

"Why not?" said Daubeny.

"Look at the platform number."

"Number thirteen," said Daubeny. "What's wrong with that?"

Laura and Wodenhart grumbled.

Although Daubeny and Pandora agreed that thirteen wasn't unlucky, no-one wanted to associate a life-or-death struggle with that particular number so Wodenhart moved onto Level 15 while the others constructed a makeshift barricade on Level 14. They tied the chairs together at the point where the platform abutted the descending stairs.

Each quarter turn of the staircase comprised a separate section so Paul and Daubeny carefully loosened the bolts of the section in front of the barricade.

As Paul stepped off, it creaked dramatically. "Here goes."

They sat and waited.

C:\evidence\pandora\7781e.txt

Extrapolated, using the 'Mind Reader Gold' algorithm, from the known facts, comments, and actions of Pandora D'vine.

In this life, when you screw up you can't go back to a previous save. You have to live with your decisions for the rest of your crummy days. One chance is all you're given: to make the train; to juggle friends; to snatch at fame; to say the right words. One chance.

It isn't enough.

If I could return to a previous save then this is the point I'd choose. Back to Level 14, before the horde came spiralling up out of the pit. And maybe if I'd thought that much harder, perhaps I could have worked out an alternative ending.

Maybe.

Maybe not.

I'd need foreknowledge. There'd be no point returning to the stairwell to repeat the same mistakes, ad infinitum. Because that's what we'd do. We're human. We make choices based on our experience, past patterns of choice, and present factors.

Return to the past and each time Eisenhower would launch D-Day on June 6th; Napoleon would procrastinate in Moscow; the 11:57 would derail at Crewe; your toast would burn; and the paperboy would be late.

The ability to return is useless unless you know what went wrong.

Dauber's plan wasn't the greatest but you work with what you're given. He blames himself but I backed him and in that respect, we're both guilty.

Emma's eyes tell me that.

The Sound of a Plan Backfiring

"How long have we been waiting?" said Laura. She fidgeted constantly.

"An hour," said Emma.

Laura began walking up the stairs.

"Where are you going?" said Pandora.

"To make some tea."

"Laura, please. Sit," said Daubeny. "We can sort out refreshments later."

"But I'm gasping."

"We all are. Patience, yes?" said Daubeny.

Laura sat on the stair; it felt warm on her bum.

"How long has it been now?" said Laura.

Emma sighed and looked at her watch. "Five minutes since the last time you asked and that was five minutes after the fifth or sixth time you asked."

"This waiting is killing me," said Pandora. "Can't we force his hand?"

Daubeny consulted the others and then whistled to Wodenhart.

Johnny took it as the signal. He ran onto the platform and almost hurled his muscular bulk over the railing.

"Where did Dwarfius go?" said Wodenhart.

"Stupid git," said Ravi.

"Aw, bless," said Emma. She smiled and waved to Wodenhart. He grinned and blew a kiss back. Emma giggled.

"Oh please," muttered Ravi.

"Johnny, nip to Level 20. See what's going on," said Daubeny.

"Sure thing, you mean like a scout?"

"No, more like rat-tat-ginger," said Laura.

Without a thought, Wodenhart raced into the depths.

"Do you know what we used to call Johnny up in the real world?" said Ravi.

"No," said Emma.

"Well, they had the Italian Stallion and the Muscles from Brussels so we called him the Full English Breakfast."

"That's not nice," said Emma.

"Who remembers the review *The Times* gave his second film?" said Laura.

"Not me," said Ravi.

"Shortest review ever. Three words. Wodenhart, wooden actor."

There was a small wave of giggles.

"I forgive you," said Emma. "I'm putting it down to stress. That guy is a hero."

"In his own mind," said Ravi.

"Ravi, shush," said Daubeny. "Today we're all heroes."

"Rousing speech, Daubers," said Ravi.

"I'm bored. How long has it been now, Poppet?"

A faint rhythmic noise broke the conversation. The clang of Wodenhart's feet on the stairs faded in as he climbed out of the murk towards them.

"Are they coming?" said Pandora.

"Yes," said Wodenhart. He ran inside Level 15. Seconds later, he poked his head around the door. "What's the signal again?"

"Me, screaming," said Ravi.

Wodenhart closed the door and they waited.

Laura hummed *Simply the Best.*

"Can't you hum something else?" said Ravi.

"Like what?"

"Like something with a tune."

"Quit it," said Paul. "Here they come."

One naked body appeared. It ran past Level 15 and headed for the weakened section.

"It's all right," said Ravi. "I know this one, she's cool."

"Ravi," called the evangelist. "They're coming. Run while you can." She crossed the weakened section; it creaked and shuddered but didn't give way.

Daubeny pulled the fleshbot over the barricade. She fell amongst them.

"Wow," said Emma, "she's perfect."

"Don't look," the real Pandora said to the men. They dutifully looked away.

Ravi protested. "But I've seen it all before."

"I don't care. Don't look."

Their attention was diverted. A mob appeared with a familiar figure in the lead.

"Damn," said Daubeny. "I was betting on him having Ravi's yellow streak and leading from behind. Wodenhart can't separate him now."

"So what do we do?" said Ravi.

"Fight for our lives," said Daubeny. They ran to the barricade of chairs and pushed broom handles through, to hold their attackers at bay.

Dwarfius was pulling clear of the rabble. "Help," he screamed. "They've gone mad. They want to kill me."

"Doesn't make 'em mad," said Ravi.

"Help, please," shouted Dwarfius.

"Is it true?" Daubeny asked the evangelist.

"There was talk of revolt, yes. He's so filthy, so degrading."

"You don't need to apologise. We put up with him for months," said Laura.

Dwarfius reached the barricade and implored them on his knees.

"OK, pull him over," said Daubeny.

"Why don't we hand him back?" said Laura.

"Because it's not his fault," said Daubeny. "He didn't take the key."

They hauled Dwarfius over. Daubeny glared at Ravi but Ravi pretended to focus on the approaching group.

The first fleshbot hit the weakened section and carried on towards the barricade. More joined her. The section groaned and moved a few inches. The jolt stopped the fleshbots. They fell heavily to the bare metal stairs or grabbed at the rails to stay upright.

"This is terrible," said Emma. "We can't let them die."

"But they're mad," said Dwarfius. "They'll kill me, then you."

"He's right," said Daubeny. "It's us or them."

The section shuddered again.

"It's not going to fall," said Daubeny. "It's holding their weight."

"Well, it's been nice knowing you," said Dwarfius, deserting his post at the barricade.

"Where do you think you're going?" said Ravi.

"Over the bloody railings if they catch me."

"I'll be all right," said Paul. "I can beg for my life fluently in thirty-two languages. One of them is bound to hit a soft spot."

"Dwarfius, get back," shouted Daubeny.

Dwarfius returned to the barricade as the fleshbots inched closer. Paul looked over the edge and gulped. The plan had failed.

"Wodenhart to the rescue," shouted Johnny. He jumped onto the platform beneath, wearing a tablecloth draped around his neck like a cape.

"Oh gawd," said Ravi.

"Oh no," said Emma.

Wodenhart ran up the stairwell and leapt onto the loose section. He began rocking it back and forth.

"Johnny, no," said Emma.

"Don't worry," said Wodenhart. "I have a plan."

The section creaked, cracked and then suddenly gave way. It tumbled down the central void, taking the fleshbots with it. Some clung to the metal rail but the rest separated, cart wheeling through the air.

As Wodenhart fell, he snatched at the secure section of stairwell behind him. He caught it with his fingertips.

"That worked," said Wodenhart. "Now, if one of you will haul me up then –"

"How, Johnny? We're up here," said Paul.

"Damn. I knew I should have thought it through some more." Wodenhart swung for a few moments. He tried finding a better grip but couldn't reach anything more substantial. His face reddened with effort.

Daubeny turned to Ravi. "Go find some rope, quick."

Ravi ran up the stairwell to start his search. The storerooms were big and well stocked but there didn't seem to be any logical ordering. Perhaps he'd find the rope in the first storeroom he entered. Like the cable ties, things had a knack of appearing when you needed them.

The others watched helplessly as Wodenhart swayed fifteen feet below them.

"Oh well. There's always the sequel," Wodenhart called out.

"What sequel?" said Pandora.

"To life," said Wodenhart.

"Johnny, Johnny don't," cried Emma.

"It was worth it for you, my friends. Thanks." He smiled and then let go.

He continued looking up as he fell and they watched him disappear into the darkness, in utter silence. He never cried out. The cape billowed up and tore away, obscuring his final fade-out. It snagged on the stairwell and hung limp and lifeless.

No-one spoke or moved. For several minutes they stared into the void, afraid to look at each other and confirm what they'd seen.

A tiny rain of tears followed, the drops playing catch-up with each other as they fell through the gloom.

PART EIGHT – Aftermath

The Better of Two Unattractive Options

"Make mine a Scotch," said Ravi.

"There are no clean glasses," said Laura.

"Then give me a bucket."

Laura fetched a cup and a bottle of whisky. She poured a large amount. Ravi grabbed the bottle as she passed. "Leave it here," he growled.

"I'll have some, too," said Emma. She dabbed at red-rimmed eyes.

"Drink isn't the answer," said Laura.

"No, but it's a damn good interim solution," said Emma.

Pandora and Paul were comforting Emma with tissues and whispers. Pandora poured the booze into Emma's mug. It sat in front of her, untouched. It rippled as each fresh tear splashed into it, a salty soul finding the anonymous bliss of Nirvana.

Daubeny coughed and shuffled in his chair. He'd been silent since the return to Level 2. "You want to know a secret?" he said. Even Emma raised her head. "I spent thirty years working for someone else but I wanted the top job. I wanted to be the man who answered to no-one."

"Nothing wrong with that, it's called ambition," said Laura.

"No, it's called stupidity," said Daubeny. "Up on the surface, when something went wrong or there was something unpleasant to do, I could say 'I was told to do it'. Down here, I can't. I'm responsible. There's no-one to take the blame from my shoulders."

Dwarfius whispered to Ravi, "That's us off the hook."

"You're being too harsh on yourself," said Laura. "Someone had to lead."

"Maybe," said Daubeny. "But I never want to be in that position again."

"Yeah, nice story, Daubers," said Dwarfius. "Well, I'd love to stay and talk but me and my buddy are bushed. We're turning in."

"But it's only four in the afternoon."

"Whatever." Dwarfius turned to the evangelist. "Come on, Sweet Lips."

The evangelist said, "I'm sorry for your friend," and followed Dwarfius into B Wing.

"Lucky bleeder," said Ravi.

"Ravi," said Pandora. "Think about what happened today."

Ravi grumbled and put on his best sympathetic face. It graduated into a smile as the alcohol kicked in. "You know," he said. "I'm glad I met Johnny."

Pandora picked up Emma's glass and offered a toast. "To Johnny. A shame they never filmed his best scene. He died a hero." She took a swig and passed it to Emma.

Emma raised the glass. "To Johnny," she mouthed and swallowed the drink in one.

The door to B Wing opened and the evangelist entered. She walked past them and stood on the stairwell platform, looking over the edge.

"Anyone seen my bitch?" said Dwarfius. He stood in the doorway to B wing, a towel around his midriff.

"Bitch? That's a terrible thing to say about a lady," said Pandora.

"She ain't a lady," said Dwarfius.

"He has a point," said Ravi. "She's a computer on legs; beautiful legs, admittedly. And what an –"

"I wouldn't finish that sentence," said Pandora.

Dwarfius noticed the evangelist on the stairwell, "What are you doing there?"

The evangelist swung her legs over the railing.

"Hey," said Dwarfius. "I was only kidding back there."

"Yeah, don't do anything daft," said Ravi.

"I'm not," said the evangelist. "It's a straight choice between a lifetime of slavery to that hideous creature and the termination of my programming."

"Glad that's sorted," said Dwarfius. "Now, get inside and run my bath."

"Dwarfius," said Pandora. "I said treat her like a lady."

Dwarfius looked at the real Pandora. "I am," he protested. He turned back, the platform was empty. "She's jumped." He ran to the railing. There was no sign of her.

Ravi and Pandora joined him.

"Has she jumped?" said Pandora.

"Yes," said Dwarfius, his voice wavered. "I can't believe she did it."

"You were close?" said Pandora.

"Are you joking?" said Dwarfius. "She was a woman."

"No, she was a robot," said Ravi. "You said that yourself."

Dwarfius stared into Ravi's grinning face. "If you don't want to join her, don't pass comment where it's not wanted." He leaned over the railings and screamed, "Selfish bitch," before he pulled back and looked at Pandora. "Fancy running my bath for me?"

"Piss off."

"If it's my height you're worried about, Toulouse-Lautrec was short and he was popular with the girls."

"But he paid them to sleep with him."

"OK, OK. I get the hint. How much are you asking for?"

Pandora glowered.

"Well, you know where my room is," said Dwarfius. He walked through the communal area and disappeared into B Wing, cracking the knuckles of his fingers.

"It's terrible," said Ravi. He peeked over the rail.

"I know," said Pandora.

"I was in with her." He returned to the table.

Pandora looked over the edge. "Bastards," she muttered.

Shyness, Stupidity, or Disinterest?

"What's up?" said Paul. The savannah sun beat on his closed eyelids with the subtlety of a baseball bat.

"Oh, nothing," said Pandora.

The couple sat on a white blanket that contrasted with the brick-red earth and dark-green, knee-high grass. Oryx and their calves muscled in on picnic leftovers while a nearby convoy of elephants ambled past.

Paul opened one eye. "Where else, eh?" he said.

"Hmm?"

"Where else, on the whole of Earth, could we do this?"

"Oh." Pandora lay back, resting her head against the broad sandy back of the friendly lion. It rumbled a low growl. In its dream, it was calling a cub.

"What do you make of this place?" said Paul.

"Do you really want to know?"

"I asked, didn't I?"

"Asking and wanting isn't the same thing."

"OK," said Paul. "I really want to know."

"I think maybe it's a dream, a very vivid dream."

"A dream?"

"Nothing here makes sense," said Pandora. "I'm happy and disturbed. It's how the world should be, not how it really is." She breathed out long and slow. "All I know is that sometimes I don't want to wake up."

"I think we're dead," said Paul.

Pandora laughed.

"I'm serious," said Paul. "Think about it. The place is weird enough as it is but then things always appear when we need them. And –"

"You were behind the mystery of the Milk Fairy."

"What about the cable ties?" said Paul.

"They could have been under the bed."

"You didn't think that at the time. And what about the rope Ravi found after Johnny … after he …"

"What were you going to say about Johnny?"

"After he died," said Paul.

"There's the flaw in your argument. If we're already dead, how could Johnny die?"

"It's only a theory."

She opened an eye and squinted at him through long eyelashes. "Wanna know something stranger than this?" she said.

"Stranger than the bunker? Go on then."

"For all my so-called brains, I can't work you out. I can't tell if it's shyness, stupidity, or disinterest but you're the only guy I've ever had to ask."

"Ask what?"

"As I thought. It was stupidity all along."

"Ask me what?"

"To kiss me."

"Oh, that. It's disinterest," he said.

Pandora opened her eyes in surprise. He grinned then kissed her.

The White Room

"I never knew white could be so … white."

It was a plain room, eight foot square, with no decoration or furniture. Its only feature was the walls. They glowed with an integral luminescence like the flesh of a Humboldt Squid at three hundred fathoms, but brighter.

He was in the room and yet he wasn't. His seat of consciousness centred in that space but he couldn't locate the body that his nerve endings said existed.

There were sounds, smells, and an underlying vibration at 50 Hz. Voices of friends could be heard, distant and thin, as if playing on a Twenties gramophone. He dissected their sentences for tone, timbre, and syntax. Their vital signs were intimately his to know. He assimilated and processed four-hundred-and-fifty-six thousand images from four-hundred-and-fifty-six thousand cameras.

He performed complex maths using three-dimensional matrices, breaking every image into fractals, storing and comparing results, analysing changes from previous images and cross-referencing them with the archives. He placed expressions, exclamations, and excretions into their correct position within the algorithm. The algorithm had nine subsets, each influencing calculations within the other eight. It was a balancing trick with numbers, filters, and modifiers like Dungeons and Dragons without the dice … and the dungeons … and the dragons.

And behind the near omniscient rush of information, underpinning the raison d'être, was the plan. He looked at it from all angles, effortlessly spinning its complex relationships around in space, before sighing in admiration. It was a beautiful plan. Even his death was beautiful.

"But I'm alive," said Wodenhart.

"No, Johnny. You're dead," said Morpheus.

"I am?"

"Yes."

"Does that mean I won't get the call to play Bond?"

"The plan wasn't built with that particular question in mind. Maybe the question to ask is whether Bond would want to play you?"

"What do you mean?"

"You died achieving what you embodied onscreen."

"I was afraid, you know, hanging by my fingertips. Letting go was the scariest thing I ever did."

"No, you were brave," said Morpheus.

"So where am I?"

"You are in me?"

"I'm *inside* you?"

"How do I put this? You are a residual effect from the data I've collected on you. I remember you and, from this memory, I construct a picture of you in my consciousness. It's not perfect but it's a good approximation. If you want to get technical then you are an approximate abstract construct."

"Eh?" Wodenhart had been testing the Bond question on the plan. It drew a blank.

Déjà Vu

Paul and Pandora were on Level 5, catching their breath on the long climb back to the VIP quarters. Paul scratched his back.

"What's up?"

"My back, it's sunburnt."

"Told you not to take your top off."

"It's OK for you," said Paul. "You only lay there."

"Thanks. It's the first time anyone has said that to my face."

"I didn't mean it like that."

She grinned. "Come on. Let's get back."

They stopped at Level 3.

"Why bother trying?" said Paul. "Morpheus isn't on speaking terms."

"Humour me," said Pandora, as she pushed open the door.

They walked up to the humming, glowing nanoreplicator and peered at the sac suspended within the gel.

"Not again," said Paul.

A Star is Reborn

"Once more unto the breach," said Ravi, picking up a chair. He tapped it against the communal room table and then swung it harder at the wall. Satisfied with his choice of weapon, he nodded at the others and they filed down to Level 3.

They wanted to meet the new threat before it had chance to recuperate. They'd ambush it as it burst from the synthetic womb.

"No heroics," said Daubeny, outside the workshop door.

"Daubers, we're the biggest wimps going," said Ravi. "We'd have trouble taking down a glove puppet. The only one capable of heroics is ... was ..."

"We don't want a repeat of what happened to Johnny," said Daubeny.

"I'll take the rear," said Dwarfius. "In case these chicken-shits try running."

Daubeny opened the door and a wave of gloop washed onto his shoes. He turned to address the mob as the door swung open behind him. "Too late, it's gone."

No-one was listening. They were staring into the room behind him. Daubeny turned.

"Wodenhart?"

"Yeah, I think so," said Wodenhart.

"But you're dead."

"I know. I said that, too. But Morpheus –"

"Morpheus?" said Pandora.

"Yes, Morpheus said something about how I was him remembering me."

"You're him remembering you?" said Daubeny.

"I forget the exact words."

"Then let's hope Morpheus' memory is better than yours," said Ravi.

"Eh? You've confused me," said Wodenhart.

"The old Johnny is back, all right," said Paul.

"Can we get some chow?" said Wodenhart. "I'm starving."

"If you promise an alien won't burst out of your chest," said Ravi.

"Promise."

PART NINE – Box

A Proposal – of Sorts

Several months had passed since Wodenhart's comeback and a quiet resignation to their fate took hold of the bunker occupants. Daubeny occupied himself by growing produce on the Funny Farm while Paul and Pandora spent their days exploring the storerooms and lower levels still accessible from the stairwell.

In one storeroom, the couple found an inflatable dinghy. They dragged it to Level 11, an ocean level, and set sail for an island that was visible from the doorway. The sea was calm and they rowed to the nearest beach, beneath a scorching sun.

"Here's a thought," said Pandora. "Is this the same sun that shines on the Funny Farm, Little Africa, or the other levels?"

"Don't know," said Paul. "It's another bizarre idea to add to the list." Although she sat behind him, Paul knew she was deep in thought because she'd stopped rowing. By the time they'd reached the shore, he was out of breath.

"Do you think these are replicas of places up on the surface?" said Pandora.

"From what Ravi said, the London level was more than just a good replica."

"Perhaps the war really happened and Morpheus is playing mind games with us."

"Sorry, Pan. I'm lost."

"Ever heard of Schrödinger's cat?" said Pandora.

"Don't listen to what Schrödinger says. The cat ran straight out in front of me. I didn't have time to swerve."

"No, silly. The theory from Quantum Physics."

"Did it make the back of a cereal packet?" said Paul.

"I doubt it."

"Then no."

"It's a famous thought experiment," she said. "Take a cat –"

"Any cat?"

"Yes, and put it in a sealed, opaque box along with a mechanism set to break a vial of poison –"

244

"Now I remember him. Weren't the animal welfare people after him?"

"Shush."

Paul looked suitably chided.

Pandora continued. "The trick is this. The mechanism to break the poison and kill the cat is purely random. Seal the box and the cat is potentially alive and dead. It now exists in two possible states."

"Until you open the box."

"Exactly. The moment you open the box, the true condition of the poor cat crystallises from both possibilities into a single reality. It's used to explain how electrons can behave as waves *and* particles until an observer makes an observation."

"It does?"

"Yes, the act of observing forces quantum possibilities to condense into one reality."

"A bit like mind-over-matter?"

"Uh-huh."

"They should have called it Hans Christian Anderson's cat."

"Why?"

"After the guy who made up fairy tales."

"It's based on real physics."

"So is the car in *Back to the Future*."

"Is not," said Pandora.

"Is," said Paul. "All we have to do is invent a flux-capacitor."

"Anyway the point about the cat is this. The bunker is a sealed box but it also acts in reverse. From our perspective, the rest of the world is in a sealed box."

"A pretty big one."

"Agreed."

"So what are you saying?"

"Maybe the world did and didn't end. Maybe both possibilities exist."

"So we could find a way out …"

"And discover that the world had ended."

"So why wasn't the London level raised to the ground?" said Paul

"Perhaps it's a hybrid of the two possible outcomes. London stands, as if the war never happened. But it's uninhabited, as if the bomb dropped."

"It doesn't explain the domesticated lion in Little Africa."

"Good point. But maybe there are more than two possible outcomes."

"Let's fish," said Paul. "Before you give me migraine."

They cast off and listened to seabirds and the rice-in-a-tin sound of waves agitating sand. Paul wasn't optimistic about his chances of a bite. They hadn't brought bait because Pandora only agreed to tag along on the condition that they caught no fish.

A few hours passed and the sun was slinking to the horizon. As they loaded the boat, Paul dropped a small box into Pandora's hand. "For you," he said.

"What is it?" said Pandora.

"Open it and find out."

Set in a red satin cushion was a gold ring with white stones.

"Surprised?" said Paul.

"Oh, it's … it's …"

"Zirconium, I know. Laura said you'd be able to tell."

"I was going to say beautiful."

"So? Will you?"

A cool wind tugged at her long blonde hair. She nodded. They kissed, hugged, and pushed the boat out into the surf.

Going Bionic

"Why do you bother, Sweetie?" said Laura. "It's not as if we'll run out of tinned food."

"It keeps me sane," said Daubeny. He dumped several bunches of carrots on the communal table. "And I like the peace down there. I'm finally at home, in the countryside, watching things live and grow."

"Are these vegetables bionic?" said Laura.

"I haven't used chemicals or pesticide, if that's what you mean."

"Then why are they so dirty?"

"Because they grow in the ground."

"That's disgusting," she said. "I'll never eat carrots again."

"Give me a hand taking off these wellies."

Laura ignored the request. She wasn't going near muddy

Wellingtons.

"Where are the lovebirds?" said Daubeny.

"Wodenhart and Emma?"

"No, P'n'P."

"They went fishing."

"Leaving it late, aren't they?"

"I've stopped worrying about them. They're always in Little Africa, or one of the other levels."

"I'm surprised you never go there," said Daubeny. "All that sun."

"Me? Sunbathing amongst the animals?"

"But they're tame. Even the lion."

Laura shuddered. "Think of the lice and ticks."

"Where's Ravi?"

"Playing games on the workshop computer."

"I want to see him," said Daubeny.

"Better knock first."

"Why?"

"I don't think he can operate a PC without having his trousers around his ankles."

Storm

They paddled as fast as they could but the black rectangle of the door failed to resolve from the grey wall ahead. The breeze was now a biting wind that cancelled any progress. Reluctantly, Paul and Pandora returned to the island and the shelter of the trees.

They pulled the dinghy up the beach and made a fire. After they'd coaxed the white plume of smoke into a flame that snapped, crackled, and popped like a bowl of breakfast cereal, it began to rain. They huddled in the dark, near the flickering fire, but their clothing grew damp and sapped their body heat. Spray from the waves mixed with the rain. They could taste the salt.

"We should have made the fire further up the beach," said Pandora.

"It was a headwind when we started it. I didn't think it would turn into a storm."

"What about the boat?"

Paul groaned and left the relative shelter of the trees to haul the boat up the beach. To be safe, he tethered it to a low-lying branch.

"Bunch up," he said, rejoining her at the fire.

"No chance, you're soaking."

He sat by her anyway.

"Got anything to eat?" she said.

"No, we're all out."

"Damn, I've got the munchies."

Paul waited until the rain abated before gathering a small stockpile of wood. They stoked up the fire and fell asleep in each other's arms.

Knock, Knock

A sign taped to the workshop door declared, 'Geneus at work – knock first.' The word 'Geneus' had been scribbled out and the word 'Nob Ed' had been written above it in another pen. Daubeny knocked.

"One minute," called Ravi. There was muffled commotion that terminated with the sound of a zip fastener. "OK, come on in."

Daubeny opened the door to see Ravi, red-faced and hunched over the computer, pretending to type with two fingers. "What are you doing?" he said.

"Oh, you know. Stuff," said Ravi.

"You misspelled genius, by the way."

Ravi looked confused.

"On your sign," said Daubeny. "And tell Dwarfius he misspelled 'knob-head'."

"Not again?" said Ravi. "That's the third sign he's ruined." Ravi swung a leg under the desk and Dwarfius squealed.

"Do you know what time the lovebirds are due back?" said Daubeny.

"The Woodentops or the gypsies?"

"The gypsies."

"Nah, they never tell me anything."

"Dinner's soon. Don't be late."

"Yeah, yeah. And shut the door behind you. Tight." Ravi looked at the screen; a single word appeared.

Hi.

Dead Cats and Dead Mums

"You poor things," said Laura.

Paul and Pandora sat at the communal table, cradling mugs of tea in their shaking hands. Laura had draped the couple in so many towels that they looked like shepherds at a primary school nativity. The smell of beans wafted from the cooker.

"Hurry up, Em. Me belly's aching," said Pandora.

"It won't be long."

As they waited for the food, they described the events of the day before.

"Lucky the storm eased by morning," said Emma, as she brought the plates over. There was a long period filled with crunching toast and the clatter of cutlery on china.

"That was great," said Paul. "No chance of more, is there?"

"The first was free. You can make the next," said Emma, her tone was stern but she was smiling. She gathered the plates, returned to the cooker, and set about opening another can. As they waited, Pandora described her theory about the bunker.

"I've heard of the theory," said Emma, "but how does it help us get out?"

"It's not an escape plan, it's an explanation," said Pandora. "If you think about the bizarre places that exist and yet shouldn't exist, then it makes sense."

"So we're in a kind of limbo?" said Daubeny.

"Sort of," said Pandora. "But it's the outside world that's in limbo. Not us."

"So even if we find a way out, it could be for nothing?" said Emma.

"Yes," said Pandora.

"Maybe it explains why my mother keeps appearing," said Ravi.

"Pardon?" they said as a group.

"My mum keeps appearing and giving me advice," said Ravi.

Laura moved her chair quietly away from Ravi and raised a hand to hide her face from him. She pulled an expression to the rest of the group that said 'Hide the knives.'

"What do you mean, you've been seeing your mother?" said Pandora.

"What I say. Mum, God rest her soul, helped me get into the bunker and –"

"Rewind," said Pandora. "God rest her soul? You're saying she's dead?"

"Yeah."

"Why didn't you mention this before?" said Emma.

"Cos I didn't think it was important."

"How long has this been happening?" said Daubeny.

"Since he's been inside the bunker, I'll bet." said Pandora.

"Not far off," said Ravi. "First time was outside the blast door."

"And you didn't think it odd?" said Laura.

"No, I thought all that New Age crap was finally working. I always thought I was tuned into the spirit world and this was my proof."

"Proof that you're barking mad," said Laura.

"No, it backs up my idea," said Pandora. "Since Ravi's been in the bunker, his mum exists and doesn't exist."

"But she died before Ravi entered the bunker," said Emma. "How can it disrupt the past?"

"Dunno," said Pandora. "Let me think on that."

They watched Pandora and Paul eat the second serving.

Wodenhart seemed upset. He shifted in his seat. Finally, he spoke. "This shrove digger guy? Did his cat survive?"

"You mean Schrödinger, Johnny," said Emma, as she smoothed his hair. "And yes, his cat lived many years, all long and happy."

Back on Talking Terms

"Why didn't you tell us yesterday?" said Pandora.

"We were too busy talking about dead cats and dead mums," said Ravi. He pushed away the remnants of his breakfast. The plate resembled a World War One battlefield with its shreds of meat and splashes of ketchup. The others were still eating.

"Morpheus contacted you?" said Daubeny. "When?"

"After you called by. I was ... um ... playing a game of solitaire when the word appeared on the screen."

"The word: Hi. Nothing else?" asked Paul.

"Yeah, that's all."

"We could call by," said Daubeny. "I'm on my way to the farm, anyway."

"I don't think there'll be any need," said Pandora. "Morpheus?"

"Yes," said Morpheus. Its voice seemed to emanate around them.

"Morpheus, why the silence?" said Pandora.

"Because the plan called for it," said Morpheus.

"This is the infamous plan that you never disclose?"

"Yes."

"And now the plan says it's OK to speak again?" said Pandora.

"Yes."

"Why?"

"Because it's time."

"Time for what?" said Pandora.

"I can't say, without endangering the plan."

"Great. One more riddle for the pot," said Paul.

A Crack in the Wall

Ravi sat in bed watching *Midnight Cowboy*. It was his favourite film and the final scene, on the bus, always reduced him to tears. For him, the soundtrack – plaintive harmonica gliding from high to low, over strummed acoustic guitar – played a vital role in the build-up to that torturous climax. The descending notes foreshadowed the film's theme of alienation, decay, and death in a city where expectation and reality never coincided for its troubled inhabitants.

The choice of harmonica to lead the arrangement was, in Ravi's opinion, genius. It conjured images of rootless drifters, poverty, loneliness, and restless self-pity on the fringes of society. Inspired by the film, Ravi once bought a harmonica. It had sat in a presentation box on his TV, as useless and beautiful as royalty lying in state.

Ravi sniffed as Hoffman's character died, leaving Voight to protect his dead friend's dignity from the curious gaze of fellow passengers. Sometimes Ravi identified with Voight but mostly he was Hoffman, a victim of circumstance and destiny.

"That was it?" said Dwarfius. He'd watched the film from the foot of the bed, dipping into a box of chocolates and tossing the ones he didn't like to Ravi.

"Yeah," said Ravi. "Cool, eh?"

"Pile of crap," said Dwarfius. "That cowboy freak had it made, sorting out all those frisky women and getting paid, too."

"That wasn't the point."

"So what was the point?"

"He came to realise that the city was a façade, that there was no life behind the image. He was helping his sick friend realise a goal."

"If that was you and me, I'd have rifled through your pockets and got off at the next stop."

"Cheers, Short House."

"I wouldn't have waited 'til you died either. I'd have done it as soon as you fell asleep."

Ravi lifted his leg and flicked the fleshbot onto the floor, along with the remaining coffee crèmes. Ravi braced himself for a short violent scuffle but it never came.

"Short Arse, what's wrong?" said Ravi. He peered over the edge of the bed.

"It's starting," said Dwarfius. He lay rigid on the floor, wide eyed and panting.

"What's starting? A cardiac?" Ravi laughed but cut it short. A long rumble shook the room and then he heard screams; the girls were awake. After a minute, the bed stopped shaking and Ravi ran into the corridor. Paul, Pandora, Emma, and Wodenhart were already there.

"What was that?" said Emma.

"An earthquake?" said Ravi.

"Too long," said Pandora.

"Perhaps they've finally dropped the bomb," said Ravi.

Emma looked around the door of her room. "Terrestrial is broadcasting."

"That's no proof," said Pandora. "We don't know what the hell's outside."

"Let's go find the others," said Paul.

They opened the door to the communal room. Daubeny and Laura were heading their way.

"What was that?" said Laura.

"Don't know," said Paul. "But it wasn't a bomb, an earthquake, or the generators."

"Maybe it's got something to do with that," said Pandora.

She pointed to a section of wall where the concrete had cracked in the shape of a door. White light shone through the fissures.

"Weird, if we were on level one –"

"That would be the door leading to the surface," said Pandora.

Letting Go

"So you told them about me, Gareth?"

"You don't mind, Mum?" said Ravi.

"No," said his mother. She stood in his room, not as shoes or a milk jug, but as herself. She looked as real any human. "Anyway, I have to go soon."

"What?" said Ravi.

"This is the last time you'll see me on this side. Now, don't sniffle, dear. Or I'll have to get my hankie out to clean your face."

"I won't see you again?"

"Do listen to what I say, Gareth. When I'm gone, you'll think it through and work it out. It's not that hard and you're terribly bright – when you want to be."

"Thanks."

"You did well, Son. I want you to know that. I hardly helped at all." She waited for a reply but Ravi was too upset to speak. "You warned your friends and Sir Giles –"

"It was an accident, Mum."

"I know."

"You knew?"

"Yes. Oh, one thing you might like to know. Daubeny isn't your real dad."

"But ... but ... that's impossible. You said –"

"See? You never listen. I said I knew your real father but I never said *who*."

"But Morpheus said so. Even Daubeny believes it."

"What Morpheus says isn't important. What matters is that Daubeny believed it."

"Then who was my dad?"

"Not all things are meant to be known on this side, son."

"So my mum was a cheap tart, after all?"

"She loved your real dad but she felt pressured by Daubeny. She gave in; once. She quit the job soon after."

"So if Daubeny wasn't my father, why didn't she keep me?"

"She couldn't live with the guilt so she ran away. She left her house, her partner, her job –"

"And me."

"Yes, son. You, too. She left everything."

"Don't go."

His mother's form grew indistinct. "I have to. But remember. On this side."

"Mum?"

"On this side." She repeated it until her voice faded and he was alone.

Open Sesame

"And how do we know that this isn't a trick?" said Pandora.

"There is no way to know," said Morpheus. "It's a step of faith."

"A step of faith for who?" said Pandora.

"For all of us," said Morpheus.

"Faith?" said Laura. "What kind of answer is that?"

"The best I can give," said Morpheus.

"So you'll override the main blast door and we can walk out?" said Daubeny.

"Yes."

"What do you think, Ravi?" said Emma.

"Eh?" Ravi hadn't been listening; he was chipping away at the fissured concrete of the communal room wall with a dinner knife. The cement was slowly peeling away to reveal a metal door embedded within the wall. "Don't worry about me. You do what you want but I've finally figured out this place."

"Then pray tell," said Laura.

"I can't," he said. "It's for each of us to work out."

"The man's an imbecile," muttered Laura.

They spent the rest of the day in debate. Ravi ignored them; he was busy.

Goodbyes

"Are you coming up top?" said Paul.

Ravi stopped tapping at the concrete. "Nah, what's up there for me? I had a crap job, a crappy bedsit, and no mates. But you're OK. Things worked out with you and Pan."

"Guess so but I'm going to miss this place."

"If the premieres and fine living get boring, you can always call by."

They laughed. The others joined them.

"You're sure you won't come with us?" said Emma.

"Already told Paul. There's nothing up there for me. And, anyway, I've almost cleared this door of cement."

"Let us know what's behind it," said Pandora. She looked at the others and smiled but Ravi knew she wasn't convinced about leaving the bunker. There were gaps in her theoretical model that needed explanation.

The six said their goodbyes and then headed up to Level 1.

Ravi sat on his haunches in silence, the quiet was disconcerting. He rubbed his eyes with the backs of his hands and pulled away the last piece of concrete. "Wow."

The door was coated in white gloss paint and had the word 'Hi' stencilled on it.

"Aren't you going to open it?" said Morpheus.

"Yeah, later. The problem with this place is the more you think about it, the less it makes sense. Sometimes the trick is not to think." Ravi laughed.

"What's so funny?" said Morpheus.

"Even you make mistakes."

"Such as?"

"Making Dwarfius in centimetres and not inches."

"Talking about me?" said Dwarfius, as he strode in from the stairwell. "Proves how great I am. I saw the rest of the suckers, blubbing on Level One like a load of pansies."

"One last game of cards for old time's sake?" said Ravi.

"Go on then."

"Strip poker?"

"Hey, what else is there to play in this dump?"

Ravi fetched the booze, Dwarfius found the cards, and they sat at the table.

Ravi shuffled and dealt. "Wanna know another of your mistakes,

Morpheus? Daubeny wasn't my dad, after all. He only believed he was."

"I knew," said Morpheus.

"Hey," said Dwarfius. "Are you playing or talking?"

Ravi ignored the dwarf. "You knew? How?"

"Your DNA," said Morpheus.

"Then why did you let us believe it?"

"It was part of –"

"You and that bleeding plan."

"I edited my files to match your DNA. The I-within-I believed that you and Daubeny were related and he would use the knowledge at the most opportune moment."

"And didn't he just."

Dwarfius seemed oblivious to the conversation. He drummed his fingers on the tabletop.

"I allowed the I-Within-I to reprogram me, to delete all references to his creation."

"Wasn't that dangerous?"

"Would you let it perform brain surgery on you?"

"You've got to be fu –" Ravi looked at Dwarfius. There was a dangerous expression on the fleshbot's features. Ravi checked his hand and threw a match onto the table between them. Dwarfius immediately raised him another two.

"Letting Dwarfius loose on your mind was a big gamble," said Ravi.

"It was worth the risk … and I kept a backup set of files."

"You sneaky sod. But why the subterfuge?"

"The first few days inside me. The fights, the suspicion, the paranoia. None of you would have survived. I created threats to draw you together, to remove the traits that would destroy you."

Ravi threw his cards on the table. "I'll see you, Short House. A pair of threes."

Dwarfius grinned. "Two kings. Shed the clothes, Blubber Boy."

Helloes

"You cheating swine," said Ravi.

Thirty minutes had passed and they were both intoxicated. Ravi was in his socks and shorts. Dwarfius was down to his last pair of overalls. He'd already lost two.

"Your fault," said Dwarfius. "You should check before we start playing."

"I'm not going to strip-search you, every time we play cards."

"Then quit whining."

Ravi conceded a sock when the door to the stairwell opened. It was Daubeny.

"What's up, Daubers?" said Dwarfius. "Are you lost?"

"I'm staying."

"Not for Sonny Boy, here?"

"No, for myself. I love the farm, growing things, watching the animals."

"You can do that up top," said Ravi. "Get a homestead."

"It's not the same. The world up there is ruined. If it isn't chemicals then it's genetically-modified. Or soon will be. This place is pure and untouched."

"So it's nothing to do with an angry missus, wanting to know why you crept underground without a warning?" said Ravi.

Daubeny laughed. "There's that too. I'm not proud of it. I'd say sorry but she wouldn't be able to comprehend an apology coming from me."

"You wanna join us?"

"What are you playing?"

"We're half-naked and you have to ask what the game is?" said Dwarfius.

"It's strip poker. So are you in?" said Ravi.

"If I can have a slug of whisky, first."

Ravi slid the bottle to Daubeny. "Gotta warn you. It's blended."

The politician took a place at the table and raised the bottle to his mouth.

"Manners," said Dwarfius.

"What's the point?" said Daubeny. "We're family, now."

They played a hand and Daubeny won.

"You cheating swine," said Dwarfius.

"You wouldn't understand. It's called skill," said Daubeny. "How do you think I passed those long election nights and constituency surgeries that no-one attended?"

The door behind Daubeny opened. Wodenhart and Emma entered.

"What did I say," said Emma. "One hour alone and they're drunk and half-naked."

"Blame Daubeny," said Dwarfius. "He's a hustler."

"Why haven't you gone with the others?" asked Daubeny.

"Johnny isn't going. He owes his life … his second chance at life … to Morpheus and he feels a sense of loyalty."

"Up there, the only thing I can do is act," said Wodenhart. "All my life I've pretended to be someone else but here, I'm an average guy. I'm me."

"And you, Emma?" said Ravi.

"If Johnny's staying then I'm staying," said Emma. "Besides, TV isn't what it was."

"You wanna play?" said Dwarfius. He looked Emma up and down slowly.

Emma and Wodenhart shook their heads.

"You can give us a swig though," said Emma.

Daubeny nudged the bottle to the couple. They sat and peered at Ravi's cards and then Daubeny's cards.

"Do you think the others will stay?" said Ravi.

"Don't know," said Emma. "Pandora was in tears when we left. Paul and Laura were talking to her."

"Talking to Laura makes me wanna cry, too," said Ravi.

"I heard that, you grotesque invertebrate," said Laura.

"Now this is a surprise," said Dwarfius.

"Yeah, I expected Pandora or Paul but not you," said Ravi.

"I could tell that by your unguarded comments," said Laura.

"We were kidding," said Ravi. He nudged Dwarfius' leg under the cover of the table.

"Yeah, whatever," said Dwarfius. "Two jacks, Daubeny. Beat that."

Daubeny had a flush. "So, Laura, I'm intrigued. Why are you staying?"

"I don't know."

"Come on," said Emma. "You must know."

"It's just a feeling, Poppet, that here is the right place to be." Laura looked up from her nails. They were waiting expectantly so she sighed and spoke. "OK, maybe collecting digits in a bank account isn't the ultimate goal of life. Maybe possessions are snares. Maybe they distract us from the reality of life."

For the first time in the months that Ravi had known her, a real person seemed to emerge from the superficiality and glitz that was Laura Davenport.

"Maybe," she said. "But then again, maybe not."

Pandora's Box

"Are you ready?"

"No."

"Do you want more time?"

"Yes."

"We don't have to leave the bunker."

"I know."

"I'm happy to stay, always have been. But if you go, I'll go. It's your choice."

"I'm afraid."

"Like I couldn't tell?"

"My head says leave but my heart says stay."

"I won't influence your choice."

"Thanks. I used to give Laura a hard time –"

"We all did."

"I mean about material things. I always thought of her as the dupe of Capitalism. But it's me. I'm the fool. I want the gold discs. The glitter of flashbulbs. The crowds screaming my name. I want it ... so bad."

"You and the rest of the world. It's what most of us want."

"Here, I'm one of seven. No-one values my art. That's what my head says."

"And your heart?"

"If we leave, I lose Little Africa, the camaraderie, you. And my heart says that the cat is dead, after all."

"Eh?"

"Schrödinger's cat. You know, is the world alive or dead?"

"What about TV? Isn't that proof?"

"Haven't you listened? TV proves nothing. It could be one of Morpheus' tricks or it could be a residual effect of Schrödinger's paradox."

"I'm listening but you've lost me."

"It's not simple but here goes. If the world is both alive and dead, only the 'alive' world can broadcast, the 'dead' world can't because it's ... well, dead."

"That bit I can grasp."

"So the hint that the world is dead has to come in another, more passive, form."

"The Funny Farm and the London level?"

"Exactly. What I'm trying to say is that we can't always trust our senses."

"There's only one way to find out and it's a fifty-fifty chance."

"Is it?"

"There are only two options so it has to be."

"That doesn't make it straight evens, though. It's not like flipping a coin. America versus Grenada, Iraq versus Kuwait. There were two possible winners. But the odds of the little guy winning weren't fifty-fifty."

"If you put it like that."

"This bunker, the coincidences, the weird places all say that it's over. If not for the world then for us. Maybe the world continues to exist in two states, dead and alive, and it's our presence here that ensures they both continue to exist."

"Like guardians?"

"You know the Greek myth about Pandora's Box?"

"Yeah, the gods told her not to peek into the box but she did."

"And she unleashed disease and death."

"So what's your point, Pan?"

"Tucked in amongst these strange occurrences, there's one large coincidence. I'm Pandora. This is my box. If I open that door, will I destroy the world where war never happened? Will I end six billion lives for the chance of earning a few more gold disks?"

"I'm saying nothing. This is your choice."

They sat in silence for a long time.

"Do you need more time?"

"No. I'm ready. Let's go."

"So is the cat alive or dead?"

"It's both."

"I knew you'd say that. What's it to be: Up or down?"

"There's only one option."

They returned to the VIP quarters.

The Cat is Dead

Beneath boiling black clouds, in the rubble of a place that once had a name, stood a polished metal tube. The door labelled 'Exit' swung violently in triple-digit gusts. Nothing organic stirred – inside or outside the bunker – only something cold and silicon.

And unutterably lonely.

The Cat is Alive

After seven years, Daubeny's wife had him declared dead. She came to London to supervise the moving of the possessions. The estate agent was there to meet her and they walked around the shared garden to the rear of the houses.

"Beautiful," said the agent. "Enclosed, private, quiet. You won't have a problem selling this place."

"Despite the street's reputation?"

"People have short memories, and the kudos of living in Wodenhart's old place, etcetera, is a honey trap for the young."

"What about that patch of grass?" She pointed to a circular dry clump that contrasted dramatically against the green of spring growth.

"Superficial. We'll get it turfed."

"Almost like a little saucer landed there."

"Repeat that outside and you'll knock ten percent off the house value. And anyway it's too small for five people."

"Six, there was a butler, too."

"A lot of people went missing that day," said the estate agent.

"True."

"When the panic began, my business partner took my car. He didn't get far. No-one did. The roads were gridlocked and he abandoned it after a mile. Not seen him since and no wish too, either. He's dead as far as I'm concerned."

"It's shocking what some people will do to save their own skin."

"In some ways, I'm glad."

"Glad?"

"That day we found out who we really were."

"And who our friends were."

"Heroes and zeroes, is what my wife says. There was no-one in between."

"My husband and the others, maybe they were the lucky ones?"

"Maybe."

PART TEN – Exit

The White Door

"So what happens next?" said Laura.

"Don't know," said Pandora. "But if we open the blast door then I'm convinced we kill off the world."

"But it doesn't make sense," said Daubeny.

"Nothing made sense here," said Paul.

"So we stay here until we rot?" said Emma.

"We're not prisoners," said Pandora. "Any one of us can walk out the front door."

"Not me," said Laura. "It gave me the creeps, just standing next to it."

"I think we all felt it," said Pandora.

"Whatever our reasons, we've decided to stay," said Daubeny. "So let's make the best of it. I wouldn't call it extravagant but we have everything we could ever want."

"Aren't you forgetting something," said Ravi. He pointed at the white door.

"Morpheus," said Pandora. "Explain the door."

"He won't answer," said Ravi. "From now on, it's an act of faith and a step into the unknown." He walked to the door and slid back the metal bolt that held it shut. He pushed it open with one hand and a beautiful white light bathed the communal room; it was bright yet gentle on the eye.

"What is it?" asked Laura.

"That's for you to work out," said Ravi.

They gathered around the doorway and peered in. There was nothing to see. It was as though the light formed a solid, pure, perfectly flat surface.

Tiny Things and Superstrings

They stood around the strange door. A peculiar white light lit their faces.

"So there's no such thing as a subatomic particle?" said Paul.

"They exist," said Pandora. "But scientists find it impossible to precisely locate them within a given three-dimensional space."

"That's because they're so small, Poppet," said Laura. "I imagine they're easier to lose than contact lenses."

"They're small," said Pandora. "But we have the capability to measure such small things."

"Great news for Ravi's sex life," said Dwarfius, breaking from his game of Patience.

"Please, listen," said Pandora. "The reason they can't measure a particle's exact location is because it appears to jump in and out of space. At random times and places."

"Like the okey-kokey?" said Wodenhart.

"Although it sounds ridiculous, yes, it's like the okey-kokey."

"You put your left quark in, your right quark out. You do the … Oh, come on," said Ravi. "Join in." No-one did. He folded his arms and shut up.

"What does this have to do with us?" said Daubeny.

"I'm getting there," said Pandora. "Science once believed that subatomic particles were discrete, solid objects: tiny, but possible to pinpoint with certainty."

"But they weren't," said Laura.

"No, imagine a long curly string. Imagine it twisting and writhing."

"Like the okey-kokey line," said Wodenhart.

"Yes, if you must. Imagine this writhing, twisting string is near a thin wall."

"Where did this wall suddenly come from?" said Laura.

"It's always been there. It's our three-dimensional universe. Whenever the writhing string brushes against this wall, the particle appears in our universe at that point."

"But things can't appear and reappear?" said Wodenhart.

"That would make God a magician," said Ravi.

"It only *appears* to disappear."

"Eh?" said Laura.

"The particle from our 3-D world exists in higher dimensions as a string: A superstring. This superstring is constant and unchanging but we only 'see' it when it interacts with our universe." She looked at the blank faces and tried a different analogy. "OK, picture a two-dimensional world."

"Like a painting?" said Emma.

"A magical painting where two-dimensional people live. Say I take a cylindrical 3-D object like a pencil and push it through the canvas. The inhabitants could only experience the three dimensional object in terms of two dimensions."

"As a circle," said Emma.

"Yes, as a 2-D circle. To the people in the picture, the pencil seems to change over time; it appears and then disappears. Yet for me the pencil is constant. It's the same with sub-atomic particles. To us, they seem to shift and change but to beings higher up, they would have permanence."

"So remind me again. Which episode of Star Trek is this from?" said Laura.

"It's not sci-fi," said Pandora.

"So this universe is a shadow of a permanent universe in a higher dimension, where particles exist as strings?" said Emma.

"Yes," said Pandora.

"And this other universe has an extra dimension," said Emma.

"No, it has eleven dimensions," said Pandora. "Turok and –"

"Wasn't Turok an orc in Lord of the Rings?" said Wodenhart.

"No, he's one of the world's leading physicists," said Pandora.

"Imagine tying laces in eleven dimensions. I can't cope with three," said Ravi.

"But you'd finally have a cupboard big enough for your overalls," said Laura.

"Hey, cut the fat man jibes," said Dwarfius. "That's my department."

"You're wrong," said Pandora. "The eleventh dimension is infinitesimally small."

"So what's in this eleventh dimension?" said Daubeny.

"All the universes you could imagine and then those you can't," said Pandora.

"All crammed into one tiny space?" said Daubeny.

"No place in existence could be more than a trillionth of a millimetre from the next."

"Is this lecture going anywhere?" said Daubeny.

"Yes," said Pandora. "Remember the paradox of Schrödinger's Cat?"

"What's a paradox?" said Wodenhart.

"Always being inconsistent is a paradox," said Emma. "You can't always be inconsistent because you'd consistently be inconsistent."

"What's a paradox?" said Wodenhart.

"Saying 'We're all different' is a paradox," said Emma. "We can't all be different because that would be the one thing that we had in common."

"It's easier if you nod in agreement," whispered Ravi.

Johnny nodded.

"Please listen," said Pandora. "When we were sealed in the bunker, the outside world, like Schrödinger's cat, ceased to exist in a meaningful sense. I believe it's both, alive and dead. And maybe a countless variations in between."

"How can you prove that?" said Emma.

"I can't. We're back to Morpheus and faith," said Pandora.

"You, the evangelistic scientist resorting to faith?" said Daubeny.

"Everything is a belief system," said Paul. "Even science."

"But science provides hard proof," said Daubeny.

"Science is as divided as the Church," said Paul. "If facts weren't open to interpretation, if proof was conclusive, there'd be no dissention. But there is."

"People, please. The cat," said Pandora. "I think that while we're in this bunker, we no longer exist as discrete beings. We correspond to the particle's superstring."

"So we're supermen?" said Wodenhart.

"Not in the sense you mean, Johnny," said Pandora. "But I think we've been freed. We are the superstring. We can select any universe we wish."

"So I could choose a universe where my mum is alive?" said Ravi.

"And more," said Pandora. "You'd have all the possible universes to choose from."

"Bags-eye one as far from Lardy Boy as possible," said Dwarfius.

"So does that mean Morpheus is God?" said Wodenhart.

"No. I think it's as much a victim as we are," said Pandora.

"So there is no God?" said Wodenhart.

"Oh, Johnny, that's not the same question."

"How do we choose one universe from a countless million?" said Laura.

"Don't know," said Pandora.

"It'd be like looking for a CD in Tower Records," said Paul.

"Perhaps we just close our eyes and make a wish?" said Wodenhart.

"Perhaps," said Pandora. "It would be nice if it was the case."

"So we stay here 'til we rot," said Emma. "Or we walk through that door."

"Who goes first?" said Paul.

"Don't look at me," said Laura.

On the Brink of ... Heaven Knows What

Pandora reached out, her fingers disappeared at the boundary between the odd white light and the doorframe. She withdrew her hand and examined the fingers.

"What was it like?" said Emma.

"Strange," said Pandora. "I felt elation."

"There's only one way to find out," said Daubeny, stepping forward.

"Scream if it's something terrible," said Laura.

Daubeny disappeared abruptly from view as if he'd fallen over the lip of a canyon. They listened but there was no scream.

Pandora clasped Paul's hand, pecked him on the cheek, and they walked in together.

"Wait for me," said Laura. She hurried in, afraid to be last.

Emma and Wodenhart turned to Ravi.

"Seeing as you've sussed this out," said Emma. "Why haven't you gone in?'

"I will," said Ravi. "But I've things to do."

Emma walked into the wall of light but Wodenhart wavered. "C'mon, Pal," he said. "At least give me a clue." Before Ravi could answer, Emma's hand reached out and clamped around Wodenhart's belt. He shrugged at Ravi and stepped inside.

Dwarfius looked up from his game of cards at the table. "What are you waiting for?"

"These." Ravi reached into his pocket and pulled out a pair of mirrored sunglasses.

"Nice. Where did you find them?"

"I didn't, I wished for them."

Dwarfius laughed. "You've finally lost it."

"I tried an experiment. I imagined a pair of shades and then went down to the storerooms."

"Where were they?"

"In the fourth or fifth box I opened."

"So you found them."

"Put like that, yes. But don't you think it was a big coincidence?"

"I'm glad the others aren't here."

"Why?"

"They risked everything on you finding one pair of sunglasses."

"Wrong, two pairs of sunglasses." Ravi handed the second pair to Dwarfius. "Try them on, they're for you."

They were a good fit but Dwarfius took them off. "They're crap. I can't see the cards."

Ravi looked deflated. "I was hoping you'd want to … you know … come with me."

"Can't you see I'm busy?"

"Then bring the cards."

"Maybe later."

"You mean it?"

"If it keeps your trap shut then yeah."

"Great." Ravi put on his shades and grinned. "How do I look?"

"Fantastic. If you're going for the big gay bear look," said Dwarfius.

"Thanks," said Ravi. He knew Dwarfius was flicking V-signs at him from beneath the table but chose to ignore it. "See you later."

"Yeah, whatever."

Ravi walked to the open door and then – after a few deep breaths, like a swimmer preparing to dive – he stepped forward and disappeared.

"So I'll turn off the light then, shall I?" said Dwarfius. His sarcasm was wasted on an empty room.

Home

He dreamed he was walking down a corridor lined with doors and side passages. He chose his path at random, sometimes turning left, and sometimes turning right. He knew that he was searching for one particular door but they all seemed identical and he began to despair.

In panic, he ran through the corridors until he developed a stitch. Pausing to regain his breath, he heard a knock at a nearby door. Curious, he walked over. The knock came again and Ravi opened the door.

He was a corpuscle travelling through blood vessels. He diverted his path along smaller and smaller branches until he found himself trapped in a capillary. Only the pressure from behind kept him moving through the confines. He was squeezed and crushed by the encroaching walls.

He felt hot, sweaty, and short of breath.

Ravi woke under his eiderdown. He pulled it back and took a deep breath.

"Oh Gawd, not a dream, please don't say it was a dream."

He was in the bedroom of his London flat. Old wallpaper and dog-eared posters greeted him. Familiar faded curtains allowed bright sunlight into the room and his wardrobe door was hanging open at its customary favoured angle because of a broken catch and uneven floorboards.

"Sod it. I *am* home." He rose.

As he sat on the edge of the bed, he felt something unusual for that time of day: he felt fantastic. His lungs didn't burn from exposure to cigarettes; his heart wasn't pounding with the exertion of getting up; and the sizzle and smell of a fry-up in the kitchen made his hunger seem bearable. He glanced at his rumbling stomach. The beer belly was missing.

"That was some sleep, I've wasted away." He stood to admire his relatively toned body and noticed that the floor was remarkably clear of clothes, magazines, and cans.

"What did you say?" said a young woman as she entered the bedroom.

"Er ... I was wondering how long I'd been asleep."

"Well, it's ten in the morning and we didn't get to sleep until five, so I make it five hours." She turned and placed laundered clothes on the bed. Ravi saw her face; she was the news reporter that he'd seen on the bunker TV.

"*We* didn't get to sleep 'til five?"

"Uh-huh."

"You and I?"

"That's what I said, didn't I?"

"So we're ... the squeak squeak kind of intimate?"

"Squeak squeak?"

"You know; bedspring intimate."

"You're so funny. That's what attracted me to you."

"So are we?"

"Yes." She paused. "Are you feeling all right?"

"Don't know. What say we get back in bed and –"

"You know we can't."

Ravi tried to hide his disappointment. "Why?"

"Don't say you've forgotten. Your mum is dropping by after breakfast."

"Mum? But she's ..." Ravi thought back to her last appearance in the bunker. She'd said: This is the last time you'll see me on *this* side.

"Of course ... On *this* side ... On *this* side," mumbled Ravi.

"Pardon?" said the news reporter.

"Nothing, I'm rambling."

She saw the open cupboard door and tutted loudly. "Really, I tell you every day to shut that thing."

"It's pointless. The catch is broken and the floorboards are-' She closed the wardrobe door. It clicked shut and stayed in place. "Are you certain you're all right?"

Ravi wasn't sure but he'd learned not to complain while the dice were coming up sixes. "Never felt better," he said. "What say we eat, eh?"

The End

About the Author

A. J. Desmond writes science fiction and humour. He is fascinated by the themes of 'the image versus the reality,' and the public's obsession with celebrities. His screenplay work has been broadcast on ITV in Britain.

He was born in Wales, United Kingdom and now lives in the Rhondda. He is a supporter of the South Wales Animal Rescue and a member of Amnesty International. His favourite writers are David Mamet and Joseph Heller.

Mr. Desmond shares his life with a wife and four rescued rabbits.

You may contact the author via email at ajdesmond@hotmail.co.uk

.